THE DARK TIME

Also by Nick Petrie

The Drifter
Burning Bright
Light It Up
Tear It Down
The Wild One
The Breaker
The Runaway
The Price You Pay
The Dark Time

NICK PETRIE

THE DARK TIME

An Aries Book

First published in the US in 2026 by G.P. Putnam's Sons,
an imprint of Penguin Random House LLC

First published in the UK in 2026 by Head of Zeus Ltd,
part of Bloomsbury Publishing Plc

Copyright © Nicholas Petrie LLC, 2026

The moral right of Nick Petrie to be identified as the author of this work has been
asserted in accordance with the Copyright, Designs and Patents Act of 1988.

All rights reserved. No part of this publication may be: i) reproduced or transmitted
in any form, electronic or mechanical, including photocopying, recording or by means
of any information storage or retrieval system without prior permission in writing from the
publishers; or ii) used or reproduced in any way for the training, development or operation of
artificial intelligence (AI) technologies, including generative AI technologies. The rights
holders expressly reserve this publication from the text and data mining exception as
per Article 4(3) of the Digital Single Market Directive (EU) 2019/790.

This is a work of fiction. All characters, organizations, and events portrayed
in this novel are either products of the author's imagination or are used fictitiously.

9 7 5 3 1 2 4 6 8

A catalogue record for this book is available from the British Library.

ISBN (PB): 9781804541692
ISBN (ePub): 9781804541654

Cover design: Gemma Gorton | Head of Zeus
Typeset by Lumina Datamatics Ltd

Printed and bound in Great Britain by Clays Ltd, Elcograf S.p.A.

Bloomsbury Publishing Plc
50 Bedford Square, London, WC1B 3DP, UK
Bloomsbury Publishing Ireland Limited,
29 Earlsfort Terrace, Dublin 2, D02 AY28, Ireland

HEAD OF ZEUS LTD
5–8 Hardwick Street
London, EC1R 4RG

To find out more about our authors and books
visit www.headofzeus.com
For product safety-related questions contact productsafety@bloomsbury.com

For Scott Wilson,
master carpenter, mentor, and friend.

I will always remember you
and the things you taught me.
Rest in peace.

The only thing necessary for the triumph of evil is for good men to do nothing.

—Attributed to Edmund Burke

1

KATELYN

Katelyn Thorsen, known as KT to friends and enemies alike, stood inside the glass doors of Anchorhead Coffee, just down the way from Pike Place Market, staring out at the rain pouring down. She'd come for an appointment, but the anonymous whistleblower she was supposed to meet never showed up. Her next stop was Queen Anne Hill, a mile away, to pick up her daughter from school.

But she couldn't make her hand reach out and open the door.

It wasn't the weather. This was Seattle in November. Rain came with the territory, and KT was prepared in a bright orange hooded waterproof jacket that went down to her knees. She even had a collapsible umbrella tucked into her messenger bag, just in case.

It wasn't the fact that her appointment, whoever he or she was, had ghosted her. It happened all the time. People reached out to a journalist, wanting to spill the tea about something, then got cold feet. KT had pinged the other person's anonymous Signal account several times but gotten no response. Waiting for an hour in the coffee shop, she'd spent the rest of the time reviewing her notes on the half dozen other stories she was working on.

She certainly wasn't hesitating because of the afternoon traffic clogging every possible route to Queen Anne Hill, the sleepy neighborhood where she lived with her daughter. Like the autumn rains, Seattle traffic was both legendary and unrelenting.

In other words, this was a November day like any other.

Except for the feeling that KT couldn't shake.

She was being watched.

It had started that morning. She'd woken at five-thirty, her mind already thinking about the two in-person interviews she had scheduled, plus the countless calls and emails.

As usual, she'd made her daughter breakfast and driven her to school, the chatty thirteen-year-old always quiet and self-contained at that early hour. Then KT had returned home, parked in the driveway, unlocked the front door, and walked inside.

Her plan had been to check out the material the whistleblower had sent in preparation for their conversation at the coffee shop. Instead, she looked down and saw, on the floor below the mail slot, a plain white envelope.

She picked it up. There was no address, no stamp. The flap hadn't even been glued down, simply tucked inside.

Probably a neighbor, she thought. Although she couldn't think of a neighbor who wouldn't simply text her.

She untucked the flap and pulled out the contents. A single piece of white printer paper, folded in thirds like a normal letter.

It was not a normal letter.

It was a message made from partial words cut from magazines and pasted to the page, all different colors and sizes and fonts. Like the ransom notes in *Columbo,* her favorite TV show as a kid.

But it wasn't a ransom note.

The cut-up words read, *Stop your investigation or we will stop your heart. We are watching. We are Legion. If you contact the police, we will kill Eleanor, too.*

Her daughter.

She pulled open her door and stepped out into the morning drizzle, the letter in her hand, hoping to see the person who'd left it. Aside from parked cars and the steady stream of traffic that flowed down Queen Anne Avenue, the street was empty.

Although what she would do if she saw someone, she had no idea. She was a journalist, and a darn good one, but the risks she took were professional, not personal. According to a recent visit with her doctor, she was thirty pounds overweight and pre-diabetic, plus her cholesterol and blood pressure were too high. One of these days, when work slowed down, she'd start exercising more than her voice box and her typing skills.

She told herself the letter writer was just a crank. She'd gotten mail like this before. Almost every investigative journalist she knew had gotten mail like this, especially the women. Vague threats, often expletive-laden or outright obscene, from people who were clearly off their meds. Her old copy editor would have had a field day with the grammar and spelling choices.

In the old days, they'd been actual letters sent to her desk at the *Star Tribune*, where KT had gotten her start covering the cops so many years ago. Now it was a nasty email sent to her public-facing address, or a text to her Signal account, or a DM on one of her obligatory socials. Her current outlet, a nonprofit group of investigative journalists that worked internationally and published online, didn't even have a physical office.

But this was different. Even after thirty years of first covering crime, then Wall Street, and then the tech industry, she'd never gotten anything dropped off at her home. And this was definitely the first mention of her daughter.

Unspoken was the fact that they knew where she lived, which was not publicly listed anywhere that she was aware of. Nor was her daughter's name. Reporting on the sad remains of the Chicago Outfit, she'd learned the hard way to safeguard her privacy. It had not been fun to meet a couple of pissed-off Italian-American tough guys waiting outside her South Loop apartment.

Although she was not in Chicago, and it was not twenty years ago. Today, every piece of information was available somewhere. Reporting on tech had taught her that. Any crank with mediocre online skills could find a way to dig up those details, or pay for them. So somebody in Seattle had found her address and left a note. So what?

Her watch pinged a calendar reminder of her Zoom call in five minutes. Then she'd have to hustle not to be late for an interview in Redmond with the new Microsoft CEO. On the way, she'd call the school to make sure Ellie didn't go home with anyone but her. Later, when she had time to spare, she'd definitely call the police. If past experience was any guide, reporting a threat would eat up two or three hours.

Sure, she'd been scared for a hot minute. But that was letting the dickheads win. So now she was just annoyed at the distraction and, yeah, maybe a little amused at the whole low-rent ransom-note quality of the thing. She took out her phone and snapped a picture of the letter, then texted it to a journalist friend in Milwaukee. "Can you believe this shit?"

After her Zoom call, the amusement lasted until she walked out to her bright orange Honda, thinking about the note again, telling her not to call the police. *We are watching. We are Legion.*

That was totally something a crank might write. How would he possibly know if she contacted the police? Her phone had decent security. The letter writer wasn't listening to her calls. The government, maybe, if they had a court order, but not a run-of-the-mill lunatic.

But if he *was* watching, would she even know? She lived on the north end of Queen Anne, in one of the last single-family houses on a busy commercial strip. In the way of Seattle real estate, someone had torn down the houses across the street and built mid-rise apartment buildings with boutiques and restaurants on their ground floors. It would be easy enough for the letter writer to wander from shop to shop, maybe linger over lunch at the falafel place, then move down to the Starbucks. The whole time with a view of her door.

Anyway, if she did call the cops, the detectives would want to talk in person. From her time on the police beat, she knew how it worked. They'd want to see the note, check it for fingerprints and other trace evidence. They'd come to the house. And if the letter writer was actually out there somewhere, watching, he would see the detectives knock on her door. Even in plainclothes, cops always looked like cops.

She could always drive to the West Precinct station in Belltown, she thought. But if the letter writer had eyes on the house? He could simply follow her car.

That was when she felt it. A weird prickling sensation between her shoulder blades. What if he *was* out there, watching?

She told herself she was paranoid. Imagining things. This didn't happen in the real world. Although she wasn't imagining the death threat. That letter was real.

She opened the car door and climbed behind the wheel, looking around for someone who seemed to be looking at her, someone she didn't recognize. But Seattle was a big city. She didn't recognize anyone.

On her way toward the freeway, she found herself looking in her rearview mirror. A lot.

Had she seen the same car, a small gray hatchback, jockeying through traffic behind her? From Queen Anne all the way across the floating bridge to Redmond?

And wasn't it behind her again three hours later, a hundred yards back, when she left the Microsoft parking lot?

It was hard to say. A lot of hatchbacks looked alike. A lot of them were gray.

But she was pretty sure it was the same car.

2

Outside the coffee shop, the rain eased up a little.

She looked around the place for the umpteenth time. In the sixty minutes she'd allotted for the mystery whistleblower meeting that didn't happen, quite a few customers had cycled through. Some grabbed a cup to go, others stopped to sit for a while. None of them seemed to pay the slightest bit of attention to a middle-aged woman with a laptop.

So why did she still feel that prickle between her shoulder blades?

After sending the photo of the death threat to her journalist friend in Milwaukee, they'd texted back and forth a few times. June Cassidy was fifteen years younger, but she'd been through a few things. She'd asked if KT needed help.

KT was scared, yes, but she still wasn't sure if she wasn't simply being paranoid. Aside from an ill-considered and mercifully brief marriage whose only positive outcome was her daughter, Eleanor, KT had been essentially on her own since college. She'd done a pretty good job of taking care of herself and Eleanor so far, thank you very much. And that's exactly why she told her friend June that she was handling it.

June had asked her to share her phone's location, just in case. Which wasn't weakness, KT thought, just an overabundance of caution. So she'd done that.

The truth was, KT had more than her share of enemies in tech. Just in the United States, the sector was valued somewhere between fifteen and twenty trillion dollars. Which meant that a bad earnings call or product review or funding round could drop company valuations, and personal fortunes, by hundreds of millions or even billions of dollars. KT's aggressive reporting had caused many such drops. Most people killed over money had died for far less. Not to mention the fact that the men running these companies—and they were almost always men—tended to be emotionally stunted assholes who were prone to a wide variety of bad behavior. Taken as a group, tech founders had a long record of being willing to do pretty much anything to expand their empires and increase their net worth.

Another problem, along with wondering whether to call the police, was that the letter had given her exactly zero indication of which investigation she was supposed to stop. None of the stories she had in the hopper seemed to connect to a reason someone might want her dead.

The Microsoft CEO profile was basically three thousand words of cotton candy she'd pre-sold to *The Wall Street Journal*. She had a litigation follow-up to her July piece about a hardware startup that had gone bust because the battery in their signature product had a tendency to explode, but she wasn't breaking any new ground there. She was doing preliminary reporting on several stories, including one about a social company that had basically been bought for parts, and another on OpenAI's big spend on data centers, plus a dozen other ideas on her tickler list that she'd barely started thinking about. It was true that you never knew where a story might take you, but as far as she could tell, none of these seemed likely to result in a scoop that would be worth killing over.

She'd barely even considered the whistleblower who'd failed to show for today's meeting. A successful journalist was a magnet for unsolicited and anonymous tipsters. Mostly they were offering a thousand varieties of useless crap. But there were enough gold nuggets in the steaming pile to make it worth sorting through occasionally. Of the latest batch, the format of the recording the whistleblower had sent was sufficiently unusual to get her interest. Except Ellie had clomped downstairs demanding her dinner before KT had a chance to listen to it.

The only story that didn't fit that same pattern was a tip she'd gotten about something called Gun Club. She'd asked around for a few months, called every source she had, but came up with nothing. Which in itself was a little strange, because tech was awash in strange drugs, biohacking fads, and bizarre political ideas, not to mention actual orgies at some of the fringier conferences. There had to be at least a few tech bros who'd discovered the joys of firearms.

In fact, the lack of response was interesting enough that, for the last few months, whenever she was working another story, she'd drop in a question at the end of the interview: Have you ever heard of something called Gun Club? The funny thing was, aside from a straight no, the most common answer was: Is that like Fight Club? Making it evident that her interview subjects knew even less about it than she did. But recently, she'd had three guys clam up and look very guilty about something, which, to KT's well-honed reportorial senses, was a signal to dig deeper. But because of her current workload, she hadn't had time to start. Currently, that story was going exactly nowhere.

Anyway, even if she did know what story to step away from, she couldn't help hearing the growly, critical voice of her very first editor, Jim Higgins, who had burrowed deeply inside her reporter's psyche. *What kind of journalist would let some crank scare her off a story?*

A live journalist, she told herself. With a daughter, safe from harm. But still. It rankled.

Her watch pinged with a new reminder that, with the current traffic, she should leave now to pick up Ellie.

She scanned behind her again. Nobody in the coffee shop was paying the slightest attention to her. She turned to look through the glass door, flecked with droplets of wind-driven rain. She didn't see anyone out there, standing in the wet. She didn't see the gray car, either. Somehow, though, the prickle between her shoulder blades had gotten worse.

It didn't matter. It was time to go. Ellie needed her. And frankly, KT needed Ellie in the passenger seat beside her, chattering blithely about whatever teenage drama had happened at school that day.

She told herself that the letter writer would surely give her more than six hours before he did something. Wouldn't he?

She pushed open the door and headed for her car.

The rain came down around her, rattling on the skin of her orange jacket. She wished she'd bought a black coat like everyone else. And a black car, or gray or white or beige. Anything but orange, her favorite color. It stood out like an emergency beacon, visible for blocks.

Confidence had always been her strength. That and her willingness to stand out. When she'd started on the police beat, she was the only woman in a man's game. She'd moved to finance, again the only woman journalist of any prominence. Then tech— more of the same. She had to be tougher, louder, more visible than the men. Some called her a bitch, a ball-breaker. She didn't care. She wore orange jewelry, had orange frames for her glasses. Orange was more than her favorite color, it was a trademark. A reminder to be bold.

Well, she wasn't feeling so bold now.

Her orange Honda was on Western Avenue, toward the end of the next block. She kept turning her head, not wanting anyone to walk up behind her. It wasn't easy in the stiff hood. She had to turn her shoulders, too, so walking was a little awkward. She'd never been a physical person. Still, she had her keys spiked out from her fist, her laptop bag on the opposite shoulder so she could shrug it off and run if somebody grabbed the strap. She wished she'd taken some real self-defense classes. Too late now. Tomorrow, she'd sign up. And start jogging, swear to God.

Western Ave was busy, traffic headed north to Belltown and south toward Pike Place Market, a tourist trap even in November. The cars were all moving, though. She crossed Lenora Street and kept walking. Less than a block to go. She hated the hood, it made her feel blind on three sides. And the drumbeat of raindrops blocked out all sound. She shucked it back. Her glasses spattered with droplets, her face and neck damp. Her hair would be a ruin. Eleanor would be merciless.

Now the rain was rolling down her forehead and into her eyes. She swiped it away, head turning. Behind her she could hear the low rumble of a big engine. Over her shoulder she saw a weird-looking pickup truck rolling slow. That wasn't good. She came to her Honda and stepped into the street at the back bumper with her keys out.

Then she saw the gray hatchback. It was parked two cars past hers, at a hydrant. There was a man inside. He opened the door, swung his legs out into the street, and began to rise to his feet. He wore a Red Sox cap and a face mask with a fanged clown printed on it. He was staring at her, eyes awash with some emotion she couldn't decode. He carried a gun in one hand.

Dear God, she was going to die. Ellie, what would happen to Ellie?

Behind her, the truck's engine revved and it surged up alongside her, angling forward toward her Honda. Then it came to a quick stop, trapping her and her car behind the pickup's hood. They weren't going to kill her, she thought, they were going to *kidnap* her. Take her somewhere and *do* something to her. She turned to run.

A man got out of the truck. He was tall and broad-shouldered in a plain black backpacker's raincoat. He didn't look at her, but at the gunman in the clown mask.

"Hey." The tall man strode forward. His hands were empty. His voice cut clearly through the sound of the rain. "Hey, you in the mask. I'm talking to you."

The gunman's attention shifted. His eyes widened when he saw the man walking toward him.

"You don't want to pull the trigger," the tall man said, a car-length away and closing. "Trust me, if you shoot somebody, it'll screw up your whole life. I should know, I've killed a whole bunch of people."

The gunman flinched and backed up into the vee of the hatchback's open door, lurching slightly as his calves hit the bottom of the doorframe. KT saw he was wearing ratty old sneakers with duct tape wrapping one toe box.

The pistol was pointed squarely at the tall man now. Still, he kept moving closer, kept talking to the man in the mask. "Give me the gun, buddy. This doesn't have to go bad. What would your mom say if you killed someone? Or your sister? Or your grandmother?"

The gunman blinked rapidly below the brim of the Red Sox cap. His Adam's apple bobbed as he swallowed. The gun began to drift off target. The tall man slowed, closing in. His face was kind, sympathetic. "It's okay, buddy. Whatever's going on, I can help."

The gunman's legs collapsed and he fell into the driver's seat, pulling his legs in after him. The tall man reached for the slamming door but had to snatch his hand back to keep his fingers from getting smashed. The hatchback was still running. The gunman jammed it into gear and hit the gas.

The tall man jumped back to avoid getting knocked over. The gray hatchback leapt into traffic, lurched into the oncoming lane followed by a chorus of horns, and vanished into the rain. The tall man watched him go.

Startled into motion, KT pulled open her own door, thinking that she needed to get away from this whole thing, but the angled truck effectively blocked her into the parking spot.

The tall man turned back toward her and walked around the hood of his truck. "Are you all right? Sorry that didn't go exactly as planned."

She still had her keys spiked in her fist. "What were you going to do?"

"Take away his gun." He gave her a wolfish grin, his eyes lit up like he was having fun. "Put him on the ground and call the cops."

She didn't understand. "You're not with the police? Who the hell are you?"

"Sorry," he said again, extending his hand. "My name's Peter Ash. June Cassidy's friend? She asked me to stop by. I was in the neighborhood."

3

She shook Peter's hand. It was big and warm and strong, and he didn't squeeze too hard like some men. She wanted to crawl into the safety and shelter of that hand for the rest of her life.

Now he was half-turned away, eyes flicking from her to the line of traffic and back. "We should go. If he circles, we don't want to be here." He reached out and opened the passenger door of his truck. Heated air wafted out.

Suddenly she realized she was shivering. "What about my car?"

He looked at her orange Honda. "Easy to spot, easy to follow." He gave her a diplomatic smile. "We'll come back for it."

She pointed at his truck. It was deep green with some kind of large wooden box built onto the back instead of the usual metal pickup bed. "That's not exactly anonymous."

"You're right," he said. "That's why I'm going to grab a rental first thing."

Eleanor, she thought. "I have to pick up my daughter."

"June told me." He put out a hand to help her into the truck. "We'll talk on the way."

He put on his blinker and pulled into traffic, then a moment later made a crisp U-turn and headed the opposite direction.

"If your guy is circling back, he'll be expecting us to go the other way."

"He's not my guy." She put on her seat belt. The truck was cleaner inside than she'd expected. The seat cover was new and the painted metal was polished to a high shine. "How did you know he wouldn't shoot?"

"I didn't." He unzipped his jacket and rapped his knuckles on his chest. "June bought me a top-quality ballistic vest a few years back. If your guy pulled the trigger, it would hurt like hell, but it wouldn't kill me. Unless he was firing armor-piercing rounds, which civilians can't get. And the odds are that most people would miss, even at that range. Adrenaline really winds you up, makes your hands shake. Takes a lot of practice to get past that."

She noticed his hands weren't shaking. He dug into his jacket pocket and pulled out a pistol, then set it on the bench seat between them.

"You had a gun? Why didn't you take it out and point it at him?"

He turned left on Lenora. "It would've made him feel threatened," Peter said. "If somebody's coming at you with a gun, and you've got a gun yourself, there's really only one way that's going to end. Besides, I could tell he wasn't a pro."

The shivering got worse. She wanted to curl up into a ball. But she was a journalist. She had questions. "How could you tell that?"

"The clown mask is an attention-grabber, totally amateur. And his sneakers wrapped in duct tape to keep the sole from flapping? Not the footwear of a professional."

"And what kind of person would be a professional?" She needed him to keep talking, to keep her mind off what had just happened.

Peter's eyes moved from the road to his side mirrors, then back to the road. "The pros are either former military or police, or someone who learned it on the street, like a gangbanger or cartel guy. Either way, an experienced killer would have been prepared for opposition. He wouldn't have hesitated. The second I got out of the truck, he'd have pulled the trigger to put me down. That done, he'd have shot you. Instead, your guy was surprised. Then he backed up and ran." He shook his head. "I'm just sorry he got away from me."

Ever the journalist, she said, "You told him you'd killed a whole bunch of people. Is that true?"

He glanced at her. An emotion playing on his face that she couldn't quite name. "I was a Marine lieutenant in Iraq and Afghanistan. For eight years, my job description was killing bad guys and protecting my people."

She couldn't stop shivering. He turned up the heater. "You'll be okay," he said. "You've had a bad moment. It'll pass."

She wrapped her arms around her knees, pulling them to her chest. Only the seat belt held her upright. She kept seeing the gunman's strange, watery eyes above the fanged clown mask. The pistol in his hand. And she was frozen, defenseless. As if, in that moment, the veneer of civilization had been peeled away and she saw a different reality. For reasons she didn't begin to understand, somebody wanted to kill her. And he'd come very close to doing it.

"Where's your daughter's school?" He put a hand on her shoulder. "Katelyn. Take a deep breath. Your daughter needs you. Where's her school?"

That got her mind working again. "McClure Middle School. Queen Anne, First Ave West, between Crockett and Howe. Do you need directions?"

"No. Can you call your daughter and tell her to stay inside, somewhere safe, until we get there?"

She blinked. "Yes." She uncurled herself and found her phone, then had an unpleasant thought. "You think that guy's still out there."

"Better to assume so." His eyes flicked to the rearview mirrors again. "I don't see his car behind us, but we should still take steps to prevent him from harming your daughter."

Her whole body clenched. Her voice sounded strangled, even to her. "You think he knows where she goes to school."

He glanced at her, impossibly calm and steady. "I was trying not to say that out loud, but it's possible. He knows where you live, right?"

She swallowed hard and called her daughter. Ellie didn't pick up. KT opened her text app and, doing her best to keep her voice steady, sent a voice message. "Eleanor, I need you to do something for me. Something weird has happened with work. I need you to stay inside the school, someplace safe, until I call you. Okay? This is serious. Text me back, please."

She hung up. Peter looked at her. "Does she usually ignore your calls?"

KT sighed. "She's a teenage girl. She ignores me every chance she gets."

"Will she listen to the message?"

KT raised her hands helplessly. "No idea. She's thirteen going on thirty, and she keeps turning off the tracking app."

"You mind if I borrow your phone?"

"Why?"

"To call the police."

"The note said if I talked to the police, they'd hurt Ellie."

"I think that genie is out of the bottle. That guy was ready to kill you. Getting the police to the school is your best chance to protect your daughter."

She looked him up and down, this rawboned and rough-looking man in the immaculate old truck, the pistol on the seat between them. "Don't you have a phone?"

"I do," he said. "But if I use yours, the police will have your number. So they can track you if things go badly."

She didn't want to ask what he might mean about things going badly. She woke her phone and held it out. He punched in three numbers.

"Are you recording? Great. My name is Peter Ash, and I'm driving a dark green 1968 Chevy pickup with a wooden cargo box on the back." He spoke slowly and clearly. "I'm with Katelyn Thorsen, the journalist. This morning, she received a death threat at her home in Queen Anne. A few minutes ago, on Western Avenue down by Pike Place Market, somebody waiting by her parked car pulled a gun on her. I managed to scare him away, but the threat included her daughter, Eleanor, thirteen years old. We're on our way to McClure Middle School to pick her up now. Can you send a couple of cars, in case he decides to try again?"

He listened for a moment. "I appreciate it, ma'am. Also, the guy was driving a gray hatchback, I think a Ford." He rattled off the plate number. "In case you run into him." He listened again. "Yes, please, send the detectives, we're happy to cooperate. Thank you."

He handed her back the phone, tucked the pistol's butt under his thigh, then gunned the big engine and began to weave through traffic. "We'll talk about why somebody might want to kill you after we get your daughter somewhere safe."

4

PETER

Peter Ash pushed hard up First Ave with the Space Needle on his right, leaning on his horn as he rolled through a series of red lights. He thought he might have seen the gray hatchback a block back, but it was hard to tell. The rain was heavy, and his side mirrors were small. The old truck's wipers did their best.

He hadn't been back to Seattle since he'd first met June, who'd lived in a garage apartment up on Capitol Hill. But he still had the city map in his head. It was a gift that he had first discovered in Officer Candidate School, the ability to study a map and retain it. In combat, it had saved him and his guys more times than he could count.

At West Roy, he ducked right for a block, then turned left and powered up Queen Anne Avenue, downshifting for the steep grade. Apartment buildings lined the road on both sides. Because of the hill, he could see more of the vehicles behind him, and the hatchback wasn't one of them. Ahead, a slow line of cars crept up the incline, blocking the road. He goosed the gas and slid into the oncoming lane, ignoring the horns and raised middle fingers.

KT was curled into herself, one hand grabbing the oh-shit handle and the other braced on the dashboard. But she didn't scream and she didn't complain, which let Peter focus on getting where they needed to go.

She'd almost lost it earlier. But she'd managed to collect herself when he mentioned her daughter. That was better than many people would be able to do after some asshole in a clown mask pointed a gun at them. June had told Peter that Katelyn Thorsen was the toughest reporter she'd ever met. Coming from June Cassidy, a very tough reporter herself, that was a major compliment.

At the top of the hill, Queen Anne Avenue became the neighborhood's main commercial strip. The south end was still sleepy and relatively undeveloped, although Peter felt strongly that the 5 Spot café should be a national landmark.

McClure Middle School was a few blocks down and one block west. Peter stopped at the corner by the park and looked north toward the school. With cars parked on both sides of the street, it was only wide enough for a single lane, and that was filled with a long line of idling cars, he assumed drivers waiting to pick up their kids. But he didn't see any police cruisers. Surely there'd been one cop on Queen Anne when he'd called.

She said, "What are you waiting for?" Her fists were clenched on her thighs.

"Too many cars," Peter said. "I don't want to get stuck in there." Thinking the guy in the clown mask could walk up the sidewalk behind the line of parked cars and Peter wouldn't see him until it was too late.

"Let me out here." She unbuckled her seat belt. "I'll find Ellie, and you can pick us up on the other side of the park."

"No." He turned left, away from the school. "Let me find a spot for the truck and we'll both go."

There were no spots this close to the school. He had to drive around the park to find a space. Getting out, he scanned for the hatchback as he peeled off his black slicker. "Take my jacket. Your guy's seen you in that orange coat."

"I told you, he's not my guy." She stood on the parking strip and peeled off her coat and pulled on his larger one. He stood bareheaded in a thin blue fleece in the falling rain. Tall and lean, muscle and bone, nothing extra. "What are you going to wear?"

He reached behind the seat and pulled out his old brown duck Carhartt jacket. "This'll do." It wasn't remotely waterproof, but the school was only a few blocks away. He ran the zipper up, pulled a faded blue baseball hat down over his damp, shaggy hair, then tucked the pistol into his pocket and slipped the keys above the sun visor. "Leave your door unlocked," he said. "Can you drive stick?"

She blinked. "Why do you ask?"

"In case something happens to me."

Her eyes widened and her voice rose. "What would happen to you?"

"Katelyn." He gave her a steady look. "Can you drive stick?"

She stared at him for a moment, then swallowed hard. "It's been a while. But yes."

"Excellent." He smiled at her. "If something happens, anything, you and your daughter run for the truck and get the hell out of Dodge. Got it?"

She nodded.

"Ready?"

"Definitely not." She pulled in a breath, let it out. "Let's go get my daughter."

Peter tended to put people into two categories. Those who stepped up when the time came, and those who didn't.

KT hadn't asked for this, but she was stepping up. For all the right reasons.

Peter liked her an awful lot just then.

★

They walked up the sidewalk, almost as if they weren't on the lookout for a possible killer. Peter kept his hand on the pistol in his pocket, his head on a swivel. Had he imagined the hatchback? Maybe. Better to assume it was out there, though.

"Where are the police," she asked softly.

"I don't know," Peter said. "They'll be here soon. A gun threat at a school will have their attention."

They crossed the road and cut through the park. It wasn't large, just big enough for a couple of Little League fields and an open space for soccer or whatever. Ahead, a slow stream of middle-school students walked toward them in groups of two and three, shoulders hunched against the rain. The big pistol didn't really fit in his coat pocket. He didn't want to start a panic. He unzipped his jacket, then tucked the gun into his waistband at the small of his back, where the hem would cover it. The cotton canvas was absorbing water like a sponge.

Passing a trio of students, they found the gate at the last baseball diamond. Past it was an ugly low redbrick and concrete building with a blue and white sign that said it was a community center. "The school is just up there," she said.

The line of cars was moving slowly, a few with doors open, loading kids. "Where does she usually wait for you?"

"Under the covered entryway," she said. "With her friends."

Peter turned to look over his shoulder again, scanning the street and the opposite sidewalk. How vulnerable these kids were, he thought. All the school shootings in the last few years, it made him sick. And here he was, walking up with a pistol. It was the other guy's fault, Peter knew, the asshole with the clown mask and the cheap sneakers. But these kids shouldn't have to deal with any of it.

"Call her again," he said. Still no police.

Her phone was already in her hand. She hit speed-dial and put it to her ear, listening. Then made a face and shoved it back in her pocket. "It went to voicemail."

Now he could see the entryway. It had concrete pillars and a broad, flat roof that ran between the community center and the school. The school was nicer than the community center, more redbrick and windows and less concrete, but it still had an industrial look. Or maybe a little like jail, Peter thought. That's how he'd felt about school, growing up in northern Wisconsin. Even then, before his wars and their aftermath, he'd always preferred being outside. Even in the rain.

Students stood in clumps under the flat roof, talking, laughing, most of them in shirtsleeves, some alone and on their phones. Kids being kids. "You see her?"

"No."

He steered KT toward the entryway, checking the street, the sidewalk. No hatchback. "Where else would she be?"

"I don't know. Inside somewhere?"

"She have a favorite teacher?"

"Yes. Mr. Huth, her English teacher. Wait, there she is."

KT arrowed through the clumps of students toward a slender girl with jet-black hair, an ancient Sex Pistols T-shirt under an unzipped black hoodie with a line of safety pins down the arms, seriously shredded jeans, and black high-top Doc Martens with bright red laces. She leaned against one of the concrete pillars, talking animatedly with a group of boys and girls decked out in similar outfits. Punk rock was back, apparently. At least in middle school.

"Ellie. You didn't get my message?"

"Uh, no?" The girl smirked at her friends, sarcasm dripping.

KT grabbed her arm. "We have to go."

The girl pulled her arm back, eyebrows scrunched in scorn. "I'm going to Susanna's house. We have a project due Monday."

Although connected to the school and the community center, the covered entryway was wide open on the other two sides. Behind him, the scrum of students and the cars with waiting parents blocked his view. Looking ahead, past Ellie and her friends, Peter could see all the way through to the next block. Partially screened by parked cars, a gray hatchback ghosted past.

"This isn't good," he told KT softly. "We need to get moving."

Eleanor looked up at him. "Who's *this* meatball?"

Her friends stared at Peter with all the disdain available to eighth graders, which was considerable. He was pretty sure "meatball" was not a positive term.

Peter gave the girl a smile and took her elbow. "I'll explain on the way. Our ride's on the other side of the park."

"Get your hands *off* me." She tried to pull away but he didn't let her. "Let me go or I'll scream my head off."

Peter let her go, then looked at her mother. "Can I tell her?"

Ellie said, "Tell her *what*, Mom? Who *is* this guy?"

KT gave Peter a nod.

He stepped between Ellie and her friends and leaned close. Despite the punk rock outfit and attitude, she smelled like shampoo and fruit roll-ups. Voice low, he said, "Shut up and listen, kid. Don't say anything. Somebody tried to kill your mom about half an hour ago. They're still out there. You need to come with us. Now."

Ellie's eyes widened. She looked at her mom and hissed, "Is he for real?"

KT held out her hand. "Unfortunately, yes. Can we go now?"

Ellie took the hand. The attitude was gone and suddenly she was just a thirteen-year-old girl, scared and wanting her mother.

5

Peter led them through the entryway to the community center entrance, then down a hallway to the exit doors on the far side of the building. He peeked out through the falling rain, didn't see the gray hatchback or anyone wearing tape-wrapped sneakers.

He'd never seen the gunman's face, just the mask and the Red Sox cap. If the guy was smart enough to track them here, he was probably smart enough to take them off to blend in. Peter was hoping he wasn't smart enough to change his shoes. If he had another pair, he probably wouldn't have worn those cheap sneakers to begin with.

If the cops had arrived, they were still out of sight. They weren't in the line of waiting cars. Maybe they'd come up on the next block. Although subtlety was never the strong suit of local law enforcement. It rarely paid off for them.

Behind him, Ellie still held her mother's hand. "Why is somebody trying to kill you?"

"I don't know." KT's voice was quiet. "They put a note through our mail slot while I was driving you to school. And a man was waiting by my car this afternoon. He had a gun. Peter scared him off."

"Holy shit," the girl said under her breath.

"Eleanor Grace. Language."

"Mom. Someone's trying to kill us and you're worried about me swearing?"

Over his shoulder, Peter said, "It's clear. Let's go." He held the door, then led them across the concrete walkway toward the trees, heading into the park between the baseball fields and a playground. He was glad of the girl's boots, although he wished she had a raincoat. None of the other girls had coats, either. Fashion required sacrifice.

He turned to check on them and realized that her hoodie was already too wet. He stopped under a big pine, its lower branches offering a little shelter. "Hold on." He shucked his Carhartt and held it out. "Put this on, it'll keep you dry."

Ellie gave him a look. Then turned her back and allowed him to help her put it on as though he was her date for the spring formal. It was big and heavy with water and hung almost to her knees. She wrinkled her nose. "Dude, this kinda smells."

"Sorry." Peter looked behind them, then left and right, and started walking again. "There's a big dog who likes to sleep on it."

The girl followed in his wake. "You have a dog? What kind?"

"A mutt named Mingus. He's badly behaved, but fiercely loyal to people he likes."

"Would he like me?"

"Depends on your attitude," Peter said. "Just like with people."

After a few minutes, near the middle of the park, they came to the end of the trees. Peter checked the perimeter and saw only more students trickling out into the neighborhood. He gathered KT and Ellie and pointed toward the next baseball diamond and the trees past the outfield fence. Beyond it was the sidewalk and street where he'd seen the gray hatchback. "That's where we're going. Walk fast, but don't run. We want to look like everyone else trying to get out of the weather. My truck's on the next block. It's green with a big wooden box on the back. Ready?"

They set out into the open along the waist-high chain-link. There was little wind, and the rain fell straight down. Small drops, close together. Peter's T-shirt was wet under the fleece, but he was too amped up to feel the cold. He had his pistol in his hand now. The girl saw it and sucked in a breath but didn't say anything.

They walked the fence line, Peter's eyes scanning through the points of the compass. He saw middle-schoolers, parents with strollers, dog-walkers. He was hoping for blue and red light bars flashing, but there were still no cops. Well behind him, more cars rolled into the pickup line, but the gunman wouldn't do that. He'd already scouted the block. Maybe he'd scouted it days ago. And now he was circling like a shark. That's what Peter would have done.

His Chevy was a liability. With the big mahogany cargo box on the back, it was too identifiable, and nowhere near as maneuverable as her little Honda. But the heavy Detroit steel would make short work of that little gray hatchback, if it came to that.

They made it to the sidewalk and turned left and kept walking past well-maintained Craftsman-style houses packed into narrow lots with garages and alleys behind. On the other side of the street, a pair of coatless boys goofed in the rain on their way home. A luxury SUV passed, then an electric sedan. No gray hatchback. No solo pedestrians in tape-wrapped sneakers.

They came to the corner and crossed the street. They were on Third Avenue West. Ahead, he could see a couple more kids walking home, backs bent under huge book bags, then the parked pickup's cargo box rising above the cab. Maybe they'd made it.

At the truck, he walked past the front bumper to step into the road. On the other side of the street, there was a long gap with no parked cars. He saw a woman on the far sidewalk with a double stroller and a little dog on a leash, talking on her phone. He had his door open and his foot on the sill when he heard an engine wind up high. He turned and saw a little gray car flying up the street toward him.

He felt a surge in his blood as the adrenaline hit. His vision tunneled down and he tasted copper in his mouth. The car kept coming. Was it a hatchback? Somehow he closed his door and stepped back to stand between the hood and the next car, shouting over his shoulder, "Get down, get down."

The pistol rose in a two-handed grip, his feet apart and set. He could see it was a hatchback now. The man glaring through the windshield wasn't wearing the mask, but he'd kept the Red Sox hat. His face was unshaven, eyes red and raw. Peter didn't want to fire because of the woman with the baby stroller, the kids walking home, the houses across the street. You never knew where a ricochet might go. But he didn't want to get shot, either.

The hatchback slowed, tires slurping on wet asphalt. Before Peter pulled the trigger, he needed to see the guy's weapon coming up. He needed to know the woman with the baby stroller was out of the line of fire. The other guy would be wired on adrenaline, too. He was an amateur. His aim would be shit. Peter was betting his life on it.

Then the hatchback was there, *BANG BANG BANG*, the guy firing early through his side window. Peter threw up an arm to shield his eyes from the flying glass as he felt a hard blow to the sternum, like getting hit with a framing hammer. He stumbled back with the wind knocked out of him and his heart racketing in his chest, but managed to scramble around the front corner of his truck behind the shield of the engine block, hand to the armor covering his upper torso, wondering if he was dying.

THUNK THUNK. THUNK THUNK THUNK. The sound of rounds penetrating sheet metal. Now Peter was pissed. Totally not cool to shoot a man's truck. He still had his pistol. Okay, Marine, time to take this asshole out. He looked over his shoulder and saw KT and Ellie crouched by the mahogany cargo box, staring at him, eyes wide.

"Run," he said. They didn't move. "*Run!*" he said again. They still didn't move. Beyond them, the two coatless boys stood staring.

Through the ringing in his ears, he heard a car door close. He found his knees and got his feet under him in a crouch. He heard a clatter and peeked around the front bumper. A pair of tape-wrapped sneakers stood in a growing pool of radiator fluid beside a spent pistol magazine. Then came the hard clack of the new magazine being socketed in place. And under it all, a woman screaming from across the street. The double stroller.

He turned in a crouch and scrambled toward Ellie and KT, shoving his pistol into his waistband and grabbing an arm in each big hand and pulling them upright and away. Down the sidewalk he ran, towing them behind him, his instincts screaming to pull his pistol, to turn and fire, but he didn't. He'd caused enough collateral damage in his military career, he wasn't about to open fire after school in a family neighborhood.

"Hey, buddy!" a cracked voice called out behind him. "Who's the little bitch now?"

Peter didn't slow or look back. Ellie and KT were moving under their own power now. He pulled them to the right between two parked cars and across the street, angling to keep the truck between them and the shooter's line of sight. The woman with the stroller had stopped screaming and was crouched low beside a blue Tesla with her children in her arms. The houses on this side were up on a low hill, their front walks beginning with a short flight of concrete steps. He picked one with a lot of tall plantings that would help hide their movement. "Up there," he said. "Go go go."

These houses all had narrow side yards with a path to the back and the garage and the alley beyond. The shooter would likely see where they were going, but if Peter could get them far enough ahead of the guy, they'd have options. He could find a place to wait, then step out and put him down without endangering any innocent people.

Although he probably shouldn't kill the guy, Peter thought. Because he wanted to ask some questions. But he might not have a choice.

6

The house was pale blue with white trim and a big front porch. On both sides were low gates, one cedar and one chain-link. Peter chose the cedar, knowing he could kick it open if it was padlocked, but it wasn't even latched. "This way."

Down on the street, he heard shouting, a man's voice coming closer. KT was slowing. He pushed her ahead of him, hoping Ellie would help keep her mother moving, then slipped through the gate, closed and latched it, and followed after them, looking over his shoulder. Under the armor, his chest hurt like hell every time he breathed, but it was a lot better than the alternative.

The space between houses was maybe four feet wide. They ran down the narrow concrete walkway through knee-high ferns wet with rain. He passed a hose hanging from a hook and threw it down in a tangle. He did the same with the wheelbarrow leaning up against the wooden siding, anything to slow the other man and buy KT and Ellie some distance.

Then into the narrow back yard like a miniature nature preserve with small trees and shrubs and mounded garden beds filled with still-green leafy plants, the whole thing enclosed by a six-foot cedar fence. Ellie had already opened the rear gate beside the two-car garage. It was directly behind the side yard with a clear line of sight.

Then the shooter put his gun arm around the front of the house and pulled the trigger blindly. *BANG BANG BANG BANG*. Peter ducked behind the back corner, protected by the house's hundred-year-old framing. The guy wasn't likely to hit them without aiming, but even a broken clock was right twice a day.

When the gunfire stopped, Peter raised the pistol and aimed just above the gate, at chest level. Also in his sights, in the house on the other side of the street, was a man staring at him from a second-story balcony like he was watching an action movie on TV. If the would-be killer went to open the gate and Peter fired on him, he might well kill the wrong man.

He couldn't pull the trigger in this shooting gallery. He turned to sprint toward the back gate. "Go," he shouted.

Ellie pulled her mother into the alley and out of sight, her voice floating behind her, high and frantic. "Mom, c'mon, please."

Running, Peter heard the other man firing again, now more deliberately, thirty yards away. *BANG. BANG. BANG*. He waited for the burning brand of a pistol round in his shoulder or butt or legs. None came.

Then he was through, slamming the gate behind him. There were splintered holes in the fence. "Time to move."

Katelyn leaned against the side of the garage, bent over with her hands on her knees, trying to catch her breath. "I need a minute."

Ellie's eyes were wide, her pale face rigid with fear. "What do we do?"

Two houses down, on the other side of the alley, a man was in the parking place beside his one-car garage, getting into a red Audi sedan. Peter hauled ass for the car, calling over his shoulder, "This way. Get her moving."

The Audi backed up into the alley. It was long and low, the engine growling. Peter knocked on the window. The driver startled, staring at him. "What the hell?" His voice was muffled coming through the glass.

"I need your car," Peter said. "Open up."

The driver gave him a scornful look. "I'm not giving you my car, bro. It's custom. Get a job." He was younger than Peter in a very expensive hard-shell jacket and what looked like recent hair plugs.

Peter held up the pistol. "Open the door or I'll break your window. Then I'll break your face."

"Shit, okay, don't hurt me." The driver put up his hands and began to climb out of the low-slung car. Peter looked past him and was glad to see the key fob in a cup holder. They wouldn't get far without it.

Ellie came up, towing her panting mother, whose face was bright red. Behind them, the sound of gunshots. Obviously the gunman had brought a few extra magazines.

Peter found the unlock button and opened the rear door. KT climbed inside, with Ellie right behind her. Two houses back, the gunman banged the gate open. The Audi owner looked at him stupidly.

"Ellie, climb into the front," Peter said. "Now."

She began to move. Peter grabbed the Audi owner and bent him over and shoved him into the back seat and slammed the door. The man was a dickhead, but he didn't deserve to die.

The gunman turned at the sound, his pistol rising. Peter slid behind the wheel, his battered chest aching from the motion, then slammed the shifter into drive and punched the gas.

The Audi leapt forward like a jackrabbit, tires grabbing the wet concrete. The car smelled brand-new, the dashboard pristine. The odometer had nineteen miles on it. The alley ended and he was going too fast for the turn; the car slid sideways and banged off a parked car but kept moving forward, the Audi's owner shouting his outrage. Another half block and Peter stood on the brakes and threw it in park. He turned to KT. "Can you drive?"

"I think so." She was still breathing hard.

He got out, taking the pistol from his waistband again. "Come around and get in. Get off Queen Anne, keep driving until you hear from me. June gave me your number."

KT came around the front of the Audi. Ellie stared at him, eyes wide with fear. He could see the pulse in her neck. She said, "Where are you going?"

Peter gave her a soft smile and backed away to give Katelyn room to get in. "Eleanor, your job is to call 911. Tell them shots fired, shooter is a man in a red baseball cap, and this intersection. Got it?"

She nodded.

KT wedged herself behind the wheel and fixed him with a stare at once grateful, terrified, and determined. "Peter, I . . . Thank you."

He nodded. "My pleasure, ma'am. Now go."

Then she hit the gas and the car flew away and Peter stood alone on the street in the driving rain like a time-tarnished statue from a long-forgotten war. Skin hot despite the rain soaking through his fleece, the .45 hanging heavy in his left hand like an extension of his arm.

He turned and began to jog up the sidewalk toward the idling hatchback, his legs feeling strong and sure. Maybe the shooter would follow him down the alley and around the corner. Maybe he'd think it was a lost cause and retrace his steps. But either way, with KT and Ellie gone, the guy would almost certainly return to his car. And find Peter, waiting.

At the hatchback, he took out the knife he kept clipped to his front pocket, thumbed it open, and bent to the front tire. With a single quick slash, he cut the valve stem and the rubber went flat.

Neither of them was going anywhere until this was over.

As Peter straightened up, he saw the guy return through the side gate of the same house and spot him in the street. It was thirty yards, a shot Peter could make.

But in the picture window to the shooter's left was a little girl in a yellow shirt, standing on the couch with her hands on the glass, looking out.

Peter lowered his pistol. "Come on down, buddy. Let's talk." Hoping he could still end this without a bullet. Or at least get this guy down on the street with the hill behind him, so nobody else would get hurt.

The guy raised his own gun toward Peter and fired too quickly, *BANGBANGBANG.*

Thirty yards was a long way when you'd been running and your pulse was jacked up and you were burning with adrenaline. Two of the three rounds cracked into the hatchback behind Peter, nowhere close to hitting him. The third was higher and he heard the whisper as it passed a foot from his ear.

Then he was in motion toward cover behind the hatchback's hood, fast but unhurried, in that slow-motion zone where the world is smooth and fluid and nothing can harm you. Peter was well aware that zone was a chemical lie cooked up inside his brain, but he was addicted to the rush of it, the feeling of being acutely alive. Otherwise he'd have stayed in the Audi and kept driving away from gunfire like any normal person would do.

But Peter was not a normal person. He was a Recon Marine, with more combat deployments than he cared to remember. Those eight years in the Corps had rewired him, turned him into a man with the war inside him like a sleeping dragon, waiting for a chance to wake up and feed.

The dragon was awake now. Peter smiled at the guy, beckoned with the gun barrel. "Come a little closer, maybe next time you'll actually hit me."

The shooter walked across the yard toward the concrete steps. The little girl in the yellow T-shirt still watched through the window, directly behind him.

Peter heard sirens now, distant and filtered by the rain. Maybe he wouldn't have to kill this guy. Although the cops might.

The shooter was coming down the steps, the pistol fully extended. "You didn't have to get in the way," he said. "All I wanted to do was keep my promise."

"Your promise? What promise?"

"Kill the lady," he said. "She was supposed to stop, but she didn't."

"Who did you promise?" Peter kept his voice calm. "Who told you to kill her?"

"I got a special message, just for me." With his free hand, he swiped off his Red Sox cap and ran his arm across his forehead. His eyes were wet and red with sagging bags beneath them like puddles of melted wax. "I was going to be a hero. But I failed. And it's all your fault. So now I have to kill you instead."

This guy was obviously a few tacos short of a combination plate. Peter kept his pistol barrel down and away. "Buddy, you don't have to kill anyone," he said. "Everything's okay. Put the gun down, let's talk. You can tell me all about it."

The sirens were louder now, a rising wail. The gunman kept descending the steps until he reached the sidewalk, walking toward Peter with nothing but concrete behind him. If Peter was going to pull the trigger with the least amount of risk to others, now was the time.

The duct tape on the guy's sneaker had come unwrapped in the rain. The loose sole flapped with every step. He was crying now. "It's *not* okay. *Nothing* is okay. I *promised*, and I *failed*."

Peter thought back to a hostage negotiation course the Marines had sent him to, years ago. "Hey, buddy, what's your name? My name's Peter. I can help if you let me. Just please put the gun down."

A dark blue police cruiser flew around the corner to Peter's right, siren screaming, another car immediately behind it. They must have seen the hatchback blocking the street because both skidded to a stop, lights flashing. On Peter's left, a black unmarked SUV with flashers in the grille came up the next block and eased through the intersection.

Peter said, "Put the gun down, buddy. Please. Hey, do you like ice cream? Let's get some ice cream."

The gunman looked at the cruisers. Officers were out of their vehicles now, crouched behind their doors, weapons out. Some pointing at the guy, some at Peter.

"Jeez, I think we should both put our guns down, don't you?" Moving slowly and carefully, Peter laid his pistol down on the hood of the hatchback and held his hands out to his sides. He knew the cops would rather he threw it away from him, but he wanted to be able to snatch it up again if the guy started shooting. "C'mon, buddy. Put your gun down and let's get some ice cream. Or coffee. Or whatever you want. A nice cold beer?" That last one sounded pretty good to Peter right now.

The shooter's arms slowly lowered to his sides, the pistol in his right hand. His face calm now, resolute.

A distorted voice came through a police loud-hailer. "Drop

the gun and step away. Get down on your knees with your hands behind your head."

The shooter didn't move.

"Put the gun down," Peter said. "It'll be okay."

"No, it won't." The shooter shook his head sadly. "You don't know what's coming."

Then he raised the pistol and fitted the barrel under his chin and pulled the trigger.

7

Peter sat shivering in the open rear door of an ambulance, head bent and aching, a silver foil blanket wrapped around his shoulders. It was full dark, still raining, and the temperature had dropped enough for him to see his breath. His knee bounced to the beat of a metronome only he could hear. Behind him, KT sat on one of the jump seats, arms wrapped around Ellie on her lap.

With all the police on the street around them, Peter figured mother and daughter were safe enough. But he'd still positioned himself so that anyone trying to harm them would have to go through him.

He'd already stripped off the body armor June had given him, and the EMTs had supplied an ice pack for the bruise on his chest, which throbbed in time with his heartbeat. The adrenaline comedown had hit him hard. He wanted nothing more than to close his eyes. But every time he blinked, he saw the shooter jam the gun under his own chin and blow his brains out.

He knew from experience that it would stay with him. Like the other memories lingering after eight years of war and the things he'd done afterward.

He had good reasons for all of it. He'd wanted to help people.

He'd tried to do the right thing. But sometimes it went wrong. Sometimes people died.

The police had come late, but they'd come in force. Along with a couple of pop-up tents with drop-down side panels to keep the rain off the cops and the body, someone had brought coffee for Peter and KT and hot chocolate for Ellie. Two detectives named Kitzinger and O'Donnell had already taken their statements separately, going over the events of the afternoon at least three times to make sure there were no fault lines in their stories. Peter had tried hard not to be separated from KT and Ellie, but Kitzinger wasn't having any of it.

He was glad he'd made that first 911 call, which had established his desire for police involvement from the jump. He was also grateful that he hadn't actually shot the guy, because that would have ratcheted up their professional suspicion. Even with witnesses to confirm his story, the cops would have taken him to the station for sure. The white static, which was what Peter called the post-traumatic claustrophobia that had showed up after his war, would flare up like a wildfire in a tiny police interview room.

Now he turned his empty coffee cup in his hands while his mind tried to make sense of the dead man's words. He was supposed to kill the lady, he'd said. Because he'd gotten some kind of message. From who? And why? And why had he ended up killing himself? *You don't know what's coming.* He'd seemed a little unhinged, to say the least.

Thinking about all of this, Peter had listened while KT had told the police about the stories she'd been working on, trying to figure out why she'd been targeted. The Microsoft CEO interview she'd done that afternoon. A piece about OpenAI's investment in data centers. A postmortem on a failed hardware startup. An analysis of startups acquired by the Big Five, and what happened afterward. And a dozen other stories she'd barely looked at, including a whistleblower who'd reached out for a conversation but never showed up for the meeting, and something about an oddly secretive group of tech bros who may or may not be into guns.

She and June could get into that later. Or tomorrow.

Tomorrow would probably be better.

Behind him, Ellie wore her mom's orange raincoat, and KT still wore Peter's. He heard KT murmuring to her daughter, then she came to sit beside him in the open doorway of the ambulance.

He asked, "Are you okay?"

"No. I want to scream." Her voice was quiet as she stared out into the darkness. "But I have to keep it together for Ellie."

Peter was familiar with that process. "You can freak out after she's gone to bed. If you like, we can get drunk."

"Oh, we're definitely getting drunk." She turned to look at him. "You seem fine. How is that possible? He shot you point-blank, you could have died. You watched him kill himself."

"I'm not fine," he said. "I just have more experience processing this kind of thing."

"What do you mean, more experience?" Ellie had left the jump seat and crept up behind them.

"Hush, Ellie." KT reached for her arm and pulled the girl to sit between her and Peter. "That's not your business."

"It's okay." Peter turned to Ellie. "I fought in two different wars. I've been shot at before."

She peered up at him, wired from her large hot chocolate. "Did you kill anyone?"

"Eleanor Grace Thorsen! Peter, I am so sorry."

Peter might have punched a civilian who asked him that question, but Ellie was only thirteen, and she'd been through a lot in the last few hours. She was practically a combat vet herself. Peter figured she deserved an answer.

"Yes, Ellie. I killed people. That's what happens in war. Why do you ask?"

She looked away. "I just, like, I don't understand what happened today. Why would someone want to hurt my mom and me? Over some dumb news story?"

"That's a very good question," Peter said. "I'd like to know the answer myself."

KT nodded. "Me, too."

The girl opened her mouth to speak, then closed it again.

"Go ahead," Peter said. "Ask your question. You've earned the right."

Ellie looked at her mom, then back to Peter. "What's it like to be in a war?"

"It sucks," Peter said.

Although that wasn't the whole truth.

Because the sun never shone more brightly than when somebody was trying to kill you. You felt alive. That was war's dirty little secret, the reason young men had fought since the dawn of time. War could be fun as hell.

Peter hated to admit that he missed it. But sometimes he did.

Which is one reason why, when June had called about the death threat, Peter had dropped what he was doing and climbed in his truck to help.

God help him.

A man appeared out of the night. Maybe sixty with a broad silver mustache, he was bulky and imposing in a long black slicker and a black cowboy hat, rain streaming from its broad brim. "Mr. Ash, I'm Captain Durant. May I have a word?" He pointed toward a tent a dozen yards away.

Peter climbed to his feet and took a few steps into the rain, which pattered on the silver blanket wrapped around his shoulders. "Here's good." He didn't want to get too far from KT and Ellie, sitting in the brightly lit ambulance. "What's a police captain doing at the scene of an attempted murder?"

Durant had the hooded eyes and expressionless face of a man who'd seen everything and couldn't unsee it. His blue-stubbled jowls lifted in a faint polite smile. "Detectives Kitzinger and O'Donnell work for me. I run our special investigations squad, among other things. I'm curious why you showed up on Western Avenue to begin with."

"I already told Kitzinger and O'Donnell," Peter said. "I was doing a project at my girlfriend's property in Klickitat County when she called and said KT needed help. So I got in the truck and headed for Seattle."

"That's not an answer," Durant said. "I want to know what kind of man drives four hours to put himself between a bullet and a woman he's never met?"

Peter shrugged. It wasn't complicated. "I like to be useful."

"You were useful overseas, too," Durant said. "I just got off the phone with someone I know at the Pentagon. He shared some details from your file. Silver Star, Bronze Star for valor, couple of Purple Hearts."

Peter didn't like talking about this. "None of that means anything. It's just politics."

"Riiiight." Durant looked at him, a butterfly pinned to a corkboard. "And that's why the rest of your file is almost completely redacted. Listen, I know you're a serious guy. So I want to be straight with you, make sure you understand something.

You saved lives today. We appreciate that, believe me. But your involvement is now over. This is a police matter."

Peter felt the muscles bunch and flex in his shoulders. His neck was tight as a bridge cable. But he kept his voice casual, reasonable. "You understand why we might be curious." He tipped his head toward KT, who'd been listening to their conversation. "Somebody tried to kill us today, and we have no idea why. We don't even know his name."

"That's why I'm here, to share what I can. The guy's name was Geoffrey Reed. He had no criminal convictions that we can find. He did have a number of arrests, however, and a history of serious mental illness, including one period of involuntary commitment in a psychiatric institution."

"But what's his connection to the stories KT was working? How did he get her home address? What about that stuff he said before he killed himself? He said he'd gotten a message. He was supposed to kill KT. Who sent the message? Why try to kill a journalist?"

"Mr. Ash—"

Peter's voice rose. "The letter said *We are Legion*. Plural. I'm concerned that there might be somebody else involved. Did you get into his phone?"

Durant's mustache twitched with irritation. "This isn't our first investigation," he said dryly. "We're inside Geoffrey Reed's phone, we looked at every app. We can't find any messages telling him to kill anyone. We can't find any messages at all, except a few texts from his sister. With his medical history, any message was more likely to come from the voices in his head. There's no conspiracy. It's easy to get somebody's home address unless they spend a whole lot of time and money keeping it out of the system."

He looked past Peter and raised his voice, aware that KT had been listening to their conversation. "Ms. Thorsen, was that a priority for you?"

"It was," she said. "Obviously, it will be a much bigger priority after today."

Peter wanted to feel relief, but he didn't. June had forwarded KT's photo of the threat letter. He kept thinking about it. "Okay, that's Reed's phone. What about the rest of his life?"

"We have a team at his apartment right now. Forensics will do a deep dive into all his electronics, including his computer and whatever else we find, just to make sure. But I have to tell you, most of the guys who do this kind of stuff, they're not right in the head. That's looking like the case with this guy Reed."

KT said, "I want access. I want to know everything you know about him. For my own peace of mind, and my daughter's."

"Ma'am, I'm sorry, but that's not possible. This is an active investigation. In the unlikely possibility that there are others involved, I can't have you muddying the waters. It might affect our ability to prosecute."

KT stood up. She was clearly fighting her own adrenaline crash, her eyes sunken and her skin pale. She was still scared, Peter could see it. But he watched with admiration as she took a deep breath and gathered herself.

"Captain Durant, I appreciate your position. I have no interest in disrupting your investigation. But somebody just tried to murder both me and my daughter. You know I'm a journalist. I have a national platform. Obviously, I'm going to write about this. The relevant question for you and your bosses is this: How would the Seattle Police Department like to be portrayed? As concerned professionals who did everything they could to help the victim of an attempted murder? Or as bumbling idiots who had credible information about a possible school shooter but couldn't be bothered to dispatch a single cruiser until long after the first shots were fired?"

Durant's face darkened. "We had a six-car pileup on Highway 99, with multiple injuries. We came as soon as we could. In addition, the department is responsible for security for the technology conference that starts in three days. And, as I'm sure you are aware, there is a nationwide shortage of new police recruits, and the SPD is significantly understaffed across all precincts."

KT put on a cheerful smile. "That's one side of the story, Captain. I can spin it a lot of ways, depending on what happens next. I want full access. Why don't you talk to your bosses and I'll call you first thing tomorrow. By then you should know a lot more about Mr. Reed."

Durant's tone hardened. "Ma'am? All due respect? You really don't want to fuck with me."

KT's smile only got larger. "Captain, you should really read my work. I've spent three decades fucking with bigger fish than you, and I'm still here. I also have the mayor's personal cell number. If I have to call him, it's going to go a lot worse for you. So do the smart thing. Get with the program or get out of my way."

Now Peter understood why KT was such a successful journalist. Beneath the middle-aged mom was a titanium core that would not bend.

Peter raised his hand. "While you're at it, is there any chance I can get my gun back?"

"It's with forensics," Durant said. "We just want to compare test firings against the rounds we dig up here."

"I told you, I never pulled the trigger."

"And I'm sure you're telling the truth, but I have to follow procedure. When it passes ballistics, I'll get it back to you."

"I don't have another weapon. What if Reed wasn't working alone?"

Durant gave him a dark look. "I'll see if I can expedite."

"Thanks," Peter said. "One last thing. Can you get someone to give us a lift to a hotel? KT doesn't want to go home tonight, and my truck took a round to the radiator."

Durant sighed. "I'd send you with a patrolman but God only knows what she'd get out of him." He pointed at an unmarked black Suburban gleaming in the rain. "That's my ride. I'll take you."

8

They stopped at Peter's crippled truck to pick up his duffel, KT's work backpack, and Ellie's school bag, which she'd dropped on the grass. He left the keys above the sun visor. He'd already called a tow service.

Trailed by two police cruisers, they drove to KT's place to grab a change of clothes and toiletries, Durant and his driver in the front, Peter and Katelyn and Eleanor stuffed into the back. Without Peter needing to ask, the uniforms checked the house before KT and Ellie went inside. It made him like Durant more. Overnight bags packed, they drove three miles to the Marco Polo Motel on Aurora Avenue with the patrol cars still in their wake.

Also known as Highway 99, Aurora was a long commercial strip running from north to south like the city's spine. The speed limit was forty here, but traffic flew along at sixty. The motel was two stories with the room doors all opening onto the central parking lot. The second floor had a long raised exterior walkway and four sets of stairs. The motel's neighbors were a questionable medical office on one side and an improbably large tanning studio on the other. Across the divided road was a discount furniture store and a tire retailer.

KT gave Peter a look. "Of all the hotels in the area, this is the place you picked?"

At least the parking lot was well-lit. He would have preferred something with actual security, but it was the only place he could find that took cash without swiping a credit card. It also had the bonus of adjoining rooms. Despite Durant's reassurance, Peter was still feeling paranoid.

"Not a lot of vacancies on short notice," he said. "It's only for one night. If you don't feel comfortable going home tomorrow, we'll find a better place."

As Peter opened his door, Durant said, "Detective Kitzinger has assigned a patrol officer to keep watch as long as he can. I can't guarantee how long he'll stay. Like I said, we're understaffed already."

Peter understood. Seattle was a big city with big city problems. "Much appreciated," he said. "And thanks again for the lift."

"Happy to help. Ms. Thorsen, I'm guessing we'll connect sometime tomorrow. If the bosses okay it, I'll brief you on what we've learned about Geoffrey Reed."

KT leaned forward and patted him on the shoulder. "Thank you, Captain. I've got your number."

Durant gave her a look. "Just don't make me regret my generosity. And check your mattresses for bedbugs."

One cruiser waited in the parking lot while they went into the motel office. It was nicer than Peter had hoped, with paint recent enough that he could still smell it. The clerk was an older guy with acne scars, a bow tie, and a handheld video game on the counter by the computer. He was entirely uninterested in his customers, which was exactly how Peter liked it. He paid for two rooms with cash, including a large refundable deposit, which left about eighty bucks in his wallet.

The clerk handed them the keys. "First floor, halfway down. No loud parties, please. Enjoy your stay."

The rain had stopped. They found the rooms and Peter got KT and Ellie inside, then raised his hand to the cruiser. The officer nodded through the windshield and backed the car into a spot a few doors down.

Peter stepped into his room, threw the deadbolt and put on the chain, then pulled the curtains over the picture window. The place was basic but clean. Two queen beds with a nightstand between them, a particleboard dresser with a small TV bolted to the top. The white static flared slightly at the covered window, but he would live with it. His chest still ached where the plate had stopped the bullet. He dropped his duffel on the dresser, then opened the connecting door on his side. KT's side was already open.

She lay on the bed with her shoes off and her daughter curled up against her. He was glad to see she'd pulled the curtains and locked the door, too.

"We were thinking pizza," she said. "El likes Pagliacci."

Suddenly Peter was starving. "Excellent plan. Get two larges, whatever toppings you guys like. Give them my room number and tell them we'll pay cash. And use Ellie's cell, just in case."

Ellie leapt up and woke her phone, fingers flying as she ordered online. KT turned to Peter, her voice low. "Are you seriously concerned that there might be someone else after us? Even with the patrol car outside?"

Peter wasn't going to tell her about the weird feeling in the pit of his stomach when he thought about the threat letter. *We are Legion*. There was no reason to scare them. "I'm just being cautious. We're probably fine. Humor me, okay?"

The way KT stared at him, he knew she wasn't buying it. "Ellie, I need to tell you something important. Are you listening?" Her voice was serious, a mom who meant business.

Ellie looked up from her screen. "I'm listening."

"If anything happens to me, if we get separated for any reason? You can trust Peter. You stick with him like glue, and you do exactly what he tells you to do, no matter what. Do you understand?"

Ellie blinked, her voice small. "What would happen to you?"

KT reached out and put a hand on her daughter's arm. "Nothing, honey. I'm saying, just in case. You can trust Peter. Do you understand?"

Ellie nodded. "I understand."

"Good. Now how long until that pizza gets here?"

Ellie glanced at her phone. "Forty minutes." Her eyes flicked to Peter. "I hope you like meatballs."

He remembered her calling him "meatball" at her school. Now she was riffing on that, messing with him. Despite his own concerns and KT's warning to her daughter, he felt something loosen in his chest. She'd be okay.

"Are you kidding? Meatballs are my favorite." He turned to KT. "I'm going to get cleaned up and call June." Although he'd texted her several times since the cops had shown up, he owed her a call. "Leave the connecting door open, okay?"

After a long, hot shower and toweling himself dry, Peter examined the bruise on his chest where the bullet had hit his vest. It was deep purple and tender to the touch. It wasn't his first time taking a round to the armor, and he knew it would be sore for several days. But he also knew he'd live, so he pulled on clean hiking pants and a Counterbalance Brewing T-shirt, found his phone on the sink, and called June.

She answered on the first ring. "Hey."

"Hey, yourself." He walked into the bedroom and dropped himself on the bed. "Sorry it took so long. The cops kept us awhile."

"I knew they would. Are you doing okay?"

Peter felt his defenses fall away, as they always did with her. "I'm still standing," he said.

"That doesn't sound good." She knew him so well. "Talk to me, Marine."

He'd already given her the basics over text. Now he walked her through the whole story, the amateur in cheap sneakers waiting at KT's car, picking up Ellie at school on foot, the amateur—Geoffrey Reed—reappearing at Peter's pickup, shooting Peter in the chest but hitting the armor. Then the scramble to escape.

"The guy was wound pretty tight. I was worried about KT and Ellie, and about civilians catching a stray round. But I should have been more aggressive."

"Everything turned out all right, didn't it? I'm just glad you were wearing that vest. I'll buy you a new one for Christmas."

"Nothing says Merry Christmas like ballistic armor." Peter sighed. "I just don't get why he wanted to kill her to begin with."

"Well, he ended his little adventure by shooting himself, so he probably wasn't quite right in the head. I'll plug him into my databases and see what I can come up with. Hey, remind KT to send me what she's working on. I'm coming to Seattle tomorrow, but I want to use the flight time to see if I can help figure out what triggered Reed."

Peter lowered the phone and raised his voice. "Hey, KT, did you send those files to June yet?"

"Working on it now," KT called.

Peter passed the message. "Also, why did Reed bother to write that threat letter if he was going to try to kill her later that day?"

"That's actually a good question," June said. "We tend to think that disturbed people are just crazy, but usually there's an internal logic to their actions, even if we can't see it." In order to write a book about a Nebraska serial killer, June had studied up on abnormal psychology. She joked that it helped her deal with Peter, too. Now she said, "Did you have anything to eat?"

"Pizza's coming." He glanced at the time. "Should be any minute now."

He heard a faint knock from the adjoining room. KT shouted, "Eleanor, dinner's here!"

Through the opening between the rooms, he saw KT walk toward the door, hair wet, wearing leggings and an oversized Minnesota sweatshirt. To June, he said, "I'll call you back," and stuffed his phone in his pocket. Then he called out to KT, "Wait, let me get it." He'd told Ellie to give the pizza guy his room number, but evidently she'd forgotten. He hauled himself off the bed, feeling the adrenaline hangover. He was still barefoot. "Katelyn, wait, please."

"I'm just going to peek through the curtain."

Then he heard the sound of breaking glass.

9

Peter didn't understand. Had someone thrown a rock through the window? There was no sound of a gunshot. "KT? What's going on?"

He ran for the connecting door and saw her on the floor in a boneless crumple. The back of her head was a red mess. Then rounds started coming through the door. Whoever was on the other side was trying to shoot out the lock. Where the hell was that cop?

And where was Ellie? She wasn't behind the bed. Peter ran to the bathroom and shouldered open the door. Ellie was dressed in enormous gray sweatpants and a black tank top, leaning toward the mirror and applying lotion to her face. "What the hell? Listen, meatball—"

He grabbed her around the middle like a sack of potatoes and ran for the connecting passage, keeping his own body between her and the gunman, holding her close so she wouldn't see her mother lying like a rag doll on the reddening carpet.

As Peter ran, the shooter kept firing at the lock. The door was splintered, but still holding because the bolt was bound up in the metal jamb. Then he must have kicked the door because it popped open hard, but bounced back from the end of the security chain.

Looking over his shoulder, Peter saw the end of a sound suppressor poke through the opening and push against the metal links. He wasn't waiting for the outcome. Unless he changed the equation, he knew how this would end. He sprinted into the adjoining room, then closed and locked the door. The only weapon he had was the folding knife clipped to his pocket. Ellie was screaming at him and pounding him with her fists.

Still holding her, he crouched down and peeked through the window curtain. He couldn't see the police cruiser. A small pizza delivery car idled in the parking lot's aisle. They had to move.

At the connecting door behind him, rounds began to punch into the lock. Ellie was still screaming. He grabbed her shoulder and put a hand over her mouth. "Eleanor Grace Thorsen. Listen to me. Somebody else is after us. We need to run. Can you do it?"

He uncovered her mouth. She stared at him with Bambi eyes. "Did . . . ? Is . . . ?"

"Later." He met her eyes. "Now we run. We're heading for the pizza car. Got it?"

She looked down helplessly. "I'm barefoot."

Peter was, too. There was a loud *chunk* as a round made hard contact with the deadbolt. "You're tougher than you think," he said. Hoping it was true. "I've got you. It's only a few yards. But we have to go now and run fast. Ready?"

She nodded. She was already breathing hard. He put his finger to his lips, then quietly unlatched the outside door and took off the chain. He wanted to take his knife from his pocket and ambush their attacker when he came through the door, but that was no guarantee Ellie would leave the room alive. The last time he'd told someone to shelter in the bathtub, it hadn't ended well.

He heard a thump. The gunman kicking at the ruined wood, trying to free the deadbolt. Peter pulled open the outside door and peeked. Nobody there. Either nobody had noticed the suppressed gunshots or they were too scared to do anything. The rain had started again, harder than before.

He took Ellie's hand and pulled her outside, closed the door behind her to buy any time he could, then turned left on the covered walkway to make it harder for the shooter to spot them from the doorway. Two rooms down, the cruiser was no longer in its parking spot. The cop had already left.

Peter turned right and slipped between two parked cars. Rain pounded on their roofs. He kept pulling Ellie forward, speeding up. Time was not their friend. His bare feet were cold on the gritty wet pavement. His T-shirt was already soaked. Then they were out in the open parking lane, creeping toward the rear of the pizza car.

It was a tiny gray Nissan with a rooftop sign and a logo on the side. The driver's door stood open, the engine was still running. It wasn't until Peter made it past the back bumper that he saw the body on the blacktop. Murdered for a damn pizza, just to make the killer look harmless.

Ellie made a high-pitched yelp. He turned to see her standing frozen behind him, soaking wet, both hands over her mouth in a full-on freak-out. Peter pulled her close, then put his hand on the back of her head and shoved her over the body and through the open driver's door into the passenger seat. As he climbed in behind her, the Nissan's rear side window spiderwebbed with a *crunch*. The shooter had found them.

Peter threw the little car in drive and hit the gas. They lurched into motion. *Crunch crunch* sounded from the rear windshield.

"Get down, get down." The girl bent double in her seat. "No, on the floor." She'd have more protection there. As she folded herself into the footwell, he looked over his shoulder and saw a man in a wide-brimmed hat and a black windbreaker squared up on the blacktop, still firing. How many rounds could this asshole possibly have?

Peter cranked the car to the left, heading for the exit now with a line of vehicles between them and the shooter. In one spot was a tan Toyota pickup with a camo-painted fiberglass cap on the back, exhaust puffing from its tailpipe. Nobody inside. An older body style. Peter took his foot off the gas.

It was the killer's truck. It had to be. Nobody left their car running in a place like this. But how the hell had he found them? The only people who knew about the motel were cops. Durant and the two patrolmen who'd escorted them there. Maybe they'd said something over the radio or put the location in a report? Peter didn't want to believe police were connected to KT's death, but he had to consider the possibility.

Or maybe the killer had followed them from Queen Anne. He could keep following them now. No matter where they went, the runty little pizza car would be no match for the powerful Toyota truck, no matter how many miles it was carrying. They'd be dead in ten minutes.

Thunk thunk. Pistol rounds in sheet metal. Or they could be dead right here. Peter goosed the gas as he turned in his seat, scanning for the shooter, found him standing in the lane where the pizza car had been parked, hat hiding his eyes, firing accurately through the line of vehicles.

Enough of this shit. Peter stomped the gas. "Keep your head down." He came to the end of the lane, but instead of turning right onto Aurora, he turned left and circled back around the line of cars to where they'd been just a moment before.

The gunman stood in the lane and watched them come. *Crunch.* A round punched through the windshield high and to the right, spitting shards. Standing his ground, the shooter adjusted his aim. Peter bent low and angled the car as if trying to get past him. *Crunch. Crunch. Crunch.* Calm, deliberate shots. Peter did not like this guy. Glass fragments fell in his hair and down his neck. He had the accelerator all the way to the floor.

Then he raised his head enough to peek over the dashboard and turned the wheel to the left. The shooter had backed away toward the parked cars, but not far enough. Peter hit him going thirty-five, throwing him up on the hood, then stood on the brake to let the guy roll forward onto the pavement. Then he hit the gas again and didn't brake until he felt the body thump under the front and rear wheels.

He threw it in reverse and looked down at the dashboard for the image from the backup camera. Twenty yards back, the guy was somehow trying to make it to his knees. He still had the gun in his hand. The hat, which he'd probably worn to hide his face from any security cameras, was gone.

Eyes on the screen, Peter goosed the engine and accelerated until he hit him again, keeping his foot down until he felt the double thump.

If that didn't do the job, the fucker was unkillable.

10

Ellie was crying softly, pretzeled up in the footwell. He put his hand on her wet head. "Wait here. I'll be right back, I promise."

Avoiding the broken glass in his bare feet, he got out and walked over to where the man lay on the blacktop. His limbs were torn open and bent the wrong way. His chest was partly crushed. His forehead had a large dent in it. The gun was five yards away. Peter knelt and put his hand on the man's neck, feeling for a pulse. Nothing. He was a middle-aged white guy. Peter was struck again how killers looked like anyone else.

Peter already had his phone and wallet. He returned to the idling pizza car. It was shredded. He opened Ellie's door. "It's over, kiddo. Time to go." She looked at him, eyes unfocused, face pale as death. She didn't move. "Come on, Ellie. I've got you." He took her arm and coaxed her out enough to pick her up in his arms.

She wrapped herself around him like an octopus, burying her face in his neck. "I've got you," he said. "I've got you." She was so small and thin. The lightness of her body, the fragility of it, terrified him. As if she was barely there at all.

He carried her over to the killer's idling pickup and put her in the passenger seat. He buckled her in, then walked around the hood and climbed behind the wheel and drove away.

Driving barefoot, he covered three or four miles very quickly, weaving through traffic and blowing past stoplights, checking his rearview the whole time. His feet were cold and his head was killing him. He wished he'd taken a pizza, then felt like an asshole. But he was alive. And starving. And Ellie had to be starving, too. Although she sure wasn't talking. Instead she sat shivering and wet with her arms wrapped around her knees, her face turned away. That was worse than screaming.

This was all Peter's fault. He'd told her and KT that they'd be safe with him. And he'd fucked it up. Maybe worse than he'd ever fucked up anything in his life. And that was saying something.

He finally saw a sign for Dunn Lumber and pulled into the parking lot beside a half dozen other vehicles. Then he found Durant's card in his wallet and pulled out his phone.

"Captain Durant here."

"A man came to the hotel." Peter put a big hand on Ellie's back. He tried to keep his voice even, but he didn't do a very good job. "He killed KT and a pizza delivery guy. The cop who was supposed to keep watch was already gone."

Ellie's shoulders heaved with silent sobs. Durant cursed. "What about the girl?"

"She's with me. I took the killer's truck. He's dead in the motel parking lot. We're in the wind."

"Okay," Durant said. "Let me make some calls. Are you north or south? We have a precinct in Northgate, at 103rd and College, and another in Belltown, Eighth and Virginia."

"When you have the scene under control, call me and I'll come back and give a statement. I also need my things and Ellie's. Then we're gone."

"Mr. Ash, you can't just leave. People are dead. You killed a man. There will be an inquest."

"Are you kidding? You told me it was over, that it was just one guy with mental health issues. This new asshole had a suppressor on his pistol. He waited until the cruiser left. He definitely had some kind of training. Whoever sent him, they have resources. Also, the only people who knew we were at that motel were cops."

"Mr. Ash—"

"No, Durant. The guy didn't stop after killing KT. He came after me and the girl, too. So there's no way I'm trusting you or your people to keep Ellie safe. I've got her now, and I'm not telling a fucking soul where we're going. I need you to run interference for me on that. And I need access to the investigation, like you promised KT."

"Mr. Ash—"

Peter lowered his voice. "Her mother is dead. You said it was *over*, Durant, but it wasn't. Not even close. The threat letter said *We are Legion*, remember?"

A pause, filled with unearthly silence. "I'll talk to the chief. We'll work something out. Give me an hour."

Peter cleared his throat. His eyes burned. "Durant."

"Yeah."

"Once I get Ellie somewhere safe, I'm going to find out what this is about. And end it. With or without your help."

Durant's voice was quiet. "We'll talk about that when you come in. I'll call, okay?"

Peter was still soaking wet and barefoot. So was Ellie. She'd stopped sobbing and stared out the side window vacantly. He could only imagine what she was thinking about.

He cranked the heat until it roared. The killer's Toyota smelled like ten years of cheap cigars. The instrument panel was covered with dust, as if their settings hadn't been adjusted in years.

He rummaged through the center console but found only the usual crap: loose change, a charging cable, cheap reading glasses, a tire pressure gauge. Nothing that might tell Peter why the guy had targeted KT for death. He should have gone through the guy's pockets. Although that would have pissed off Durant, and Peter couldn't afford to do that. Despite Peter's demand for the captain's help, there was zero guarantee he'd get it. Durant's bosses might well override him. In their minds, they'd be right to do so. They'd certainly want to keep the Toyota as evidence. At the very least, Peter needed a new ride.

He also really needed a weapon. He leaned over and popped the glove box. No gun. Just a thick owner's manual in a cracked vinyl document folder. Below that, held together by a rubber band, lay a thick stack of folding paper maps, the kind that were common in gas stations before the era of smartphones. All the Western states, starting from the Dakotas down to Texas.

Beneath the maps was a small black rectangle. A cheap smartphone. He found the button to turn it on and was rewarded by a prompt for a four-digit passcode. Not Peter's skill set. He wiped it on his shirt to get the fingerprints off, then dropped it on the center console's junk pile.

It immediately fell on the floor. He picked it up again. His stomach rumbled, reminding him that he was starving. Without thinking about it, he tucked the phone into his cargo pocket. Then put his hand gently on Ellie's shoulder. "Hey. Can we talk a minute?"

She didn't turn to look at him. Her voice was flat. "What."

"I know you're hurting," he said. "But we have a few decisions to make. First, food. Are you hungry?"

"No."

"Well, I'm starving. And pretty soon, you will be, too. But I don't want to go inside a restaurant. There's a drive-in burger place just up the road. What do you think?"

"Whatever."

Her voice was a bottomless pit. Peter was pretty sure he didn't have the skills for dealing with this poor girl. But right now, he didn't have a choice. Time to adapt and overcome.

He put some cheer in his voice. "Okay, let's do that. Maybe a milkshake?"

Burgermaster was a Seattle institution with a broad ketchup-red carport that would shelter two dozen cars from the worst of the weather. Peter found an open spot on the end, out of sight from the road, where they could escape in two different directions.

The drive-in chain had significantly upped its game since Peter had last eaten there, now making their burgers from local grass-fed beef. "Man, this looks good," he said. "What do you think?" She didn't respond. She still wasn't looking at him.

A carhop walked over. Peter ordered bacon burgers, fries, onion rings, milkshakes, and handed over a third of his remaining cash. Then he took out his phone again and punched in a number.

"Jarhead. What up?"

Peter felt his breath come more easily, just hearing Lewis's voice, slippery as motor oil and twice as dark. "Something's happened and I need a favor. Like, now."

"Lay it on me, brother."

"A good vehicle. Something capable and reliable and relatively invisible. Legally registered, but not in my name or yours. Here's the hard part. I need it in an hour, two at most, dropped near Fortieth and Aurora in Seattle." Around the corner from the motel. "And a roll of tinfoil, if you can swing it." He'd have asked for a gun, but he needed something clean and most of the people Lewis knew wouldn't be.

"Lemme make some calls. Sit tight."

"Thanks," Peter said, but Lewis was already gone. He hadn't even asked why. They had a lot of history.

The food arrived, and Peter adjusted the windows so the trays could hang off the outside. His mouth began to water immediately. He took a bite of his burger. Paradise.

Ellie's meal was right in her line of sight. He nudged her shoulder. "Maybe a few bites? You'll feel better, I promise."

She shook her head wordlessly. He didn't like this new quiet version. The Ellie he'd met at her school was snarky, confident. Even after running from Geoffrey Reed, she'd asked him some pretty ballsy questions. But now she'd lost her mother.

He took another chunk out of his burger. Basic survival tactics, eat when you can. "Mmm, bacon. You're really missing out. I hope you're not a vegetarian."

She ignored him.

He took a big slurp of his chocolate shake and felt the sugar charge into his system. "Wow. Only a crazy person would turn down that milkshake."

She shifted in her seat to get even farther away from him.

He set down his burger, took two French fries off his tray, and stuck one up each nostril. He turned to face her. "These fries are delicious." His voice came out funny.

Her head floated sideways, her eyes slanted at him. He heard a puff of breath. Not a laugh, exactly, but something.

He dropped the fries out his window. "Please," he said softly. "Just a few bites. You need the energy."

She didn't answer. But her hand floated out to her tray, pulled a fry from the paper packet, and stuck it in her mouth, chewing mechanically. After a moment, she reached out and took another one.

He took the lid off the container of ketchup and placed it on the dashboard, then set the bag of onion rings beside it and tapped her on the shoulder. She ignored him. But a moment later, she grabbed the rings and the ketchup and put them on her own tray.

Progress.

11

By the time they were done eating, Ellie had powered through all her fries, most of the onion rings, and more than half her enormous burger. Peter put his milkshake into the dovetailed wooden box on the seat that he used as a cupholder, tapped her on the shoulder, and pointed. She put her cup beside his, then leaned back and closed her eyes.

Waiting for the carhop to collect the trays and trash, Peter took out his phone, found a number, and made a call.

"Semper Fi Exteriors, this is Manny."

"It's Peter. Got a minute?"

"Ashes, mi hermano. What's going on?"

"I'm in Seattle, trailing trouble. I could use a hand."

Manny Martinez had been one of Peter's platoon sergeants in Iraq, an extremely capable man. Now he was married with four daughters and a thriving construction business. He'd helped Peter and June with something a few years back.

"Anything for you, Ashes. You want to come to the house?"

"I'm not bringing my problems to your doorstep, putting Carlotta and the girls at risk. What I need is a weapon, preferably one that isn't registered to you, in case I have to do something.

Also, I'm out of folding money for a hotel room and I don't want to use a card. Do you have any cash in the house?"

"Yeah, I keep a little somethin' for 'mergencies. But you don't need a hotel room, 'mano. My sister, Stella, just left for Colorado. She's doing another Ironman. Her place in Ballard is empty until next Tuesday."

Four nights without clerks asking for his ID. "That'd be great, brother. Then hang on to your cash. I've got some in the truck, I just can't get to it until tomorrow."

Manny gave Peter the address and told him where to find the key. "Anything I should know?"

Peter looked at Ellie, staring out the window again. "You see the news today?"

"I got KING 5 on right now. The shooter on Queen Anne Hill or the double murder at that motel?"

"Both," Peter said.

"Dang, that's bad. I'd offer to call my guys, put a fire team together, but we're shut down for hunting season and they're all in Montana or Wyoming." Most of Manny's employees had served with Manny and Peter. They were, among other things, avid elk hunters. To Peter's knowledge, there was no more heavily armed and dangerous group of roofers on the planet.

"Okay," Manny said. "I'll grab some hardware from the shop and meet you at Stella's place. Gimme ninety minutes."

"Actually, things are a little fluid right now," he said. "I picked up a, uh, high-value package. Kind of delicate." He glanced at Ellie again, but she didn't seem to be listening. "How about tomorrow, 0900?"

"Roger that. You can catch me up then. But you better get your butt over here for supper before you blow town, or Carlotta gonna wring my neck."

Peter was still watching Ellie. "I have a better idea. Could Carlotta come tomorrow, too?"

The carhop still hadn't come for the trash, so Peter got out of his seat, collected the trays, and carried them to the garbage can. Instead of heading back to the truck, he lingered on the covered walkway, his bare feet freezing on the cold concrete. He didn't want to make his next call where Ellie could hear it.

June picked up quickly. "Hey, Marine. How was the pizza?"

"There was another shooter," Peter said. "At the motel. He killed KT."

"Dear God," June breathed. "What about Ellie?"

Peter looked back at the truck. The girl still had her head back and her eyes closed. "I've got her with me. It's bad, Juniper."

June let out a low moan. She and KT had been close. KT had been June's mentor, teaching her the basics of investigative reporting. But really, Peter knew, more like a big sister.

Then June cleared her throat, pulling herself together. "I get in at noon tomorrow. We'll sort this shit out together."

"I wish you'd stay home," Peter said. "I have enough to worry about with keeping Ellie safe. These guys came out of nowhere, and I still have no clue what this is all about."

"Listen, Marine, if you want to know why they went after KT, you need me there to figure it out. So fuck you, I'm coming."

Peter sighed. He knew better than to try to talk June out of doing something she was determined to do. Also, she was right. He did need her. In more ways than one. "Okay," he said. "Text me your flight info, I'll pick you up."

"You bet your ass you will. I'm calling Lewis, too. Maybe he can get on the same flight. Did you reach out to Manny?"

"He's coming over first thing. But I don't want to involve him any more than I have to. He's got a wife and four daughters. I'm not willing to put him at risk."

"You know Manny'd do anything for you," she said.

"I know," he said. "But Ellie's already lost her mother. I won't have Manny's four girls lose their father, too."

"What are you going to do with Ellie?"

"I have no idea. Did KT have any family in the area?"

"No. Her parents were back in Minneapolis, but they're both dead. She had a brother in Portland, but he had a heart attack last year, and he'd never married."

"What about Ellie's dad?"

"He's been out of the picture for a long time. I don't even know his name. The last I heard, he was working for a software company overseas somewhere. The police will reach out to the State Department, they'll try to find him. Given the legal system for minors, she'll most likely end up with her dad when the dust settles."

Peter looked at Ellie again. So young, so fragile. Losing her mother, especially like this, was really going to mess her up. He hoped her father was a good guy.

If he wasn't, Peter would have to set him right.

He always felt better on the move, so after he and June said goodbye, he got back on the road, circling restlessly until Durant called.

"The motel is secure. How long will it take you to get here?"

Peter was heading south past Green Lake. "Ten minutes, maybe less. You talk to your boss about me? About my security concerns, and access to the investigation?"

"I did."

Peter frowned. "That doesn't sound good."

"Just come in, we'll talk."

"Durant. You did hear me before."

"I heard you, Mr. Ash. It's complicated. Just get here, okay? Ask for Detective Kitzinger. The scene officer will send you back."

The motel parking lot had been transformed with pole lights and crime scene tape and multiple forensics vans and fifteen or twenty police vehicles in the lot and along the street. When you included the dead killer, it was a triple homicide.

Traffic was down to a single lane. Peter tried to turn in at the motel entrance, but it was blocked by a patrolman in a slicker with a flashlight. Peter stopped and lowered his window. The rain had let up and the air smelled fresh and damp. The cop came over, shone the light in Peter's face, then did the same to the girl, who put up a hand to shield her eyes. "Sir, this is a crime scene, you'll have to move on."

"Detective Kitzinger is expecting us." Peter gave his name.

"One minute." The young cop stepped back, spoke into his shoulder mike, listened, and returned. "She'll meet you in the motel office, sir. You can pull into the entrance just ahead of me."

Peter maneuvered past the cruiser and reversed into the lot, getting as close as he could while still making sure the truck faced away from the dead. Now came the tricky part. He turned to the girl. Her face was shiny and tight. She looked like she was five years old.

"This will be hard," he said. "We'll have to talk about what happened. They're going to ask a lot of questions."

She seemed small and alone. "But you'll be there, right?"

"The whole time."

They found Detectives Kitzinger and O'Donnell in the lobby. O'Donnell was a thickset, Irish-looking guy in a blue waxed cotton ballcap and jacket whose round and cheerful face meant that he would always have the role of good cop. Kitzinger, in contrast, was thin and taut as a barbed-wire fence, her narrow mahogany face fixed in a mix of skepticism and suppressed outrage.

They were talking to a uniformed sergeant and Captain Durant, who still wore his black cowboy hat and raincoat. He looked drawn and grim. The room no longer smelled like fresh paint. It smelled like wet, angry cops. People had been killed, and good police took that personally. The fact that they'd left KT and Ellie without protection only made it worse.

Kitzinger softened slightly when she saw Ellie and walked over to greet her. "I'm so sorry about your mom. Are you up to talking about what happened?" She tipped her head toward the office behind the reception desk. "Let's go back there, get a little privacy."

Ellie glanced at Peter. "Um. Can he come, too?"

Normally, Peter knew, a parent or guardian would be present during the questioning of a minor child. At the moment, with Ellie's mother recently murdered and her father out of the picture, Peter was the closest thing she had to a guardian, legal or otherwise. Ideally, the SPD would bring in a detective experienced at interviewing distraught juveniles, and a mental health professional to help minimize the damage. But this was the real world, with its after-hours crime scenes and limited budgets. And the damage was already about as bad as it could be.

Kitzinger's eyes were fixed on Ellie's face. "Of course," she said. Despite her attempt at softening, she still radiated an intensity that was almost palpable. She'd been the same when she interviewed them after Reed tried to kill them. She was invested. Peter liked that.

Kitzinger led the way to the office. O'Donnell waited until they'd passed and followed behind, with Durant last. The room was small. The white static didn't like it, or Durant blocking the doorway with his bulk, but there was nothing to be done but take a deep breath. They sat in uncomfortable chairs around a small table and Kitzinger walked Ellie through what had happened, asking clear, concise questions. Ellie's voice was thin and remote. Kitzinger recorded the conversation on her phone and O'Donnell took notes.

When Ellie was done, Kitzinger turned to Peter, this time moving back and forth in the narrative, missing nothing. She was very good at this, Peter thought. He made sure to emphasize what he'd said earlier, that the killer had a suppressor on his pistol and some kind of tactical training, which put him in a different category than Geoffrey Reed. Captain Durant was silent.

Finally Kitzinger leaned back in her chair and glanced at Durant, who nodded. "Okay," she said. "The security footage confirms most of what you're telling us. After the uniform got called out to a bar fight in the U District, the Toyota rolled into the lot. The pizza delivery guy was right behind him. The shooter left his truck, had a quick conversation with the pizza guy getting out of his car, then pulled his gun. We assume he was improvising, but he seemed to have had some practice. He didn't hesitate, and he didn't waste a shot. His hat shielded his face from the cameras, and he didn't look up to see where they might be. If you hadn't killed him, we'd have almost nothing."

"Do you have a name?"

Kitzinger said, "We can't release that yet."

"The man tried to kill us." He tipped his head at Ellie. "He killed her mother. We have the right to know his name."

Kitzinger looked at Durant. He nodded sourly. She said, "Scott Enderby. He lived in Magnolia, about two miles from Ms. Thorsen."

At the mention of her mother's name, Ellie made a small noise.

Peter put a careful hand on her shoulder. "You okay, kiddo?"

She looked at her hands folded in her lap. "I want to see her."

Kitzinger was shaking her head, her face softer. "Eleanor, that's really not a good idea."

Peter had more than his share of experience facing death. He got out of his chair and knelt on the floor before the girl so he could see her eyes. Tears ran down her cheeks. "Talk to me, kiddo. Why do you want to see her?"

She swiped at her face with the backs of her hands. "I want to say *goodbye*, you meatball."

Well, hell, Peter thought. What was he supposed to say to that?

He looked at Durant, who sighed, closed his eyes, and pinched the bridge of his nose. "Detective O'Donnell, can you go make that happen?"

As O'Donnell stood to leave, Kitzinger pointed at Peter's and Ellie's bare wet feet turning blue with cold. "Hey, Patrick? While you're at it, see if the scene techs are done with their shoes and socks."

12

Captain Durant followed O'Donnell out. Kitzinger stood up and pulled Peter out of the room, out of Ellie's earshot. "She should talk to somebody," she said. "We have a social worker on the way."

"Good idea. She's a mess." Peter leaned to one side so he could check on the girl. She sat slumped in her chair, head down. "After that, Durant said she could stay with me until we figure this whole thing out. I'll watch out for her."

She raised her eyebrows. "The captain agreed to that? What about Ellie's family?"

"As far as I know, the only family is her father, but he's been out of contact for years. I'm told he's overseas somewhere."

Kitzinger nodded. "We'll find him. Until we do, the regs say she's supposed to go into temporary custody."

"That's not happening. What if they come after her again? This last guy was good. What if the next guy is better?"

She looked at him impassively. "You're not the only person who can protect her. We're the police. That's our job."

"And you've done a hell of a job so far, haven't you?"

"We'll talk about it after the social worker shows up." She tipped her head to one side, looking at him like a radiologist staring at a CAT scan. "You've been through a lot, too. Are you okay?"

She must have seen something in his face. "I'm fine," Peter said. Although he wasn't.

She nodded, but not in agreement. Her eyes told him she'd seen every possible human reaction to every possible shitty situation. "Okay. Keep in touch. Especially if anything new comes up." Kitzinger had given him her business card the first time she'd questioned him.

She went back outside. Peter returned to the office and sat alone with Ellie while the coroner and the forensics team did their work. He texted June the name Scott Enderby, living somewhere in the Magnolia neighborhood. Forty-five minutes later, O'Donnell came in with their boots and socks and a hotel towel so they could dry their feet. When their feet were warming again, Peter leaned slightly toward the girl so that their shoulders touched. Times like this, a little human contact went a long way. She leaned back against him hard.

Finally Kitzinger returned and went to Ellie. "Do you still want to see your mother's body?"

"Yes." Ellie's voice was small. She grabbed Peter's arm. "You're coming with me, right?"

"I'll be right beside you, all the way."

Kitzinger led them from the office and down the covered walkway toward the rooms, telling them to keep their hands in their pockets and to watch where they stepped. Numbered plastic evidence markers stood on the pavement where brass shell casings lay shining. The rain had started again. A line of pop-up tents stood over the ruined man in the parking lane, the dead pizza driver, and the battered pizza car. The whole scene lurid under the blue and red flashers of the police cars and the bright portable floodlights of the forensics team.

They reached the room where Katelyn Thorsen had been killed. The door stood open with the lockset hanging out of it, surrounded by splintered holes. The window glass had partially fallen from the frame where the killer had fired through it. Four evidence techs stood at a distance, out of the rain, waiting. It was an extraordinary courtesy, allowing this.

Kitzinger stopped and turned to block their path. Her face softer again, although the vibrating intensity was the same. "Ellie, I really wish you wouldn't do this. It's going to be hard. Are you sure you want to remember her like this?"

Ellie looked up at Peter wordlessly, tightening her grip on his arm. For a skinny girl, she had some strength in her.

"It's up to you," he said. It would be traumatic up front, for sure. But he knew from his own experience that, over time, facing it would be better than running from it. Soon enough, other memories would rise and take over. Older memories, better memories. Her mother at her best. That was how it had happened for Peter, with his friends who'd died in combat. He'd learned to work at it, which helped.

She nodded to herself, then turned to Kitzinger. "I need to see my mom."

The detective tightened her lips, about to say something else, but didn't. Instead she gave way and let the girl through, Peter in tow.

Thankfully, Katelyn Thorsen no longer lay in a crumpled heap. She was still on the floor, but she'd been rolled onto her back and covered with a bedsheet. The top of it was splotched with red where it covered her face and chest. The carpet was soaked with congealing blood. Orange evidence tape dotted the walls, noting where rounds had penetrated. KT's laptop and phone were on the floor beside more evidence markers. Each device had been hit by multiple rounds.

Before Peter could say anything, Ellie released his arm, stepped forward, and bent to pull back the sheet. Nobody had cleaned or otherwise prepared the body. Her mother lay with blood on her Minnesota sweatshirt and two bloody holes in her face. Her head seemed strangely flat. The back of it was gone.

Ellie's mouth worked silently. A prayer, Peter hoped. Although they had never worked for him.

"Goodbye, Mom," she finally said. Then, with great care, she raised the sheet back to where she'd found it and returned to Peter's side. "Let's go."

Peter turned to Kitzinger. "I need Ellie's things, her toiletries."

The detective pointed toward the connecting door. "In the next room."

He walked past the splintered wood and saw the girl's things in the corner beside his duffel and coat. Peter said to Kitzinger, "Thanks for your accommodation here. I really appreciate it."

She nodded an acknowledgment. "Captain Durant's outside. He's taken a personal interest in this one. He wants to see you."

With great deliberation, Ellie put on her mother's jacket. Peter pulled on his own raincoat, then picked up their bags, and they went out into the drizzle. Durant stood in the parking lot, outside the tent sheltering the broken corpse of the dead shooter. Water dripped from the brim of his hat. His black coat flickered with the stuttering brightness of the photographer's flash. He came to meet them, took Ellie's arm, and steered her away from the carnage. "Detective Kitzinger, please take Ms. Thorsen to the office to wait. The social worker is on her way."

Ellie, looking tiny in her mother's orange raincoat, shook her head and stepped close to Peter. "I'm not going anywhere without him."

Peter said, "I'll be right here, Ellie. Also, Detective Kitzinger is going to find your dad."

Her whole body seemed to clench. "My dad's an *asshole*. He doesn't even want to *talk* to me. I haven't seen him in, like, five years. He lives in China or something. He doesn't even answer emails."

Kitzinger put her hand on Ellie's shoulder. "Let's just go meet the social worker. Work all this out."

Ellie ducked to slip her grip, then stepped close to Peter and grabbed his arm again. "*No.* I'm staying with *him.*"

The legal system was brutal with regard to minors, Peter knew. Without the father or other blood relatives, the best option was KT's close friends, and June hadn't thought she had many of those in town. The parents of Ellie's friends would be the next step, but after four violent deaths, would any of them want to take in the girl and put their own family at risk, even with police protection?

Barring sainthood, probably not. And Peter didn't blame them.

Which meant the girl would almost certainly end up in temporary foster care until somebody agreed to be her guardian. The guardian would have to pass a rigorous background check and numerous site visits. That process could take months. And none of it would help her cope with the fact that two people had tried to kill her, and one of them had killed her mother.

Peter looked at Durant. "We talked about this. She's coming with me until we know what the hell is going on."

"That's not how it works," Durant said. "Until we learn what her mother intended for her daughter and find a suitable guardian, Eleanor Thorsen is a ward of the state. You just killed a man, so you're not exactly a prime candidate for guardianship.

But before you object, she'll have protection until we wrap this whole thing up."

"She was supposed to have protection tonight," Peter said. "Look how that turned out. In fact, as far as I can tell, the cops were the only people who knew we were at this damn motel. Somebody told Enderby how to find us. What if there's somebody else out there?"

The captain's face was impassive. "I don't like it, either, but that's how it's going to be. The social worker will find her a bed and stay with her. I'll detail multiple officers to stand guard, twenty-four seven."

Ellie's face was pale, as though she was about to be sick. Her grip on Peter's arm was strong enough to bend steel bars.

"We had a deal," Peter said. "You were going to run interference with the bosses. So I could keep Eleanor safe."

"I said we'd talk about it," Durant snapped. "This is a homicide. Minors without relatives go with Child Protective Services until a long-term solution is found. She's a ward of the state. The rules don't change just because some civilian wants them to."

Peter frowned. KT would have used her journalistic muscle to leverage the higher-ups. But KT was dead. He had no leverage against Durant and the cops. He knew from his eight years in the Corps that trying to force institutions to change usually just made things worse. Orders were orders, even the stupid ones.

But he was no longer a Marine. He didn't need to follow orders anymore.

He tipped his chin toward the wet parking lot. "I need to talk with Ellie. Give me a minute?"

"Don't be long," Durant said. "And before you forget, you'd better give Detective Kitzinger the keys to Enderby's pickup."

Peter fished out the keys and handed them over. He remembered that he still had the cheap phone in his cargo pocket. He'd intended to hand that over, too.

But he didn't.

Instead, with his duffel still on his shoulder and Ellie's little bag under his arm, he tugged her hand and led her out into the disordered maze of official vehicles, red and blue lights flashing, engines idling, exhaust plumes rising.

They passed the Toyota and Peter noted the plate number automatically. As they came to a big white forensics van, Ellie asked, "Where are we going?"

"Away from here," Peter said.

"What about the police?" Her voice was small and quiet.

Peter reminded himself that she'd been through a lot. "Would you rather go with the social worker? I would understand if you did. It's your choice. I can take you back."

"No. Mom told me to stick with you. That's what I want."

"Then it's decided," Peter said. "Although maybe we should walk a little faster."

He led her past the forensics van and lengthened his stride. At the narrow sidewalk, they turned and walked south into the relative darkness and calm of Aurora Avenue.

While they were waiting in the motel office, Lewis had texted Peter an address.

Right around the corner, parked under a rain-haloed streetlight, a midnight-blue Chevy Tahoe gleamed darkly in the rain.

The doors were unlocked and the keys were above the visor. There was a fresh roll of aluminum foil on the driver's seat. Leather interior, all the bells and whistles. How Lewis had made this happen, Peter had no idea, but he was grateful as hell.

He threw their bags into the back seat, fired up the engine, made sure Ellie had her seat belt fastened, and got the hell out of there.

A mile away, he stopped, tore off a long sheet of tinfoil, and wrapped up all three phones into a single brick. The aluminum would cut off any attempt to track the signal.

Because he didn't know who else might have the number to the phone from the Toyota.

And Durant had the number to Peter's phone, and Ellie's.

Peter wasn't sure exactly which law he'd just broken by walking away with a minor who was a ward of the state, but he was pretty sure it was a big one.

13

He took narrow side streets, weaving north and west through Fremont and Phinney Ridge into the sleepy neighborhood of Ballard. Ellie leaned her seat back and looked out the window at the passing houses. The Tahoe was a boat, but more agile than Peter's old pickup.

It was almost ten P.M. when they got to Stella Martinez's sage-green bungalow on Twenty-Fifth NW. The front yard was a riot of plantings. Peter reversed the Tahoe into the side drive and eased it all the way to the rear of the lot beside the oversized garage, assessing his surroundings for security risks.

There were houses close on both sides, each with plenty of exterior lights brightening the night. Six-foot wooden fences kept the back yards private. Past the garage was a four-foot retaining wall with another six-foot fence on top, this one designed to be difficult to climb. Behind that was an apartment building with a gated sidewalk entrance. Any intruder would have to go through Stella's front door or walk up the driveway toward the back. So not bad, for a single-family house.

The key was exactly where Manny had said it would be. Peter had met Stella several times, but had never been to the house. In fact, it was his personal policy to stay as far from

Stella Martinez as possible. She'd been a drill sergeant in the Army, teaching unarmed combat for ten years before leaving to supervise Manny's office. Now she ran triathlons and hundred-mile ultramarathons to keep herself in shape. Her last serious boyfriend had been hospitalized for exhaustion. All Manny's guys were scared of her. Peter was, too.

He unlocked the door, then went back for Ellie. She was asleep on her feet. With her overnight bag under his arm, he got her into the kitchen and up the stairs to the single bedroom. He kept the lights off, not wanting to alert the neighbors in case Stella had told them she was out of town. He drew the curtains, then pointed Ellie toward the bed. "Sit."

She sat. He bent and untied her Doc Martens, slipped them off. Her socks were white with yellow smiley faces on them. "The bathroom is through that door. I'll be downstairs if you need me. Okay?"

She nodded, her eyelids sinking. He stood and backed out of the room, closed the door silently behind him, and crept down the steep, narrow stairs.

What in hell was he going to do with a thirteen-year-old girl?

He couldn't stop thinking about that letter made from cut-up magazine pages. It had just the right amount of goofball for a note from a crackpot. Reed had that vibe in person, for sure. But when you added a second shooter into the mix, someone a lot more capable, it felt like something else. Something bigger. A deliberate strategy. A calculation.

He wandered the darkened house, looking for a landline and finding nothing. He needed to talk with June but didn't trust his cell outside the tinfoil. His hand itched for a weapon. He should have asked Lewis to arrange for one in the Tahoe.

He went back to the spare bedroom, set up as an office. With a slab-glass desktop over matching blue file cabinets and a crisp wall of bookshelves filled with exercise manuals and fitness guru memoirs, everything was extremely squared away.

Knowing Stella was right-handed, he opened the top right-hand file drawer. A nickel-plated 9-mil SIG Sauer automatic lay on an oil-stained dishtowel. An excellent weapon, fully loaded with a round in the chamber. He carried it into the living room and stretched out on the couch. He could have made a pot of coffee to keep him on watch for the night, but he knew he'd need rest to be useful tomorrow.

So he found a blanket in a chest, put the SIG on the floor beside him where his hand would find it naturally, then laid his head down.

He knew what was coming.

He hadn't felt like this since losing four members of his platoon to an ambush along the Tigris.

Despite the lack of coffee, he wouldn't sleep, not yet.

Instead he closed his eyes and watched helplessly as Geoffrey Reed put his pistol to the underside of his chin and blew his own head off. Then he was at the motel, with KT crumpled on the floor, the back of her head missing. Then he had the screaming girl under his arm, racing past her mother's dead body and out to the pizza car while Scott Enderby fired at them with purpose and deliberation. He felt the first thump of the little hatchback making contact, then the double thump as he ran the man over, going forward and again in reverse. Then he was in the tall corn beside the Tigris, looking at four dead Marines.

He took slow, deep breaths and let the memories cycle, again and again, with all their fear and anger and pain. Acknowledging it all, doing his best to accept it. He felt the wave of guilt wash across him, his responsibility for KT's death and Ellie's loss of her mother, and accepted that, too. From his years of dealing with his wars and their aftermath, he knew that pushing away emotions and memories only made them worse.

When they finally began to fade, he called up a mental picture of the long sandy beach where he and June had gone camping the summer before, walking barefoot in the warm, shallow water, hand in hand. He held that image in his mind's eye as his breath filled his chest, again and again.

Eventually, he slept.

He startled awake in the dark, the pistol ready in his hand. A slim form stood swaying by his feet, backlit by the streetlight shining through the sheer curtains. He put the gun down and sat up. "Bad dream?"

Ellie nodded, her voice thick with sleep. "Can I stay down here?"

"Of course." He looked at the clock. It was two in the morning. He stood. "You take the couch."

She sank into the cushions and curled up on her side. "Where are you going to be?"

"I'll be right here." He draped the blanket over her shoulders, then sat cross-legged on the floor beside her, the gun in his lap.

She reached out and grabbed his arm with both hands. Then her breathing softened and she was asleep.

When he woke again, it was just beginning to get light. He lay on his back on the carpet with the pistol at his side. Above him, Ellie was snoring, tangled in the blanket, one arm hanging down with his shirtsleeve bunched in her small fist.

Gently, Peter detached her grip, then climbed to his feet and stared down at her. Blinking in the new day, he realized he was entirely unequipped to give her what she really needed. He was no kind of parent. He was an uncle of sorts to Lewis's two boys, but Ellie was a girl and she'd just lost her mother. Clearly, she needed more than Peter could provide. Especially if he was going to keep chasing this thing, whatever it was.

14

He figured she'd be asleep for a few hours yet, so he left a note saying he'd be back soon. He put Stella's pistol in his belt and the foil brick of phones in his jacket pocket, then headed out the back door, locking it behind him. He considered driving, but didn't want to wake the girl by starting the Tahoe's big engine. Instead he walked down the block on foot, heading for a coffee shop he'd spotted last night. The clouds were low overhead, their hanging tendrils shrouding the houses in mist.

With a large coffee in hand and a bag of pastries tucked inside his jacket, he jogged across the busy street to a bank branch with a decent overhang. Then he set his coffee on the pavement and took his phone from the foil.

Once it found a signal, the notifications began to pile up. Captain Durant had called six times and left four voicemails suggesting with increasing urgency that Peter get in touch. June had sent eight texts, each more profane than the last.

He texted back, "Call when you can." She'd have premium Wi-Fi on the plane and would use Signal to reach out.

Thirty seconds later, his phone rang. "Marine, where the motherfucking fuck have you been?"

June's vocabulary would make a drill sergeant blush. Like KT, her first job as a journalist was on the police beat, and she claimed she'd learned to swear so both cops and fellow reporters would take her seriously. That might have been true, but mostly Peter thought June cursed for the sheer joy of it.

"Sorry," he said. "I had to go dark for a while."

"I don't like the sound of that," she said.

"The cops were going to make Ellie go with someone from Child Protective Services. She really didn't want to. And I was worried about her safety. So she went with me instead."

"She went with you?" June groaned. "You mean you took her. Bad idea, Marine."

"I know," he said. "I just couldn't leave her there. Her mom is dead. She's all messed up. I couldn't protect them. It's all my fault."

"CPS is set up for kids with trauma, Peter. You're not. You have to take her back."

"It's complicated." He picked up his coffee and took a sip. "She said her dad's somewhere in China, that she hasn't seen him in years. That he doesn't want her. She'll end up in the foster system unless somebody steps up or KT made some kind of plan. Did you two ever talk about this stuff?"

"We talked about a lot of things, but not her ex. She sent me a copy of her will after they split up, just so I'd have it. I dug it out of my hard drive. Turns out her brother was supposed to be Ellie's guardian in case something happened. But he's dead. So like it or not, until the court figures things out, CPS is it."

Peter sighed. "I just feel so bad for Ellie. She doesn't deserve this."

"Nobody does," June said. "Listen, Lewis is sitting right next to me. You're still meeting us at the airport?" One of her profane texts had included her flight information.

Having Lewis in Seattle would make it easier to convince Manny that Peter had things covered. "I'll be there," he said. "Did you have time to dig into Reed and Enderby?"

As an investigative journalist with the nonprofit Public Investigations, June had access to multiple subscription databases that contained every scrap of information that money could buy, which was quite a lot. It was often more recent and more accurate than law enforcement databases. The only details she couldn't legally obtain without someone's permission were criminal histories and medical records. If the person was dead, however, she'd been known to find a way around the rules.

"There wasn't much on Geoffrey Reed. His online presence was faint at best. He was twenty-eight, worked part-time at a convenience store by the airport, and lived in what appears to be an apartment over his sister Sylvia's garage. No college, long periods of unemployment. His only significant job was eighteen months as a contract employee for a software staffing company, but that was years ago. Never married, no kids, no car. That gray hatchback was owned by an elderly neighbor who probably didn't even know it was missing. No bank account or credit card. He was on Facebook, but not particularly active. Mostly reposting other people's stuff."

"That threat letter had this odd line. *We are Legion*. It sounds familiar."

"I looked it up. It's from the Bible, Mark 5:9. Although it's not accurate. The real quote is *My name is Legion for we are many.*"

"Why would he get the quote wrong when he went to all the effort of cutting and pasting words from magazines?"

"You got me," June said. "The quote is spoken by a man possessed by demons. Maybe that's how Geoffrey Reed thought of himself."

"Was he religious?"

"Judging by his social media, I would say no. Although we should ask his sister about that."

"What about the other killer, Scott Enderby?"

"Far as I can tell, Reed and Enderby were complete opposites. According to Enderby's LinkedIn profile, his current profession is 'investor.' Before that, he'd been a senior VP at a social startup called Chatrbx. His financials are strong, with more than a hundred grand in his checking and about twenty-five mil in his investment accounts. The house in Magnolia is paid off and valued at two million bucks. He had two school-age kids and an ex-wife who works in business development at Adobe. He was forty-seven."

"Did you find any points of connection between the two?"

"Not yet. But they had to know each other, right? Two attacks on the same person on the same day, that's not just some fucked-up coincidence."

Peter thought of Enderby in his wide-brimmed hat and black windbreaker and textbook two-handed shooter's stance, firing at him in the rain. He'd killed two people and was doing his best to kill two more. It made no sense at all. Enderby had too much to lose.

Then Peter wondered why a guy with twenty-five million dollars would drive a beat-up Toyota pickup that stunk of cigar smoke. "What vehicles did you find registered in his name?"

"Let me check my notes." He heard her flipping through the pages of her notebook. "A sporty little BMW Z4, a Dodge Ram 2500 truck, and a Rivian SUV. All between two and four years old."

"No Toyota?"

"No. Why?"

"Because that's what he was driving at the motel," Peter said.

"I don't suppose you got the plate number."

Peter pulled it from his memory. "Can you check the registration?"

"Doing it now. The Toyota? It's not Enderby's. It's registered to a guy named Gerald Latimer." She gave Peter a street address in Tacoma, a city south of Seattle. He heard her fingers on the keyboard. "Looking up Latimer, I'm not seeing any activity for the past five years. Which means he's either dead or missing. The cops will know for sure."

"Huh," Peter said. "How did Enderby get the truck? Did he steal it from Latimer? Or buy it under Latimer's name?" Either way, it meant there was more to Enderby than his life in tech.

It also meant that, unlike Geoffrey Reed in his easily traced elderly neighbor's car, Scott Enderby had tried a lot harder to get away with murder.

Peter thought again about that threat letter. "Did you start looking into the stories KT was working?"

"I didn't get everything. The upload quit."

"Enderby shot up her laptop and phone," Peter said. "Very convenient."

"I guess he didn't want the cops looking at her files."

"Did she keep anything online?"

"I'm sure she did, but she didn't share her passwords. KT was my friend, but she didn't always play well with others. I did get her tickler list, a half dozen story folders, and another folder with a bunch of interview audio and transcripts."

Peter knew the terminology because June used the same system, which she'd learned from KT. A tickler list was a document listing every story she was working on, whether nearly finished or still in development, along with every other idea she was considering developing, no matter how small or unlikely. A story folder held the collected background notes, audio interviews, emails, images, and web links already accumulated for a given story. It also included a master document with an ongoing summary of key details and links to the other items in the folder for easy reference.

"I've already been through her tickler list and story folders," June said. "Her current projects seem pretty straightforward. There's a CEO profile for the *Journal*, a postmortem on a failed device startup, something about startups that get bought by big companies, and early reporting on OpenAI's huge spend on data centers."

"Is there anything on the whistleblower she was supposed to meet yesterday?"

"Just a few lines," June said. "She didn't know the whistleblower's name or what he wanted to talk about. Apparently he sent something to her PO box, but either she hadn't gotten it or hadn't updated the list."

"None of that seems worth killing for."

"Maybe, maybe not. With that failed device startup, a lot of VC money went down the tubes. A whistleblower can cost companies millions or billions, and their information can lead to criminal prosecutions. I could see Enderby having some investments he was trying to protect, or secrets he wanted to keep. But Reed barely had a pot to piss in. What's his connection to this?"

"Good question," Peter said. "Did you get through the folder of audio transcripts?"

"I did. More than a hundred interviews conducted over the past nine months for at least a dozen different stories. Which was strange, because usually an interview would land in a particular story folder, not be thrown in with all the others. It took me a while to find the common thread. Which was another strange thing, because KT was usually very direct. If she wanted to know something, whether you worked for a tiny startup or ran one of the Big Five, like Apple or Google, she always went straight at you. It was part of what made her a legend, that fearlessness. It also made her a lot of enemies. Her reporting actually helped tank multiple companies. But this thing she was looking into, whatever it was, she'd wait until the end of the conversation, then drop in a question out of the blue. She did it in a whole bunch of interviews on a whole bunch of topics over the course of maybe a month."

"What was the question?"

"'When did you get involved with Gun Club?' Kind of like, when did you stop beating your wife? Which was also a classic in-your-face KT question."

"Huh." Peter remembered KT mentioning this to Durant. Something about tech bros with an interest in guns. "What kind of answers did she get?"

"Straight denials, all the way through. Denial of the premise of the question, in fact. *What gun club? I don't even own a gun.* You can't get tone of voice through a transcript, though, right? So I went back and listened to that part of those interviews. I believed almost all of them."

"Almost?"

"Except for three guys. Each of them paused just a little too long. As if they had to think through their answer. But in the end, they didn't say what everyone else did. Instead, they said, *I'm not involved.*"

"Like they knew what it was. But didn't want to say."

"Exactly. So those guys are the first people we want to talk to. One is relatively small-time, but the other two are serious industry players. Maybe asking those questions is what put KT on the killer's radar."

"Are you following up with those contacts?"

"Emails already sent," she said. "If one of them had something to do with KT's death, I'm going to put his head on a spike."

Peter got it. He felt the same way. But there was a problem with June taking over KT's stories. "You're putting yourself at risk," he said. "If you touch a nerve with one of those guys, they'll come after you next."

"I sincerely hope they do." He could hear the fierce smile in her voice. "Because my boyfriend's gonna kick their ass."

15

When Peter got back to the house, Ellie was still sacked out. He put the pastries on a plate and fired up the coffee maker. At five to nine, he was sitting at the kitchen table with his second cup and the foil-wrapped phones when a big Ford pickup with a ladder rack and a Semper Fi Exteriors logo on the side rumbled up the driveway. He'd already returned Stella's SIG to the desk drawer.

Manny walked in without knocking. He was average height with thick, sloping shoulders and legs like tree trunks. He wore clean black duck Carhartts and a red North Face hard-shell jacket with a fresh shave and a high fade sharp enough to cut. He carried a crumpled brown paper grocery bag in one hand. "What, no hug?"

Peter rose and wrapped his arms around his friend, feeling his calm, steady strength. "Good to see you, brother. Thanks for coming." Manny's cool head in a firefight had saved their lives many times over. Peter had always thought that, in a major earthquake, with houses toppling and bridges collapsing, Manny would be the only thing standing still.

"Carlotta's here, too, she wanted to see you. But she's on the phone with a client." He handed Peter the bag. "Semper fi, Ashes."

Peter sat back down and dug inside. He found a Smith & Wesson .357 revolver with two speed loaders and a box of fifty rounds. "Nice. How much do I owe you?"

"Don't you start with that crap, 'mano. And in case you're gonna ask another stupid question, I got it at a gun show in Idaho and haven't had time to register it, so it's clean."

He took a mug from a shelf and filled it from the coffee maker, then went to lean against the counter but caught himself, pulled a fat envelope from his back pocket, and tossed it onto the table. Rubber-banded stacks of greenbacks spilled from the open flap. "Ten thousand, mixed bills, what I had in the safe at home."

"Manny, I told you—"

Manny gave him a benevolent look. "Ashes. Shut the fuck up. Wasn't for you, I'd have been dead years ago, along with most of my guys. So I'm here, 'mano. Let me help."

Marines, Peter thought. Gratitude filled his chest like oxygen. "Thank you, brother. I appreciate it."

Manny waved it away. "Now tell me what the hell we're dealing with."

But Peter was looking at the doorway to the living room, where Ellie stood, nervous as a cat.

He couldn't imagine what it would be like to wake up the morning after watching your mother get killed. First stretching, feeling rested, feeling good. Maybe thinking that the day was like any other. Then a moment later remembering that your whole life had been blown apart. That maybe you would never be okay again.

She'd clearly slept in her clothes. Her hair was wild and her face was puffy from sleep, giving her a slightly feral air.

He said, "Good morning, Ellie. This is my friend Manny Martinez. Manny, this is Ellie Thorsen. Katelyn Thorsen's daughter."

Manny said, "I'm sorry for your loss, Ellie."

She didn't look at him. Instead she eyed the pistol and the envelope of cash. "What's going on?"

"I got some pastries if you're hungry," Peter said. "Do you want to take a shower, maybe change your clothes?"

She nodded. "Can I have some coffee?"

Peter didn't know how to answer that. The girl was thirteen. "Uh, did your mom let you have coffee?"

"All the time." She straightened up and stood with her hands thumbs-forward on her narrow hips. Suddenly she looked like a young woman. "I have the Starbucks app on my phone."

Peter turned to Manny, the father of four daughters. Manny threw up his hands. "Don't look at me. My oldest is eleven and she still likes juice boxes."

"Thanks for nothing." Peter took a mug from the cupboard and set it by the coffee maker.

Ellie stepped forward, filled the mug, and stirred in enough cream and sugar to make a pint of gelato. "Where is my phone, anyway?"

"We'll talk about that when you come back," Peter said.

She grabbed two Danishes from the plate and headed for the stairs. "I'll be down in twenty minutes."

Peter heard a car door slam and looked out the window. A black-haired woman in a bright yellow raincoat and matching gum boots bustled toward the house. He met her at the back door.

"Peter!" Short and round with pronounced curves, she wrapped her arms around him. When Carlotta Martinez gave you a hug, you damn well knew it. Then she held him out at arm's length and stared him full in the face. "How are you? Tell me what happened."

Carlotta was a clinical psychologist turned headhunter for tech firms looking to hire in-house mental health professionals to help their stressed-out, overachieving executives. She still had that therapist's empathetic look.

As the sound of the upstairs shower gurgled through the thin ceiling, Peter told them the story from the beginning. The threat letter, the attempts on KT's life, the gunman's success at the motel. Peter barely getting the girl out with her life. His conviction that there was something larger going on.

When he was done, Carlotta said, "All that must have been hard on you."

"It was a lot harder on Ellie." Peter's response was sharper than he'd intended.

Carlotta nodded calmly. "That may be. But you know it's not your fault, right?"

"Of course it is," Peter said. "I said I'd protect them both and I failed."

Manny put his thick hand on Peter's arm. "You didn't pull the trigger, Ashes. It's not on you. You did the best you could."

Peter sighed. "Yeah, yeah."

"That's why she's here now," Carlotta said. "Instead of with the social worker or a friend of the family. Because you feel responsible for her."

"I *am* responsible for her. She's got nobody else. Her dad's out of the picture. If I hadn't taken her, she'd be stuck in the system."

Carlotta raised her eyebrows. "What do you mean, you took her?"

"Um. The social worker from CPS was coming to get her, but Ellie didn't want to go. She wanted to stay with me. So we left."

Carlotta shook her head. "I love you, Peter, but this is a very bad idea. Manny and I both know how relentless you can be when you aim yourself at something. Not to mention the fact that you are not exactly domesticated at the best of times." She looked at Manny. Something unspoken passed between them, and he nodded his agreement. They'd been married fifteen years.

Carlotta turned back to Peter. "If it's okay with you, why doesn't Ellie come stay with us? You can figure out what's going on while Manny plays bodyguard and I find her a therapist to talk to."

"I'm pretty sure I broke a few laws when I took her," Peter said. "I don't want that to come back on you."

"Not a problem," Manny said. "If the shit hits the fan, we deny everything and blame it all on you."

"That sounds about right," Peter admitted.

Carlotta beamed. "Then it's settled. Ellie can come home with us."

"Screw that." They all turned to see Ellie standing on the carpeted stair landing, in clean jeans and a white Taylor Swift sweatshirt. Her hair was wet but brushed. Her Doc Martens hung from one hand. She glared at Peter. "I'm staying with you. I don't even *know* these people."

16

Peter said, "Ellie, this is Carlotta Martinez. I've told her and Manny what happened with your mom. They've got four daughters. It will be better at their house than with me, I promise."

She came down the last four steps and faced him, eyes hollow, teeth bared. "You *promise*?" Her voice rose. "Like you *promised* to protect me and my mom? To keep us safe?"

On the rage-meter, she'd gone from zero to sixty in a heartbeat. Clearly that coffee had been a bad idea. Peter took a breath, let it out. "You're right, I did promise. And I failed. I don't blame you for being angry. I screwed up. I'm really sorry."

"That won't bring my mom back."

"No," he said. "It won't. Nothing will. But I'm going to keep digging into your mother's death. Things might get ugly. That's why you should stay with Manny and Carlotta. You'll be safer with them than you'll be with me."

"I told you, I'm not *going* with them. I don't even *know* them."

Peter kept his voice gentle. "Kiddo, you barely know *me*. We just met yesterday, remember? Look, I get that things are really screwed up right now. But I need to find out why those people went after you and your mom. I can't do that and protect you at the same time."

She lifted her chin. "Well, I want to know, too. So I'll just come with you."

"Eleanor Grace, you are thirteen years old—"

"Don't you *Eleanor Grace* me, meatball. You're *not* my dad, and you're sure as *hell* not my *mom*. So you don't get to tell me what to do." Her face was red. She thumped her sternum with the flat of her hand. "I'm my own person. I decide. Me. Get it?"

Then she burst into full-blown tears. Shoulders heaving, snot streaming, skinny arms wrapped around her narrow chest.

Carlotta went to her and put her hand on the girl's shoulder. "I'm so sorry, Ellie—"

Ellie knocked her hand away, shrieking, "Don't you *fucking touch me*."

Carlotta jerked back as if she'd stuck her finger into an electric socket. Then Peter was across the room with his long arms around the girl, pulling her close, voice soft and low. "I've got you, kiddo. I've got you. It's going to be all right."

Even though he knew that wouldn't be true, not at all, not for a long time. And maybe never.

After a few moments of hiccupping, Ellie pulled free of Peter, then ran to the bathroom and slammed the door without a backward glance.

"I'm sorry," Peter said. "She's upset. She didn't mean anything by it."

Carlotta gave him a look. "Of course she did. It's okay. She's thirteen. Two different people tried to kill her. Her mother just died. Plus, the emotional roller coaster of puberty. So put yourself in her shoes. How would you feel?"

Peter glanced at the bathroom door. "Like shit. I get it. But what's the right thing to do here? I don't want to just abandon her."

"Sending her home with us isn't abandoning her, Peter. It's caring for her. By allowing us to care for her." She gave him a sad smile. "And, all due respect, you're getting your ass handed to you by a thirteen-year-old girl. She is living inside a hurricane of emotions. Careening around the city with you, trying to figure out why her mom got killed, that won't help. She needs a stable environment. She needs a therapist."

Peter made a face. "I really screwed this up. I should have let her go with the social worker."

"No," Carlotta said. "At the time, you probably did the right thing. The only thing you could do. You thought she might still be in danger. You didn't trust the police, maybe for good reason. You didn't think the system would help her. It often doesn't."

"Then why do I feel so damn lousy about sending her off with you and Manny?"

"Oh, Peter." She stepped forward and put her hand on his cheek. "Ellie's not the only person who's been through the wringer. I know you feel guilty, like you've failed both KT and Ellie. So you've doubled down on protecting her. But this isn't combat, and she's not one of your Marines. It's more complicated than that."

She went up on her toes and kissed him gently. Then she slung her purse across her shoulder and headed for the door. "We'll be outside when she's ready."

Manny shrugged into his jacket. "She'll be safe with us, Ashes. I'll protect her like my own."

"I appreciate that," Peter said. "Lewis is coming to watch my back, so you're off the hook for hazardous duty."

"You wouldn't say that if you knew what it was like to have four daughters." Manny laughed, then gave Peter a powerful hug. "Keep in touch, okay? Whatever you need. And take care of yourself."

After the pickup's big diesel fired up, the bathroom door opened and Ellie stepped out. Her face looked scrubbed clean, as if she were five years old and had never skinned a knee. "Are they gone?"

"Not exactly," Peter said. "I'm going to make a deal with you, okay? You're going home with Manny and Carlotta." She opened her mouth to protest, but he held up a hand and kept talking. "You will be safe with them. Manny and I were in the war together. He might look like a teddy bear, but he's a warrior, the best of the best. He'll protect you with his life. And Carlotta will find you someone to talk to, someone who can help you."

"That's not a deal." Her jaw was set. "That's you telling me what to do."

"That's your part of the deal. And it's non-negotiable because I am a grown-ass man and you're thirteen years old. But here's my part of the deal. I will check in with you every day. I will make sure you're doing okay. And whoever is responsible for the death of your mother, I will find them."

She frowned. "What if I don't like Manny and Carlotta?"

"I've known them a long time. They're good people. Better than me, honestly. You'll like them, I promise."

She made a face, obviously trying to find a way out of it. "I need more clothes, but I don't want anyone going through my closet. And I need school stuff, too. I don't want to get behind."

Maybe it was a good sign that she was thinking about school. "I have to make a phone call, so Manny and Carlotta will take you home to get some things. I'll meet you there. But after that, you're going with them, not me. And listen, they're taking a real risk to watch out for you, so please try to be nice, okay?"

She stared at him, her face red. He thought she was going to explode again. Instead she blinked furiously, then abruptly came and wrapped her skinny arms tightly around him. With her voice muffled by his chest, she said, "Okay, meatball. You win."

He retrieved her bag, walked her out to the truck, then stood watching as they drove away. He knew it was the right thing to do. But that didn't mean he had to like it.

How was it possible to get so attached, so quickly, to a prickly thirteen-year-old girl?

17

Peter hopped in the Tahoe and headed out, unwrapping the tinfoil brick as he drove. Turning onto Twenty-Fourth NW, a corridor of new mid-rise condos, he could see the big Semper Fi pickup a few blocks ahead. Traffic was heavy, as usual. The cloud cover had darkened, but the rain was holding off.

Waiting at a light, he checked his phone and noted new voicemails from Captain Durant. He made sure Ellie's phone and the burner were wrapped up again, then returned the call.

The captain answered immediately. "Where the fuck is Eleanor Thorsen?"

"She's safe," Peter said. "Any luck finding her father?"

"Not yet. But you're in a great deal of trouble, Mr. Ash. Detective Kitzinger is writing up an arrest warrant as we speak. And she is seriously pissed about your stupid stunt with that poor girl."

Peter felt the white static flare. "Come on, Durant. A social worker wasn't going to do her any good. I'm on your side."

"Felony child endangerment, kidnapping of a minor, and otherwise generally being an asshole," the captain said. "State guidelines say eight to ten years. Although being an asshole is obviously a life sentence."

"Somebody's had their coffee this morning," Peter said. "I have a question for you. When your tech guys went through KT's phone and laptop, did they find anything about something called Gun Club?"

"Why on earth should I talk to you?" Durant asked. "In about five minutes there will be a felony warrant with your name on it."

"Because I'm one of the good guys."

"So you say," Durant grumbled. "Anyway, the electronics are toast. The shooter put most of a magazine into them. And that's not your concern, anyway. You need to bring young Ms. Thorsen to CPS right now. If you do, and if she is unharmed and not further traumatized by whatever rathole you slept in last night, I can talk to the prosecutor and possibly knock the charges down to a misdemeanor. Otherwise I will make it my personal mission to send you away for a very long time."

"Durant. This thing is not over. A friend looked up the killer's Toyota. I have some new information."

"I don't give a damn about your new information. We found the connection between Enderby and Reed. Enderby's recycling had two magazines that were all cut up. We're pretty sure he made the threat letter."

Peter remembered the ransom-note quality of the thing. "You think Enderby was behind the whole thing?"

"It fits our theory," Durant said. "Enderby wanted Katelyn Thorsen dead. He hired Reed to pull the trigger. When Reed screwed up, Enderby did it himself."

"You got all that from some cut-up magazines? How would these guys even know each other?"

"Reed was a contract employee at Enderby's startup for a year and a half. There's your connection."

"Still, Reed didn't seem like a pro to me. Did he have any unexpected cash?"

"We haven't found direct evidence of payment," Durant admitted. "But Enderby's bank records show high four-figure cash withdrawals every month going back three years. The nerd squad is still working on the communications angle. They'll find something on the dark sites. Enderby worked in tech, so he presumably knew how to cover his tracks."

"Sounds pretty thin," Peter said.

"We'll get there, trust me. We also have a motive. Enderby was a major investor in a couple of failed startups. Katelyn Thorsen's reporting hit both companies hard. One went into bankruptcy and the other is on life support."

"You think she was killed over a couple of feature articles?"

"According to Enderby's ex-wife, he lost twelve million dollars. People have been killed for less. He had a basement full of guns. His ex said he was angry about a lot of things. Maybe he just decided that it was KT's fault. We know he was a subscriber to her column."

"Durant, everybody in the industry subscribed to her column. She'd been writing scoops about tech companies since before Facebook, before Google. She had bigger enemies than Scott Enderby. There has to be more to this. What about the part of the letter that told her to stop her investigation? That means a story she was still working on, not something from the past. So what's that investigation, and what was Enderby's connection to it?"

"We don't know yet, but we'll find something. Or else that was just to get us looking in the wrong direction. Enderby was a smart guy. If he wanted to pin the killing on a former mental patient, what better way to do it?"

"Okay, but when Reed failed and killed himself, why did Enderby feel like he had to step in? Nobody knew he was involved. Why put himself at risk? Why not just find another mental patient to do his dirty work? And hell, if his beef was with KT, why did he keep coming after Ellie and me?"

"Kitzinger is still looking into that," Durant said. "There's more to do, but we're wrapping it up. The word's come down from the top. There is no further threat to Eleanor Thorsen. You need to bring her in."

Peter thought about the phone he'd taken from the Toyota's glove box. "This is total bullshit," he said. "You still don't have anything that really links Enderby to Reed. No communications, no financials. Enderby had a silencer. Where did he get it? Was that gun registered to him? I know that Toyota wasn't. Don't you think that's strange? And how in hell did Enderby find us at the motel?"

"Don't rain on my parade, Mr. Ash. The killer is dead, you took care of that. Call it a win. Bring me Eleanor Thorsen and you can go back to your life."

Peter's jaw was tight. "How can you quit like this? A journalist was murdered. Over a story she was chasing. That's a big deal."

"The chief of police thinks so, too. And the mayor. That's why they held a press conference this morning to announce that we've concluded our investigation into these unfortunate murders."

"Durant, you're hanging Ellie out to dry. She's thirteen. Her life is in danger. This isn't over and you know it."

"It's over because the mayor says it's over. The killer is dead, and we have a large tech forum, the so-called Conference for the Future, that starts on Monday. Executives, entrepreneurs, and thought leaders are coming to Seattle from all over the world, and they'll spend millions in the city's hotels, restaurants, and bars. We don't need to make our visitors nervous with a few unanswered questions."

"So you're just going to ignore them?"

"Of course not, Mr. Ash. I've been a cop for thirty-eight years. Kitzinger and O'Donnell will keep digging until they have as much of the story as they can find."

"What about the Toyota Enderby was driving? I had a friend run the plates. It's not in Enderby's name."

Durant sighed. "We know, Mr. Ash. It's registered to a gentleman named Gerald Latimer, who lived in Spokane. He passed away a number of years ago. Apparently the registration was never updated."

"So who paid to keep it current?"

"We assume Enderby. The registration address is a storefront in Tacoma. Detective Kitzinger asked Tacoma PD to take a look. It's vacant, and has been for a long time. It's a dead end."

"If that's the case, then what does that tell you about Enderby?"

"That he was a slippery bastard who took every possible precaution in order not to get caught."

"So he's been planning this murder for years, is that what you think?"

"I don't know, Mr. Ash. Maybe he borrowed the truck. Maybe he stole it yesterday and it hasn't been reported yet. When you've been doing this job as long as I have, you learn that not everything points to a tidy conclusion. As I said, Detectives Kitzinger and O'Donnell are still checking into loose ends. You, on the other hand, are done digging. Let it go or I'll add charges of obstruction to the list. And don't bother the detectives, either. They have jobs to do. They won't take your calls. Plus soon there will be a warrant for your arrest. So if you want to bother somebody, call me."

Peter heard a voice in the background, something about a meeting.

Durant sighed. "I have to go. Crime never sleeps. But I hope I've made myself clear, Mr. Ash. Bring that girl to Child

Protective Services downtown before she's further traumatized by watching you get proned on the sidewalk, handcuffed, and thrown into the back of a cruiser."

Peter had been about to offer to put the social worker in touch with Carlotta Martinez, but now he had even less faith in the cops than before. "I hear you, Durant. Loud and clear."

Then he turned off his phone and, as he crossed the Fifteenth Avenue bridge, tossed it out the passenger window, over the railing, and into the ship canal below.

18

Peter followed Manny down McGraw and parked across the street from KT's little house. Peter locked the Tahoe and walked up to the big Semper Fi pickup as Ellie got out on the passenger side.

Manny rolled down his window. "I'll keep an eye out here, just in case."

Peter and Ellie waited for a break in traffic, then jogged across the road, the .357 bouncing slightly in his waistband. As they went up the front walk, she said, "I want my phone back."

She was a teenage girl, of course she wanted her phone. "Here's the thing," Peter said. "If you go with the social worker, I'll give you the phone back. But otherwise, I have to keep it wrapped in tinfoil. The police can track the signal. They'll know where you are and come get you."

"You're kidding," she said. "They can do that?"

"They can. So it's up to you, whatever you want to do."

She sighed and glanced back at Manny and Carlotta for a moment. "My mom always said it wasn't good for me to spend so much time on my phone. That I needed to learn how to turn it off." She swiped a forearm across her eyes. "I mean, I knew she was right. You spend four hours on TikTok and you feel like shit. But I never thought this was why I'd give it up."

He put an arm around her and gave her a squeeze. Then they climbed the porch steps and Ellie unlocked the front door.

It was a modest 1920s bungalow, with two small bedrooms tucked under the eaves and another on the main floor set up as an office. Even from the front hall, Peter could tell that the police had been through the place. The sofa cushions were askew, books replaced sloppily on the living room shelves. But the searchers seemed to have made an effort to keep things relatively neat, which hopefully made seeing it easier on Ellie.

She stood uneasily with one foot on the stairs, keys in her hand, looking around at the only home she'd ever known. "I'm not coming back here, am I? Not to live, I mean."

Peter didn't answer. He knew it wasn't really a question.

She went upstairs to pack. He went to the kitchen, planning to go through the fridge and put perishables into the garbage for pickup. He noticed the Nespresso coffee maker was pulled out from the back of the counter, as if KT had just filled the water reservoir. He put his hand on it to push it back into place and realized it was warm.

He opened the top and pulled out the spent coffee pod.

That was warm, too.

The cops wouldn't use a coffee maker at a crime scene. Plus they'd likely cleared out hours ago.

The coffee maker should not be warm.

Peter pulled the .357 from his waistband and moved toward the front hall. "Ellie? You doing okay up there?"

No answer. Revolver up and ready, he stuck his head into the living room, then the dining room, saw nobody. The front hall closet held only coats and boots. KT's office was in the back of the house, but it would have to wait. He turned toward the stairs, his voice louder now. "Ellie? What's taking you so long?"

Still no answer. He turned and began to ease up the steps. Slow and smooth, his back to the wall. At the landing, he heard a voice. It was coming from the front bedroom. The door was open. He charged in and saw Ellie at the dresser, singing softly to something on the clock radio, dumping clothes into a giant suitcase open on her bed.

She looked at him. "What?"

He put a finger to his lips, peeked behind the door, then sidestepped to the closet. A chaos of clothes, but nobody hiding. He checked under the bed. Nothing. Her eyes were wide. He pointed to the far corner, out of the line of fire. She went.

He slipped past her and eased open the bathroom door. Nobody inside, nobody behind the shower curtain. He ghosted toward the rear bedroom. The door was ajar. The closet was open with clothes hung neatly. Nobody there. Nobody under the bed.

He went back to Ellie's room. Over the radio, she whispered, "Dude, what the hell?"

"I think someone was here," he said softly. "Might still be here. Stay put. I'm going to check the rest of the house."

Then down the stairs to the kitchen again, where a doorway led to the half-bath and KT's office. The half-bath was empty. KT's office was empty. But it had clearly been searched, and not by the same people who had searched the rest of the house. Some of the desk drawers and file cabinets were still open. Papers and notepads and other desk litter lay scattered across the carpet. Books had been pulled from the shelves. The trash can had been upended on the floor.

He went to the desk. On the glass top was a dark ring, maybe three inches across. The kind of thing the bottom of a coffee cup might leave behind. He put his knuckle to the ring. It was still wet.

He spun out of there and went toward the back hall, where a short flight of steps led down to the back door, a row of coat hooks, and more steps down to the basement. Peering into the gloom, he realized that all the lights were off. A bad bet to hide down there with no other way out. He turned to check the back door. It was the original two-panel door, varnished pine, over a hundred years old.

It was standing open a half-inch. A cold breeze wafted through. The jamb was cracked where someone had pried it open.

He looked down at the floor. No trace of rain at the gap.

It hadn't been open long, Peter was sure of that.

He took a deep breath, then yanked open the door and blew through the opening, checking left and right, then scanning the small yard. No garage. No plantings big enough to hide behind. Nobody waiting to kill him. Whoever this guy was, he'd had at least two chances at it. If he'd heard them coming up the front steps, he could have pulled the trigger when Peter and Ellie first entered the house. If he'd been in the back of the house, searching KT's office, he could have killed Peter when he walked into the kitchen.

The yard was fenced, but there was a gate standing half-open to the neighbors behind. That and the driveway were the only ways out. Peter peered around the rear corner of the house, saw nobody, and jogged to the street with the pistol half-hidden behind his leg. The rain was still holding off. Traffic was stopped at the light. He looked both ways and saw nobody on foot.

Manny's window rolled down again. Peter called, "You see anybody come out here?"

Manny shook his head. Peter forked his fingers at his eyes and pointed at the house. Manny nodded and got out of the truck, unzipping his jacket to reveal a pistol on his belt.

Peter turned back to the house and sprinted toward the rear gate. He peeked through and saw nobody. The house was another bungalow, slightly larger, in serious need of paint. He ran down an overgrown path toward the driveway and then to the sidewalk. He looked south and saw nothing. He looked north and saw a figure toward the end of the block, walking away. He began to run, closing the distance.

Ahead of him, the figure glanced back, saw Peter coming. A man, and he held something in one hand. Like a coffee mug.

Peter turned up his kick and found another gear. He was wearing hiking boots, but they were a newer pair, light and flexible. The pistol in his hand put him off-balance, but he adjusted. It was a whole lot easier than running with an M4 carbine and full armor.

The figure's face had been light, but his hands were dark. Peter realized he was wearing gloves. The guy moved his arm to the side and something fell. Then he turned the corner and disappeared from view behind a long row of lilac bushes.

Peter sprinted to the end, then slowed to see what had fallen. It was a broken mug in a black puddle on the pale sidewalk. The guy had taken his coffee to go, then dumped it. Peter raised the Smith and peeked past the bushes, not wanting to get shot in the face, expecting to see the figure running hard.

Instead, the sidewalk was empty. Peter kept moving forward, hampered by the need to check behind every car along the curb. He saw nobody. Whoever the guy was, he was fast.

Before he reached the end of the block, a bright car peeled out of the last parking spot and cranked around the corner. Peter sprinted to get a better look. All he saw was a pair of streamlined taillights vanishing over a rise.

He hadn't even heard an engine start. Seattle was filled with electric cars, sleek and silent.

Well, hell.

THE DARK TIME

*

As Peter jogged back to the house, it began to rain. He waved to Carlotta, parked across the street. Heading up the front walk, he realized the front door was standing wide open. He raised his pistol and climbed the steps. "Are we good?"

"We're good." Manny stood in the front hall with his pistol held at low ready. From there he had sight lines to the kitchen and back entryway and all the way out front to Carlotta in the pickup. "Find anything?"

Peter shook his head.

Ellie was on the landing, her face pale. "What happened?"

"Someone was here. Looking through your mom's office, I think."

"Did he take anything?"

"I don't know. I lost him. Are you okay?"

She gave him a pointed look. "I'm not the one who lost him."

Peter snorted. "Next time, you chase him."

"That's the bodyguard's job." She clattered down the stairs. "We should go check my mom's office. See if we can figure out what he was looking for."

It was a good idea, Peter had to admit. "Manny, you're on security."

"Roger that."

She led him through the kitchen to the office door, where she stopped and scanned the room. "What's that?"

19

Peter stepped past Ellie and into the ransacked office. She was pointing to a cassette-tape case on the floor by the wall. Peter knelt and took a closer look. The clear plastic case was empty. It was also cracked. Above it, at shoulder height, was a small triangular divot in the plaster.

Peter licked his fingertip and pressed it to the divot. When he pulled it away, loose grains of plaster were stuck to his skin. He put his nose to the wall and sniffed. Renovating houses, Peter had torn out a great deal of old plaster. It had a distinctive smell when you first broke it open, like wet concrete and dust bunnies. The smell didn't last long. He was pretty sure the divot was fresh.

The person he'd chased had been wearing gloves, so Peter didn't think he'd left any prints, but he took a tissue from the box, then carefully picked up the case, checking the corners. A little paint still clung to one. It wasn't hard to figure out what had happened. Someone had thrown the case against the wall, cracking it.

Ellie stepped closer and peered at it. "What is that thing?"

If the searcher had found what he was looking for, would he have thrown the case against the wall? Peter didn't think so. He'd have kept the tape in the case and taken it with him. Which meant the case had been empty already. Which meant the tape might be somewhere in the house.

"You haven't seen this before?"

"Never," she said. "I don't even know what it is."

"It was designed to hold a cassette tape. An antique form of media storage. It made music truly portable for the first time. You could make copies of albums you liked, even make mixtapes for your friends."

As a teenager, Peter had run a lot of miles on the gravel roads outside of Bayfield, listening to Johnny Cash and Willie Nelson on his dad's ancient Walkman. That was almost twenty-five years ago, and it was old technology even then.

"Like an iPod, but, like, primitive?"

"Exactly. Except the tape needed a player, something you'd put the cassette in. It might be big, it might be almost as small as the tape itself." He glanced around the office, checked drawers and shelves, finding nothing. He turned to Ellie. "Can you think of anything in the house that might be able to play this thing?"

"I have no idea," she said. "Why would she even have something like this?"

"Good question." He thought a moment. "Does your mom have a box of old electronics somewhere?"

She blinked. "In the basement? The graveyard of technology. That's what my mom calls it."

He noticed she was still referring to her mother in the present tense, as if she were still alive. Which made him realize he was doing the same thing.

He tucked the plastic case in his jacket pocket and resettled the revolver in his waistband. "Lead the way, kiddo."

★

The basement stairs were steep enough that Peter had to duck to make it down without banging his head. When Ellie flipped on the lights at the bottom, he saw a cramped space with a cracked concrete floor and exposed floor joists above. An oversized dehumidifier hummed softly in the center, keeping the space dry. The walls were lined with mismatched metal shelving units.

The shelves were full. Everything appeared to be neatly organized. Two entire shelf units held cardboard boxes filled with reporter's notebooks, labeled by the dates covered. They went back thirty years. Two longer units had rows of ancient desktop towers and round old monitors. Then clunky laptops not much smaller than a portable typewriter. The laptops got progressively newer and smaller until the last few looked like something you'd buy today. Everything was clean and free of dust. Not a technology graveyard, Peter thought. More like a museum.

"I don't see any music players," he said.

"Over here." Ellie yanked a pull-chain, lighting a bare bulb in an old porcelain fixture, then led him past the furnace and water heater toward the front of the house. On the far side, under the living room, was a worn-out throw rug, a tattered wingback chair under a tarnished reading lamp, and set of makeshift shelves made from planks and cinder blocks. Like a dorm room, Peter thought. Maybe a reminder of KT's younger days.

On the top shelf was a stereo receiver, turntable, and speakers. Each component was probably older than Peter, but he knew Harman Kardon was high-end stuff. A row of vintage vinyl filled the shelf below, except for one section that held a cassette player Peter recognized from his dad's old setup. Expensive modern headphones were plugged into the jack.

"Sometimes she comes down here to listen to her records," Ellie said. "She says there isn't really room for all this stuff upstairs. But I think she just likes to be down here by herself every once in a while."

Peter crouched by the cassette player and peered through the little window. There was a tape inside. He hit the eject button and gingerly pulled it out. KT had either rewound it, or she hadn't listened to it yet. On one side, there was a small label. In the precise numerals of an engineer, someone had written a date. Two months before.

KT had gotten the threat letter yesterday. June said KT had gotten hate mail before. If that's what this recording was, Ellie didn't need to hear it.

He dropped the tape back into the player, then picked up the headphones. "I'll listen to it first," he said. "In case it's something ugly."

She put her fists on her hips. "You think I can't handle it?"

He kept his voice calm and gentle. "I think you're handling a lot already, kiddo."

"My mom's fucking *dead*, meatball." Her face was turning red again. "How much worse can it be?"

He was having trouble with the speed of her emotional pivots. Earlier that day, she'd been scared to be alone. Now she wanted to run the show. "Ellie, please. I'm trying to protect you."

"Really? Like you protected my mom yesterday?" Her eyes were bright and welling with tears. "Fuck that. It's *my* life. *I* get to decide."

He had no idea how to respond to that. Clearly Carlotta was right, he was not equipped to deal with a thirteen-year-old girl in crisis. Before he could come up with anything, she reached past him and hit the play button, then yanked the headphone plug from the socket.

The first sound was the hiss of the tape. It was strange and sibilant and very different from the digital deadness of modern media. It sounded old. Or maybe it was a recording of a recording.

Then came a voice.

20

"Hello, friends. This is your humble messenger. I am so very glad to talk with you again. As I record this in our mountain home, the sky is blue and the sun shines brightly on the greenhouses. Progress continues on the new cabins. We are almost ready."

The voice was round and rich and full of warmth. The tape hiss gave it depth and gravity. KT's sound system was pretty good.

"Each of you has found the message in your own way. Perhaps your religious tradition no longer spoke to you. Perhaps no religion spoke to you. Perhaps your faith still carried you, but it was not enough. You craved something that was profoundly missing. A community of like-minded people. True friends who know your fear, your pain, your anger, your loss."

The words spilled forth effortlessly, like water from a spring, the most natural thing in the world. The voice of a radio announcer late at night, Peter thought, but without the careful consonants. Instead it was folksy and friendly. Maybe a pastor at a country church, untrained but born with a gift for connection. Certain of his gospel, and his audience.

"For we have all suffered under the yoke of modern life. Even those who appear prosperous face the struggle to put food on the table, to maintain our dignity, our humanity, in the face of the industrial machine. You all know what I mean. Prices are through the roof, but most people's pay has not gone up in years. Once upon a time, you could feed your family through the skill of your hands, the strength of your arms. Now two jobs are not enough to pay your bills, let alone build a life, buy a home of your own. The world has changed, and it's going to keep changing. The future will not be better than the past. The industrial machine wants everything we have to give. It will take from us until we die."

The voice rose and fell, one moment a hoarse whisper, the next a battle cry. With the tape hiss, it was hypnotic, like a message from another century. And so intimate, as if the speaker's words were for you alone. The combination was undeniably powerful, Peter thought. You wanted to believe it.

"And this, friends, is why we have chosen to step away. We are survivors, plain and simple. We choose to make our own lives, together. Not as cogs in the machine, interchangeable, disposable. Used up, one by one, bones crushed, flesh torn from flesh, so that the mechanical beast is lubricated by our very lifeblood. That is not who we are, not who we will be. When the time comes for the beast to grind to a halt, we will take all necessary action.

"But not yet, friends. I am thinking of you all. I know we are not all together yet. Wherever you are, I am certain you are doing what must be done to make this community strong. It would not be possible without your efforts. I do not say this lightly. I know it to be true, as do we all."

Ellie's eyes were wide. Her mouth hung open. Her hands fluttered up from her sides, moths rising to a flame. "What *is* this?"

Peter put his finger to his lips. Ellie clamped her mouth shut. The voice continued.

"It is difficult to spend your days in the bowels of the machine, away from the warmth and kindness of our community. It is all too easy to feel small and powerless. A single stick, thin and frail, is easily broken. As we have all been broken before. But if you take many such sticks and bind them together, as we are now bound together, we are stronger than steel. Stronger than the machine. Stronger than the change that is coming for us, inexorable and unyielding as fate.

"I know your tasks are not easy, friends. You are afraid. You feel alone. But you were chosen to join us because you are special. You are capable. And you are needed. So I am certain you will prevail, no matter the hardships. No matter the cost. We all rely on you to do your part to help us prepare for what is coming.

"And the dark time *is* coming, friends. The time of undoing. The time of remaking. Soon your messenger will call you home. We will survive the coming darkness together. More than survive, we will thrive, by going back to the old ways. We have prepared for this. We have made a place for ourselves. A kingdom. Where you are loved, without hesitation, without condition.

"Soon we will be together. I cannot wait to see each and every one of you. Until then, please stay safe, and stay ready. Remember the protocols. Check your messages twice a day. I may call on you at any moment. Because together, we are one. Together, we are Legion."

The hairs rose on the back of Peter's neck. *We are Legion.* The same phrase from the threat letter. Not a misquote from the Bible. A quote from this recording.

"Thank you, friends. As always, I am your humble messenger, signing off. Until next time, please know in your heart that I love you all."

The voice ended. The recording hiss went on for another fifteen or twenty seconds, then abruptly cut off.

Ellie bounced from one foot to the other, as if standing shoeless on hot asphalt. "What the heck was *that*?"

Peter bent to peer at the cassette player. The tape was still passing from one spool to the next. He stopped the tape, then pressed rewind. "I think we just found the reason your mom was murdered."

He pressed play again. The second time, he still had no idea what to make of it. The message or the messenger. *The dark time is coming. The time of undoing.*

Whatever that meant, it couldn't be good.

21

HOLLIS

Hollis Longro sat in the borrowed car, now parked a block from the journalist's house, rain beating down on the sunroof, furious with himself. His phone was in his lap, the app downloaded and open. He'd just sent an update. Now he was waiting for a response.

The Messenger had come up with the plan, with Hollis's help. The Messenger had made a recording for Reed. Hollis had delivered the tape and given Reed the gun. He'd thought it might be hard to convince the kid, but it wasn't. Reed was a true believer. He'd been terrified of the Dark Time for years. He wanted to prove that he could do what was necessary when it arrived. All Hollis had to do was tell him to clean all traces of the Movement from his apartment and quit taking his medication.

Geoff Reed wasn't a perfect choice, but his medical history would provide a convenient explanation if he was caught. They hadn't thought it would be so difficult to kill a middle-aged reporter. It wasn't Hollis's fault that Reed had failed. It wasn't even Reed's fault. It was the fault of the tall man in the green truck.

Hollis had been on the next block when Geoff had made his first try. After watching the young man flee, he'd had to get on the phone and coach him into trying again. Reed had failed again, and Hollis had stood in the crowd watching the police deal with the aftermath. Thankfully, Reed was talented in other areas and had already finished his two essential tasks. The Movement would go on without him.

At least Reed had understood his failure and followed the Messenger's final instructions. The young man wasn't strong, especially off his medication. He'd have told the police everything. The Movement couldn't afford that, not now. Despite everything, the kid had still gone out protecting them all.

Hollis had a backup plan, of course. The Messenger had insisted, and he'd been right, as he was right about so many things. They'd risked too much and come too far to not take this breach seriously. Scott Enderby had gotten himself a fair amount of private tactical training and, like Reed, was looking to prove himself in the real world of bullets and blood.

Enderby had managed to kill the woman, and to damage her electronics as instructed, but he hadn't gotten her bag or the tape. He hadn't taken out the tall man, either. Instead, the tall man had killed Enderby and taken the daughter. Which only made things worse.

Hollis had taken the cut-up magazines from Reed's trash and put them in Enderby's recycling as an insurance policy. It was the Messenger's idea. At the time, Hollis thought it was overkill. But now, after watching the press conference that morning, it was clear that the Messenger was right again. The mayor had taken the win. The law had no clue about what had really happened.

But the tape was still out there somewhere.

Hollis had gone to the reporter's house to find it. He hadn't time to search properly. All he'd found was the empty case, and he'd suspected that the tall man or the daughter had the tape itself. When the tall man showed up at the house and chased Hollis down the sidewalk, he became certain of it.

The tall man was a serious problem.

The Movement had other people in Seattle. But they were the kind of people who thought they could buy their way through the Dark Time. Too soft to do what was necessary. Definitely too soft to take on somebody like the tall man.

Hollis had reported all this to the Messenger a few minutes ago.

Now, sitting in the borrowed car, with the rain beating down on the glass, the phone chimed with a response.

The Messenger was furious. Failure was unacceptable. The stakes were too high. They couldn't be exposed now, when they were so close to executing their plan. To making history.

His next instructions were unequivocal.

Capture the tall man. Capture the girl.

Get the tape.

Then kill them.

No loose ends.

It wouldn't be easy, Hollis thought. He'd had seen the tall man in action. Hollis needed more men. He needed a few of the Hardcore Originals.

By the time they arrived, he'd have a new plan.

He had the beginnings of one right now.

From his parking spot down the street from the journalist's house, he watched as the tall man hugged the girl and got into a dark SUV. Then he watched the girl and a brown man in a red jacket climb into a big pickup truck with a ladder rack and a company logo on the door.

Semper Fi Roofing.

That would give him a place to start.

22

PETER

With the cassette tape in his jacket pocket and the .357 in the console, Peter rolled north behind Manny's pickup, eyes flicking from rearview to rearview, making sure nobody was behind them. He was looking specifically for a sleek blue car, but he'd gotten such a brief look at it, and only from the rear, that he wasn't sure he'd know it if he saw it. Suddenly Seattle seemed to be full of sleek blue cars.

Manny led him to a strip mall on Eighty-Fifth, where he waited while Peter stepped into a phone store and picked up a half dozen cheap burners. He gave one to Manny. Peter was no tech wizard, but his adventures with Lewis had convinced him that most phones could be tapped or traced, and the best defense was to use a phone nobody knew about. If this thing went south and Peter ended up behind bars, at least he wouldn't take his friends down with him.

When Manny headed home with Carlotta and Ellie, Peter stayed to watch their wake for any sleek blue cars entering traffic behind them. Nothing stood out, so he spent a few moments getting his new phone set up and charging. After texting June and Lewis so they'd know how to reach him, he searched online for old-school stereo shops. The first one he called, Hawthorne Stereo, had exactly what he needed.

Including the fifteen-minute crosstown drive to Sixty-Third and Roosevelt, he was back on the road in twenty. But he still had an hour to kill before he had to pick up June and Lewis. So he swung back to Ballard, running the gauntlet of huge new condo buildings until he reached Vintage Vic's Vehicle Repair, where the tow company had taken Peter's wounded pickup. It was south of Leary Way, in the small remaining semi-industrial section still packed with dented sheet-metal workshops where people still made or fixed things, like cars, boats, and heavy machinery. Peter wondered how long it would be until condos took over Seattle entirely.

At the mechanic's, Peter pulled the Tahoe close to the bay doors, got out with the .357, and took a long look around. It was still raining, so there were few pedestrians, and he saw nobody lingering in a car. It would have been easy enough for Captain Durant to find out where the Chevy had been towed. Peter considered it a mildly encouraging sign that a detective wasn't waiting for him there, although the shortage of manpower amid the impending tech conference was a more likely explanation.

Vintage Vic was a skinny dude with watchful eyes and a non-ironic mustache, wearing a tie-dyed T-shirt under his mechanic's blues. He shook Peter's hand and walked out to take a look at the truck. He glanced at the bullet holes, but didn't comment.

Peter had found the old Chevy abandoned in a barn in central California when he was still a Marine. Between deployments, he distracted himself from memories of war by rebuilding the pickup from the ground up. Normally he would replace the radiator himself, but he didn't have the tools or the shop space or, frankly, the time. Just sourcing parts could take a week or more.

Thankfully, when Vintage Vic popped the hood to survey the damage, he seemed to know what he was looking at. He also wanted a credit card up front, which Peter didn't mind, but he didn't want to use his own. Instead, he borrowed a screwdriver, moved the .357 from the small of his back to the front of his pants, and slid under the truck's chassis to open the secret compartment he'd welded to the frame.

He'd already taken out the pistol the day before, to deal with the threat against KT. That was the gun Durant had taken for the forensics techs after Reed killed himself. Now he removed a plastic bag with a rubber-banded stack of used bills in multiple denominations, totaling ten thousand dollars. He'd already returned the rest of Manny's cash when he'd given him the burner phone.

There was also a smaller plastic bag that held a worn leather wallet with a driver's license and credit cards in another name, the new identity that Lewis had put together a few years ago when Peter happened to be wanted by Interpol. The Red Notice had been taken down, but Peter had hung onto the wallet. Because you never knew what might happen.

When he scooted out from under the truck, Vintage Vic eyeballed the clear plastic bags, mustache twitching from side to side like an anxious mouse. "So, like, how sketchy are you, man? Like, for real."

It was a fair question. "Not the kind of sketchy you need to worry about." Peter pulled a Visa from the alternate wallet and held it out. "Is that going to be a problem?"

"Nah." Taking the card, Vintage Vic turned his gaze to the bullet holes in the sheet metal. "Finding a fresh quarter panel might take a while. You want me to Bondo and repaint?"

He'd have to repaint the whole truck or the panel wouldn't match. "Don't worry about the quarter panel," Peter said. "Just get it roadworthy as soon as you can."

As he climbed back into the Tahoe, Peter thought again about the question Vintage Vic had asked. The honest truth was that he had done more than his share of morally questionable things. Many had been as a commissioned officer in the service of his country, doing his best to carry out the mission and protect his guys. He had complicated feelings about those years, a potent mix of pride and shame that he knew other veterans shared.

He'd done other questionable things after his wars were over. He'd broken many laws. He'd killed men and faced no justice except in his darkest dreams. But it was always to protect someone in trouble, someone innocent. Somebody like Ellie.

About those later years, he had no regrets of any kind.

His breakfast Danish seemed like a long time ago, so he backtracked a few blocks and stopped at a place called Mean Sandwich for takeout, deciding on the hot pastrami with red cabbage slaw for himself and a couple of cold subs for June and Lewis, thinking they would taste better in an hour than a hot sandwich gone cold.

He planned to eat on the road, but when he saw the stacked pastrami he knew he'd need two hands and a bib or he'd end up wearing it. He ate standing up by the front window, watching the street, conscious of the .357 at the small of his back.

When he was finished, he wanted a nap. He stopped again for coffee a block away, then headed for the airport, absurdly grateful that the Tahoe, unlike his elderly pickup, had real cupholders.

Arriving early, he parked in the cell phone lot and unpacked his purchase from Hawthorne Stereo, a high-end compact portable cassette player made by a company called We Are Rewind. As he plugged it in to charge, his burner buzzed with a text from June. "Is this the limo company? My driver is late."

He crept through arrivals traffic until he spotted a slim freckled redhead and a large dark-skinned man with a tilted smile. He pulled to the curb, popped the rear hatch, and stepped out into the rain. June ran into traffic, jumped into his arms, wrapped her strong cyclist's legs around his waist, and kissed him hard on the mouth. "Hello, stranger." They hadn't seen each other for two weeks.

Holding her up, he cupped her round backside with both hands. "I beg your pardon, miss, but I'm spoken for."

"You bet your sweet ass you are." Her eyes were green and filled with wickedness. She kissed him again, this time with a little tongue. "Hey, is that a banana in your pocket or are you just happy to see me?"

"Man, you two need to get a room." Lewis wore a shadow-colored rain jacket with no visible logo that made no sound when he moved. It repelled the rain so efficiently that droplets didn't even seem to land on him, although they did bead slightly on his cropped black hair. His tilted smile widened. "Glad you ain't dead, Jarhead."

Peter lowered June to the pavement and bumped fists with Lewis. "Me, too."

Lewis was a semi-retired career criminal who'd made a small fortune robbing high-level dope dealers and, after leaving that business, a larger fortune while saving Peter's ass. He'd learned his killing skills during a tour with the Army, which included a couple of deployments to Iraq. He was the most dangerous man Peter had ever met. And given the nature of Peter's friends from the Corps, that was saying something.

Once they were rolling, Peter handed out the sub sandwiches. "I have updates."

While they ate, he told them about the police brass declaring the investigation over, the intruder at KT's house, and finding the tape recording with Ellie. He held up the cassette player, realizing just now that he didn't have headphones so they could listen to it.

June reached up from the back seat, grabbed the device, and turned it in her hands. "Peter, it's got Bluetooth. You can connect it to the car speakers."

"I just bought the damn thing," Peter said. "I didn't have time to figure it out." In fact, the idea had never occurred to him. Modern technology was not his strong suit.

"I guess I know who's the brains of the outfit." Lewis poked at the media console until the device connected.

June pressed play. The tape hiss filled the cabin, low and visceral, the analog sound of a bygone age. Lewis turned up the volume. Then the voice began. "Hello, friends. This is your humble messenger. I am so very glad to talk with you again."

They listened in silence. The voice rose and fell, intimate and hypnotic. It spoke about the ravenous industrial machine, about the dark time that was coming. When it was over, they sat in silence for a moment. Finally June said, "*We are Legion*. That connects to KT's death threat."

Peter nodded. "This has to be the story she was digging into."

"Yeah," June said. "Does it sound to you guys like some kind of prepper manifesto?"

"Some kind of end-time manifesto," Lewis said. "Although you notice there ain't no real mention of God or the Rapture, right? Sounds to me like they ain't just getting ready for the Dark Time, whatever the hell that is. They gonna make it happen themselves."

23

Peter had already navigated out of the main airport complex and onto Pacific Highway, a busy four-lane surface road with the elevated light-rail line on one side and a long string of chain hotels and cheap airport parking on the other.

Lewis said, "Did you tell the cops about that tape?"

"I wanted to talk to you guys first."

"I think you have to share it," June said. "It's a game-changer."

Lewis frowned. "Problem is, you don't exactly trust the cops to do the right thing. Plus they might limit our moves, get all up in our business."

"Police departments keep intelligence files on fringe groups," June said. "So does the FBI. What if someone already knows who these guys are? All we're doing is helping them connect the dots to KT's murder."

"The mayor and the chief of police don't seem too keen on connecting the dots," Peter said. "They just want the political win. Plus they have their hands full with the tech conference coming up. Although I have to say, Durant seems to want to do the right thing."

Lewis shrugged. "Sharing with him might earn you some goodwill on the whole felony-kidnapping thing. Let him see you trying to be part of the solution."

"I had that thought, too," Peter admitted.

"Okay," June said. "Play the tape again and I'll make a recording on my phone. Then I can forward it to the captain."

Peter parked behind a drive-through espresso place to limit the road noise on the recording. The message was no less disturbing on the fourth listen. He gave June Durant's number and she texted him the audio attachment, identifying herself as a journalist and a friend of KT's.

Waiting for a response, they sat in the warm car while the rain poured down and talked about next steps.

"I still haven't heard from those three guys KT interviewed," June said. "I've pinged them twice. They may never get back to me. We'll probably need to find them. Which means I need to do some more digging, get their phones and cars and home addresses, so we can walk up on them in person."

Peter said, "Geoffrey Reed worked around here, didn't he?"

"Just up the road," June said. "At the Speed Mart." Then her phone rang. It was Durant. She put it on speaker and set it on the center console.

"Thank you for sending that recording, Ms. Cassidy. How did you come to have it?"

"Peter Ash gave it to me. He and Eleanor Thorsen found a cassette tape at her house when they returned to get her things. A man was in the house, searching the office. When Peter and Ellie walked in the front, the man went out the back. The lock had been forced."

"Is Mr. Ash with you right now?"

Peter and June had already decided that they wouldn't let Durant know Peter was on the call. With a felony warrant on his head, Peter's presence at her side would make her an accessory after the fact.

She put a hand on his thigh and squeezed. "We're in touch,"

she said. "He thought it would be good for you to know what happened. That it would convince you to reopen the case."

"Unfortunately, it's not up to me, but I'll share this with the relevant parties. Tell Mr. Ash not to get his hopes up."

June's voice rose. "Captain, someone broke into Katelyn's house after her killer was dead. The recording provides an entirely new angle of investigation. What more do you need? Another dead body?"

Durant sighed. "Ms. Cassidy, I appreciate what you and Mr. Ash are trying to do. And I will pass this information on. But the truth is, my hands are tied. We're short on manpower and the Conference for the Future begins in two days. Ten thousand attendees are already arriving, filling our hotels and restaurants and souvenir shops. The city doesn't need any bad press, especially about motel killings and attempted murders on a public street in broad daylight."

"So if Peter keeps looking into this, he's on his own. That's what you're saying?"

"Quite the opposite. Mr. Ash is already facing an arrest warrant for felony child endangerment and kidnapping of a minor. If he doesn't step away and allow our investigators to do their jobs, he'll also be charged with obstruction. So I would say he'd do better to worry about himself."

"May I ask," June said, "if your techs have found anything pertinent on KT's phone or laptop?"

"Their last report was not optimistic," Durant said. "But I can share something Detective Kitzinger discovered today. One of the victim's neighbors had a doorbell camera. A recording showed Enderby's Toyota parked on Ms. Thorsen's street when we arrived to get her a change of clothes. It left right after we did. Our working assumption is that Enderby followed us to the motel. He was not tipped off by anyone from the SPD."

June looked at Peter. "I'll pass that on. It's good to know your detectives are still chasing down loose ends."

"We are. But as I already told Mr. Ash, don't get any ideas about reaching out to my people. Detectives Kitzinger and O'Donnell are quite busy and are not authorized to speak with journalists. We're badly understaffed as it is and I don't want you interfering with their work." Durant cleared his throat. "One more thing. I'm sure you're aware that Eleanor Thorsen has gone missing. She was last seen with Mr. Ash. Do you know her whereabouts?"

"I'm sorry, Captain. I can't help you on that."

"Because of her mother's death, she's officially a ward of the state. We're concerned about her emotional well-being. Mr. Ash told me he would bring her to Child Protective Services by lunchtime, but we haven't seen her yet. If you know where she is, you should tell me now."

June looked at Peter. He shook his head. She said, "If I learn something new, I'll definitely be in touch. And I might reach out with more questions, if you don't mind. I'm working on a piece about KT's death. You understand that it's in your department's interest that you talk to me."

"That's what every journalist says, Ms. Cassidy. Right before they hang the cops out to dry."

And with that, Durant ended the call.

June leaned forward between the front seats. "I don't think the captain is happy with you, Peter."

"I'm not that happy with him, either. Why the hell aren't they diving deeper into this thing?"

"Policing is always political," June said. "Especially at the command level. It sounds like he's getting a lot of pressure to stick with a certain result."

"Why don't we just bypass Durant and release the tape to one of the local TV stations?"

"All we have is that tape," June said. "Everything else is speculation. We can't prove anything. And if you think Durant is pissed at you now, if you release that recording, the department bosses will have the whole day shift out looking for you."

Peter knew she was right. Actually, he didn't mind the official lack of interest at all. It meant he was free to chase this thing on his own.

June said, "The detectives probably won't talk to me because I'm a journalist, but they may still talk to you, no matter what Durant told them. They also might be more interested in new information than Durant will admit."

Peter thought about it for a moment. Calling Kitzinger would piss off Captain Durant, but with a warrant out for Peter's arrest, that ship had already sailed. Making contact was also a risk because if Kitzinger wanted to roll him up, she could trace his burner. But that would likely take a while, and it was better than using June's phone and putting her in legal jeopardy. He pulled out Kitzinger's business card and made the call.

It went to voicemail immediately. He said, "Detective Kitzinger, this is Peter Ash. Call me back when you have a minute, I have some new information about Katelyn Thorsen's death."

As he put the phone away, Lewis said, "You believe Durant about the killer following the cops to the motel?"

Peter put the car in gear and eased around the espresso shack to the street. "It's a reasonable explanation. Two police cruisers sandwiching a big SUV, it's an easy follow. Especially because the driver of the rear cruiser would have had no reason to look for a tail." There was a gap in traffic. He hit the gas and pulled onto Pacific Highway. "Let's go back to Stella's house and get June set up so she can keep digging. Once she figures out how to find the people KT interviewed, we can make a plan."

"That reminds me," Lewis said. "I didn't bring a piece. I need to make a stop before things get loud."

"We can do that now if you want," Peter said.

Lewis smiled, his teeth bright. "Better at night."

June said, "I think we just passed the convenience store where Geoffrey Reed worked."

"Should I turn around?"

"No. But his sister's house isn't far. Why don't we stop and see if she wants to talk?"

24

Sylvia Reed lived in a working-class neighborhood less than a mile from the airport. Tucked between several freeways, the small ranch house hid behind a high green hedge with glossy leaves that shone darkly in the soft rain. A cluster of inexpensive vinyl patio furniture had been pulled into the mouth of the narrow driveway, blocking passage through the hedge. A soggy handwritten NO TRESPASSING sign was taped to a chair back. Behind the house, a two-story garage loomed.

A pair of newer vehicles were idling at the edge of the street, a heavily logoed KING 5 TV van with a microwave mast on the roof and a silver Pathfinder with a press card on the dashboard. Both drivers eyeballed Peter through rain-spattered windows as he eased past.

There were no curbs or sidewalks, just a muddy verge and abrupt knee-deep drainage ditches flanking the cracked asphalt. At the next intersection, Peter made a U-turn and pulled in behind the Pathfinder, opening his door as a huge Delta jet screamed overhead, almost close enough to touch. The engine noise made Peter's teeth hurt.

June hopped out of the car and marched toward the furniture barricade. Peter hustled to keep up. As they passed the KING 5 van, its window dropped down. The driver wore a beard, a flannel shirt, and a wool hat. The passenger was a younger man with excellent hair, disturbingly regular facial features, and a spray-tan. "Be careful," he called to them through the driver's window. "She's not doing interviews, and she's got a shotgun."

Peter raised a hand in thanks, then broke into a jog to catch up to June, feeling the weight of the .357 in the back of his waistband. "Maybe this is a bad idea." He'd already been shot once by a member of the Reed family and didn't want to repeat the experience without a vest.

June kept walking. "Part of the job, Marine. You worry too much." She wasn't wearing a vest, either.

"I'm serious. We don't know anything about this woman. Maybe she's as crazy as her brother." They were almost at the tangled pile of patio furniture. He went to grab June's elbow.

She twisted away and slipped through a narrow gap between an upended picnic table and the hedge. Then she turned to face him from the far side, still backing toward the house. "Sylvia Reed works at a middle school. Which makes her practically a saint. Are you coming or not?"

"You're not bulletproof, June."

She flared at him. "You aren't, either, and that didn't stop you yesterday."

"Yesterday I didn't have a choice. Today I do. Can we pick our battles?"

Her face was stony. "KT was my friend." She turned away and headed toward the tiny front porch. In the picture window, the long white vertical blinds began to sway.

Peter shoved the picnic table aside and charged through the enlarged opening. "June, let's talk about this." He heard nothing behind him but knew Lewis would be right on his heels.

The storm door opened. A gray-haired woman stood in the

opening with a worn-looking 20-gauge snugged against her shoulder, barrel rising. Her face was tight, her voice loud and angry. "I told you people to leave me alone. Now get the hell off my property or so help me, I'll fire both barrels."

Peter believed her. He slowed, feeling his boots slip in the long, wet grass. "Don't shoot. We're going." He put his hands out, palms forward, trying not to seem threatening, but kept advancing. "Come on, Juniper. Let's go."

But June didn't stop. She climbed the steps to the edge of the porch and pushed back her hood. The rain fell on her face and her cropped red hair. The shotgun muzzle was almost at her chest.

Peter was a few strides back, reaching for her arm, when she said, "I'm sorry to bother you. I was hoping we could chat for a minute. My name is June Cassidy."

The woman put her finger on the double triggers. "I have nothing to say to you. Leave now or I will shoot."

"I'm sorry for your loss," June said. "I lost someone yesterday, too. Katelyn Thorsen was my good friend. I'm trying to understand why your brother tried to kill her and her thirteen-year-old daughter."

Something passed across the woman's face, an emotion vast and ungovernable. The shotgun wavered for a moment, then steadied and turned toward Peter, centering on his chest. "And who are you?"

He froze. This could still go any number of ways, depending on her state of mind. Her finger was tight on the triggers. He had no idea what loads she had in that thing, but at point-blank range, even birdshot could kill him.

In for a penny, he thought. "Ma'am, I'm the one who saved their lives."

Her eyes closed and her face began a slow collapse. The shotgun didn't move. Peter stepped sideways from the line of fire, then reached out and captured the barrel. She let him tug the gun from her hands. He watched the air go out of her.

She said, "I guess you better come inside."

June glanced back at Peter. He broke open the 20-gauge and pulled out a shell. Number 4 buckshot. They'd have put a hole in him the size of his fist.

Lewis held out a hand for the shotgun. "You go with them. I'll keep an eye out."

Peter followed June and Sylvia Reed through the small cluttered living room to the kitchen. A windowed breakfast nook had a view of the garage and the overgrown back yard. The noise of jet engines rose again, and dishes clattered on open shelves as another big plane roared close overhead.

Peter and June sat at a small white table and Sylvia fussed over an antique coffee maker, its logo long since worn away by years of washing. While it hissed and roared, she rattled through chipped yellow cupboards, taking out mugs and spoons and paper napkins, then opened the fridge and stood there looking at its contents as if she couldn't quite remember what she was doing there.

Peter knew the feeling after his own losses at war. You did familiar chores without thinking, your mind wandering in a vain attempt to seek understanding that it would never find.

Sylvia Reed was stocky and plain in a Costco fleece and jeans with a silver cross on a chain around her neck. Despite the gray hair, she was younger than she looked, thirty-five at most. Her brother was only twenty-eight. Her eyes were the fractured red of someone who'd been up all night crying.

Finally she poured the coffee and sat, staring at the garage apartment out back, hands restless on her lap. "You want to know why my brother did what he did," she said. "The detectives were here twice already, asking all sorts of questions. I wish I had answers, but I don't."

"Your brother," June said. "Tell us about him." She leaned slightly toward the other woman, her voice calm and quiet.

Sylvia Reed sighed. "If you met Geoff on the street, you'd think he was okay. But he wasn't. Not for a long time."

"I'm sorry," June said. "That must have been hard. In what way was he not okay?"

"As a kid, he was really smart. Like off the charts. Taught himself to program when he was twelve. He never even went to college. He got a software job right out of high school. The hours were long, but he loved that job. And he made twice as much as I did.

"He was a sweet kid, but he was always volatile. He had these fits of anger where he'd break things, shout at people. Afterward he'd feel terrible, blame himself. He never really told me what happened, but one day there was an incident at work. He got fired. He couldn't find another job. It was really hard on him. And he was really hard on himself."

The roar built as another plane flew overhead. The whole house seemed to shake. She stopped talking until it subsided, then picked up as if nothing had happened.

"After that, things got worse. He had his own apartment in those days. I would go visit, and the place would be filthy. He'd stopped cleaning. I'd tidy up, do the dishes, run the laundry. I had to beg him to take a shower and brush his teeth, and most of the time he wouldn't. He stopped talking to me. He spent all his time on his computer."

"What about your parents," June asked. "Did they help?"

Sylvia shook her head. "It's just the two of us. Anyway, Geoff ran out of money and stopped paying rent on his place. When the deputies came to evict him, he physically attacked one of them. He actually bit the poor man. That's why he ended up in the hospital. They said he'd had a psychotic break. The diagnosis was schizophrenia."

Peter thought about Lewis and Dinah's two boys, Charlie and Miles. Both were bright and curious and full of life. He couldn't imagine the heartbreak of seeing someone you loved go through that change.

Sylvia pointed out the window at the garage apartment. "After his release, he moved in over there. The medication seemed to help. He was calmer, less reactive, although he didn't like the pills. He said it was living in a fog bank. But I watched him swallow them twice a day, just to make sure he actually took them. He always did. A couple of years ago, he said he could handle it himself, so I stopped monitoring him. He'd already gotten that job at the Speed Mart. And he'd actually made a friend, one of his regular customers. They went camping together a few times."

She sighed. "Now I wonder if Geoff had already decided to do something like this. He stopped letting me visit him in the room over the garage. He came here for dinner a few nights a week, that's how I kept an eye on him. But I should have seen the signs." She put her hand over her mouth. "Dear God, what if he'd succeeded? What if he'd killed you?"

She closed her eyes, collecting herself. "I'm sorry. It's just a lot. He's—was—my brother. I loved him." She cleared her throat. "Now then, Ms. Cassidy, what else did you want to talk about?"

Peter had some questions, but June beat him to it. "Geoff's camping buddy, the customer from work. Do you know his name?"

"The detectives asked that, too, the second time they came, after your friend died. Geoff called him Ollie."

"Did you ever meet Ollie?" June glanced at Peter, knowing he was wondering if the friend was Enderby.

Sylvia shook her head. "He only came through town every

month or so. Geoff said he was a traveling salesman. I don't know what he sold or who he worked for."

Peter said, "You said Geoff spent all his time on the computer. What kinds of things did he do?"

"I don't really know. Geoff called it research. He had a lot of interests. The police took his laptop, you know. When they went through the apartment."

Peter asked, "Did your brother ever say anything about the Dark Time, or the end of the world, some kind of apocalypse?"

Sylvia's hand went to the cross around her neck. "The Bible talks about the End Times, in Matthew and Revelation. Geoff used to like the story of the Rapture. But he left the church a long time ago, after our dad walked out on us. It was hard on Geoff, he was only fifteen. I thought the Gospel would help him, but he wouldn't even step into our church, let alone sit and pray."

"Your brother said something to me before he died. That he'd gotten some kind of message. It told him to kill Katelyn Thorsen. Does that mean anything to you?"

"The police asked the same question. I have no idea what he was talking about."

"What about somebody called the Messenger? Did he ever mention that?"

Her forehead wrinkled in thought. "I don't believe so. Although the Bible is filled with references to messengers. John the Baptist, angels, Christ himself. Anyone bringing the Word of God. Did he use that word, 'messenger'?"

"It was someone else." Peter took the cassette tape from his shirt pocket. "Do you know if Geoff had any of these?"

"Oh, sure." She nodded at the garage apartment. "He had a whole bunch over there. He used to trade concert bootlegs with his friend Ollie."

June said, "Would you mind if we took a look?"

25

Sylvia Reed needed some convincing. Her brother hadn't allowed her into the place for months. After he died, when the detectives came, she'd stayed in the house. She hadn't wanted to watch them pick through Geoff's things. She knew she'd have to go up there eventually, but she wasn't ready.

"I understand why you wouldn't want to come with us," June said. "But we'd really like to look. We won't take anything, I promise."

Sylvia narrowed her eyes. "Why are you asking all these questions, anyway? I told you everything I know about Geoff. Why do you need to see where he lived?"

"We just want to understand him better," June said. "Seeing his apartment will help us with that. Maybe it will help you, too."

Sylvia sighed. But she rose from her seat, took a set of keys from a drawer, and opened the back door. Outside, she led them across the yard to the garage. The rain fell steadily. The unmown grass bent under the weight of accumulated droplets.

As they climbed the sagging wooden steps to the second-floor apartment, the roar of another jet began to rise. Sylvia stopped at the landing with a hand on the rail, as if to steady herself against the noise. As the plane's white belly flashed overhead, the engines were deafening. The light fixture over the door vibrated, flashing on and off. Peter hoped the house had been really cheap.

When the sound subsided, Sylvia tried keys from the ring one by one. "To be honest, I'm afraid of what the place will look like. The last six months, Geoff wouldn't even let me come over to clean the bathroom." She found a key that fit and turned it, then pushed the door open into the darkness and stepped aside to let them pass.

Peter went first, finding a switch on the wall and turning on the lights. It was a single room tucked under the eaves. Kitchenette on the left, one corner walled off for a tiny bathroom. In the alcove behind it, an unmade double mattress lay on the floor by a bookshelf. A sagging sectional sat against the far wall with the seat cushions set aside in a heap. On the right under the front window, an expensive gaming chair sat by a cheap folding table that held a giant computer monitor and a tangle of orphaned cables. A partial case of Monster Energy drink sat on the floor below.

There were no dishes in the sink. The trash can was empty. There was a faint smell, maybe dirty clothes, maybe body odor. But otherwise the room seemed pretty clean.

Sylvia peeked over June's shoulder. "Huh. The police must have tidied up."

Peter and June exchanged glances. The police never left a place neater than they found it. Maybe Geoff had known he wasn't coming back. Maybe he'd been planning to kill himself all along and hadn't wanted to leave a mess. Some suicides were thoughtful like that.

Sylvia walked in and turned on a few more lights. The walls had been patched repeatedly and without regard for appearances. Two of the four windows had bad seals and were fogged between the panes. The kitchen cabinets were shabby and the Formica countertop was peeling.

"I wish I could have made it nicer for him," she said. "I couldn't afford to. I can barely afford the house payments. It's not like he paid rent." She sighed. "The worst thing is, I really thought he was getting better. I thought I might get my life back. Now that he's gone, part of me is relieved. It was so much work, taking care of my brother. The worry, the appointments. I couldn't even date, not really. Then I catch myself and think, you're a monster. Your brother was mentally ill and now he's dead."

Peter had plenty of friends from the service who were caring for partners wounded at war. The invisible wounds were often the most difficult to care for. "You're not a monster, Sylvia. It's hard taking care of someone else. Especially over the long haul."

She swiped angrily at her eyes. "Tell me about it."

June gave her a moment, then said, "Where did Geoff keep his cassette tapes?"

"With his books." Sylvia walked into the alcove and stared at the shelves. "They're gone."

"How did he listen to them?"

"He had a cheap little player by the bed, but that's gone, too."

Peter said, "Did you ever listen to the tapes?"

"He played me some of the music on his phone. Old-timey music, fiddles and banjos." She made a face. "I can't abide a banjo."

"But that was on his phone. Did you ever listen to one of the actual tapes?"

"No," she said. "I guess I didn't. But where did they go? The police didn't take them. They're not on the inventory sheet they gave me."

Peter looked at June, knowing what she was thinking. That maybe Reed had disposed of them or given them to someone else in case he was captured or killed. Because if the police had the tapes, the investigation wouldn't go away.

"Peter." June stood looking at the wall by the desk. It was covered with images and computer printouts tacked up haphazardly. "Come look at this."

He walked over. The images were captioned photos printed from news stories. Many showed houses and businesses in various stages of destruction. Some had been wrecked by wind or water, others were blackened and burned. The captions told of hurricanes and tornadoes and wildfires. More photos showed melting electrical wires in Texas, the riots in Portland and Minneapolis, people breaking down the doors of the Capitol building in D.C. There were articles about climate change. Artificial intelligence. A half dozen wars. Famine in Africa. Some of the text had been marked up with stars and circles and arrows.

June started taking pictures with her phone. "Peter, what do you think?"

"He seemed very concerned about the state of the world."

Sylvia came to stand beside them, hand to her mouth. "I've never seen these before."

"He didn't talk about this stuff with you?"

"Never."

To one side, a glossy brochure was taped to the wall. The brochure was for a company called Resilient Systems, something to do with renewable energy. It was folded over to show the picture of the company founder, a middle-aged white guy with strange eyes that seemed to bore through the camera lens to somehow stare directly at you. June took a photo of it. "How about this brochure?"

Sylvia sighed. "A few years ago, he got obsessed with putting solar panels on the garage. Even if I could afford it, which I can't, it rains nine months a year here, so it really never made financial sense."

Another plane flew overhead, drowning all conversation. Peter stepped back to the big bookcase. The particleboard shelves were sagging under the weight of the contents, jammed in there every which way. Programming manuals covering six different computer languages. Thick textbooks on electrical engineering and industrial power systems. How-to books on farming and hunting. Animal husbandry. Log home construction. Build your own drone.

A lot of interests, as his sister had said. The kind of brilliant self-taught person who went on to become an inventor. Or something else.

The how-to books were all together on one shelf. They were smaller than the textbooks, but a few of them stuck out a few inches. Peter pulled them from the shelf. Tucked into the space behind was a narrow stack of what looked like pamphlets. Peter reached in and extracted them.

They weren't pamphlets. They were old paper maps, the kind you used to buy at gas stations, held together by a rubber band. He flipped through the stack. It looked like all fifty states.

He'd seen a similar collection of maps in the Toyota's glove box.

He put the books back where they had been. Using his body to block Sylvia's view, he tucked the maps into his jacket.

June had told Sylvia they wouldn't take anything from the apartment.

If the maps turned out to be nothing, he'd bring them back with an apology.

Somehow Peter didn't think they'd be nothing.

26

With June and Sylvia Reed watching, Peter went through the rest of the small apartment. It didn't take long. The closet had a camouflage-patterned jacket and pants, but nothing you couldn't find at Bass Pro or Cabela's. The cupboards held mostly sacks of rice and dried beans. The fridge had only a half-empty carton of chocolate milk. Under the kitchen sink, he found a small plastic toolbox with an assortment of specialty screwdrivers and pliers, along with a small soldering kit. For working on computers, Peter assumed. Behind the toolbox were four empty boxes that had once held heavy-duty motorcycle chains.

He held one up so Sylvia could see. "Did your brother ride a motorcycle?"

She shook her head. "I have no idea what those are doing here."

Peter found no weapons, not even a pocketknife. He went through the bookshelf again. Just engineering texts and guides to surviving the end of the world.

They thanked Sylvia and left. The rain had let up. Lewis was waiting on the front porch with the shotgun. Peter left it inside Sylvia's front door.

June said, "What'd you take from Geoff's apartment?"

"You saw that?" Peter reached inside his jacket and pulled out the maps. "There was a bundle just like this in the killer's glove box." He handed them to her. Then he remembered the burner. He pulled the foil-wrapped phones from his pocket. "There's a cheap phone in here. I found that in the glove box, too."

June groaned. "You took evidence from the scene of a murder?"

"By accident." Mostly.

"Oh, if it's accidental, the cops won't mind at all."

"Sarcasm is not your best quality," Peter said. "Any chance you can get the phone unlocked? Might be something useful on there."

She rolled her eyes and took the foil packet. "I'll ask Robert later. We're besties now."

Robert was an old friend of Lewis's. He ran a small consulting company doing white-hat security intrusions for corporate clients. On the side, he did a few things for Lewis. As long as Lewis promised not to tell him anything he didn't want to know.

It was after four, and with the low clouds and rain, it was already getting dark. Peter looked at Lewis. "You wanted to make a stop for some hardware. When and where?"

"After dinner. In the foothills. I got a guy."

Lewis always had a guy.

They walked down the driveway and through the gap he had made in the makeshift barricade. As he paused to pull the plastic furniture back into place, the KING 5 reporter climbed out of the van, hair perfectly arranged.

The guy in the Pathfinder got out, too. He was stocky and unshaven, carrying a professional-looking camera with a fat white lens. "She let you in, huh? What'd you say?" As he walked closer, Peter saw his cheeks were mottled by the broken veins of a serious drinker.

"Who are you with," June asked.

"Freelance," he said. "I sell to all the websites, video and stills." He raised the big Nikon. "Say cheese."

Peter felt something boil to the surface. Anger at what had happened to KT and Ellie. A feeling of helplessness at Sylvia Reed's distress. Before the other man could bring the viewfinder to his eyes, Peter stepped in and twisted the camera from his hand.

"Ow, fuck. What the hell?" The freelancer held his wrist.

"Most people don't like strangers taking their picture." Peter turned the Nikon over, found the card slot, popped the waterproof plug, and pulled out the data card.

The freelancer's face was red. "Are you kidding me? I got good shit on there."

Peter snapped the data card in two, dropped it in the mud, and stepped on it. "The woman has lost her brother. Leave her alone. Go home." He held out the camera.

The freelancer snatched it up. "Fuck you, pal. This is a public street. I have every right to be here."

Peter moved in. "Time to go."

Something in his face made the freelancer step away. "What the hell is wrong with you?"

Peter moved closer and growled, "Get in your car or I'll put you in it."

Muttering under his breath, the freelancer stomped back to the Pathfinder.

Peter turned to the KING 5 reporter, who'd gone pale under his spray-tan. "You, too. Go film a car accident or something."

The reporter opened his mouth, then closed it again and hurried back to the van.

Watching them both drive away, June said, "You feel better, Marine?"

Peter glanced back to the house. The vertical blinds were parted at the front window. He raised a hand. The blinds swung closed. "Maybe a little."

June said, "What if it was me out here, trying to get an interview?"

"You wouldn't be," Peter said. "Not waiting like some vulture. Preying on Sylvia Reed."

June patted him on the chest. "No," she said. "I wouldn't."

As they walked toward the Tahoe, June's phone rang. She stepped away to answer. When she returned, she said, "That was Carlotta. We're having dinner at their place tonight."

Peter felt something ease inside him. He'd get to see Ellie. He'd see the Martinez girls.

When the world seemed ugly and cruel, a houseful of kids was often the best antidote.

Because of rush-hour traffic, it had been dark for an hour by the time they arrived at the pocket neighborhood north of Ballard. With their small lots on winding, tree-lined streets, the houses tended to be modest, single-story homes with one-car garages. Most had at least one vehicle parked along the road.

Manny and Carlotta lived in a sixties ranch at the top of a hill. Their back yard opened onto a heavily wooded drainage called Carkeek Park. The summer Carlotta was pregnant with the twins, Peter had spent a month working with Manny and the guys to get an addition framed and finished in the rear of the property. June had been there with Carlotta's sister when the babies were born.

Peter found the turn, then crept down the street, trying to find the house in the dark. When he spotted the Semper Fi pickup and turned into the driveway, the Tahoe's headlights swept across the windows. Before he managed to put the vehicle in park, the front door opened and Manny's square, solid form peered out into the night, a pistol in his hand.

Peter smiled. A true Marine Corps welcome.

Three houses down on the other side, between a short-bed pickup and a Korean subcompact, a sleek blue car was tucked under the low branches of a sprawling cedar.

Hollis Longro sat in darkness, watching. It had been easy enough to find the address where the truck was registered. His time with the Movement had given him valuable contacts.

It was a shame the Hardcore Originals wouldn't arrive until tomorrow.

They could have rolled up the tall man and his friends all in one go.

But Hollis wasn't concerned. There would be other opportunities.

Now that he knew where the tall man had stashed the girl.

27

Dinner with the Martinez family was chaotic but wonderful. Peter was glad to see that Ellie seemed to be doing all right, spending most of her time interacting with the two-year-old twins. Luna, eight years old in a bright pink fleece and pigtails, peppered the guests with questions. Marta, eleven, sat with her legs curled up beneath her, reading a Garth Nix book at the table, although every once in a while she'd pipe up with a sharp observation that showed she'd been paying close attention to the grown-up talk.

It was after eight by the time the dishes were done. As they were saying their goodbyes, Ellie pulled Peter aside for a fierce hug. "You were right," she whispered, face pressed into his chest. "They're good people."

"What, better than me?" he asked softly.

She pushed him away with an epic eye roll. "Omigod, meatball. *Totally* better. Like, not a contest."

"How are you doing without your phone?"

She shrugged. "It's fine."

It was nearly nine by the time they reached Stella's little house and dropped June at the back door with the old paper maps from Reed's apartment, the foil-wrapped phones, the cassette tape, and the player. She wanted to get back on her computer, crack the burner, and start digging into this Messenger thing. She would also reach out to the three guys who had reacted strangely to KT's questions.

After she locked the door behind her, Peter left with Lewis to see a man about some guns.

They took I-5 south to the 405, traffic light and fast at that hour. Peter pushed the Tahoe hard through the rain.

They hit Highway 169 and turned southeast, away from the city lights. Peter said, "This thing with Ellie and KT is turning into a real mess. You know you can sit this one out, if you want."

Lewis had been shot four times the winter before. The recovery had been long and difficult.

"Naw," he said. "I'm good, brother." Putting some street into it.

"I'm serious," Peter said. "I know it messed with you, getting hurt like that. It would mess with anyone."

Lewis looked at him, his dark face nearly invisible in the darkened vehicle. "Would it mess with you?"

"Of course it would," Peter said. "In fact, it did. You remember when my PTSD was so bad I could barely go inside without a panic attack. All those years in uniform, kicking in doors, going house to house, it fucks with you."

"But it didn't stop you."

"No," Peter said. "But this isn't the bad old days, when you and your crew were running and gunning. You've got two boys now. And Dinah. What about them?"

Lewis turned forward to look through the windshield for a moment, the wipers slapping back and forth, the road dark and wet before them.

"That night in the snow," he finally said, "Charlie and Miles learned who I really am. What I'd been back in the day, what I'm capable of now. When I woke up in the hospital, I realized I'd been working real hard to hide it from them. To protect them, I guess. But that wasn't the right way to go. The right way is to show them how a man can be, what he can do, when he's got good reason."

"When he loves his family," Peter said.

Lewis nodded. "But it's more than family, ain't it? It's everybody else, too. A man's got to stand up and be useful in this world. Use his skills. Make a damn difference." Lewis looked at him now, eyes bright in his dark face. "You taught me that."

"I did?"

"Yeah, you jarhead motherfucker. You did. So here I am."

"Well," Peter said. "I appreciate you, brother."

Lewis nodded again. "Long as we having us a moment, I notice you pretty tightly wrapped. Ready to beat that photographer to death with his own camera."

Peter stared out at the lights of Maple Valley. His words felt stuck in his throat, or somewhere lower.

Finally he said, "I was supposed to protect her. I was supposed to protect them both."

"Yeah," Lewis said kindly. "Put you right back in the sandbox, didn't it? Losing one of your people got that white static all fired up."

Peter sighed. He'd lost a lot of guys in Iraq and Afghanistan. Young men under his command, men whose lives were his responsibility. Men with wives and families. It never got easier. But this was different.

"KT didn't sign up for war," he said. "Ellie didn't sign up for any of it. And now . . ."

Lewis nodded. "Her momma's dead and her life's turned upside down. But it coulda been worse. She could be in the hospital or in a pine box. Instead she's with Manny and Carlotta. They good people, brother. She'll get through it."

Peter hoped that was true. "Except that man from KT's house is still out there. And the voice on that tape? Whoever these assholes are, they're planning something big."

Lewis clapped his hand on Peter's shoulder. "That's exactly why we here, Jarhead. Put our skills to use. Need be, put some bad dudes in the dirt."

"Roger that," Peter said. "But that thing you said before? I just want to be clear. I'm your role model?"

Lewis flashed that tilted smile and whacked Peter on the chest with the back of his hand. "Sheeeit, I knew you was gonna make it weird."

"Good talk," Peter said. "Let's go buy some guns."

At Summit, Lewis pointed him east into the unincorporated foothills, trees looming midnight green at the roadsides. Aside from a few lonely subdivisions carved out of the woods, there was little sign of humanity. The night grew darker. The trees grew taller, closing in.

They slowed through Ravensdale, then again through Kanaskat, which was barely a wide spot in the road. The subdivisions were long behind them. Out his window, Peter could see the flat blackness of the Green River behind the trees, with flashes of white at the gravel bars. They passed logging trucks parked in dirt turnouts, their booms and trailers looking like prehistoric creatures in the wet night. As they gained elevation, the rain turned to sleet.

The Tahoe thumped across a narrow bridge, the river now on their right. Lewis looked at his phone. "Next left, coming up fast. Might be hard to see."

Peter slowed, then slowed more. Even so, he was past the turn before he saw it, just a small gap in the trees. He braked, reversed, then cranked the wheel. Someone had used a bulldozer to cut a road into the slope of the hillside, angling upward. A long time ago, judging from the size of the trees grown up beside it. Heading up into the darkness, bouncing over the rutted gravel, he was glad the vehicle was four-wheel drive.

"Tell me who we're buying from," Peter said.

"Couple of small-time ex-army peckerwood brothers I knew back in the day. Worked for the company armorer, repairing weapons. Knew their stuff. Now they in business for themselves. Got a machine shop way up in the woods, stamp their own AK receivers, build new guns with replacement parts sourced from Poland and Bulgaria."

"Ghost guns," Peter said. "No serial numbers, totally untraceable."

"You got it. Worth serious scratch, if you don't end up getting killed by your customers. So these guys play rough, they don't like outsiders, and they paranoid as hell."

"You don't know anyone else out here?"

Lewis snorted. "Jarhead, these mountains are full of wingnut groups. You got your race-war militias and eco-anarchist collectives and everything in between, and they all armed to the teeth. Even the damn hippies got AR-15s. And every last one of 'em thinks the moon landing was faked and the president's an alien. But I've known Nickels and his brother since the Army, and far as I can tell, all they care about is money, and we got plenty of that. Not to mention, we ain't got time to make new friends."

"We're just going to knock on their door?"

"I messaged 'em from the plane. Nickels said they might part with a few things if the price was right. They call him Nickels because he carries a roll of coins in his pocket, always ready for a fight. And he never did like me much, anyway. You best keep that .357 ready."

"Did you forget we only have the one pistol? What are you going to use?"

Lewis smiled brightly. "I'm gonna give them the Denzel Washington."

"What the hell is the Denzel Washington?"

"Just follow my lead, Jarhead."

The land opened up and yellow lamplight filtered through the evergreens ahead. The road came to a crest and they arrived at a clearing carved out of the trees. A two-story log home moldered beside a large sheet-metal pole barn. In the mud yard, three big Dodge Ram pickups stood high on knobby tires, gleaming in the rain.

"Tap the horn," Lewis said. "Stay in the truck. Keep the engine running."

28

Peter didn't need to tap the horn. A man came around the side of the pole barn in a green M65 jacket with a long gun at his shoulder. He had skinny legs and blond hair showing under his bucket hat. The rifle had the distinctive curved magazine of an old-school Kalashnikov and a fat suppressor on the end of the barrel.

Lewis dropped his window and put his hands out. "Yo, Nickels. It's Lewis."

Nickels came closer, pale and squinting in the headlights. His voice was thin and high. "Let's see the money. Or else turn that rig around and get the fuck out."

Lewis gave him a wide smile. "My brutha. Put up that gun. I got the dough if you got the hardware. 'Less you dudes don't want to get paid today?" Lewis was laying on the street thicker than butter on a biscuit. Maybe this was what he meant by the Denzel Washington.

"How much you got to spend?" The sleet melted on Nickels's coat and ran down onto his pants, which from the darkening color were likely not waterproof.

"Enough," Lewis said. "Can we at least talk someplace out of the damn rain? I'm getting wet, leaning out the window like this. Hell, you must be soaked to the bone."

"You got the money on you?"

"Told you I did, man. Who you think you talkin' to?" Lewis opened his door and stepped out, looking around. "I always did like this place you got up here. Room to breathe, right? None of those uppity city folk to bother you. Man, I got to get me a joint like this."

If this was the Denzel, Nickels wasn't buying it. The AK stayed steady. "Stop right the fuck there. Show me your hands. Who's that driving?"

Lewis stopped and held his hands out from his body. Nickels was twenty feet away. "Nobody you need to know, man. A good dude, reliable. Keeps his mouth shut." Lewis took a step toward him. "You know I paid you boys a lot of coin over the years. I ain't looking for no bargain." He took another step. "I need three long guns and three pistols, extra mags for all of 'em. Everything new, no history, no serial numbers."

Nickels's voice hardened. "Tell him to get out of the truck. Keep showing me those hands, both of you."

"What's the damn problem, Nickels?" Lewis took another step. "I told you, he's cool. You gonna show me some inventory or what?"

"Get your pal out of the truck or I'll shoot him where he sits."

Peter didn't like how this was playing out. Even from that distance and through the windshield, he could see something in the man's face. He opened the door, laid the .357 on the door's armrest, and showed his hands. "Don't shoot. We just want to do a little business."

Nickels turned the gun on Peter for a moment, then pivoted back to Lewis with his finger on the trigger. They were fifteen feet apart. "Now take your coat off, nice and slow. Then show me the money."

"I ain't taking it off, man. It's raining." Lewis sounded indignant. As he unzipped his jacket and held it open, he took another step closer. "I ain't strapped. The cash is in my coat pocket."

Nickels took three steps back, settling the rifle deeper into his shoulder and putting his eye to the iron sight. Maybe not such a dumb peckerwood. His voice sharpened. "Take out the money and put it on the hood of the truck. Any funny moves and I blow your fucking head off."

"I thought we was doin' business, Nickels. This feels more like a stickup."

"It's going to be a killing if you boys don't do what I say. Now take off your got-damn coat and put the money on the hood."

This had gone from bad to worse. It was all about the money. The AK had a thirty-round magazine. After Nickels dropped Lewis, he'd empty it through the door and into Peter. There was a lot of acreage for burying bodies out here.

Behind Nickels, the pole barn door opened and a second man stepped out. Raising another long gun.

Shit, shit, shit. Peter tasted copper in his mouth. Before he could think twice about it, he picked up the .357 and stepped bareheaded into the rain, keeping the big pistol out of sight behind the door. "Fuck it, Lewis. Let's go. These guys don't have shit."

Nickels began to pivot toward him, gun up and ready. "Hands up or you're dead."

Lewis moved so fast he was a blur. He grabbed the rifle barrel with one hand and pulled it down and away. Under pressure, Nickels pulled the trigger. A jet of orange fire shot from the suppressor into the trees. Then Lewis stepped in close and gave him a hard elbow in the head. It sounded like thumping an overripe melon with a wooden mallet. Nickels fell on his ass in the mud and Lewis had the weapon.

"Lewis, behind you." Peter raised the .357 toward the second man and thumbed back the hammer. The metallic click cut like a razor through the sound of the rain. "Drop the gun," he shouted. "Drop it or I'll shoot." He was maybe forty yards away, not the easiest shot with a four-inch barrel.

The man didn't reply. He didn't even hesitate. The gun kept rising.

Peter pressed the trigger. The .357 leapt in his hand. The man with the rifle staggered back, but he still held the weapon.

Peter thumbed back the hammer again and tried to squint the rain from his eyes. By then, Lewis had managed to reverse Nickels's rifle and raise it. He beat Peter to the trigger with three rounds on full auto. The man fell forward and was still.

At Lewis's feet, Nickels was on his knees clawing under his Army coat. Peter sprang forward and kicked him in the stomach. Nickels flew back.

Peter tore open the coat and pulled an automatic pistol from the holster on his belt, then got back to his feet, weapon ready, eyes scanning for another shooter. Lewis did the same.

They stood there in the deepening mud, breathing hard. The rain came down as though it would never stop.

There were three trucks at the house, but so far only two men.

29

JUNE

After locking the door and checking out Stella's house, the first thing June did was fire up her laptop in the dining nook. She didn't have Stella's Wi-Fi password, but she didn't need it. Because her work was often sensitive—and because, years ago, she'd been hacked at a Starbucks, which for a tech journalist was fucking embarrassing—she'd started using a mobile hot spot, which allowed her to connect securely to the internet from any place with a cell connection.

She'd already texted with Lewis's friend Robert, and knew that he was up late, working. June had plenty of computer skills, but Robert's knowledge was light-years ahead of hers. She let him know she was online, and he sent her a permission box to allow him to access her system remotely. She clicked yes. If you can't trust a professional white-hat intrusion specialist to peek inside your shit, who can you trust?

Waiting for his software to sync, she peeled open the tinfoil and removed the burner Peter had taken from the killer's Toyota. Rewrapping Ellie's phone, she shook her head, thinking again what a bad idea it was to take evidence from a murder scene. She'd have been pissed at Peter for doing it, but she knew he hadn't done it lightly.

Mostly it was a serious indication of how much losing KT was messing with his head. June got that. Losing a good friend was messing with her, too. She hoped the phone would give up some secrets that Captain Durant wouldn't have otherwise shared. Or—and she knew she was rationalizing here—maybe Durant's people wouldn't even have bothered with it.

When you've already decided what happened, why continue to actually investigate?

Following Robert's instructions, she plugged the burner into her laptop with a spare cable from her bag, so he could use his pro-grade tools to unlock it from his hacker lair.

"Ready," she texted. "How long do you think this will take?"

"A few hours, tops," he replied. "These cheap phones don't have strong security. You're lucky it's not an iPhone. Those are a lot harder."

She sent him a few kiss emojis along with a reminder to send her a bill, then pulled out the bundle of old maps Peter had taken from Reed's apartment, similar to the bundle he'd found in the Toyota's glove box. Pulling off the rubber bands, she flipped through the collection. He had one for every state except Alaska and Hawaii. Very strange. She unfolded the top map, which was for Washington state.

It was covered with markings. They were like hieroglyphics or alien pictograms, made with ultra-fine-tipped pens in multiple colors. Dense in places and sparse in others, each dense section was linked to others by ruler-straight lines. Like an org chart or genealogical diagram, only far more complex.

Adding to the mystery was a column of numbers written down the side of the map in the same spidery hand. Each row was fourteen digits long with no breaks. Too many digits to be telephone numbers. Maybe account numbers? Or email addresses? There were ten sets, each unique.

She opened the next map, Oregon. It had a similar set of hieroglyphics and column of numbers. California was the same. And Arizona. And Nevada. What any of this meant, she couldn't even begin to guess.

Although maybe there was no sense to be made. Maybe the diagrams were just the product of Reed's tangled mind, referencing some abstract internal structure that only he could see. He sure had put a lot of work into it, though. She'd share the diagrams with Peter and Lewis. Maybe they could figure it out.

She folded up the maps, put the rubber bands back on, and set them aside. Moving on to the next task, she pulled out her tablet and opened a voice transcription app, one of many recent technologies made possible because of a leap forward in artificial intelligence.

As AI got better and better, all kinds of companies were taking advantage of the tech to make more capable software. June didn't do much reporting on AI, but she kept up on new advances. It was a little freaky, she thought, for the present day to start catching up to science fiction. Some obvious benefits, but oh so many possible disaster scenarios.

June wasn't particularly worried about a *Terminator* moment, where the machines revolted, made robots that looked like Arnold Schwarzenegger, and tried to wipe out humanity. She was more worried about the number of jobs that could be lost over a relatively short span of time and what effect that might have on society. If AI advanced as quickly as the experts expected, it would be like NAFTA on steroids, and it would cut across every sector of the economy. Every AI company was racing for the brass ring, the mother of all killer apps and the enormous fortunes it would generate. Nobody seemed to be thinking much about the long-term ramifications.

Even if one company did decide to slow down, twenty more would leap forward. All the journalists in the world wouldn't change that. There was simply too much money involved. Government oversight had been neutered by hundreds of millions in campaign contributions. Even without it, regulation would never be able to keep up with the rate of change. The genie was officially out of the bottle.

Sighing, she found the digital audio she'd made from the Messenger cassette and uploaded it to the transcription app. It immediately began to spit out text. She copied and pasted into a document and then, because poor sound quality tended to amplify mistakes, began to work her way through it, checking for errors.

There were remarkably few. They must have updated the app again, she thought. Before long, they would be able to transcribe your thoughts. No joke, there were actual companies working on that, with some early success.

She tried to be hopeful about all this rapid technological evolution. She wasn't always successful. And June was good at technology. She actually *liked* it.

What if you were someone who *didn't* like it?

What if you were truly afraid of what the future might bring?

You'd be someone like the Messenger.

She went through the cassette tape transcript, looking for key words and phrases. The Dark Time. The Industrial Machine. The Messenger. She noticed there was no mention of Gun Club, but she added that to the list. Then she ran web searches for each one, looking for mentions online. Once she found those, she could backtrack, find more people to talk to. With any luck, she'd find the Messenger himself.

Working her way through dozens of pages of results, she found plenty of hits. "Dark Time" led to a Google Chrome extension, a music sequencer, books about the cold war, and a hip-hop duo. "The Industrial Machine" led to large machine shops, computer-controlled equipment, and, oddly, a vast world of sewing enthusiasts. "The Messenger," which seemed the most promising, led to a movie, a video game, a TV show, and multiple magazines from previous decades. "Gun Club" led to, yes, ten thousand gun ranges and shooting clubs.

None of it seemed remotely close to what she was looking for, a group of freaked-out people working toward some kind of cataclysm.

She went to a half dozen social media sites and tried again. Lots of results, so presumably there might be some signal in the noise, but if so, she couldn't see it. She tried the usual encrypted communications apps, WhatsApp, Signal, Telegram, and a few others, looking for any public groups with those key words, but nothing popped up there, either. Not even anything with common coded language, which some extremists had learned to use to keep from getting blocked by various apps.

After several hours of this, June shoved back her chair and began to pace the house. She was a good researcher, with years of experience and an affinity for the web, but she'd found zip, nada, bupkus. She didn't get it. Enderby and Reed were tech professionals. Wouldn't they use the technology at their disposal?

Sighing, she went back to the dining nook and picked up the cassette player, ejecting the tape and turning it in her hands. This was technology, too. Old technology, but it still worked.

Also, it was analog, not digital. Which made it inherently more secure, because it was simply harder to copy and distribute. If you wanted to throw a monkey wrench into the so-called Industrial Machine, maybe this was the best way to go about it. Build a physical network and distribute cassette tapes, person to person, to the secret faithful. With everything offline, there was no electronic chatter.

That was basically what Osama bin Laden had done after he went into hiding, she thought. He'd sent handwritten letters and analog recordings into the world using an elaborate system of secret couriers, which prevented the United States from tracking any electronic signals back to his hideout. The messages were distributed hand to hand until they reached the radical imams and their madrasas. He'd directed his entire international operation that way. Despite the intensive efforts of the most fearsome military and intelligence apparatus the world had ever seen, bin Laden had escaped detection for almost ten years.

Also, if you were going to communicate in secret, audio was an especially powerful way to do it. Perhaps the most powerful, because of its intimacy. Wearing headphones, it felt like a whisper in your ear, or a voice in your head. Perfect when you wanted to convince scared or angry people to do crazy shit.

Plus, for tech workers like Enderby and Reed, this old-school vibe was probably part of the appeal. Couriers and audio messages and secret meetings. It would make them feel like spies. Or revolutionaries.

Man, when she found this Messenger guy, she was going to bitch-slap him so hard he'd forget his own name.

If Peter and Lewis didn't put a bullet in his head first.

30

June had still not gotten a reply from any of the three people who'd given strange responses to the question about Gun Club. She'd emailed them again and was busy finding their phone numbers and home addresses when her phone pinged with a text. It was Robert, telling her the burner was unlocked and giving her the new access code.

She sent back her thanks and a promise of breakfast at Wonderland when she returned to Milwaukee, then unplugged the phone and sat down to work her way through it.

Typically, the security provided by burners was their anonymity. Unconnected from any known account, data paid for in cash, destroyed after a few days or weeks to start the cycle again with a new phone and new number. On top of that natural protection, or maybe because of it, people who used burners tended to watch their words in text and email. So she didn't have high expectations. Maybe a few cryptic texts, a couple of phone numbers. Someplace to start.

But she hadn't expected the phone to be completely empty. No call history, no text history, no browser history. No emails. No contacts. No previous searches archived in Google Maps. And zero other apps. In fact, the only indication the phone had ever been used was a scratch on the battery cover and the absence of the usual manufacturer-added bloatware, which often harvested user information and was a colossal pain to remove. She'd seen her share of burners, and this was the cleanest she'd ever come across. Why work so hard to sanitize an anonymous phone you were going to smash with a hammer and toss in a dumpster?

She thought about the cassette tape again. The Messenger and his people were going to a lot of trouble to stay under the radar. But something nagged at her.

She went back to the recording transcript and read through it one more time. Here it was, toward the end. Check your messages twice a day, he'd said. Clearly the slow-motion cassette network wasn't the only means of communication. Inevitably, some things would have to be dealt with more rapidly, or one-on-one—hence the burner. And she knew it had been in use. But there was nothing in its memory. So where were the fucking messages, and how did you check them?

Grrrr. She got up and paced the house. She put water in the kettle for tea, then paced some more, waiting for it to boil.

What if they were loading an application fresh, every time they wanted to use it? And then deleting it afterward?

That was a little excessive, even for the truly paranoid. But it was a pretty good way to keep a clean phone. And even if deleted, most apps stored each phone's details on company servers, so they'd remember your information when you reinstalled them.

The most popular encrypted apps were Signal, which June used herself, along with WhatsApp and Telegram. There were dozens more. But even if she found the right app, she'd still need a username, password, and phone number. Without those, she couldn't log in.

Unless, she thought hopefully, the truly paranoid had gotten a little sloppy.

She navigated through the security settings to the password manager. There was a single entry. No name for the app and no username for the account, but there was a password and a ten-digit number. Ten digits would be the phone number you'd need to log in. Gotcha, you lazy fuck.

She loaded Signal but got nowhere. Then WhatsApp. Same result. Then Telegram. Fingers crossed while it loaded. Then she opened it.

The login prompt came up. The app filled in the username automatically from the server. June felt the rich flush of pleasure that came from figuring something out.

The username was Duke Nukem, after the hero in the old-school first-person shooter game. Enderby, she assumed, rolling her eyes. Such a bro. She entered the phone number and password from the phone's password manager and was rewarded with a chat screen. She was in. She did a little victory dance bump and grind, wishing Peter was there to help her celebrate.

The fact that these guys used Telegram was unsurprising. For years, Telegram had been the app of choice for criminals and extremists of all stripes. The company was known for, and had often bragged about, ignoring all governmental requests for information.

Until the owner had been arrested in France and thrown in jail. It had taken only a few days for him to change the company policy. But because of the way it organized private groups and public channels, not to mention zero content moderation, it was still the preferred communication app for certain groups.

The interface gave her two chats to choose from.

The first chat was a group called Gun Club. Aha! This was what KT had been searching for. But there were no messages, and all the other members were hidden. June figured it was set to self-delete. Teenagers and criminals really loved that feature.

The second chat was still up. It was one-on-one between Duke Nukem and another user named Circuit Rider. There were only four messages.

From Circuit Rider: "Plan A failed you're up. Good luck my friend."

The reply from Duke Nukem was a thumbs-up emoji and a flexing biceps.

An hour later, Circuit Rider had responded. "Truck 2 blocks s of house. Keys on floor. Wpn in glove. Leave car w keys."

Then Circuit Rider followed that up with: "Take or destroy electronics and notes. Leave nobody. M's orders."

The reply was a squirt gun emoji and a grinning face.

If this was in fact Enderby's phone, by looking at the times on the messages, June could put it together easily enough. Reed had just killed himself and Enderby was being activated as Plan B. Circuit Rider had left him a truck and a gun. She assumed the truck was the Toyota. And Enderby had left his car for Circuit Rider.

Holy crap. She dropped the phone on the counter, thinking hard about the ramifications.

Between the message content and the timeline, she'd gotten confirmation of a deeper conspiracy with at least one more person involved. If she gave the phone to Durant, he could probably get the investigation reopened.

The problem was that, because Peter had lifted the phone from the murder scene, handing it over to the police would get him into even more trouble than he already was. And legally, because of the break in the chain of evidence, the phone and its contents were also now inadmissible as evidence.

Regardless, she'd also learned something else. The Toyota hadn't actually belonged to Scott Enderby. It had belonged to the third conspirator, the person who called himself Circuit Rider.

Maybe that's why the ownership was so murky. It had been registered to someone named Gerald Latimer, but Durant had told Peter that Latimer had been dead for years. However, the registration had been renewed at the Tacoma address multiple times. She could run down any connections there, maybe get a name that way.

Then she realized she might have a much more direct connection to the third conspirator. If Circuit Rider hadn't already dumped his phone, maybe June had a way to communicate with him. Using the same app.

She looked down at the phone and scanned the messages. Her eye caught on the last sentence.

"Leave nobody. M's orders."

Those last four words made her shiver.

Leave nobody, June was pretty sure, meant *Kill everybody*.

Good Lord, she thought. Who the holy hell are these people?

31

PETER

One-handed and with no apparent effort, Lewis picked Nickels up by the front of his coat. "Who else is here? They don't have to die like your brother."

Nickels looked over at the crumpled form on the ground by the shed. "You killed Craig?"

"All you had to do was sell me some damn guns. I had the money. But you had to get greedy." Lewis shook Nickels like a rag doll. "Who else is here?"

"Nobody, man, just me and Craig. Take what you want and go."

Peter pointed toward the vehicles by the house. "Who drives that third truck?"

"I'm telling you, nobody." Nickels's voice cracked slightly. His eyes slid up and away. He was lying.

They were running out of time. If someone was in the house or shed, it was quite possible that they hadn't heard the suppressed AK fire. But the .357 was very loud. Like an announcement, or a starter's pistol. Nickels and his brother being what they were, Peter was certain they'd have weapons stashed within easy reach throughout the compound.

"We start in the shed," Peter said. He press-checked the slide on Nickels's pistol, the Beretta civilian version of the Army M9, and found a round in the chamber. He reversed it and held it out to Lewis. "You keep hold of Nickels. I'll take the rifle."

At the closed shed door, he bent to check the dead man's pulse. Nothing. Peter left him in the mud. First things first. His heart was racketing in his chest, adrenaline burning in his veins like gasoline.

He moved to the knob side with Lewis behind him, holding Nickels with the pistol at his back and a fist bunched in his coat collar. Softly, Lewis said, "You make a sound, you die first."

Peter cracked the door and took a quick peek. Heavy steel workbenches and big floor-mounted machines lined both walls. Some of it a century old, some looking brand-new. He didn't see any people, but he also couldn't see the whole space. He took a breath and flowed through the opening and into the long, dim room, rifle up and ready in his hands.

He'd done this countless times in the sandbox. Except he'd always had a stack of heavily armed Marines at his back. Still, Lewis was as good as any three-man fire team. Even with Nickels to deal with.

He eased forward, knees bent, weapon up, eye at the iron sights, sweeping the space as he advanced. Cement floor with rubber mats at the workstations. A milling machine, two drill presses, a shaper, a stamping press, all of them a hundred years old and greasy with cutting oil. A pair of newer computer-controlled lathes. Racks of raw metal. Three tall fireproof cabinets with flammable stickers on them. Toward the back, a half dozen pieces of advanced equipment he didn't recognize. Pistols on bench tops and long guns leaning everywhere he looked. But no people. In the far corner, a door stood open. The rest of the back was taken up by what looked like a gas forge, with a draft hood and a crucible. Whatever these guys were doing, they were serious about it.

"Clear," he said. "Going out the back and over to the house."

"Right behind you. Move, Nickels."

"Wait." Nickels was pale and wet and breathing hard. Behind them, they'd left a trail of muddy bootprints. "There's someone in the house."

"Who," Lewis said.

"Mama. You go in there, she'll fire on you. Especially if she knows Craig's dead. He always was her favorite. You'll have to kill her. I don't want that."

"Will she come out if you call her?"

"She's not stupid," Nickels said. "Are you gonna kill us?"

Lewis growled, "You and Craig started this shit, remember? All I want is what I came for in the first place. Three long guns and three pistols with extra mags. Looking around your shop, I see you got plenty to spare."

"Swear you won't kill us, Lewis. Give me your word."

Lewis sighed. "I won't kill you 'less you make me. You have my word."

Peter said, "Nickels, do you have your phone on you?"

"In my pocket."

Peter put the AK on him. "Nice and slow."

Carefully, Nickels found his phone, pulled it out, and cursed softly. "She already called twice. What should I say?"

"Tell her to stay in the house. Put it on speaker."

The phone only rang once. The answering voice was sharp and high. "Dickie, what's going on out there?"

"Nothing, Mama. Just trying out a new sidearm."

"Don't you lie to me, Dickie. I can see a damn body out there by the shop."

Nickels closed his eyes. "Stay in the house, Mama. I'm dealing with it."

"Your brother's not answering his phone. Let me talk to him."

"He's busy, Mama. Promise me you'll stay in the house. I'll be there soon."

Through the speaker, they heard a door close, then the rattle of raindrops on a metal roof. She'd gone out onto the porch. "Just tell me Craig Jr. isn't dead."

"Mama, please. Go inside and let me deal with this."

"Dickie, I'm your mama. You don't tell me what to do, it's the other way around. I already called your cousin Vance, he's on his way." They heard the squelch of mud, the soft patter of rain. She was off the porch and in the yard.

Nickels hit the mute button. "Let me go out there. I'll take her weapon and bring her in the back. I won't try anything. I swear it. I just don't want you to hurt her."

"Who's Vance?"

"Trust me, you don't want to meet him."

"How long until he gets here?"

"Thirty minutes, give or take."

Peter glanced at the clock on the wall. They needed to be gone in fifteen. He looked at Lewis, who nodded, then said, "If he shows up early, Nickels, it's on you."

Nickels nodded and unmuted the phone. "Mama, I'm on my way out the back. I'll meet you, okay?"

Peter walked him to the door, making sure he didn't pick up a gun along the way, then stood just inside the shed, peering around the corner. Under the floodlight's glare, he saw Nickels hustling toward a narrow figure in an ancient felt hat and an open raincoat over a flowered bathrobe with gum boots on her feet. She carried a sawed-off shotgun, gleaming black in the rain.

"Mama, wait." Nickels put a hand on the weapon, but she pulled away and kept walking. With that street-sweeper, she could clear a room without even aiming.

Peter didn't want Nickels to have it, either. He put the AK to his shoulder and stepped into the rain. "Drop the gun, ma'am."

She stopped in her tracks and glared at him, the shotgun half raised. "You wouldn't shoot a woman."

"If you lift that weapon another inch," Peter said, "I absolutely will."

Nickels put a hand on the gun again, now shielding her with his body. Peter could hear him talking but not what he said. Finally Nickels turned, holding the weapon by the barrel, then let it fall to the mud. "Come into the shed, Mama. It's okay. They won't hurt us."

As Peter backed away from the doorway to let them pass, she gave him a venomous stare. "My son is dead, isn't he?"

Peter didn't need to say anything. She already knew the answer.

32

Inside, the older woman dropped the wet hat and her phone on a metal worktable, folded her arms, and looked Peter and Lewis up and down with utter contempt. Her face was seamed as though from a carver's knife, the skin stretched taut and thin as parchment. "My nephew is on the way. You two better get the hell out while you can."

"Call him back," Peter said. "Tell him it's a false alarm."

"Only one person tells Vance what to do, and it's not me. If he says he's coming, he's coming. And he's bringing some friends."

Peter glanced at the clock on the wall. "How long until he gets here?"

"Any minute," she said.

"Dickie already told us half an hour," Lewis said.

His mama gave Nickels a withering look. Then she turned it on Peter. "What do you idiots want?"

"I'm sorry about your son," Peter said. "I told him to put the gun down but he didn't. It was him or me."

"You think that makes me feel any better?" Her voice was high and bright. Her piercing eyes reminded Peter of a raptor's. "Anyway, I don't need your damn condolences. Between war and cancer, this hard old world already took two husbands and two sons. Now it's taken Craig Jr. I've no more grief left. So I won't be giving you the satisfaction of my tears."

Lewis turned to Nickels. "Like I said, we need three good rifles and three pistols, clean and new. Two extra mags for each. And a couple boxes of ammo. Tell me what you've got and give me a price."

"You're really going to pay me?"

"A fair price. Even though you were gonna hold me up. Where's your inventory?"

"We're not selling guns." Nickel's mama raised her voice, brassy and sharp. "We need every last one of 'em. Because of people like you. Barbarians at the gates. Your time is coming, and sooner than you think."

Lewis gave a tired sigh. "Nickels, the clock is ticking. Where are the weapons?"

Nickels led them to the three fireproof cabinets. Each had a hardened padlock, but Nickels had the key in his pocket.

Lewis opened the first cabinet and gave a low whistle. "You boys been busy," he said. It held two tight rows of AK rifles, twenty in all, with a grab rack of Beretta pistols and two full shelves of neatly labeled plastic reloader's ammo boxes. Lewis opened the next cabinet. More of the same.

The third cabinet was different. It held a dozen Benelli combat shotguns and four M24 sniper rifles. One shelf was full of the same plastic ammo boxes labeled for the M24 and the shotguns. The other held boxes labeled 7.62x39 AP.

Lewis stood back to take it all in. "This isn't a gun collection, it's an armory. What the hell are you keeping all this for?"

"Just in case," Nickels said.

Peter's eye had caught on the ammo boxes. *AP* usually stood for armor piercing. Peter pointed. "Grab one of those."

Lewis pulled down an ammo box and popped the cover. He tipped it to show Peter. Inside were fifty rounds, long and deadly, with the telltale black tips used to differentiate an armor-piercing round. On the brass, someone had handwritten *AP* in black marker.

"Holy shit." Peter looked at Nickels. "Armor-piercing rounds are restricted to law enforcement. Where'd you get these?"

Nickels didn't answer, a small smile playing at the corner of his mouth.

Lewis's eyebrows went up. "You're *making* them? In this crappy little shop?" Armor-piercing rounds were made with super-hard tungsten carbide instead of lead or steel. It was a complex and highly technical metallurgical process.

Nickels shook his head, but the pride on his face was unmistakable.

Peter looked back at the shop equipment. The century-old milling machines were functional but cheap. The new machines, whatever the hell they were, would have been very expensive. He turned to Nickels. "Who's funding all this? Who are the rounds for?"

Nickels shrugged. "Business is good. We sold off some inventory and invested in new machines."

"Bullshit," Peter said. "You either have a customer or a partner. Who is he?"

Nickels started to speak, but his mom overrode him. "Dickie, you keep your big mouth shut. You two, this is none of your business. Take your guns and go. This world will catch up with you soon enough."

Peter's jaw was knotted up, his stomach sour with bile. Armor-piercing rounds of that caliber had only one purpose, to punch through body armor, killing soldiers or cops. When he blinked, he saw Ellie staring at her mother's dead body. He walked over to Nickels, put the .357 right in his face, and thumbed back the hammer. "Answer the question or join your brother. Who are you making the AP rounds for?"

Nickels raised his chin. "Go ahead and kill me. Kill my mama, too. That's nothing compared to what he'll do if he learns we talked."

The older woman had the same defiant look as her son. "Do your worst, barbarian. We won't betray him. And not because of what he'll do to us. But because we believe he's right." She glanced at the clock. "Vance is on his way. He'll be loaded for bear. You want to live, you better git."

Peter put the pistol barrel against Nickels's forehead. "Give me a name."

Lewis put his hand on Peter's gun arm. "Peter."

Peter felt the air go out of him. He stepped back and decocked the pistol. "Let's take what we need and get the hell out of here."

Lewis found a roll of baling wire and bound their wrists behind their backs, then sat them on the ground and bound their ankles. That done, Peter chose three AK rifles and three Beretta pistols from the third cabinet. He found a plastic storage crate and loaded it with spare magazines, sound suppressors, and ammunition. "How much?"

Nickels gave them a price and Lewis didn't even haggle, just took a wad of folded bills from his pocket and counted hundreds onto the counter.

Peter found another crate and began to fill it with boxes of armor-piercing rounds.

"I need those," Nickels said. "There'll be hell to pay if you take them."

"Tell me who's buying and I'll leave them." Although he wouldn't leave them. He couldn't live with himself.

Nickels flexed his jaw and shook his head. Peter loaded the rest of the AP boxes started carrying gear out to the Tahoe. By the clock, they'd only been inside the shed for fifteen minutes. Peter had no desire to meet Cousin Vance and his friends.

They left the dead man in the mud.

Back on the highway, Peter said, "I thought you said these guys weren't crazy."

Lewis shrugged. "People change."

"You think they rob all their customers?"

Lewis shook his head. "It don't make sense. There'd be retribution. The kind of people looking for untraceable full-auto assault weapons ain't the kind of people you want to piss off." Lewis looked out the window into the speeding darkness. "Unless that old lady just kills 'em. You suppose we went back in daylight we'd find some shallow graves?"

"Maybe they don't care about long-term consequences," Peter said. "They're just raising cash any way they can. And they're accumulating a serious arsenal, including armor-piercing ammo. Like they think the end of the world is coming any day now."

Lewis looked at him, eyebrows climbing high. "Motherfucker. You think?"

"All that stuff about barbarians at the gates? Your time is coming? Sound familiar?"

"You think these ding-dongs are connected to the Messenger. The Dark Time and all that."

"Maybe, maybe not. But you told me these guys sold to everybody, right? And they're scared of somebody. How many freaky assholes can there be around here planning something big?"

"We should've looked for cassette tapes." Lewis flashed him his tilted grin. "You want to go back and see Mama, search the house?"

Peter thought about all those guns in that machine shop. Then he thought about Cousin Vance and the kind of friends he probably had, how ugly it would get if he and Lewis went back up there. Somebody else would die for sure, and no guarantees on who it might be.

"No," Peter said. "I most definitely do not."

33

HOLLIS

Well after midnight, Hollis Longro sat in the electric SUV outside a Walgreens. With the leather driver's seat tipped way back, hat over his eyes, phone on his lap, he waited for the borrowed vehicle to charge.

Although it wasn't borrowed anymore, he thought. The owner was dead. The Rivian was Hollis's now.

He liked the electric SUV more than he cared to admit. It was a lot more comfortable than his old Toyota pickup. The acceleration was insane. Driving it felt like the future, or how he'd thought the future would be when he was a kid. But he'd been wrong about that. The future wasn't sleek or cool or easy. It was the world's largest axe, just waiting to fall.

He did miss the Toyota. He'd put a lot of miles on that truck in the last few years, riding the circuit, delivering the Messenger's news and recruiting members to their cause. It had served him well. But now it was gone. Like so many things.

Eight years ago, when it all started, the man wasn't calling himself the Messenger yet. He was plain old Gary, an unemployed electrical engineer standing on a wooden box on the sidewalk in front of the shuttered pulp mill, trying to warn people about what was coming.

He didn't call it the Dark Time then, either. Or the Time of Undoing. He came up with those later.

But the ideas were there from the beginning. The ravenous Industrial Machine, eating humanity to fuel its own growth. How things had changed from the world they had grown up in. How the future would keep changing for the worse unless they did something about it.

The Messenger had been right back then, and he was even more right now. The last eight years had only proved his point.

That day outside the mill, Hollis was walking past the man on the box, fighting the hunger in his belly and the anger in his heart, when something made him stop and listen. He'd thought the man was a preacher, the way he talked. Hollis kept waiting for the mention of Jesus, or the Bible, but it never came.

Which was fine with Hollis. He'd given up on the Lord, but not before the Lord had given up on him. He'd tried the Army to get some job training but he didn't learn anything that would get him work in the real world. He knew he needed college but he couldn't make himself sit in class or at a computer all day. So he'd worked at a succession of factories and mills that had closed, one after the other, until there was no place left for a middle-aged guy like Hollis. His wife left before the unemployment ran out. He had to sell the car. He never could afford to own a house, so he had nothing left to lose. Except hope. By the time he met the Messenger, he'd definitely lost that.

But there was something about the man and the story he told. The changing world they lived in, how it was no longer made for regular people, working people.

Hollis found that he was hungry to learn the reasons for the slow-motion disaster he was living through. The economic forces arrayed against him. The Industrial Machine, always growing. The people who owned the Machine, profiting from the relentless future that never stopped coming at you. While regular people slowly lost everything they had spent their entire lives working for.

He was even hungrier to learn what he could do about it.

First, prepare.

Then, act.

When the man on the box finished speaking and stepped down, Hollis had introduced himself and asked how he could learn more.

Instead of answering, Gary had looked him in the eye, introduced himself, put his strong hand on Hollis's slumped shoulder, and asked about Hollis's own life.

It was a small thing. Almost nothing, really. But it had been such a long time since anyone had treated Hollis Longro like a human being. It overwhelmed him, the sense of gratitude. As the words tumbled out, he'd wept and Gary had wept with him.

Hollis returned to the shuttered mill the next day and listened again. And again the next day, and the next. Every day for a week. Until Gary told him he was going to Wenatchee to spread the word there. Would Hollis like to come with him and meet the others?

It turned out that Gary wasn't alone. There was a Movement. Tiny, but growing.

Hollis had asked what he had to do.

Not a thing, Gary said. Just be yourself. We'll figure out a use for you.

And so they had.

Gary didn't always talk on street corners. Sometimes, he went to people's houses, where he would stand in the living room and talk to whoever showed up. Sometimes two or three people, sometimes a half dozen. And so the Movement grew.

Gary had a plan from the beginning. Build the community. Buy some property in a remote area, as much as they could afford. Get self-sufficient. Prepare for the worst.

The second part of the plan came later.

Even in the early days, Gary had asked for donations. People were happy to give what they could. It was the Message, of course. But the sound of his voice was a big part of the appeal, that country preacher sound reminding people of a gone-away time, when communities were whole and people really knew one another. There was something about his eyes, too. His presence. When he looked at you, you mattered. Almost as if, when you stood in his sight, you became fully real.

In the beginning, the donations were small. These people didn't have much. But it was enough to put gas in the car and food in their bellies. When they weren't sleeping in somebody's guest room, they stayed at the cheapest hotel they could find. All that time together on the road, Gary always talking, always looking at Hollis like he was a true and cherished friend, like he was somehow more important than Hollis could ever know.

Over time, the Message spread and the Movement grew. As the years passed, and the Machine began to grind up more and more people, the Messenger began to refine the Message. The pandemic came, and it was easier to imagine a Dark Time coming, a Time of Undoing. Wildfires and back-to-back hurricanes only added to the sense of the world gone wrong. Then artificial intelligence went mainstream, and people could feel the Machine getting bigger, stronger. It was only a matter of time before it grabbed up anyone and everyone, grinding them into meat pulp.

Even the tech people, who should have felt like the winners in this winner-take-all contest, saw the writing on the wall and began to pay attention. With that small but affluent audience, donations grew. By then Hollis had found his role. The Messenger was the voice and the vision. Hollis was the man who made the plan work. The cassette tapes were his idea. So was the subscription model with various levels of membership, depending on the size of your donation. The tech boys loved it. Survival as service, they called it.

Three years ago, with money to spend, Hollis and the Messenger started looking for land. They finally found an old summer camp, a legacy parcel tucked in the middle of twenty thousand acres of national forest.

A place to make their stand when the shit hit the fan.

That's when the Messenger began to develop the second part of his plan. Hollis helped.

Closing his eyes, he walked himself through it, step by step, reviewing it for flaws. He and a select few of the Hardcore Originals would do their part, then make their way overland to the camp in the first hours of the Dark Time. As he sat imagining it, how they would stand fast and hold together while the Industrial Machine fell apart, his phone vibrated in his lap. A message.

He opened the app. From BigGuns.

"Running late. There's been a setback."

"What kind of setback?"

"A robbery. Killed my brother. Took the Specials."

Hollis swore loudly. "Sorry about your brother," he typed. "How many Specials?"

"Everything we'd kept back. The rest was already gone. But they were asking questions."

"What did you tell them?"

"Not a damn thing, even with a gun to my head. But they know something."

They couldn't know about the Messenger, Hollis thought. Nobody outside the Movement knew about him. He almost never left the camp anymore. That's what the tapes were for. To protect him, to keep the secret.

Except that dead reporter knew about him, didn't she? She had the tape. And now the tall man had it, Hollis was sure of that.

He wrote, "What did they look like?"

"Two men, one white and one Black. Good with guns. Driving a big American SUV."

Hollis ground his teeth. He'd had seen the same two men a few hours ago, driving away from the roofer's house with a woman. "We'll deal with them soon. Where are you?"

"On the road. I had to bury my brother. Cousin Vance is with me."

Hollis sent a thumbs-up, dropped the phone in his lap, then picked it up again. This was part of the Industrial Machine, making these devices addictive on purpose, stealing your mind and monetizing your attention. But they were also useful. Wondering about the others, he went to Google Maps and found Location Sharing.

He saw the Messenger's blue dot at the camp headquarters, exactly where he should be. BigGuns and Vance were on the highway near Kent. Reed's locator had gone dark when the police took his phone.

But Scott Enderby's was lit up.

He opened Telegram and went to his chat with Enderby. The app showed that his phone was logged on. Hollis didn't understand.

He wasn't naïve enough to think the mayor's announcement about the end of the investigation meant the police wouldn't follow up as many loose ends as they could. But why the hell was Enderby's phone in Ballard, and how had they figured out Telegram? He could imagine a signal going out when the police tried to get into the phone, but the forensics lab was downtown. And why would they be looking at it in the middle of the night?

He deleted Telegram, then went back to Maps and zoomed in on the Ballard location, getting the street address, then pulled up the King County Assessor's website and ran a search. The property was owned by someone named Estelle Martinez.

He knew from a previous search that the roofer had the same last name. It was common enough. But this was no coincidence.

The tall man had the phone.

And now Hollis thought he might know where the man was staying.

Hollis had done some killing in the early years, to protect the Messenger and move the plan forward. As the Movement grew, he'd let the Hardcore Originals take over the bloody work. But when the Dark Time came, he'd have to pick up a gun again. So why not now?

He'd need Nickels and Vance to take on the tall man directly, especially if the man had brought in a friend. It was almost two A.M. His reinforcements would arrive before too long. With everyone in the house asleep, it would be a lot easier.

He plotted a course to the address.

Twelve minutes out.

He got out of the car and unplugged the charger. He was at ninety percent.

More than enough.

34

JUNE

Still waiting for Peter and Lewis to return, June got back online to finish digging up contact information for KT's three interview subjects. Place of employment, home address, phone numbers, automobiles, it was all easy enough to find using her subscription databases. Then she mapped out a plan of attack for the morning, trying to calm her nerves.

Ever since KT had been killed, she'd been on edge. Yes, her friend had died, but it was more than that. Someone had assassinated a journalist for reporting the wrong story. That was the kind of thing they did in Russia, or China, or the cartel-controlled parts of Mexico. Not in America. Not until now.

June glanced again at the clock on the wall. It was two in the morning. Where the hell were Peter and Lewis? She wasn't the kind of girlfriend that wanted to know where her boyfriend was at all times, but an illegal gun buy qualified as special circumstances. Too much could go wrong.

Knowing he'd have his burner silenced if he was in the middle of something, she sent a text. "Where r u?"

The reply came immediately. "Almost back. All good."

She went to the living room and pulled aside one of the

curtains to peer out at the street. No headlights yet. The rain was coming down in buckets.

She opened the front door and walked onto the small porch, her breath steaming in the cool night air. She'd always liked the sound of a heavy rain. It rattled on the porch roof and pummeled the rhododendrons in the yard. Fat droplets splashed off the wet pavement like a river learning to levitate.

Then her eye caught a faint movement across the street, where a good-sized madrone tree grew. The unpruned branches hung low, the glossy green leaves blocking out the streetlights, leaving a deep shadow below. Beside the trunk with the distinctive peeling bark, she saw a faint pale flash. She focused harder. It was a face, now fading from view as its owner eased himself deeper into the darkness.

She felt abruptly cold. What kind of freakazoid would stand out in the rain at two o'clock in the fucking morning?

Oh, she thought. That kind of freakazoid. The kind that might arrange for the death of a journalist and her daughter. Somehow Circuit Rider, or someone connected to him, had found Stella's house.

Trying to look casual, she glanced left and right, hoping for Peter's headlights and seeing none. The street was empty of parked cars. If the freakazoid had a ride nearby, she didn't see it. She backed inside, closed and locked the door, then worked her way to the kitchen, turning off lights as she went. Hoping he'd think she was going to bed.

Peter had told her about Stella's pistol. She went into the darkened office, pulled it from the drawer, and checked the magazine. The SIG was bigger than the .22 target pistols she practiced with at the range, but it fit her hand well enough.

She had waterproof trail shoes on her feet. Her gray raincoat was hanging on a hook. She put it on, unlocked the back door, and stepped out into the darkness.

If she'd learned anything from Peter, it was that the best defense was a good offense.

Fuck you, freakazoid.

KT was her friend.

The madrone tree was across from the driveway apron, so June walked the other direction, around the rear of the house toward the privacy fence blocking the back yard from the neighbor's driveway. She'd been a rock climber since she was a teenager, so the six-foot fence was no obstacle, even one-handed. She held the SIG ready in the other.

Staying close to the house, she crept toward the street, sheltered from the rain by the roof overhang. If he hadn't moved, she'd be hidden from his position until she cleared the big evergreen rhododendron bushes by the porch, when she'd be fifty or sixty feet away from him.

At fifty feet, she could put nine rounds into the center circle of a target.

She wouldn't shoot first. She wasn't an assassin. Besides, it might just be a local perv or an insomniac walking his dog. If that was the case, she'd tell him to put his hands up and step out where she could see him, and wait for Peter and Lewis.

But if he pointed a gun at her, she'd put a bullet in him.

She scanned ahead and to her left, knowing he might have relocated, but she didn't see him. There were other plantings to shelter him on either side of the madrone. Or he could have crossed the street and was now tucked behind the rhododendrons, waiting for her.

She felt her heart beat, the blood pulsing through her veins. She'd always been an adrenaline junkie, but she never would have done something like this before meeting Peter. She'd have hidden under a desk and hoped the freakazoid would go away. But her adventures with Peter had sparked something in her. Not fearlessness or aggression, but a powerful desire to take ownership of her life and safety in a whole new way.

She approached the corner of the house. He wasn't behind the bushes.

A wash of light came up the street, followed by the sound of tires on wet pavement and a big engine softened by the rain. Peter's Tahoe. Shit. She stepped out past the big bush with her weapon at the ready, still looking for the freakazoid, hoping Peter and Lewis would recognize her when the headlights caught her.

The Tahoe turned to enter the driveway, then braked abruptly. Peter popped out of the driver's seat, a pistol in his hand. "What's the problem?"

She gestured with the SIG. "A man behind that tree. Watching the house."

Peter pivoted immediately toward the madrone and began to approach it, gun up and ready. She did the same. She heard the passenger door close and knew Lewis was with them, too.

Behind the tree, the darkness shifted. There was a faint liquid shimmer as the fractured rays of the streetlight caught something, the retreating wet surface of a hooded jacket.

"Don't move," Peter shouted.

The shimmer broke and ran for the space between the neighbors' houses.

Peter went after him, shouting, "Lewis, take the car and meet me."

Lewis sprinted around the rear of the SUV to the driver's door. "June, come on."

He pulled the back door open as he passed. She dove inside as he threw the big SUV into drive, stomped on the gas, and bounced over the parking strip to the street, the motion slamming the door shut behind her. She crawled forward to the front passenger seat as they flew into the darkness, the wipers slapping fast but the rain still too heavy for decent visibility. Then he doused the headlights, making the night even darker.

He braked hard, turned left, goosed it, then turned left again, rounding the block. Past the next intersection was a set of streamlined taillights, receding. Lewis ghosted forward at speed, flicking on his headlights. Peter stood panting at the curb, hands on his knees.

Lewis slowed just long enough for him to pop the back door and slide inside. Then Lewis put his foot down again and began to pick up speed.

The taillights were a block ahead, then a block and a half. Despite his acceleration, Lewis was losing ground. The speedometer was at sixty, then seventy, the big SUV bucking wildly as the road camber changed at the intersections. With cars parked on both sides, it was essentially a one-lane road.

Peter reached into the cargo bay, came back with a pair of antique-looking assault rifles, and handed one over the seat to her. She said, "What the hell am I supposed to do with this?" She was good with a pistol, but was not a fan of heavy hardware.

"Hopefully nothing." Peter leaned forward and his fingers found the controls for the sunroof. As the glass peeled back, he stood up in the back seat with his upper body out of the car, the rifle raised. His voice filtered down from the night. "Where'd he go?"

"Turned left," Lewis said. "Hold on."

June grabbed Peter's leg as Lewis braked hard, shedding enough speed to make the turn without fishtailing or plowing into a parked car. Between Peter's body and their speed, not much rain fell through the open sunroof. She saw the taillights two blocks ahead, angling left onto Twenty-Fourth NW without slowing.

Lewis jammed the accelerator to the floor and the Tahoe leapt to follow. Twenty-Fourth NW was two lanes with a third in the center, and he made the turn without braking, the heavy SUV sliding on the wet pavement. The only other moving vehicle was the same set of taillights, now at least six blocks ahead, appearing and disappearing as the wipers slapped across the windshield, struggling to clear the rain.

The speedometer was at eighty, then ninety. The other driver was still adding distance. Peter called down, "Lewis, punch it."

"I am," Lewis called back. "This thing is a boat. That car up there is a rocket."

Eight blocks ahead, or ten, the brake lights flashed bright for a moment, then the taillights vanished around a corner. A stoplight was coming up fast. Lewis braked hard to follow, Peter still banging around in the open sunroof. June unbuckled her belt and knelt on the seat with one arm around his waist to help stabilize him. If they wrecked at this speed, they'd both be dead.

Lewis cranked the wheel and the Tahoe slewed sideways, Lewis correcting for the skid. They were on Eighty-Fifth now, a two-lane flanked by single-family houses and older apartments and parked cars.

Lewis hit the gas and the engine roared. They were at the crest of a gentle hill. Ahead, June saw only empty road. "Lewis," she said.

Lewis growled and bared his teeth at the windshield, then took his foot off the accelerator and the big SUV began to slow.

Peter dropped down and reached forward to close the sunroof. His face and coat were wet but his pants were mostly dry.

"Whatever that car was, we never had a chance of catching it."

"No," Lewis said. At the next intersection he made a U-turn, then began to head back the way they'd come. "How'd he find the house?"

June thought of the burner phone in her pocket and cursed. Now she knew why Google Maps was the only app loaded. She hadn't thought to check it. Now she opened it to Location Sharing and saw that the app was sharing location data with another number. But that number wasn't reciprocating. She cursed again, turned off sharing, deleted the app, then threw the phone down, disgusted with herself.

"It's my fault." She should have known better.

They drove in silence toward Stella's little bungalow. The rain unrelenting. All of them knowing the house was no longer safe.

June really didn't want to sleep in the Tahoe. "I'll start looking for hotels."

"No need," Lewis said. "I already got a spot."

June elbowed him. "What, you're too good for us?"

He flashed her that tilted grin. "Habit from the bad old days. Always have a backup. Your place gets blown, you got another hole to hide in."

"I don't like to think of it as hiding," June said.

Lewis snorted. "I bet you don't."

Peter leaned forward into the gap between the front seats. "That's twice that guy has run from me."

Lewis nodded. "First time, at KT's place, he wasn't there for you and Ellie. He was looking for that tape. You startled him, he ran. I get that. Second time, he'd locked in on the burner. The only people who could have it were the cops and you, and the cops wouldn't have taken it to that little house in Ballard. So he was targeting you specifically. But why not go inside?"

"I think he was scouting us," Peter said. "Even testing us, seeing how we'd react. Getting a sense of our strength."

"Maybe waiting for reinforcements," Lewis asked. "Man seems to like using other folks to do his dirty work."

Peter nodded. "My guess is, the next time we see him, he won't be holding back."

35

PETER

Lewis approached Stella's place using an inward spiral pattern, Peter and June looking hard for any car with familiar taillights in case the guy had circled back to wait for them. They saw none. Still, they entered the house carefully, guns out, clearing it room by room. It was empty.

They grabbed their stuff and got out fast, leaving Stella's pistol in the desk drawer and putting the key back where they'd found it. Peter would text Manny in the morning, so he could alert Stella with Peter's apologies. They'd pay for her hotel room until this was over. He didn't tell June about killing Nickels's brother. It could wait until the morning.

Lewis's backup hotel was the Columbus Motor Inn on Ninety-Fifth and Aurora. It was a lot like the Marco Polo, fifty blocks to the south, where KT was killed, but with the added benefit that some of the parking was out of sight of the main road. Lewis went into the office while Peter and June waited in the car. It was after three in the morning. KT had been dead for less than thirty-six hours. It felt like an eternity.

The room was utilitarian but clean. Before the static could flare too badly, Peter got into the shower and June climbed in with him, her fingers tracing the bruise where the armor had stopped

Reed's bullet. As the hot water warmed them, she wrapped her legs around his hips and they moved together, finding comfort in each other's bodies. In the night, he woke as she sobbed softly for her lost friend. He took her in his arms and they fell asleep like that, her head on his bare chest, his strong arm around her naked waist, each of them a place of solace and protection for the other.

By noon the next day, they'd collected Lewis, thrown their bags in the car, and driven to Pete's Eggnest on Greenwood for breakfast. They sat at a window table in the corner out of earshot of the other diners.

June said, "You never told me how it went with the gun guys last night."

"It went sideways," Peter said. "They were planning to rob us."

Lewis snorted. "Motherfuckers would've killed us. Lucky it went the other way."

June gave Peter that look that went clear through him. Like she could see the architecture of his soul. "You had to kill someone."

Peter nodded. He needed to talk about it, but this wasn't the time or the place.

June understood. "Why did they want to kill you?"

Lewis shook his head. "They wouldn't cop to anything. Whoever they're in with, they're too scared to talk. But they're into something, that's for sure. Jarhead thinks they might be connected to the Messenger. Either way, they had enough guns to outfit a small nation."

"That's not good." June cupped her coffee mug in both hands, warming them.

"It gets worse," Peter said. "They were making armor-piercing bullets. A lot of them."

Lewis sighed. "These guys used to be small-time, selling ghost guns to the local wingnuts. But black-tips are a whole different deal. The equipment to make that shit is spendy as hell. Whoever they're dealing with, they've got money."

"You didn't get any names?"

"The guy's mom called the cavalry," Peter said. "We had to get out of there."

June looked at both of them. "Those armor-piercing rounds are cop killers," she said. "You think they're planning some kind of attack?"

"That tech conference starts the day after tomorrow," Peter said. "The Seattle PD will have a major presence. Everybody will be wearing body armor. AP rounds would do a lot of damage."

June closed her eyes. "What would they be trying to accomplish? Aside from murdering a lot of people."

Peter thought about what the Messenger had said on that cassette tape. "They want to destroy what he called the Industrial Machine, right? Maybe they think killing a bunch of tech moguls would do that."

"That's nuts," Lewis said. "We got too many companies working on too many projects. Even if they manage to kill five hundred people, they won't make a dent in the tech talent we got in this country."

"Didn't you hear that recording?" June asked. "I'm pretty sure they *are* nuts. So who knows what the fuck they're up to?"

That stopped the conversation cold.

After the waiter came to refill their coffees, promising their food would come soon, June caught them up on her progress from the night before. She started with the old maps Peter had taken from Reed's apartment, their weird multicolored hieroglyphic markings. She gestured at the cluttered breakfast table. "When we get someplace we can spread out, maybe you guys can make sense of them, because I sure as hell couldn't."

Then she took out the Toyota burner and showed them the Telegram messages. "He calls himself Circuit Rider," she said. "I think the Toyota is actually his, not Scott Enderby's, which is why I found that weird registration history. The owner of record appears to be dead. Which means Circuit Rider's been hiding his ownership for years. This thing has been brewing for a long time. And now he's driving Enderby's car, a Rivian electric SUV. Which is why he got away from us so fast last night. Those new electrics accelerate a lot faster than a regular car."

"We should tell Durant," Peter said. "Maybe he'll put it on the radio and the cops will start looking."

"About that." June gave him a look. "If we tell Durant what we know and how we know it, you're in even more trouble."

"Don't have to be that way," Lewis said. "We say the guy came after us and we ran him off, got his plate that way. Turns out to be the dead guy's."

"What about the Telegram messages," June asked.

Lewis shrugged. "Dumb motherfucker dropped the phone when he was running away. You picked it up and saw his messages. Now you doin' your duty as a citizen, keeping Durant in the loop."

"You're disturbingly good at this," Peter said.

Lewis smiled that tilted smile. "Life of crime, you pick up some skills."

June pointed her fork at them. "You guys are missing the point. We have the address on the Toyota's registration. We can go there and look around, see what we can find. Maybe track down the owner or leasing agent, see if they remember something."

"If Circuit Rider even had a real connection to that address at all," Peter said. "Maybe he just used it as a drop, stopping in to ask the receptionist if any mail had come for him. Anyway, Durant said it's vacant, remember?"

"Don't be Mister El Negativo," June said. "Maybe Circuit Rider's got a key. Maybe it's their secret clubhouse or something. We won't know until we go down there."

Lewis held out his coffee mug. "You still the brains of the outfit."

"Damn right." She clinked his cup. "And there's more." She held out the phone so they could see the open app. "We can message this Circuit Rider asshole on Telegram."

Peter looked at her. "If he hasn't pitched his phone already. Anyway, what would we say?"

"Aside from cursing him out?" She frowned. "I don't know yet. I'm working on it."

Peter's breakfast burrito arrived, along with Lewis's Greek scramble and June's strata.

They dug in. "Why don't we divide and conquer," Peter said, his fingers greasy with chorizo. "I'll call Durant and go down to Tacoma, check out that address. You and Lewis track down those people KT interviewed, see what they know."

"That was my thinking." June looked at Lewis. "We'll need another ride."

Lewis gave her a tilted smile. "Already got one. Made a call last night. Should be parked down the block."

Peter shook his head in mock disgust. "See, now you're just showing off."

36

Peter dropped June and Lewis at the other car, a used white Lexus SUV that looked like a tank, then headed south in the Tahoe toward Tacoma to find the address where Enderby's Toyota was registered. They'd lingered over breakfast, and the mid-afternoon traffic was unusually heavy.

Although he'd just seen Ellie at dinner the night before, he'd promised to call her every day, so while traffic crept along, he pulled out his burner and called the phone he'd given Manny. If Peter ended up getting charged with kidnapping a minor or whatever else Durant could come up with, there was no reason to implicate his friend by calling his personal cell.

Manny answered on the second ring and quickly put Ellie on the line. "Why does he call you Ashes?"

"Long story," he said. "How'd you sleep?"

"Okay, I guess? I dreamed about my mom."

"A good dream or a bad one?"

"It wasn't about, you know, the motel, if that's what you mean. We were sitting at our kitchen table, eating pizza. A normal night." She sniffled. "Just thinking about her makes me want to cry."

"It's okay to cry," Peter said gently. "Part of the process."

"I still can't quite believe she's really gone. It's like the world changed completely in two minutes. And then I'll start playing with the twins and forget for like an hour. How can I forget my mom is dead? What's wrong with me?"

"There's nothing wrong with you," Peter said. "Losing someone you care about, it's messy. It hurts, then it doesn't. Then it hurts again."

"When will it *stop* hurting," she asked. "I want it to stop."

He wasn't going to tell her that it never stopped hurting. Now wasn't the time for that. Instead he thought about his post-traumatic stress, and the people he'd lost, and what he'd learned that helped.

"Don't resist the pain," he said. "Feel your feelings. Lean into it. Cry when you need to cry. That's how you honor her memory. That's how you begin to move forward. To heal."

She sniffled again. "Well, that sucks."

"Yes," he said. "It does. But if you fight it, things get worse."

They were quiet a moment. Traffic crept past downtown. "I guess Carlotta's taking me to see a therapist today?"

"That's great," Peter said, thinking about the Oregon shrink who had set him on the path of working through his PTSD. Had saved his life, really. With how he was feeling about KT's death, Peter knew he should call the man.

"I'm nervous," Ellie said. "What's it like? Have you ever been?"

"Many times," he said. "It's just a conversation. With a very kind person who understands what you're going through. You'll be great. And if you don't like the therapist, Carlotta will find you a different one."

"Can't I just talk to you?" Her voice was small.

"You can always talk to me, kiddo. But you should also talk to someone who's trained to help people with stuff like this. Someone who actually understands teenage girls."

"I mean, you're not *so* bad." She sniffled again. "Can you come to dinner tonight?"

"I'll do my very best. Call you later, okay?"

Then he hung up and called Captain Durant.

Because there was nothing more fun than getting yelled at by an angry policeman.

Peter's call went straight to Durant's voicemail. He left a message, saying he had updates.

As with calling Detective Kitzinger, it was a risk using his burner to call the captain. Although the police would need a court order to track his location, and Peter was betting that Durant had more pressing things to do.

Next he tried Kitzinger again, reasoning that she already knew his number, but this time she must have rejected the call because her phone didn't even go to voicemail.

He was taking the exit toward the Tacoma Dome when Durant called back. "This better be good, Mr. Ash. The Conference for the Future starts in under twenty-four hours and my plate is very full."

"I'm just checking to see if you've heard anything about Ellie's father."

"Nothing yet. Although something tells me that's not your only question."

"It's not." Peter told him about the man watching Stella's house. "I lost him, but I managed to get the plate. June looked it up. The car belongs to Scott Enderby, the motel killer."

"Mr. Ash, we've had this conversation. You need to stand down."

"The guy left a phone behind," Peter said, not specifying which guy. He didn't want to give Durant any added motivation to chase him down. "It had an app on it with encrypted messages.

The messages make it clear that there's at least one more person involved in KT's killing. And that Toyota pickup you thought belonged to Enderby? The messages make clear that it belongs to this new guy. He calls himself Circuit Rider."

Durant gave an audible sigh. "Mr. Ash, why are you telling me this? Perhaps you don't remember, but this investigation is officially closed."

"That's not all of it," Peter said. "I went into the foothills east of Maple Valley and talked to a pair of gun guys who are supposed to be plugged into the wingnut community. They wouldn't admit to any connection to the Messenger, but they had a serious arsenal of illegal Kalashnikovs."

"Well, that's concerning," Durant said. "It's also out of my jurisdiction. Give me the names and address and I'll call the local sheriff personally, get somebody up there ASAP."

"There's more. These backwoods armorers had the equipment to make black-tip rounds. Armor-piercing. Restricted to law enforcement and military only."

"I know what black-tip rounds are, Mr. Ash. Did you just see the equipment, or did you actually see the ammunition?"

"Oh, I saw it," Peter said. "A thousand rounds. It's in the back of my rig right now. But I think they made a lot more than that."

Durant swore loudly. "And these gun dealers just let you take it? Or did you have to shoot somebody?"

Peter didn't answer. If he'd judged Nickels and his mom right, he was pretty sure they didn't want the police sniffing around. They'd probably already buried the body where it would never be found.

Durant heard what Peter hadn't said. "And you didn't call the police? No, you fled the scene." The captain swore again, even more loudly. "Mr. Ash, you have broken so many laws, I wouldn't even know where to start charging you."

"You need to reopen the case," Peter said. "I think KT's murder is connected to the tech conference. Whoever these people are, I think they're going to hit it. I think KT was looking into it, and that's why they killed her."

Durant was obviously struggling to get himself back under control. "Nobody is hitting the tech conference, Mr. Ash. The Seattle PD and the FBI are all over it. The vice president is coming, so the Secret Service is involved, and NSA is monitoring electronic chatter. We're talking to every informant we have. There is no threat. You are imagining a conspiracy where none exists."

The captain sighed, his tone softening. "You should really be worrying about yourself, Mr. Ash. You were already in serious trouble because of the Eleanor Thorsen situation. Now you're doing God knows what else. So I'm going to say this one time and one time only. Even if you don't care what happens to you, Eleanor Thorsen should be in a safe place. Because if something happens to that girl, it'll be on your head. And I'm the one who'll bring the axe down, trust me on that."

"Durant—"

"No, no. You listen to me. Do yourself a favor and turn yourself in, along with poor Eleanor. You pick the place. I'll meet you wherever you like. I really do think you're trying to help. If we can meet soon, in the next few hours, I might even be able to get the charges dropped."

"I'll think about it," Peter said.

"You're in a deep hole, Mr. Ash. You know what they say about finding yourself in a hole, don't you? Stop digging."

"I hope you're right about the conference," Peter said. "Because if you're wrong, those armor-piercing rounds are going to kill a lot of good police."

Then he hung up.

37

JUNE

June sat in the passenger seat of the used Lexus, laptop open and mobile hot spot on the dashboard, reviewing her notes about the men she'd begun to think of as the KT Three.

Although everyone else KT asked about Gun Club apparently had no clue what she was talking about, these three were the only ones who'd actually denied being involved. June hoped that, if she could talk to them in person, at least one of them would tell her something useful.

Lewis turned south toward Montlake, a favorite neighborhood for tech workers because of the easy access to the Evergreen Point Floating Bridge across Lake Washington to Redmond, where Microsoft's huge campus sprawled. The UW Medical Center was on their right and Husky Stadium loomed up on their left. "Who's this first dude we trying to find?"

"Troy Boxall," June said. "Started a Twitter clone called Chatrbx out of college, had maybe one or two original ideas, ran it for five years, and sold to Meta. His take was about thirty million. In tech, that's chicken feed."

She'd emailed Boxall three times, requesting an interview. He'd finally responded with a two-word all-caps reply, "FUCK OFF." Very on-brand for a tech bro, she thought. KT's notes had his cell, so June had also tried texting him, but he'd either blocked her or was ignoring her. His social media was full of pictures of his fitness regimen and his Tesla Cybertruck. Unsurprisingly, there appeared to be no wife or girlfriend. Digging into her databases, she'd found his house in Montlake but no other real estate. He didn't seem to travel much, so she hoped to find him at home.

"Chatrbx," Lewis said. "Where Scott Enderby was a senior VP."

June nodded. "And, according to Durant, where Reed worked as a contract employee. Although normally a contractor wouldn't socialize with the C-suite, the company was small, so they probably all knew each other."

"Why was KT talking to him to begin with?"

"She was writing a piece about all the startups bought by the Big Five and cannibalized for parts. Half the time, they just used a few pieces of technology and scrapped the rest."

"Creative destruction," Lewis said.

June had heard this expression many times from startup founders and venture capitalists, talking about technology-driven change. Few seemed to realize that the concept originated with Karl Marx, who'd thought it would eventually lead to the end of capitalism.

"Or buying up and shelving potential competitors on the cheap, depending on your point of view. Anyway, Troy Boxall didn't seem to give a shit one way or another." June flipped through her notes. "He told KT, 'I got paid, what do I care?'"

"Five years of his life and he didn't give a damn what happened to it?"

"Guys like Troy are always in it for the money. Thirty years ago, he'd have gone to Wall Street. Now all the big money is in tech. And the road to getting rich is a lot shorter."

Lewis crossed the Montlake Cut and turned right onto Hamlin, a lush, tree-lined street with large and meticulously maintained older homes. Three blocks down, across from the Seattle Yacht Club, he pulled to the curb. "How you want to do this?"

"Well, I already know he doesn't want to talk to me. But I also know he's home, because he just posted a selfie with his protein smoothie. So we'll knock on the door and start a conversation."

"What if he don't want to talk?"

She patted Lewis's muscular arm. "That's why I brought you."

They walked past the high screen of trees and up the drive, where a large black Bronco stood beside a blocky gray Cybertruck, charging in the rain. The house was a big ugly box with a dark brick exterior and strange metal shutters beside the windows.

"You see those?" Lewis pointed at the shutters. "They're steel, for security. Mounted on hinges so you can close them over the windows and lock them from the inside. In case a mob shows up with pitchforks, I guess."

June looked closer. "What are those rectangular openings in the metal?"

"Gun slits." Lewis shook his head. "Motherfucker's paranoid as hell."

He had a camera doorbell, too, which would capture them on video. June rang it a half dozen times, hearing the elaborate chime through the sidelights. Lewis said, "You looking to piss him off from the jump?"

"I just want him annoyed enough to come to the door." She rang again and kept ringing.

After several minutes, the door opened with a jerk. "What the fuck?"

Troy Boxall wore tight workout clothes that showed a vastly overdeveloped musculature. His arms were so bulked up he probably couldn't straighten them. At twenty-nine, he already had a receding hairline.

He also carried a pistol-grip shotgun hanging from one hand. "Get the fuck off my property before I call the police."

Lewis gave June a quick questioning glance. She shook her head slightly, not wanting to provoke the man. She was pretty sure the shotgun was just for show, anyway.

So she flashed him the smile that had worked on tech bros before. "Hi, Troy. June Cassidy, with Public Investigations. I've been trying to reach you. We need to talk."

"Huh." He tipped his head to the side. "I thought you'd be uglier."

She resisted the urge to kick him in the balls. He couldn't answer her questions if he was curled up on the floor protecting his damaged manhood. She'd also heard far worse bullshit in her years interviewing tech bros, and you couldn't kick them *all* in the balls—could you?

She kept her smile pleasant. "May we come in? I'd like to ask you a few questions."

Boxall shook his head. "You are persistent, I'll give you that. Almost as persistent as that other girl reporter, but apparently she's no longer with us." He smirked. Was he baiting her? Did he know something about KT's death? Now she wanted to punch him in the face. He probably got that a lot.

But he didn't close the door. It was the shotgun, she thought. It made him feel in control, overconfident. It was an opportunity.

"We are Legion," she said, watching his face closely. He didn't react. "Tell us about the Gun Club," she said. "Tell us about the Messenger."

Now he smiled merrily. "I'm not telling you shit. 'Cause obviously you don't know shit."

But he didn't deny his involvement, June noticed. Boxall

glanced disdainfully at Lewis, who stood silently beside her with the contained and implacable stillness he had. She'd had learned in the last few years that his stillness was more than lack of movement. It was a focused readiness for whatever might come. Boxall clearly had no idea what Lewis was capable of. Few people did.

"I know a few things," she said. "I know about Circuit Rider. I know he ordered Scott Enderby to kill Katelyn Thorsen. I have the Telegram texts to prove it."

"That's enough." Boxall raised the shotgun to his hip and put his free hand on the slide. "Time for you to go."

June didn't think he'd pull the trigger. She wanted to rattle him.

"You used to work with Enderby at Chatrbx, didn't you? I wonder if the cops can connect you to that murder." She made a guess. "I'll bet you a thousand dollars you're on a Telegram chat with him."

She must have guessed right, because Boxall began to rack the shotgun's slide to bring a shell from the magazine into firing position. Before he could complete the action, Lewis was in motion, flying forward and twisting the weapon effortlessly away.

Then he stepped back with the shotgun hanging down as if it had been his all along. "Never did like a pistol grip," he said. "Kick like a mule, hard to control. Do a lotta damage up close, though. But you got to keep a shell in the chamber."

Boxall put his hands out to his sides. But he didn't back away from the doorway. His face red and bunched like a fist. "You have no idea what kind of shitstorm you're facing."

This was no way to interview anyone, June was well aware. But she was tired of being nice. "Tell us about the Messenger," she said again. "Tell us about the Dark Time."

Boxall choked out a laugh. "Or what, he'll shoot me? On camera?"

The doorbell. She sighed. "Lewis, ditch the shotgun." She knew he still had the Beretta under his jacket.

He gave her a deadpan look, not happy with giving up an advantage. But he racked the slide, ejecting shell after shell until the gun was empty, then tossing it aside onto the wet grass.

Boxall didn't lower his hands. Instead he reached to his right, out of view behind the doorjamb. When he brought his hand back, it held a shiny chrome automatic pistol pointed directly at Lewis.

"I do believe I'm within my legal rights to shoot you." A cruel smile played on his lips. "I've never killed a man before. It'll be good practice for the Dark Time."

38

Lewis took a step forward, but Boxall took a step back, the chrome automatic steady in a two-handed grip. "Don't even think about it, you fucking prick. Hands up."

June saw something twitching inside the tech executive, a kind of madness rising to the surface.

Lewis saw it, too, and raised his hands. His jacket rose up, exposing the Beretta tucked into the back of his pants. He glanced at June.

She knew Lewis would have a round in the chamber and the safety off. All she'd have to do is reach out and grab the pistol. Then she flashed back to the previous winter and the horror of watching him get shot. "Not worth it, Lewis. Back away."

His face a mask, he retreated one step, then another.

"Keep going," she said. If he went left toward the driveway, Boxall would have trouble keeping an eye on them both. If Lewis moved far enough, he'd be out of sight and could pull the Beretta.

Instead, he came to a stop, knees slightly bent, ready. "I'm not leaving you."

He was still within range of the camera. June looked at Boxall. "He dropped the shotgun. He backed away. Legally, if you shoot him now, you'll be fucked. Everything's on camera. With your money, you'd be a flight risk, so they'll deny bail. Do you really want to be locked in a prison cell when the Dark Time comes?"

The twitching thing behind his eyes stared back at her for a long moment. June could see how badly it wanted to pull the trigger, had been wanting it for a long time. Then he blinked, making some internal calculation, and the thing inside him sank down, waiting for another day.

"You better keep your nose out of our business," he said. "Or things will get ugly in a way you really won't like."

"Things are already ugly for you," June said. "You're down two guys. And your little secret plan is coming out. Come clean now, maybe you'll get a reduced sentence."

He laughed out loud. "You're funny, girl reporter. You think you know something but you have no idea."

"So educate me," she said. "Tell me the timeline, at least."

A strange smile grew on his face. "Sooner than you think. We moved up the schedule. You better look to your own future instead of fucking with ours."

Then he stepped back and closed the door in her face.

She backpedaled onto the wet lawn and sucked in a deep breath, heart pounding. "That was my fault," she said. "I shouldn't have asked you to lose the shotgun."

"And I shouldn't have done it. Lesson learned." He eyed the house. "In retrospect, I should have learned it after what Peter said about Enderby's skills at the motel. These tech goobers may be amateurs, but they sure ain't playing."

"You always told me amateurs are more dangerous than professionals because you can't predict what they'll do."

"Guess I forgot." He flashed her a tilted smile. "Next time, remind me."

Unzipping his jacket, he bent to pick up the shotgun. With the hem of his shirt, he wiped off any prints he might have left. "You believe what Boxall said about moving up the schedule?"

"You saw how happy he was just thinking about it," she said. "So yeah, I do."

"Me, too." He dropped the shotgun into the mud and turned to go. "Guess we better figure what the hell that means, and in a hurry."

They walked back to the Lexus, pulled a U-turn, and drove away.

Their next stop was the University of Washington, where Sanjay Mishra ran a robotics lab. In the last thirty-six hours, June had emailed him, texted him, and called his cell. She'd never gotten anything back. In fact, his voicemail was full, so she couldn't even leave a message.

"I read about this guy," Lewis said. They were back on Montlake, heading north across the bridge toward the university. "Writer seemed to think he was a pretty good dude. Kinda the opposite of Troy Boxall. A family man. He put real money into tech scholarships for poor kids. Plus he made stuff that was actually useful, like the first fully functional robotic hand."

"The hand was only the start," June said. "Mishra's new project is to use humans with teleoperated equipment to train robots on complex manual tasks. After thousands of repetitions by dozens of human trainers, the robot AI has enough data to perform the task on its own."

"Like how training data enables chatbots to outperform a human being on the LSAT," he said. "After learning enough tasks, the AI will begin to teach itself, develop new skills on its own. The robot revolution is right around the corner." He caught her looking at him. "You know I invest in tech, right? I try to keep up on the latest."

Because of his physicality and the aura of violence that surrounded him, it was easy to forget how smart Lewis was. On his own since the age of fifteen, and parentless long before that, he was entirely self-educated.

She smiled at him now. "Black man with a library card." Referencing his favorite quote about the most dangerous man in America.

He gave her a smile back, full and genuine. "Damn right, Junebug."

They drove past the UW sports complex, then turned left on Pend Oreille Road and angled up into campus proper. In the last twenty years, academics had increasingly turned their research into for-profit businesses, often partnering with their universities and VC outfits to do so. The result was to turn powerhouse institutions like the University of Washington, along with MIT and Carnegie Mellon and many others, into de facto tech incubators.

Sanjay Mishra was right in the middle of it. With his name on more than a hundred patents, he'd already spun off three robotics companies. He was in the process of leaving academia to fully commercialize his research and make a fortune in the process. And the world would change forever, again. For the better, she hoped.

His lab was on the fourth floor of the Paul Allen building, a big new complex for computing and robotics. She knew he wouldn't work from home because he had four small children. They rode the elevator up and emerged in a small reception area, where a tubular young man in a fleece quarter-zip sat behind a desk. "Help you, folks?"

"June Cassidy to see Sanjay Mishra," June said. "We have an

appointment." By which she meant that she would have made an appointment if Mishra had gotten back to her.

"Uh." He flushed slightly. "Professor Mishra's not in today."

June figured she'd have to talk her way into the appointment, but didn't think they'd be denied outright. Beside her, Lewis straightened his posture, dipped a hand into his pocket, and brought out a business card, which he handed over. Instead of his usual street-inflected drawl, he had the clipped tones of an Ivy League graduate. "Colonel Lewis, Department of Defense. Where is Dr. Mishra?"

"Oh, gosh. I don't know." The desk man's face got pinker. "One moment?" He picked up the phone and punched in numbers. "Someone from the Department of Defense is here? For Professor Mishra?"

June raised her eyebrows at Lewis. He pretended not to notice.

Two minutes later, a small capable-looking woman with jet-black hair came through a set of glass doors. "I'm Jennifer Wong, the lab administrator. What's this about?" The desk man handed her the card.

"I'm afraid that's confidential," Lewis said. "We need to speak with Dr. Mishra."

The administrator looked at the floor for a moment, then back up at Lewis. "I would also like to speak with Professor Mishra," she said. "Five days ago, he left the lab early, saying he had a meeting off campus and would be back the next day. I haven't heard from him since. He's not responding to text or email. I called his wife and she hasn't heard from him, either."

"I see. Have you spoken with the Seattle police?"

"Yes. They said he's an adult and entitled to change his plans. They told me to call again if he's been gone for more than a week."

Lewis took a pen from the reception counter, retrieved the card from the administrator, and scribbled something on the back. "That's my personal number. Have him reach out the minute you hear from him."

Back in the elevator, June said, "Colonel Lewis?"

He gave her an elaborate shrug. "We in a hurry, ain't we? Just trying to move shit along."

39

PETER

It was almost three-thirty by the time Peter found 507 Puyallup Avenue in a row of attached storefronts not far from the BNSF freight yard. Parking on the street, he could hear the clang and roar of locomotives rearranging boxcars into new strings. This was the Tacoma Tideflats, an industrial area near the docks where refineries, chemical plants, and the big pulp and paper mills had once been located. The mills were a major area employer for decades, but they'd shut down one by one, moving operations to wherever labor was cheapest.

With the .357 at the small of his back, Peter stepped out into the rain, sniffing the air. He had a Marine buddy who'd grown up in family housing at Fort Lewis, on the east side of town, back when the paper mills were in full operation. He'd talked about the smell of his childhood, a pungent sulfurous stink known locally as the Tacoma Aroma. With the mills gone, and environmental laws now requiring smokestack scrubbers for the last remaining oil refiner, the Tideflats now smelled only of rotting seaweed and bunker oil exhaust from the huge dockside container ships.

507 Puyallup was nestled between an empty pawn shop and a for-profit plasma donation center. The storefront was cinder

block with peeling paint and weathered plywood over the windows and the glass entry door. It had seen better days and certainly looked vacant. Peter doubted the Tacoma cops had gone inside.

The plywood over the door had a rough cutout for the knob and three separate deadbolts. Peter tried the knob but it didn't turn. Without his green Chevy, he didn't have the tools to get through the door. He put his eye to a gap, trying to see inside, but saw only darkness. How had Circuit Rider managed to pick up his tabs and registration? There was nobody here to accept the mail. And hadn't been for some time, judging by the condition of the plywood.

Peter supposed the man could have gotten his tabs in person at the DMV, but to do that, he'd have to show a legal ID. Which would defeat the purpose of the elaborate fake registration routine. Circuit Rider must have been up to some nefarious shit to want to go to all this effort to hide the vehicle's ownership.

At the far right end of the storefront was another entrance door, a steel security model. The knob had been replaced by a metal cover plate. He wasn't getting in that way, either. But the door had a mail slot. Peter pulled open the flap and bent to look inside. A modest scattering of envelopes and circulars littered the floor. Somebody was still getting mail here.

He turned left, walked past the vacant neighboring building, then turned right and around the corner. Ahead was the fenced-off railyard. But first came the entrance to a narrow lane that ran behind the row of attached storefronts. He walked into the alleyway, the railyard fence to his left, rain pattering down on his jacket hood, boots crunching over weed-heaved blacktop and broken glass.

The back of the building was in worse condition than the front. Dense weeds grew waist-high along the cinder block, which had stairstep settlement cracks big enough to fit his finger. Two old steel divided-light windows flanked a single loading dock guarded by a roll-up door. The windows were covered by steel exterior security bars and the glass had been painted from the inside. He stepped into the wet weeds with his stomach against the cement lip of the loading dock, then put both hands on the corrugated metal door and pressed upward. It didn't move. And now his pants were wet.

Again, if he had his tools, Peter could have gotten inside. He stepped back into the alleyway to survey other possibilities, shaking his head and thinking this trip to Tacoma was a fool's errand. Until, looking at the roll-up door again, he realized it had no handle. So there was an electric opener on the inside. Where would the button be?

The most common location was directly beside the door. Most people were right-handed, he thought, so it would most likely be on the right side. Viewed from the outside, it would be on the left. For reasons of building code going back at least forty years, the controls should be mounted forty-eight inches off the finished floor.

Glancing around to make sure he was unobserved, he bent and picked up a rock the size of a golf ball. The loading-dock lip was roughly four feet off the alley pavement. He eyeballed four feet above that, picked a pane on the left, stepped back, and threw—and was rewarded by the musical chime of breaking glass. The kid's still got it.

The lip of the loading dock was less than a foot deep with no handholds. It took him several tries to climb up and keep his perch. Finally he stuck his arm out and gingerly plucked the remaining shards from the crumbling window putty. When the twelve-inch opening was clear, he reached through, hooked his elbow, and began to feel around inside.

There. A familiar rectangular shape, with three square buttons. The top two would be green, the bottom one red. His dad's shop had one just like it. Hoping the power was still on, he pressed the top button.

With the creak of breaking rust and the rattle of poorly lubricated rollers, the loading dock door rose. Peter took the .357 from under his jacket, took a deep breath to calm the static, then stepped carefully inside.

40

The air was cold and smelled of mold. He was in a storage room. Empty shelves lined the walls. The concrete floor had a broad, shallow puddle in the center. He looked up and was rewarded with a drip of water in his eye. The roof was leaking, the ceiling stained black with mold. The noise of a passing diesel locomotive drowned out all sound.

The light from the open loading dock door was dim and watery. With vacant commercial buildings, the owner would usually pay for light and heat until the space was rented again, although this place felt like it had been vacant for years. He glanced around for a switch, found one on the far wall and flipped it. Nothing. He looked up and saw that the fluorescent overheads had no bulbs.

A tiled utility room in the corner stood open. Along with the furnace and water heater, it had a toilet, a stained slop sink with a cheap saucepan in the bottom, a handheld shower fixture attached to the sink spout, and a floor drain. Above the sink was a shelf of ancient cleaning supplies and a shriveled bar of soap.

At the back of the storage room, a passage led to the rest of the building. The door had been removed from its jamb. On the far side was a drywalled hallway painted a bright sunshine yellow, the bottom half spotted with mildew. He found another light switch, but again it didn't work. He turned on his phone's flashlight and stepped forward, still holding the .357. Halfway down the hall was a closed door, probably an office. At the far end he could see a large front room with a soft glow filtering through the gaps in the plywood over the windows.

He figured it was a former showroom of some kind. All the fixtures had been stripped, leaving holes in the walls and gaps in the floor tile where some kind of counter had once been. There was nothing to identify the business that had been here. Here, too, the floor was puddled with moisture and the ceiling discolored from another leak.

Tucking the .357 into his waistband, he walked to the front wall to scoop up the pile of mail from the floor below the delivery slot. By the light of his phone, he flipped through the envelopes, circulars, and catalogs. Office supplies, janitorial services, warehouse equipment, generic stuff. He was hoping for something that might provide a clue to Circuit Rider's identity, but it was all addressed to "Office Manager," "Owner," or "Occupant."

So much for the mail. At least he'd figured out how Circuit Rider could pick up his vehicle tabs. Maybe he was a former tenant who'd kept his keys? It would be a reasonably safe mail drop. From the condition of the place, Peter figured the owner hadn't set foot in this property in years.

He left the mail in a pile and headed for the back room. In the hallway, he passed the closed door and tried the knob. It was locked. On closer inspection, both knob and door were newer, and of decent quality. There was even a deadbolt. Peter didn't get it. What was the point of replacing this knob and locking this door when the place was boarded up and the roof was leaking in two places?

Only one way to find out. Peter walked through the storage room, hopped off the loading dock, and scanned around for something heavy. He saw a large chunk of broken concrete lying in the weeds at the base of the fence to the railyard.

He needed two hands to pick it up. It weighed about as much as a sack of Quikrete. Peter had carried hundreds of those sacks in his life, and would no doubt carry many more. He hoisted the chunk onto the loading dock floor, climbed inside, picked it up again, then returned to the locked door. Mindful of the location of his toes, he swung the massive chunk directly at the deadbolt.

The door popped open on a dark room. He dropped the concrete chunk on the tile floor, then reached through the jamb and felt around for a light switch. Expecting nothing, he flipped it on and was surprised when a bank of fluorescent overheads lit up, nice and bright.

He'd thought it might be an office, filled with some remaining inventory or supplies worth protecting. Instead he saw a pair of metal bunkbeds with thin mattresses, an electric space heater, a mini-fridge with an ancient hot plate on top, and what he assumed was the door to the back room set over sawhorses and used as a worktable. On the wall over the table, attached with a thumbtack, was the same glossy brochure for Resilient Systems that he'd seen in Reed's apartment, folded in the same way. The same face stared out from the glossy paper with those same penetrating eyes that somehow seemed to look right inside you.

Peter looked down at the contents of the worktable. Scattered snippets of wire with insulation in a half dozen colors, the remains of several rolls of tin solder, spent tubes of epoxy, and a paper plate holding a random assortment of machine screws. Someone had been repairing something. Or building something.

The paper plate sat on a book. He moved the plate. The book was a cheap printing of the Unabomber Manifesto, well-thumbed with underlined passages on every page.

The Unabomber was a former mathematics professor turned Montana hermit who had railed against the industrialization of America. His bombing campaign had lasted from 1978 to 1995, killing three people and injuring twenty-three more. He was finally caught when *The New York Times* published his so-called manifesto and his brother recognized the writing style. The Unabomber Manifesto had since been republished many times. It was a touchstone for many disaffected oddballs and school shooters.

Aw, hell, Peter thought. This just gets better and better.

He looked up at the brochure again. Despite the slightly bulging eyes, there was something about that face, something warm and compassionate. *Garrison Bevel, Founder of Resilient Systems.*

He reached across the desk and pulled the glossy paper free from the thumbtack. It was a single legal-size page, folded in half and printed on both sides to make a simple four-page booklet. Bevel's photo was on the second-to-last page. The paper had softened and the gloss had dulled at the edges, as if it had been taken down and handled frequently.

Folding the booklet back to its intended form, he flipped through from the beginning. He saw stock images of downed utility lines, smiling customers, and rooftops covered with rectangular black panels. *Solar power with battery backup. Live in comfort through even the longest power outage.*

The back page touted Bevel's engineering degrees and his career with Pacific Gas and Electric, along with a graphic suggesting that your solar investment would pay for itself in just a few years, which seemed a little optimistic in the rainy

Pacific Northwest. At the very bottom was the company contact information. Email, phone, and physical address.

507 Puyallup Avenue, Tacoma, WA.

The storefront he was standing in right now.

Holy shit. He turned back to the photo of the founder. He looked again at those eyes, that face. He felt something click.

He couldn't prove it, but he felt pretty damn sure that Garrison Bevel was the voice on the cassette tapes. Garrison Bevel was the Messenger.

41

JUNE

June already had Sanjay Mishra's home address. He lived about two miles from the university on a tree-lined street in Ravenna, across from the ravine park that gave the neighborhood its name. He owned two small Craftsman-style houses that were joined together with a modern glass addition. June guessed if you had money and four kids and you wanted to be able to walk to work, that was a pretty good option.

When they knocked on the door, a woman answered immediately. She had long blond hair, a ski-jump nose, a peaches and cream complexion, and a scowl. She carried a fussing baby on her hip with another clinging to her leg. "You bloody buggers better not be trying to sell me something. I just had this one down for his nap." She sounded like a woman pouring pints in an English pub.

June handed her a business card. "I'm sorry to bother you, Mrs. Mishra. We're looking for your husband. I understand he's been out of the office for a few days. Is he home today?"

Her face crumpled for a moment, until she recovered, holding herself together. "No, he's not home—he's bloody *missing*. I can't bloody reach him."

She stepped back, ushering them into the comfortable clutter of the house. It had been opened up into one large room, with a bright kitchen, a wooden train set looping a sectional couch, and unfolded laundry heaped on the dining table. The two children stared at June with enormous eyes.

"I tracked his mobile to a parking lot in feckin' Sumner, of all places. I loaded up the kids and drove all the way down there yesterday, found his feckin' car with the mobile under the seat. I can't imagine why he'd leave it behind. He lived on that damn thing. I was always on him to put it down."

She blinked hard, then furiously swiped away a falling tear. "Silly bugger's never gone this long without checking in. We usually talk three or four times a day. I didn't think he even knew where Sumner was. I called the coppers and they couldn't be bothered."

Then she caught herself. "What the bloody hell do you lot want with my Sanjay?"

June gave the woman a sympathetic smile. "My name's June Cassidy. Mrs. Mishra, we think your husband might be involved in something we're looking into."

"Call me Sally, please. Is Sanjay in trouble?"

"We hope not. Did he ever mention something called the Gun Club?"

"I don't believe so." She hugged the fussy baby closer. "Now you're scaring me. My husband is a good man."

"What about somebody called the Messenger?"

"No. What on earth is this about?"

"Did your husband ever talk about preparing for some kind of natural disaster?"

Sally Mishra made a face. "Had a midlife crisis, if that's what you mean. Got all worried about living in an earthquake zone, filled our basement with bottled water and tinned food and nappies and all kinds of other supplies." She shrugged, bouncing the baby on her hip. "A couple of years later, he was on to something else. We'll be eating tinned beans until we're ninety."

June fished into her pocket and came out with the Messenger cassette. "Have you seen your husband with one of these?"

"That was Midlife Crisis 2.0," Sally said. "He got interested in jam bands." She made air quotes and shuddered. "Phish and Widespread Panic? I can't stand that shite. But he started trading tapes of live shows with people through the mail. He plays them on his walk to work."

June raised her eyebrows at Lewis. Geoff Reed had told his sister he collected bootleg tapes, too. She said, "May we see his collection?"

Sally Mishra stared at her. "Who the bloody fuck are you people? And what is this all about?"

"Better you don't know," June said. "Not yet. We need to see those tapes."

Sally scowled again, but she detached the toddler from her leg, took the child's hand, and led them all through the glass addition, which was set up like an English solarium with plants and couches, and into the other house, where a back bedroom had been converted to a home office. It had a reading chair by the window, a large wooden table with a giant monitor and related computer clutter, and floor-to-ceiling shelves.

Mouth set, the baby fussing on her hip, Sally pointed at the shelves, where a rack for cassette cases stood about three-quarters full. Beside it was a portable tape player and a pair of cheap headphones.

June walked over to the rack. Like the tape case from KT's, these were unlabeled, with the blank white facing out. She took one from the rack and opened it. The cassette inside was the same brand as the one from KT's house. On one side was the same kind of label with a date written in the same spidery hand.

The dates were different, though. She pulled the next few cases from the rack and opened them. They were organized sequentially, each dated roughly a month from the one before. She counted forward and found a single empty slot. After that was a single final tape case. She checked the date on the last one. It was for the month after KT's tape.

The dates fit. The tape had come from Mishra's collection. June would bet her life on it.

Sanjay Mishra was KT's whistleblower.

She turned and saw Sally staring at her, the baby fussing louder now. "I know you're not interested in a ring of bloody jam band bootleggers. Please, please tell me what this is about."

June felt for the woman, but she couldn't allow herself to be human just yet. She kept her voice businesslike, as if she couldn't see Sally's distress. "Just a few more questions. Did your husband ever travel without his phone before?"

Sally Mishra swallowed. "A few times, yes, when he went to meet with some startup founders. He said they were a little paranoid about their big idea getting out. They made him put his phone in a kind of security pouch to cut it off from the cell network. I thought it was odd, but he told me the startup might be a game-changer. It only happened a few times. And only for the day. Never overnight." Her eyes were brimming.

"In the last few weeks or months, did Sanjay seem upset about anything?"

Sally knuckled away the tears. "Not that he'd ever talk about," she said. "I mean, we're English. But a wife knows. Maybe two weeks ago, something changed. He was different. Tense. Five days ago he said he had a meeting and I haven't heard from him since."

June looked at Lewis. He nodded. She took a deep breath.

"Sally, we believe your husband got involved in something unfortunate. My guess is, he probably thought it was a good thing, something to help your family in case of a disaster. Then, I would like to think, he realized it was not such a good thing. That it was dangerous. And he did something that he hoped might put an end to it. He reached out to a colleague of mine. And now that colleague is dead."

Sally held the children to her like an anchor, like they were the only things keeping the tide from washing her out to sea. "And my husband?"

June cleared her throat. "We're looking for him. Do you have any contact information for these startup people he went to visit?"

"I already looked," Sally said. "I checked his phone, I checked his computer. His work and personal calendars. I know all his passwords. We didn't keep secrets, at least I thought we didn't. But I found nothing."

June had a thought. "May I see his phone?"

Sally led them back through the solarium to the kitchen and took a phone off the counter. She put in the password, then handed it to June, who immediately went to the alphabetic list of apps, looking for Telegram. It wasn't there.

June went to the app store, found Telegram, and began to download it, holding her breath.

When it was finished, she opened the app.

It went directly to the chat screen. Mishra had deleted the app just like Enderby had. When it loaded, it had remembered the phone. Unlike Enderby, Sanjay Mishra had put the details in his password manager. And now she could see any messages.

There were only two. The first was with Circuit Rider, a single text dated six days ago.

"I understand you've chosen to leave our community. Would it be possible to have an in-person exit interview about your reasons? It will really help us improve the experience of other members. Tomorrow, 10am? Usual place? Won't take long."

Sanjay had responded an hour later with a thumbs-up.

The second set of messages was from somebody calling himself WILKS, dated four days ago, after Sanjay's disappearance. It had never been opened. And it was in all caps, the text equivalent of a shout.

"RE OUR PREVIOUS CONVERSATION, RECOMMEND YOU TAKE NO ACTION. NEGATIVE CONSEQUENCES HIGHLY LIKELY."

The next message arrived an hour later. "STRONGLY RECOMMEND YOU DO NOT ACT. TOO DANGEROUS. PLEASE RESPOND."

Then another message a few hours after that. "SANJAY WHERE ARE YOU?"

Sanjay Mishra had never responded.

Now the only question was whether he was still alive.

June turned to Sally. "Do you have any family nearby? Anywhere you can go stay?"

Sally burst into tears.

They walked out to the Lexus under a threatening sky, Lewis carrying the rack of cassette tapes. "Some dude calling himself WILKS, on a private chat with Sanjay Mishra?"

"Only one guy that could be," June replied. "Isaac Wilkinson."

Of the people KT had interviewed, he was the third person who'd disavowed knowledge of the Gun Club. From the messages above, he was clearly a part of this, too. June was pretty sure she knew where to find him. The question was, would he see her?

42

Part of the legend surrounding Isaac Wilkinson, the founder of Savant, was that he'd basically lived at the office for years, sleeping on a cot in a storage room, working impossibly long hours even after he'd spun off a half dozen companies and made a half dozen fortunes. Adding to the myth, when the new company headquarters was being constructed, the Savant publicity team had gotten a lot of press over the fact that Isaac, as he was universally known, had told the architects to include a personal residence on the top floor, so he'd never have to leave work.

Unlike many innovators who transitioned to investing in other people's startups, Wilkinson had never stopped innovating. He'd had a hand in almost every significant technological development in the last thirty years. His current focus, according to a recent article KT had written, was artificial intelligence. And Savant was leading the pack.

The new eight-story headquarters in Fremont, just uphill from Gas Works Park with unobstructed views of Lake Union, was a surprisingly artful assemblage of glass, steel, and concrete that spanned two city blocks. It had won the Pritzker Prize for architecture the year before, and seeing it in person, June understood why.

Lewis found a parking spot across the street. The rain had started up again, beating steadily against the windshield. "You ever interview him?"

"Not me," June said. "He's notoriously private. KT is the only journalist he's talked to in decades. They met when Isaac was fresh out of Stanford creating his first company and have been fairly close ever since. Everything I know about him, I learned from her."

"So, what's our in? Guy like Isaac's gotta have serious security."

"We wait," June said. "Kill the engine."

Lewis cracked the windows to avoid condensation on the glass, then did as she asked. "What're we waiting for?"

"You'll see."

They didn't have to wait long. Thirty minutes later, a man walked out of the headquarters main entrance at a rapid clip, then turned away from them and strode purposefully into the blowing rain. Directly behind him were two athletic guys hustling to keep up. They wore black ballcaps and stylish black hip-length raincoats that didn't quite hide the pistols on their belts.

"That's him," June said. "Get me closer."

"What's he doing?" Lewis eased out into traffic and past the walkers.

"He takes three or four walks a day, rain or shine. He told KT it's how he does his best thinking. Pull a U-turn at the next intersection."

Lewis did as she asked, then double-parked, flashers on, as Isaac Wilkinson approached. He wore an ancient red raincoat, the color faded to a soft pink, over black rain pants and well-worn hiking shoes. His dark brown face was weathered. His felted wool rain hat looked like it had been sat on several hundred times. The overall effect was of a hiker who'd walked out of the woods after thirty years in the wilderness.

"You're joking," Lewis said. "That's Isaac Wilkinson?" Isaac wasn't one to pace the stage publicizing the company's latest products. There were few pictures of him. According to KT, he didn't care for publicity.

June opened her door and hopped out. "Stay in the car or you'll spook his security."

Wilkinson was moving faster than he seemed. By the time she walked around the Lexus and between two parked cars, he was already past her.

"Isaac Wilkinson," she called to his back. "Can I have a few words?"

Wilkinson didn't seem to hear her, but one of the security men pivoted with his palms forward, eyes assessing her with cool professionalism. "Back away, miss. If you want to speak with Mr. Wilkinson, call his office for an appointment."

June gave him her best smile and picked up her pace, the treads of her running shoes gripping the wet pavement nicely. The guard's lips tightened and he reached for her wrist, trying for a control grip.

She swept his arm aside, then slipped beneath it, thumping her elbow into the back of his head as she passed, the blow hard enough to make him stumble and begin to fall. Ever since a certain asshole had locked her in a car trunk a few years back, she'd been training in mixed martial arts. It was always fun to put her skills to use outside the gym.

Wilkinson kept walking as if nothing had happened. Behind her, she heard the first guard curse softly as he caught himself and began to recover. The second guard, slightly older, had already jumped ahead of her to shield his boss, backpedaling as he raised the hem of his raincoat and unsnapped his holster strap, fingers made clumsy by the cold and wet. "Stop right there or I'll shoot."

"Don't," Lewis said, suddenly there on the sidewalk with the big Beretta in his fist, staring down both guards. Something in his face or his voice froze them both in place. "Ain't nobody need to get hurt. Five minutes and we're gone."

Wilkinson, a scarecrow in baggy clothes, hadn't stopped or even seemed to notice, striding into the rain. Past the second guard now, June leapt forward to catch up, then put a hand on his arm. "Isaac. I know what happened to Sanjay Mishra."

He stopped abruptly and stared at her. Lines were carved deep around his mouth and eyes. Raindrops beaded up on his round eyeglasses. "I don't know you."

"June Cassidy. I'm with Public Investigations." She released his arm and put out her hand. He ignored it. "I worked with Katelyn Thorsen. She was my friend."

He ran the outside edge of an index finger across the lenses of his glasses like a windshield wiper, then studied her face. After a moment, he spun on a heel to regard his frozen security detail.

"Stop fucking around back there." He pointed across the street at a small building with dark wood siding. "We're getting coffee. Try to keep up."

Then he set off into traffic, his long legs propelling him through the line of fast-moving cars as if they didn't exist.

The Stone Way Café was bright and clean, with large windows and only two other customers, an older woman with a book and a young man with a laptop.

Wilkinson led June to a large corner table by the front window. There was a RESERVED sign on it. He didn't seem to notice. She pointed to the sign. "Should we sit somewhere else?"

He looked at her as if at a particularly dim specimen of a much stupider species. "It's reserved for me. I own the restaurant."

Of course he did, June thought. Wilkinson's net worth was somewhere north of a hundred billion dollars. He really should have had a larger security detail.

He shed his coat, scattering droplets everywhere. "You two." He pointed at a table near the door with another reserved sign. "Sit."

His security men's disapproval showed in their faces, but they did as directed, dividing their attention between Lewis and the street outside. Lewis returned their gazes with a small tilted smile, leaning indifferently against the long marble service counter. The Beretta had vanished.

June opened her mouth to speak but Wilkinson put up a hand. A server approached unasked with six different coffee drinks on a tray, as if she'd somehow known he was coming. She set the tray on a lazy Susan in the middle of the table, the only one in the entire restaurant, then left without a word.

Wilkinson leaned forward and spun the lazy Susan twice, examining the options and finally selecting something in a tiny white porcelain cup. He gestured irritably at the remaining beverages. "Take one and tell me about Sanjay."

June ignored the drinks. "He's almost certainly dead and I think you know why."

Wilkinson looked out the rain-beaded window. "Why do you believe he's dead?"

"He's been missing for five days. His wife traced his phone to his car in a parking lot south of town. On it, I found a Telegram message sent six days ago from someone calling himself Circuit Rider, asking for a meeting. He told his wife and his office manager he'd be gone for the day. I think he went to the meeting. It was clear from the text that he was leaving the group. I believe he also gave one of the Messenger's tapes to Katelyn Thorsen shortly before she was killed."

"I cannot fault your logic," he said, still staring out at the rain. "There is a high probability that Sanjay is dead."

"I saw your texts to him. Tell me about your involvement with the Messenger. Have you heard the recordings?"

"I have a large collection," he said. "I was the one who invited Sanjay into the Movement." He turned to look at her again. His face was taut but otherwise betrayed no emotion. "If he is dead, it is my fault."

June said, "Tell me everything you know about the Messenger's group."

Wilkinson glanced disapprovingly at his watch. "That will take longer than five minutes."

June remembered KT telling her that Wilkinson was probably somewhere on the neurodivergent spectrum. Very good at technical ideas, very good at numbers, not very good at people. But still human.

So she waited, knowing he wanted to talk.

43

Finally Wilkinson sighed. "Very well. What do you know about the so-called technological singularity?"

June felt like she was back in school. As a journalist whose job was to talk with very smart people who understood things she did not, this happened with regularity.

"The singularity," she said, "is the idea that multiple technologies—artificial intelligence, biotechnology, and nanotechnology—will advance in a mutually reinforcing explosion of innovation that will become uncontrollable and irreversible. The result would be that humanity either makes a great leap forward or destroys itself."

"Very good," Wilkinson said, his face indicating that perhaps she was not as dim as he'd previously thought. "It is not a crackpot theory. NASA has a conference on this subject every year. The current best thinking is that this explosion of innovation will arrive some time in the next five to twenty years. In my opinion, the possibility of a negative outcome is significant. Perhaps as high as fifty percent in the next hundred years."

She held up her hands like a traffic cop. "Hold on. Your P(doom) is fifty percent?"

The risk arising from uncontrolled technological development was a popular topic in the tech world. AI researchers had coined the notoriously under-defined pseudo-mathematical term P(doom) to express the probability of a civilization-ending outcome. Fifty percent was much higher than the average.

"Then why," June said, "are you still working on AI?" In the singularity scenario, artificial intelligence was the precursor technology that would accelerate innovation in all other fields. That theory was already beginning to prove out in a number of scientific areas.

"Because the entire world is working on it," he said. "And if a true superintelligence is possible, we need to achieve it before the Chinese. And the Russians, and the Iranians, and the North Koreans. All of which have proven to be deeply flawed, repressive, and destructive regimes."

"American history is hardly without its flaws," June said dryly.

He tipped his head, acknowledging that truth. "The US has often acted quite badly, I agree. Going back to well before the nation's founding. That notwithstanding, and not withstanding our current political challenges, America—let us say the Western allies—have a history of valuing human freedom in a way that many other nations do not. The nation that wins this race will be able to set the world's agenda in an unprecedented way. QED, better us than them."

"How did you arrive at a P(doom) of fifty percent?"

"Computer modeling. Of course, there are too many variables to make any single model the clear winner. Depending on the application, almost every transformational technology, past, present, and future, can be used to help humanity or harm it. Including the original transformational technology, fire. When burning in a stove or firepit, it cooks food, it warms on a cold night. When burning out of control, it destroys forests, prairies, communities."

Wilkinson became more animated as he warmed to his subject. "Best case, if humanity can actually begin to work together for some kind of common good, with commonsense regulations and safety controls in place, we truly could see the next human renaissance. The end of disease. The end of hunger. Clean, abundant energy. Lifespans extending for decades longer. Universal education. Widespread prosperity. We can repair the planet, colonize the solar system. The infinite expansion of human potential."

"That sounds pretty good," June said.

"However," Wilkinson said, "given the current behavior of humanity as a whole, the modeling shows that positive scenario is increasingly unlikely. Evolutionarily, *Homo sapiens* is wired for tribalism and short-term thinking. Elected leaders sow division for personal gain. Late-stage capitalism prioritizes profit despite significant human and social costs. Climate change is also a factor. We are already seeing increased wildfires, strengthening storms, torrential rains, drought and desertification, and food shortages. Taken together, these factors are likely to lead to increased competition between nation-states and state-scale corporate actors. Which leads to social destabilization, not to mention resource and religious wars. Which we are already seeing, wouldn't you agree?"

"Ukraine," June said. "The Middle East. Africa."

"Exactly. The common result across all existing models is that the singularity is coming. The genie is out of the bottle. All we can do is work to mitigate the downstream effects. The inevitable job losses and social upheaval. Things are already changing too quickly for most people. There is a widespread desire to turn back the clock. We see that in political movements across the world. Unfortunately, the rate of change will only accelerate. This is the reason the so-called prepper movement is growing.

It's an entirely rational response to instability and uncontrolled change."

Now June understood why Wilkinson had started down this conversational path. "That's why you got involved with the Messenger's movement. You were hedging your bets in case the coin flipped the wrong way."

"As any rational person would," Wilkinson said. "Relative to my net worth, the cost of a membership was negligible. And unlike my large holdings in British Columbia and New Zealand, I could, if necessary, simply bicycle to the Messenger's camp, which is advertised as being within a hundred miles of downtown Seattle."

New Zealand was the billionaires' safe space. Because of its geographical isolation and record of good government, many of the wealthiest men on the planet had bought vast estates and built secure compounds there during the pandemic.

"You've been to the camp?"

He shook his head. "My security team wouldn't allow it. When you take the tour, you can't bring anyone with you. They take your phone and blindfold you, so you don't actually know where the camp is. You are entirely in their power. So I sent Faraday in my place." He glanced back at the older of the two security men. "Tell her about it."

Faraday was dark-skinned, mid-forties, and clean-shaven, with that air of contained watchfulness common to many cops and combat vets June had known.

"It was always with a group, maybe forty of us, the rest of them tech workers," he said. "There were only a few opportunities to visit each year, and the others were excited. We met in the parking lot of the Auburn mall. There were ten guys from the camp, and they loaded us into a beat-up old school bus with duct tape patching the seats and the windows painted over so you couldn't see out. Plus the blindfolds, which only added to the mystique. They patted everyone down, made us leave our phones and wallets in our cars. You couldn't take a bag with you, either. They were dead serious about keeping the location secret. If you didn't like it, they'd escort you off the bus."

"Great marketing," June said. These were old sales tricks going back to the days of door-to-door salesmen. Like the cassette tapes passed hand to hand, the scarcity of the product would make it feel like an exclusive club. And the strange hardships of leaving their stuff behind, the blindfolds, the ratty old school bus, and not actually knowing where they were going, would be very different from their normal environment of wealth, comfort, and privilege. It would make them feel like outsiders. Basic human psychology would make most people want to be part of the in-group.

"I checked my watch before they put on my blindfold and after they gave the okay to take it off. The whole thing took sixty-eight minutes. Call it ten minutes to get everybody settled, so maybe an hour of drive time? There didn't seem to be a whole lot of turns at the beginning, so I don't think they were trying too hard to throw us off."

Lewis spoke for the first time. "But I'm guessing you picked up some clues."

Faraday nodded. "The last time I went, it was full summer. I sat as close to the front as I could, so I could feel the sun through the windshield. Mostly we seemed to go southeast. And when we got off the bus, it was clear enough that I could see Mount Rainier rising to the southwest. So I could make some educated guesses about locations. Draw a circle on a map, at least. Until the nineties, that was the largest unpopulated area in the continental US. There aren't many roads in. But it's still a lot of open country, couple thousand square miles."

"What about the compound itself?" June was taking notes.

"I'd guess it used to be a summer camp, maybe even an old Boy Scout camp. There's a main lodge, a bunch of old cabins, but also new cabins, new greenhouses, a huge solar array. It was the weekend, so I don't know if anyone lives there full-time, but I saw at least a hundred people working on the place. Everyone was armed. I've been three times in the last three years. Each time, they'd made more improvements. It's pretty impressive. They clearly have a lot of funding."

"Did you get any names? The guys on the bus, the people living there?"

Faraday shook his head. "The tech bros didn't want to out themselves. The people who put us on the bus or who lived there only gave us first names. A guy named Hollis seemed to be running things."

"What about the Messenger," June said. "Did you meet him?"

"All three times. Mid-sixties, Caucasian, educated. Never gave a name, he was just the Messenger. Kind of spooky eyes, but definitely magnetic. Empathetic, charismatic. You wanted to be near him. He'd put a hand on your arm or shoulder when he talked to you. The way his people looked at him, it was like he was the messiah."

June thought back to the recording Peter and Ellie had found. "Did he talk about the Dark Time?"

"That's most of what he talked about, although he didn't give any details. When I was out there last July, he said it would come next year, maybe as soon as the spring."

"Was he trying hard to convince you? Like one of those crackpot preachers who claim to know the hour and date of the apocalypse?"

"More like he had it written in his calendar," Faraday said. "Very matter-of-fact. That was right before he took us to the armory, showed us how many guns they had." He looked at Lewis. "A crap-ton, by the way."

"Here's what I don't get," June said. "If you're not supposed to know where it is, how do you know where to go when the shit hits the fan?"

"There's a protocol," Faraday said. "They say they'll send an alert to the members, with GPS coordinates and detailed directions."

June frowned. "What if it's a natural disaster that happens without warning, like an earthquake or tsunami? There won't be time to send an alert before the cell network goes down."

"Don't matter," Lewis said. "Whatever happens, they gonna know about it ahead of time. Because they the ones gonna pull the trigger."

"I agree," Wilkinson said. "It's one of several reasons I'm seeking alternative options."

"What are the other reasons?" June said.

"All the weapons. As if preparing for war rather than self-defense. Also the recordings, which became steadily more dire, more apocalyptic. I decided the group was dangerous. More likely a problem than a solution. After Faraday's last trip in July, I decided to end my participation."

"And you told Sanjay Mishra." June was guessing, but the barren look on Wilkinson's face told her she was correct. "Why did they come for him, but not you?"

Wilkinson looked out the window again, the rain streaming down the glass, his coffee forgotten in his hand. "Because I didn't tell the Messenger about my decision," he said quietly. "Unlike Sanjay, I continued paying for my membership. Unlike me, Sanjay was a man of principle. He agreed with me about the threat. He was going to reach out to a journalist. I suggested Katelyn Thorsen. In that way, I am responsible for her death, as well."

The coffee shop was silent for a moment. Then June said, "What do you think they're planning? Maybe something to do with the tech conference this weekend?"

"It's possible," Faraday said, "but I doubt it. Have you heard those recordings? The Messenger has something more ambitious in mind. He seems to think he's planning the end of civilization as we know it. But I have no idea what that plan entails."

"Whatever it is, it's coming soon," June said. "Lewis and I just talked to a guy named Troy Boxall who says they moved the date up."

Lewis frowned. "Faraday, did you ever go back out to the compound, get more intel on what they're up to?"

"Isaac stepped back, so I did, too. At the time, I thought I was too busy." The security man shook his head and lowered his eyes. "Now I think I just didn't want to know. I wanted to pretend everything would be fine."

June turned to Wilkinson. "Would you talk with the police? We're having trouble getting them to take this threat seriously. A call from Isaac Wilkinson might get their attention."

"I already called the Seattle police on Isaac's behalf," Faraday said. "Four days ago. I spoke with a captain who said the area was outside his jurisdiction. He told me he'd speak to the appropriate county sheriffs and someone would get back to me. But we've heard nothing since."

June's stomach sank. "The captain you spoke to. What was his name?"

"Captain Durant," Faraday said. "Why do you ask?"

44

HOLLIS

Hollis Longro pulled the Rivian into the parking lot of a modest office building in Greenwood and found a place two slots down from the blue minivan. He glanced at his watch, gauging the time. Unless they'd already slipped out the back, he had about forty-five minutes to wait. Nickels was due any minute.

Hollis didn't want to do what he had to do next. It was never easy, being the right hand of a visionary. He reminded himself that he'd done worse things for the Movement. A leader needed to be capable of doing whatever was necessary. The Messenger had taught him that long ago. Actually, what the Messenger had said was that if Hollis couldn't kill a man, he didn't belong in the Movement. So he'd done what the Messenger had asked, again and again. No matter how he felt about it. Now he couldn't imagine leaving, where he might go, what he would do.

He hadn't liked ordering Enderby to kill the girl. She'd done nothing to them. She was just a girl. But the Messenger had insisted. And the cause was just. Otherwise, humanity would be lost to the Industrial Machine forever.

Besides, this wasn't on him. It was the Marine's fault. Peter Ash. At least now Hollis had a name for that relentless fuck, thanks to his old friend on the cops, one of the Movement's Hardcore

Originals. They'd met when the Messenger and Hollis and a few others were sleeping in the old Resilient Systems storefront, living rough and dreaming about the end of the world. Rather than roust them, Tom Durant had joined them. He'd already owned a copy of the Unabomber's Manifesto and carried it with him everywhere. At the Messenger's direction, he'd moved to the Seattle PD, where he'd moved up through the ranks to captain, where his duties included supervising the department's domestic terrorism unit. That position allowed him to steer any attention away from the Movement.

The Messenger had kept the storefront because certain things still required a physical address, like vehicle registration. Using a vacant building was a good way to discourage questions, not to mention providing a private place to meet.

And now the Dark Time was almost here, months earlier than planned. Hollis was still getting used to the idea. He thought he'd have more time to prepare himself. Part of him had always wondered if they would actually go through with it. Had hoped that, perhaps, the Industrial Machine would relent and the plan would become unnecessary.

He lowered the car window and lit a cigarette and remembered how they had gotten to this point, right at the brink.

It started a few weeks ago, when Troy Boxall texted him, saying that the journalist, Thorsen, had called him for an interview about the company he'd sold. At the very end, though, she asked a gotcha question about Gun Club.

Boxall had said he was too smart for the journalist, had sworn he'd stonewalled her, claimed total ignorance. Hollis was used to this very tech-bro response, many in the Movement thinking their material success translated into brilliance in all other things. But it didn't matter whether Boxall was overconfident. To be successful, the Movement needed to work in darkness. If Thorsen knew to ask about the Gun Club chat group, she already knew too much.

Even more significant, Hollis thought, was the fact that Boxall was one of the few people who actually knew the plan. He'd helped Reed pull off the intrusion that would give them the access they needed to carry out the plan on a truly national scale. Boxall appeared devoid of any moral compass. If he was taken, Hollis had no doubt he would tell everything to save his skin.

They had to deal with Thorsen, that was clear. But Nickels and his brother were busy making the armor-piercing rounds. Vance was the Messenger's bodyguard and couldn't be spared. Hollis was too valuable to the Movement to risk himself. In the end, the Messenger had thought Geoff Reed would be perfect. He'd already finished his computer work. He wanted to prove himself. Enderby was the backup, useful but ultimately disposable.

Still, removing the journalist was only part of the problem. They also had to deal with the traitor to the Movement, the person who'd shared their secrets.

It wasn't difficult to find the betrayer. Whoever he was, Hollis assumed he had a prior relationship with Katelyn Thorsen. He searched online for Movement members she had written about in the past, and two dozen names came up. Sanjay Mishra was one of them. He was the only member who'd recently canceled his subscription.

Hollis had always been a little concerned about Mishra. He had the wrong values, for one thing. He'd put technology he'd invented in the public domain rather than profiting for himself. He'd also given away a substantial amount of money. All of which told Hollis that Sanjay Mishra simply wasn't self-interested enough. He cared too much about people he'd never met. Which was not how the Movement worked.

The Movement worked because people knew what was

coming and wanted to secure a protected place for themselves and their loved ones. They knew that, in a dangerous world, safety was only possible in a small, well-prepared, and tightly knit community. Caring about people outside the community was a waste of limited resources. In retrospect, Mishra had always been a bad fit. And now he knew far too much.

So Hollis had reached out and asked for a meeting. He'd called it an exit interview. He'd never made it past high school, but he was smart enough talk to the tech people in their own language.

Mishra had agreed to meet in a parking lot south of town. The clouds had briefly cleared and they'd stood outside and talked. After a few minutes of bullshit, Hollis had asked him point-blank if he'd talked to Katelyn Thorsen about the Movement.

Mishra said no. But something showed in his face and Hollis knew there was more. You sent her a cassette, he said. It was only a guess, but Mishra's frozen expression told him the rest.

Right there in the parking lot, Hollis took out the Taser and got him in the neck.

Unlike some in the Movement, Hollis didn't enjoy hurting others. But sometimes it was necessary. The betrayer went rigid from the voltage and fell back against his car. Hollis lifted him into the Toyota's back seat and leaned in to tape his wrists, ankles, and mouth. He'd thrown a blanket over the man and told him to stay still and keep quiet or he'd get zapped again.

Then he'd driven the betrayer to the camp.

The Messenger's People would have their justice.

The Messenger's People were the ones who had joined the Movement early. Unlike the techies, they were true believers, not only in the truth of the Messenger's vision, but in the Messenger himself.

In every case, they had experienced the limitless cruelty of the Industrial Machine and were committed to the necessary action to free the world from it.

The Messenger's People were working people, a community of sixty-three families and a dozen singletons, four hundred strong. The Messenger himself had selected them from many possible candidates, because of the knowledge and skills they brought with them, essential during the Dark Time to come.

They were men, women, children, and even a few grandchildren. Most were skilled in multiple areas, even the kids. They were hunters and trackers, ranchers, farmers, loggers, master gardeners. Carpenters, masons, plumbers, electricians, mechanics, machinists, teachers. They also had eight nurses, three doctors, even a dentist. Many had been soldiers. All were familiar with firearms.

This was not a political group. They were beyond politics. That system had been bought and sold years ago. Nobody was coming to help them. Everyone in the community was in agreement on that. Instead of politics, the Movement was about belief in the Messenger and his vision for the future. They were the cornerstones of the new world to come.

All had signed the Messenger's Protocols, every man, woman, and child over the age of ten, using their own blood as ink.

Many of the most skilled had already relinquished their lives, sold everything they owned, and moved to the camp to prepare for the Dark Time. Others still worked in the Machine, sending money in every month.

None of them knew what would bring on the Dark Time, of course. That was a carefully guarded secret. Only the Hardcore Originals knew about the larger plan. Hollis, Nickels and his brother, their cousin Vance, and a few others. Reed and Boxall had learned the secret after their recruitment. Their knowledge and computer skills were essential to the plan.

Reed was one of the few tech people the Movement truly needed, however. In fact, in the Messenger's vision, the tech people were actually fueling the Industrial Machine, hollowing out America, hastening the inevitable end. They would not be notified when the Dark Time was truly upon them. To the Messenger, they deserved to die.

The only thing the tech people provided was funding. After a sizable deposit, they paid monthly dues ranging from one to six thousand dollars. A thousand-dollar subscription paid for a single bed in a bunkhouse and food and water for one. For two thousand, you'd get a private room, a private bath, and food and water for two. Six thousand got you a cabin for four. Everyone would get electricity, running water, two years of rations, and armory privileges, of course. Or at least that was what the tech people thought they were getting.

They always chose the more expensive options, too. Many of them were quite wealthy. Hollis felt not a single pang of guilt for fleecing them. The tech people were causing the problem. It was only fair that they help provide for the solution.

And they were providing. The average monthly subscription was just over four grand. Taken together, it added up to a monthly income of almost two million dollars.

When the Dark Time came, money would be irrelevant. So the Messenger's People were spending it as fast as they could. They'd laid in a huge supply of dried food, dug multiple wells, and added enough solar panels and storage batteries to power the expanded camp several times over. They'd built enough bunkhouses and cabins and greenhouses for a future population of two thousand souls. They had a backhoe, a bulldozer, and a tanker truck. They had thousands of gallons of diesel and gas in buried tanks, and enough propane to last for years. They had an armory of twelve hundred rifles, twelve hundred pistols, and four million rounds of ammunition, plus whatever other goodies Nickels had found on the open market.

Moving up the timeline was not a significant problem. The Messenger was already reaching out to their allies across the country. They'd already been planning for spring, after they got the greenhouses planted, but November was better.

When the Dark Time came, the food supply would collapse in a matter of days. The remains of the government would have to focus on that problem. But without adequate refrigeration and fuel for transportation, they'd be shoveling shit against the tide. Canned goods and bottled water would only last so long. Mass starvation would thin the herd. Winter would only accelerate that process.

They were ready.

But first, they had to deal with the betrayer.

With four men working together, they hauled Mishra from the truck, stripped him naked, and lashed his wrists and ankles to the ringbolts set into the punishment wall.

They left the traitor standing alone while the Messenger's People went to the river to collect stones. They stood at the water's edge, selected water-worn rocks, weighed them in their hands. Larger rocks for the men, smaller rocks for the women, smaller still for the children. Three each.

The rain had stopped and it was a fine day, but people did not laugh or smile. It was a solemn occasion. They were addressing a grave breach in their community. The punishment must fit the crime. So said the Protocols. The community must survive. Even if one of the members did not.

They carried their stones up the hill to the punishment wall. They arrayed themselves in a semicircle around the bound man, their stones at their feet. The Messenger stood before them and expressed his sorrow and regret at what must happen.

The failure was his own, he said, for placing his trust in such a weak vessel. He knew the other members were not weak. They were strong, especially together. As he spoke, he made a point to look at each of them, one by one, man, woman, and child. When the Messenger's eye met Hollis's, he felt again the electric force of the man, and a profound gratitude for being included in his vision.

Then the Messenger stepped away from the wall and into the semicircle. "Now is the time for punishment," he said, his voice rising. "Who will cast the first stone?"

Hollis had chosen one slightly smaller than a baseball, round and smooth from the river. He didn't like being a part of the punishment, but he'd signed the Protocols, too. It was his duty. More than that, as the Messenger's right hand, he needed to set an example.

He stepped forward and threw.

Four hundred stones followed. Then eight hundred more.

It was the principle of the firing squad, the Messenger had explained to them all early on. No single person was responsible for the punishment. Instead they bore the weight together, in the old way. The ritual was powerful. Rather than divide the community, it brought them together.

Mishra was not the first man who had been tied to the punishment wall. Nor would he be the last. Anyone who broke the Protocols was subject to punishment. Four men had been found stealing community property. A fifth had thought that his wife should be exempted from the Messenger's personal initiation, no matter that he'd signed the Protocols that enumerated the Messenger's privileges. Two other men had tried to leave with their families. Hollis had found those punishments especially difficult, because of the women and children.

But not all crimes were capital crimes. Others, such as laziness, greed, or excessive drunkenness, led to beatings. Depending on the severity of the offense, the Protocols dictated the diameter of the stick and the number of blows. Then, as evidence of the Messenger's mercy, the punished would be received into the bosom of the community again, his wounds salved. If he had no man or woman to share his bed, one would be given to him until the scabs fell away. None of those punished had ever offended again.

It was proof of the Protocols, of the vision, of the Messenger himself. The way of the future.

The Dark Time was coming. It was inevitable.

Sitting in the Rivian in the office building's parking lot, Hollis finished his fourth cigarette and stuffed the butt in his pocket. A spot had opened up next to the blue minivan, so he'd moved to occupy it. He glanced at his watch. Four forty-five. It wouldn't be long now.

There was a knock at the window and Nickels's cousin Vance slipped into the passenger seat. The SUV's springs sank with a groan. Vance was a big boy, and not a bit of it fat.

Nickels climbed into the back. "We parked five blocks away, like you said. What's the plan?"

Hollis told them.

"In broad daylight?" Nickels asked. "On a busy street? Just the three of us?"

Vance turned to look at him and Nickels shut up.

"The clock is ticking," Hollis said. "We need to take some players off the board. We have another journalist sniffing around. And we need those damn black-tips you lost. This thing won't work without that armor-piercing ammo. Unless you got a better idea?"

Nickels shook his head. "No, I'm in. Anyway, I got my own axe to grind."

Hollis stared at him. "This isn't personal, Nickels. This is about the Movement."

Vance spoke for the first time, his voice like gravel in a gearbox. "Everything is personal, Hollis. Especially the Movement. But don't worry. It's just more motivation."

The office building's door opened and a sturdy brown man stepped out, eyes roving alertly. A moment later, he gestured and a woman and young girl followed him into the parking lot.

"This is us," Hollis said. "Remember, we need them alive." He pulled up his mask, picked up his pistol, and opened his door.

Vance and Nickels did the same.

That's when the shouting started.

45

PETER

In the storefront office, Peter began to methodically search for anything else that might tell him what the Messenger was planning. He flipped through the pages of the Unabomber Manifesto and found nothing. He checked under the bunkbed mattresses and patted them for telltale lumps, then checked the seams where someone might have sewn up an opening. More nothing.

He returned to the front room and double-checked the junk mail, then went through the storage room, moving the empty shelves one by one to make sure there was nothing beneath or behind them. Then he stuck his head into the utility closet again, looking for anything unusual or out of place. The slop sink with its shower attachment caught his eye. He shone his flashlight into the floor drain and saw water gleaming in the p-trap. In a vacant building, with normal evaporation, it should be bone dry.

He went to the toilet and opened the lid. It, too, still had water. So did the cheap saucepan in the bottom of the sink. He thought about the hot plate and the mini-fridge in the office. Someone had been living here.

Were they *still* living here?

He went back to the office and opened the mini-fridge. It held two cans of Monster Energy drink and a partial carton of chocolate milk. Just like Reed's fridge in his apartment. He opened the carton and took a cautious sniff. It still smelled good. Once opened, milk would go bad after a week. Someone had been here less than a week ago.

Not wanting to miss anything, he stepped back for a wider view of the room and realized someone had stacked an assortment of empty cardboard boxes under the worktable. He picked one up and shook it out over the table, dumping the contents. He found only the packing cardboard and plastic bag that had been wrapped around whatever had been inside.

He examined the box itself. There was no identifying information on the outside. Just a notice that the contents contained lithium-ion batteries. From the size of the box and the packing cardboard, it would be a large battery, almost the size of a shoebox.

He stuffed the waste back in the box, then picked up the next one. It was identical to the first, with the same battery notice. Shaking out the contents, he found the same packing materials and plastic bag. Another battery, he figured.

The next two boxes were a different size, with Chinese printing on one side. He shook them out. More packing materials and plastic wrapping, but nothing else. The last box was different again. He shook it out, too. Same nothing.

Except one of the bags made a faint clicking sound as it hit the table. He sifted through until he found what had made the noise. A clear plastic propeller, thin as a blade, more than a foot long.

Batteries and propellers. He thought back to a title on Geoffrey Reed's bookshelf. *Build Your Own Drone*. He remembered Reed's toolbox with its many screwdrivers, pliers, wire cutters, and other hand tools. Including a soldering iron.

Reed had been here. Recently. Peter was sure of it. Using the storefront as his workshop. Building a drone.

Judging by the propeller, it would be a big one. Or maybe two of them, because there had been two batteries. But why?

He thought about the war in Ukraine, where Ukrainian soldiers had taught themselves to weaponize drones. Surely there were instructions on the dark web by now.

Then he thought about the upcoming Conference for the Future at the Seattle Center.

He pulled down his shirtsleeve and wiped off everything he'd touched that would hold a print, including the light switches and the crushed lock. Walking back through the storage room, he hit the button to roll down the door. As it began to descend, he slipped beneath it and hopped down into the weeds. The rain had picked up again. As he walked down the alley, the wind shifted into the northwest, carrying with it the fetid smell of rotting seaweed.

He knew Reed wasn't coming back, because he was dead. But whatever was going on, others were involved. Maybe Circuit Rider was staying here, cooking on the hot plate and showering in the utility room. Maybe he'd just stepped out for groceries.

Peter climbed into the Tahoe and drove a block, then pulled a U-turn and parked in front of the shooting range, where he had a clear view of both the storefront's main door and the alley entrance. He killed the engine and sat with the .357 on the console and his fists clenched on his thighs, thinking of KT's last few moments. Thinking of Ellie.

If he was lucky, one of these assholes would show up.

Peter was going to do his best not to kill him.

But if it happened, he sure as shit wasn't going to feel bad about it.

Waiting, he called Captain Durant, left a message saying what he'd found and that he was keeping watch outside. Time passed slowly. Impatient, he checked his phone several times. Durant didn't call back.

Instead of hitting redial, Peter texted June's burner, keeping one eye on the street. "Just left the storefront. I found another brochure for Resilient Systems, just like at Reed's apartment. The owner's name is Garrison Bevel. He might be our guy. The company used to be located at the storefront. Also I think someone used the storefront to build some kind of drone. Call me when you get this."

He saw the three dots that meant June was looking at his text. A moment later, she responded. "I'm talking with someone who met the Messenger. Learning a lot. Call you when I'm done."

A few minutes later, another text arrived, all caps. "CAPTAIN DURANT MAY BE INVOLVED. AVOID AT ALL COSTS."

Well, hell, Peter thought. Suddenly, Durant's unwillingness to help made all kinds of sense. The problem was that he'd just left a message telling Durant where he was. The captain didn't know what Peter was driving, but his was one of only four cars parked on two city blocks.

Then his phone rang.

It was Manny. "Three men ambushed us at the shrink's office. They took Carlotta and Ellie."

Peter had never heard Manny sound frantic before, but he was frantic now.

"Shit. Are you hurt?"

"No. They had me dead to rights, Peter. I never even got my gun out. They put hoods over their heads and threw them in a blue car. They even shot up Carlotta's van so I couldn't follow."

Peter could hear the pain in his friend's voice. Like what Peter felt for losing KT, only a thousand times worse. And it was all Peter's fault for getting him involved. He clamped down on his shame and anger. "Damn, Manny. I'm so sorry. What can I do?"

"They knew your name, Ashes. They want you and the black-tip ammo. They'll trade both for Carlotta and Ellie. They said to check Telegram for where and when. They said you'd know what that meant."

Peter felt the dragon wake inside him. "I don't, but I think June does. I need to call her. Ping me your location, I'm coming to pick you up."

Manny cleared his throat, struggling to regain his equilibrium. Finally he said, "I can't ask you to trade yourself for them, Peter."

"You don't have to ask, brother. I'm on it. We'll get them home safe. No matter what."

Just like the old days, Peter thought, starting the Tahoe's engine. Never leave a man behind.

In his civilian life, Peter had extended that ethos to everyone he cared about. If you were in his orbit, you were an honorary Marine.

Man, woman, and child.

46

JUNE

June was still talking with Wilkinson when her phone rang.

It was Peter. She didn't pick up. She didn't want Wilkinson to walk out while she still had questions.

Her phone rang again. She looked at Wilkinson. "I'm sorry, I need to take this." She put Peter on speaker. "What's up?"

"Someone took Carlotta and Ellie. They want to make a trade for me and the ammo we took from the Gun Club. They said to check Telegram for the details."

June closed her eyes. After everything that had happened to Ellie, now this? And Carlotta? They must be scared to death.

"Hold on." She pulled the burner from the foil and opened the app. There was a new message with a photo. The bottom dropped out of her stomach when she saw it. "I got a picture of two women in hoods, like fucking ISIS prisoners. They want you in Auburn at five-thirty. If we call the police, Ellie and Carlotta die. If you don't bring the armor-piercing ammunition, Ellie and Carlotta die. If you bring anyone else with you, if they find a tracking device, if they see anyone following—"

"I get it," Peter said. "Ellie and Carlotta die. Do they say anything about an exchange of hostages?"

"Nothing," June said. "Just instructions for you."

"Okay, we'll play by their rules. Traffic's a mess. Getting to Auburn in that time frame won't be easy."

Now June felt like she was going to throw up. "Peter—"

"I have to get moving, Juniper. I don't have time to grab Manny. He's in Greenwood, I'll text you the address. Whoever you're with, show them the brochure picture of Garrison Bevel and see if he's the Messenger."

"Peter, wait. Are you really going to do this? Put yourself in these lunatics' hands?"

"It's not Ellie's or Carlotta's fault they're in this shit situation. It's mine."

"No, it's Circuit Rider's fault, the Messenger's. *They* kidnapped two innocent people. Not you."

"So you think I should do nothing? Abandon Ellie and Carlotta? Leave Manny to find them by himself?"

She let out the breath she'd been holding. She didn't like it, but she knew he was right. Also, the man she loved would never abandon someone he cared about, no matter what it cost him. "Of course you should help. But maybe you shouldn't hand over that armor-piercing ammunition."

"Right now, Juniper, I don't have a choice. So I'm going to do what I need to do, and have faith that you and Lewis and Manny will figure out how to save my ass and stop the bad guys. Did you learn anything useful today? Like maybe where they're taking me?"

She told him about the confrontation with Troy Boxall and his declaration that the Dark Time was coming sooner than planned. She told him about Sanjay Mishra, the fact that he was missing and almost certainly KT's whistleblower, and what she'd learned from Isaac Wilkinson about the so-called Movement. "The Messenger has a compound, we think an old summer camp somewhere about an hour from Auburn, probably in the mountains to the east. Also, the place they're meeting you is the same place they picked up their members for the grand tour of the compound. So I'm guessing that's where they'll take you, too."

"Unless they have another hideaway," Peter said. "It won't be the storefront, because I already told Durant I've been inside, so he won't risk your knowing about it."

"From the descriptions I have of the compound, it's isolated and self-sufficient. If they're going to pull the trigger on the Dark Time, whatever the fuck that is, I'm pretty sure they'll go there to weather the storm. Problem is, we don't actually know where it is. Although I have some ideas about finding it. I'll do some digging online while Lewis drives."

"Sounds like a plan," Peter said. "Will you send me a screenshot of the meet details? I don't want to get this wrong."

"Sending it now." Her fingers flew across her screen. Then she got up and walked away from Wilkinson and Lewis and the two security men, turning off speaker mode for privacy. "Listen, Marine?"

He heard something in those two words. "I know. I'm sorry about this."

"That's not it." She cleared her throat, thick with emotion. "I just. I can't lose you."

"You won't," he said gently. "We've been through worse."

"But . . ." She couldn't finish the sentence. She was afraid that if she spoke her greatest fear out loud, it might come to pass. Clearly some of his combat superstitions had rubbed off on her.

"Juniper Cassidy." His voice was soft and low and calm. "You will figure it out. You will find me. I have faith in you. And in Lewis and Manny. There's nobody else I'd rather have on my side. Hell, I'm feeling sorry for the Messenger's people already."

She pulled in a shaky breath. "Okay," she said. "We're on it."

"Gotta go, June. I'll see you soon, okay?"

And then he was gone.

She put the phone down and took a moment to wipe her eyes, then turned back to Lewis. "You get all that?"

He nodded. He had the Beretta in his hand again, radiating potential energy and violence. In other men, that would have terrified her. In Lewis and Peter and Manny, it made her feel safe.

Faraday, the senior security man, was staring at them. He saw it, too.

Wilkinson said, "You're going after this entire organization on your own? With one of you as a captive, in exchange for two kidnapped women?"

"Yes." Lewis looked at Faraday. "Could use a hand, if you're up for it."

Wilkinson said, "I can't have my security detail involved in something like this."

Faraday gave him a short nod. "Understood, sir. Tell HR to backdate my resignation by at least four months. That should give you a buffer in case the optics go bad."

Wilkinson blinked. "You don't have to do this. You could come to New Zealand with me and the rest of the team."

"No, I can't," Faraday said. "Twenty-five years ago, I took an oath. Working for you doesn't negate that." He put out his hand and Wilkinson took it. "Be safe, Isaac."

"Come see me when it's over," Wilkinson said. "All of you."

Faraday nodded, then turned to the younger security man. "Take Isaac back to the office. Tell Carl he needs to beef up the detail, at least four guys at all times. And get him in the air to New Zealand tonight. Whatever the Messenger and his people have planned, if they're successful, things will go to hell in a hurry."

Lewis stood in the open doorway. The rain came down hard outside, and the cold, wet wind pulled all the warmth from the bright little café. "We need to go."

June said to Wilkinson, "Thank you for your time."

Then she walked out into the storm without looking back, Lewis and Faraday hard on her heels.

47

PETER

With two minutes to spare, Peter turned the Tahoe onto the service road for the enormous outlet mall. Its vast parking area was bounded on two sides by a band of wetland and the cloverleaf intersection of two state highways. The other two sides were lined with fast-food restaurants, a movie theater, and a Walmart superstore.

Forty acres of discount retail, Peter thought. American as apple pie. And all of that was just a single node in a seemingly endless sprawl of freight warehouses, corporate distribution centers, big box stores, airplane parts manufacturers, construction supply wholesalers, stacked shipping containers, and semi-trailer sales offices, all the ugly essentials that made the modern economy function.

According to Circuit Rider's Telegram message, the meet was in the farthest corner of the lot, where the oily runoff from all that blacktop drained into a series of retention ponds. Peter pulled over by the guardrail and turned on his flashers as instructed. Night was coming on.

The rain fell in buckets. On the far side of the guardrail, the retention pond gleamed darkly under low clouds, its surface dimpled like hammered iron. The mall itself was at least four hundred feet away and there were no other cars visible from that part of the lot. Either the place had fallen on hard times or the mall's designer had vastly overestimated the amount of parking required.

He didn't know for sure if Durant was actually involved with the Messenger and Circuit Rider. But assuming he wasn't got Peter nowhere. Assuming he was, Peter still had no clue how much of what Durant had told him was actually true. Whether the investigation into the murders at the motel truly was ongoing, or even whether there was a warrant out for Peter's arrest because he hadn't left Ellie with the social worker.

After hanging up with June, he'd reached out to Detective Kitzinger again. She still wasn't picking up, but he was able to leave a long message detailing everything they'd learned, including the contents of the cassette tape, the burner phone, Durant's possible involvement, Ellie and Carlotta's kidnapping, and Peter's plan to trade himself for their safety. He tried not to sound too much like a guy wearing a tinfoil hat. He also gave her June's number and said she had a copy of the recording. Peter hoped Kitzinger was a good enough cop to follow up, regardless of orders from her boss.

He was doing his best not to think about handing himself over to these assholes. The white static wasn't happy. Peter assumed Sanjay Mishra was dead, which meant they'd killed at least three people to make this happen. Peter was betting there were others. Like most soldiers Peter knew, his greatest wartime fear was not that he might get killed, shot, or blown up, but that the enemy would take him captive. There were too many online videos of jihadis torturing prisoners before beheading them. In every mission on every deployment, Peter had made a point to keep one last bullet set aside for himself. So he could control the manner of his own death.

He was no longer at war, but that same fear remained with him. The fear of being helpless and alone at the hands of bad people.

In the distance, a pair of headlights made the same turn onto the service road that Peter had made. Half-hidden by the rain, it headed directly for him. After a few moments it resolved itself into a black Bronco with big knobby tires and fog lights mounted on the roof.

Peter got out of the Tahoe to watch them approach, making sure his empty hands remained visible. The sheeting rain beat down on his hood and the shoulders of his jacket. At the prospect of what was to come, the white static began to crackle up his spine like a battery under the skin.

The Bronco came to a stop twenty yards away. The passenger door opened and Durant stepped onto the pavement. He wore the same black cowboy hat and long black coat he'd worn at the motel, but now he had a heavy black pistol in his right hand.

"Take off your jacket and turn around," he called. "Slowly."

"I need to talk to Ellie and Carlotta," Peter called back. "I need to know they're free."

"You're not in charge, Mr. Ash." Durant leveled the gun at Peter's chest, then tipped his head toward the Bronco's open door. "My friend is on the phone with the others right now. Remove your coat or the females will suffer."

"You'd allow that to happen?"

"It was my idea," the captain said. "You can't make an omelet without breaking a few eggs."

The veteran cop had been a patrolman and a detective. He had decades of practice in situations like this. His hand was steady, the gun was ready. Peter couldn't take him down now if he wanted to. Besides, he'd left the Beretta in the Yukon.

He unzipped his jacket and let it fall. "Are you going after the tech conference?"

Durant's mustache lifted in a slight smile. "No, but it was fun to watch you get wound up about it. There's far too much protection from multiple agencies. I can't run interference on it the way I did on the Katelyn Thorsen investigation. Besides, it wouldn't make a dent in the problem. The Zuckerbergs of this world, the true tech oligarchs, will pull into the sheltered parking garage in armored limos with their security details. You might get one of them, even two, but you'd just make martyrs out of them. You won't slow the march of technology. The problem is systemic. We need a larger, more long-term solution. Ted Kaczynski had the right idea all along."

"The Unabomber? What the hell happened to you, Durant? You're a sworn officer of the law."

"The law is a joke, Mr. Ash. Innocents fall victim and the guilty walk free. I see it every day. The world is becoming lawless. Nobody respects the police anymore. They think we're the bad guys. The courts prevent us from getting justice for victims. We can't get decent recruits. We're paid peanuts to risk our lives for a lousy traffic stop."

Peter actually agreed with him on this point. Being a cop was a difficult and dangerous job. Not unlike being a soldier. But he couldn't agree with Durant's conclusions. "So rather than work to change things, you're just going to fuck everything up?"

"People have tried to change things for generations. The world has only gotten worse. As ever, those with money and power think only of themselves. Do you really believe all this new technology will change that? It won't. It will only make things worse. Until a few men are kings and the rest of us are slaves. The Movement's actions will prevent that from happening. It's a question of morality. We're restarting society from the ground up." Durant gestured with the barrel of his pistol. "Raise your shirt and turn. I need to see if you're carrying."

Peter hiked his fleece past his belly button and spun on his heel. The rain was cold on his face and neck. He knew it would soak through his fleece sweater before long. "Restarting society, huh? Sounds like ending the world as we know it. How will that make anything better?"

"People will no longer be slaves to the Industrial Machine. We know freedom won't be easy. We'll have to work hard. Every individual will be responsible for the safety and well-being of everyone else. Penalties for failure will be swift and merciless. But the rewards will be immense. Community, purpose, and meaning. Folks will own their lives again. They'll be truly free. Exactly what's missing in the Machine world now."

Durant had really drunk the Kool-Aid, Peter thought. "So how will it happen, the Dark Time? What's the plan?"

Durant's mustache lifted again, the smile larger this time. "If the Messenger wants you to know, he'll tell you." He gestured with the pistol again. "Now, take off your clothes, all of them. Not a stitch remains. It's the only way I'll know you're not carrying a tracker."

"It's forty degrees and raining."

"Don't worry," Durant said. "We'll get you wrapped up again in no time."

Starting with his boots, Peter began to strip.

When he was fully naked, soaking wet, and already beginning to shiver in the swirling wind, the Bronco's driver stepped out.

He was bulky and stiff in camouflage pants and hunting jacket that still held the creases from the packaging. He had a hungry smile on his face and a Taser in his hand. He walked toward Peter, the smile widening. "Hold still, shithead. This is going to hurt."

He aimed and pulled the trigger. The pinpoint prongs snaked out on their thin wires and hit Peter in the sternum, right below the purple bruise from the stopped bullet. His heart seized and he couldn't breathe. His chest burned from the current, his entire body rigid as every muscle clenched in excruciating agony. The fact that he was naked and wet only increased the conductivity.

He rocked back on his heels, unable to maintain his balance. Right before he tipped like a felled tree, the current cut out. His heart stutter-started and his muscles released. Then his legs collapsed and he dropped to his knees on the asphalt. The whole thing had only taken five seconds but it felt like an eternity.

He was dimly aware of Durant holstering his pistol, then opening the back of the Bronco and returning with a heavy green canvas utility tarp. He shook out the fabric at Peter's side. "This will warm you up," he said.

Peter no longer needed to get warm. After the blast from the Taser, he was sweating profusely. The pain was fading but he knew he'd ache for days. He reached to remove the prongs, but the fat man triggered the Taser a second time.

Peter went rigid again, his chest on fire, his helpless heart clenched like a fist.

"You like that?" The fat man's voice seemed distant. "Follow instructions or I'll give you another. Or maybe just because I feel like it."

"That's enough, Troy," Durant said. The voltage stopped. Peter fell forward, panting. The white static crackled into his brain, demanding that he react, fight or flight. But he knew he could do neither, not if he wanted Ellie and Carlotta to live.

"Mr. Ash, remove the electrodes and lie face-first on the tarp and cross your wrists behind your back." Durant pulled a pair of handcuffs from his coat pocket. "I know what you're capable of. I need to contain you. For the sake of the females."

Peter did as he was told. His skin was on fire where the prongs had punctured. Durant knelt on his bare back and cuffed his wrists. "I told you to leave it alone, Mr. Ash. Now you pay the price. Where are the black-tips?"

"In the back of the truck." Peter's voice was a rasp.

Durant stood. "Your sidearm and your phone?"

"In the glove box."

Durant nodded at Boxall, who popped the Tahoe's hatch and carried the ammunition and the AK to the Bronco. He made a second trip and returned with Peter's pistol, wallet, phone, and keys, which he handed to Durant.

Opening the wallet, Durant looked at the cash inside. "No way you came by this honestly."

Peter choked out a laugh. "That's funny, coming from you."

Durant slid the cash into his own pocket, then threw everything else into the retention pond. "Is anybody waiting to follow us?"

"No."

"If you're lying, Boxall will take it out on the females. And he likes it."

"I'm not lying."

"We'll see about that." Durant took a step back and Boxall stepped in close and punched the Taser directly into Peter's side. The pain drove all other thoughts from his head. When it was over, Durant and Boxall were pulling the tarp over him and rolling him up like a burrito.

When it was done, he could barely move. Was there enough air in this thing? At least the tarp was canvas rather than plastic. The claustrophobia closed in. He heard the sticky sound of tape coming off a roll as the canvas cinched tight above his head and below his feet.

Someone grunted and he felt himself rise into the air, then thump back down. He was in the back of the Bronco. The white static flashed like lightning in his brain, panic rising, blinding his mind. The Bronco lurched into motion and began to pick up speed. Frantic, hyperventilating, his chest in a vise, he managed to remember to hold his breath. He counted to eight, then released it slowly. Then another breath, deeper this time, another count of eight, followed by another long, slow release. Again, then again, and yet again. Breath by breath he settled into his mind again, not fighting the static. Allowing it to be. *Hello, old friend. Stay cool. We can handle this.*

This time, instead of calling up a mental picture of the sandy beach where he and June had walked not long ago, he pictured Ellie's face when she talked with her mom about pizza at the motel, before everything went to hell. She looked calm and confident and safe. Even though he knew, right now, she was none of those things.

Still, seeing her, he felt his heart rate begin to slow. He had a purpose.

I'm coming, he told her. And I'll make them pay.

48

JUNE

June tried not to think about Peter, trading himself and the armor-piercing rounds for Ellie's and Carlotta's lives. Instead, while Lewis fought traffic on the way to Greenwood Avenue, where Manny was waiting, she pulled the Washington state map from her bag and opened it up. Geoff Reed's circles and lines and hieroglyphics were all over the place, but there was nothing in the rough area Faraday had given them for a location of the Messenger's compound.

Although that gave her an idea. Faraday had thought it was an old summer camp. Refolding the map, she opened her laptop, connected it to her mobile hotspot, and ran a simple search for the sale of a summer camp. In a smaller community, that would be a newsworthy event, especially if it was a Boy Scout camp. She found several mentions of camps sold in the last ten years, but again, nothing even close to the right area. Hmph.

She'd already shown Faraday the photo she'd taken of the Resilient Systems brochure pinned to the wall at Reed's place, folded to the picture of the owner. Faraday had confirmed Garrison Bevel as the Messenger. Now she logged onto her subscription databases, trying to find traces of the man.

Unfortunately, Bevel seemed to be a ghost. She found no

physical address, email, telephone number, real estate, or vehicles in his name. He had no credit history or available banking information. He had no presence on social media or any of the business networking sites. She tried Resilient Systems with the same lame-ass result. Most government websites only kept business information for five years. The company's own website was long gone.

The only mention she could find was a letter to the editor he'd written to the *San Francisco Chronicle* after the 2018 Camp Fire, which destroyed the town of Paradise, killing eighty-five people and causing over eighteen billion dollars in property damage.

As it turned out, Bevel was once an engineer at Pacific Gas and Electric. The letter called out the utility company for poor equipment maintenance. Bevel claimed he'd warned executives of the risk for years, but had lost his job because he wouldn't be quiet. He said he had a simple plan to solve the wildfire problem, citing the ideas of Dr. Theodore Kaczynski, who he referred to as a mathematician and a philosopher.

So the Messenger's inspiration was the Unabomber, June thought. A convicted madman. That's just fucking great.

Of course, the Camp Fire was just one of many fires caused by utility company failures. PG&E was by far the worst culprit, and in the end was found legally liable for multiple wildfires. A private company, it declared bankruptcy because of its inability to pay for damages. After restructuring, it still only paid a fraction of what it owed. And utility-caused fires continued, including the Lahaina fire in 2023 and the Texas Panhandle fire in 2024.

So Garrison Bevel had been proven correct, at least about this.

Just the kind of thing to give a disturbed individual a messiah complex.

Unfortunately, he appeared to have the personal magnetism to turn his obsession into a movement.

In Greenwood, they found Manny pacing in the parking lot. The family minivan lay dead and bleeding on the blacktop. There were no police.

Lewis flashed the lights and slewed to a stop. Before the big Lexus stopped rocking on its springs, Manny pulled open the passenger door, his usually calm face a mask of fear. "Please tell me you know where they are."

"Working on it," June said. "Nobody called the cops?"

Manny climbed into the heavy vehicle. "It happened so fast, I don't think anyone even noticed. Plus they had suppressors on their pistols, so the gunfire was relatively quiet." He looked over at Faraday. "Who's this?"

Lewis made the introductions. "We only got two long guns and three pistols. Can you add to that?"

Manny gave a grim nod. "Get to my place, I'll set us up."

Lewis hit the gas and turned the wheel and the Lexus leapt into traffic through a chorus of angry horns. "Your girls safe or do we need to find someplace to put them?"

"They're still at school. Carlotta's mom is coming down from Bellingham to pick them up. She'll drive them to a friend's cabin in the Cascades until this is over." Manny pulled on his seat belt and turned to look over his shoulder at June. "You got an update on Ashes?"

She glanced at the time. "The meet was an hour ago. They have him now."

Manny swore softly. "I'm so sorry, June."

She looked at him. "Not your fault, Manny. It's ours, for bringing your family into this shit."

"Screw that," Lewis said. "Those motherfuckers killed two people, then kidnapped two more. That's on them, not us. We're just trying to make it right."

At Manny's house, he and Lewis went inside and emerged a few minutes later with several equipment cases and two long duffels that clanked as they were loaded into the Lexus.

Climbing behind the wheel, Lewis said, "Where we going, Junebug?"

She was back on her laptop. "I don't know yet. Head south."

With no luck tracking down Garrison Bevel, she turned her efforts to the Tacoma storefront, which Peter said was still being used as some kind of base of operations. Because he said it didn't appear to have been rented since Resilient Systems had been there, she wondered if Bevel might actually own the building. Plugging the address into her databases, she found the taxpayer's name, 507 Puyallup Ave LLC, with a mailing address in Spokane. Exactly the kind of purpose-made corporation that landlords used to legally and financially separate one property from another. She knew Lewis had done the same thing, back when he was still acquiring apartment buildings.

She also knew that, for every registered corporation, the state of Washington required the name of a so-called registered agent, along with both a mailing address and a physical address. So she went to Washington's secretary of state's website and ran a search for 507 Puyallup Ave LLC.

When the company came up on her screen, she saw both its physical and mailing address in Spokane, the same as the taxpayer's address. She scrolled down to the registered agent. It was something called PNW Registered Agents, which was a service that business owners used as a proxy, in order to keep their personal information off public records. She went to the PNW Registered Agents website, but there was no way to search for customer names. Which made sense, because privacy was the whole point.

If Bevel had gone the registered agent route with the Tacoma storefront, he'd almost certainly have done the same with the compound, wherever it was. She knew it wasn't in Bevel's name, because nothing was in his name. So she was unlikely to find it that way.

Although there was another possible path. She went to the Washington State Department of Revenue and plugged the same LLC into the search bar. Here, instead of a registered agent, there was a section for "Governing People," because the state wanted a contact person in case of legal issues or nonpayment of corporate taxes.

For 507 Puyallup Ave LLC, the governing person was someone named Ann-Marie Wildman.

That was a possibility, June thought. She went back to the DOR site and plugged the name into the search under "Governing People," hoping to find Ann-Marie Wildman on another corporation with, hopefully, a real address.

But the name turned up on several hundred companies, which mean Wildman, like PNW registered agents, likely ran a service for people setting up companies who didn't want their name visible to the public.

June searched for Wildman on her subscription database. She found only two people with that name. One was affiliated with a wildlife refuge nonprofit in Florida. The other ran a business called Wildman Legal Services LLC from an address in Renton, a sprawling suburb southeast of Seattle.

June thought again about Peter, who was by now almost certainly a captive of the Messenger's people. She had to find out where they were taking him.

Wildman Legal was the only lead she had.

She was about to break any number of laws.

"Lewis? I think I just found the Messenger's lawyer. I have an address."

PETER

The Bronco's engine labored in low gear as the struts fought the steep and rutted road. In the cargo bay, wrapped in the tarp and dealing with the static, Peter barely noticed it. He kept his focus on his breathing, and the mental picture of Ellie.

Finally the Bronco leveled out and came to a stop. He heard both doors close, then felt a blast of cold air as hands grabbed the taped ends of the tarp. They dragged him out of the cargo bay and let him fall to the ground with a hard thump.

"Hold on, hold on," a man's voice said. Someone pulled at the ends and the tarp loosened slightly. Then someone took hold of the loose edge of the canvas and gave a great yank, unrolling the burrito until Peter sprawled out cold, naked, and handcuffed in the freezing mud.

He was in an open gravelly area where pickups and SUVs were parked at haphazard angles, lit by the yellow glow of two sodium pole lights. A wet snow fell softly, just beginning to stick to the evergreens ringing the space. Through the trees, he saw the faint silver mesh of a chain link fence topped with razor wire.

Nickels and another man, bearded and very large, stared down at him. The large man was holding the muddy tarp bunched in his fist. "He don't look like much to me, Nickels."

"He killed my brother, Vance. He stole our shit. So I'm gonna do him some damage." Nickels wound up and kicked Peter hard in the stomach.

Peter saw it coming and managed to tense his abdominals, but it still hurt like hell, especially after the full-body clench caused by the Taser. Better than getting kicked in the head, though that was likely on the menu. He might have made it to his feet and taken Nickels down, even with his hands taped behind his back. But the large man, Vance, was another story. For him, Peter would need both hands and a baseball bat. Or an elephant gun. Plus, fighting back right now wouldn't help anyone.

So he simply looked at Nickels and said, "Where's Ellie? Where's Carlotta?"

Boxall, the Bronco's driver, still wearing full camo, looked eagerly over Nickels's shoulder. "Can I get in on this?"

Durant walked up in his cowboy hat and black slicker. "Fuck off, all of you. Except you, Vance. Get him up. The Messenger's coming."

Vance bent and grabbed Peter's arm roughly and jerked him upright. "You better behave."

Peter's bare feet were ice cubes in the mud. The Bronco's cargo area hadn't been heated, and now he was fully exposed and trembling with the cold. "Durant, where are Ellie and Carlotta? We had a deal. Let them go."

Durant nodded at Vance, who casually backhanded Peter in the face, almost knocking him to his knees. "No talking," the big man growled.

Behind them, a familiar warm voice said, "Stand aside, men. There is no need for this violence."

The others shuffled back and Garrison Bevel stepped into view, his face older but familiar from the brochure photo. His thick shock of hair had turned white and stuck up in all directions as if he'd jammed a knife into an electrical socket. His long face was canyoned like a desert landscape marked by eons of erosion. In person, his eyes were large and luminous, and he stared at Peter as though he could see something deep inside him, something essential and unique. Even bound, naked, and seriously pissed, Peter could feel the magnetic force of the man.

Nickels spoke up. "Sir, this man killed my brother. I want justice."

"Rightly so, my friend. And you shall have it. But not like this." The Messenger didn't take his eyes off Peter. He had the same rich and sonorous voice as in the recordings, at once theatrical and utterly natural. Behind him, more people had begun to gather.

"You all signed the Protocols," he said, playing to the small but growing crowd. "We have a method of justice, do we not? You will have a chance to express your grievance, all of you, when he is taken to the punishment wall."

"I brought the black-tip ammo," Peter said. "Release my friends."

The Messenger smiled. "I have changed my mind. They will stay here. When the Dark Time comes, they'll be safer with us."

"Is that how you lead this movement?" Peter asked. "With lies and broken promises? What other promises have you made to these people that you will choose not to fulfill?"

The Messenger's smile stayed in place, but something hardened in his eyes. "You are mistaken, friend. I am simply thinking of what would be best for young Eleanor and Miss Carlotta. But you are correct in that we had an agreement. So tomorrow, when the Dark Time comes and the Undoing begins, I will give them a choice." He gestured at the stunted evergreens and the falling snow. "To be out there in the darkness, in the chaos and hunger and violence, or to remain here, in the light, where they will have food and shelter and safety. A community."

The group murmured its agreement. They were young and old, men and women, Black and white and shades of brown, but they shared a weather-beaten quality, their cheeks hollowed and their shoulders bent under invisible weights laid there by a hard, uncaring world. Peter could see it in their faces, the need to believe in something. To believe that they mattered.

Peter felt the pull himself. He had his own share of sorrows from his time at war. Good friends dead for reasons that no longer made sense to him. He often felt it had all been for nothing.

How easy it would be to fall under the Messenger's spell, he thought. To take your hands off the wheel and allow someone else to steer your life. Rather than wrestle with your own doubts and fears, the uncertainties of fate and the relentless economic and social changes that came faster every year.

No matter that the Messenger was driving them off a cliff. Before gravity took over, they would have a brief sensation of flying.

The Messenger watched Peter closely, as if he could hear the thoughts flickering through the naked captive's mind. His eyes grew soft and kind. "My goodness, you must be freezing. Let's get some clothes on you." His voice rose to reach the crowd. "Can anyone spare a garment for our friend Peter? Pants, shoes, a warm coat?"

Behind him, another man appeared, thin under a black hardshell jacket and watchful as a coyote on a bombing range. "Here, sir." He held out an old Army coat, a pair of cargo pants, and Army surplus boots without laces. "I took the liberty of checking out a few things from inventory."

The Messenger smiled. "Ah, Hollis. As always, you anticipate every need. Vance, please free our friend's arms and help him dress. Then we can show him to his accommodations."

"Hollis." Peter looked at him as if over iron gunsights. "Or do you prefer Circuit Rider? It's so good to put a face to the name."

Hollis didn't speak, just returned the stare with studied indifference. Whatever awful shit the Messenger had planned, Peter was confident that Hollis was the one to make sure it happened.

When the killing started, Peter would do his best to include Hollis among the dead.

50

Durant removed the handcuffs, but because Peter was so cold, he could barely dress himself. His naked body was covered with mud and there was no way to clean it off. His trembling fingers fumbled with the zippers and buttons. The boots were several sizes too small, and he almost fell trying to cram his feet inside. Vance had to hold him up with one arm. The lack of laces was irrelevant because he could never have managed to tie them.

Disappointingly, once he had the coat on, Durant put the cuffs back on, this time with his hands locked in front of him. Still, cuffs or no cuffs, even with the mud coating the inside of the boots and pants and coat, he felt himself beginning to warm under the heavy clothes.

The Messenger looked at him as if pleased with what he saw, then held out his hand like a game show host toward a prize. "Your female friends are this way. Vance, Hollis, Captain Durant, please join us."

With the others close behind, Peter and the Messenger walked side by side down a wide gravel path strung with lights between two long rows of simple cabins. The first ones were new and built for the ages with stone walls and metal roofs. The last cabins were older and sinking unevenly into the mud. Raw stumps poked up where big trees had once stood. Every south-facing roof was covered with solar panels. Light blazed from every window.

As they walked, Peter saw people heading toward the cabins, clothes and hands dirty from physical labor. They stopped and lowered their heads. Like the crowd in the parking area, Peter could see the weight they carried.

As the Messenger passed each man or woman, he touched their arms and shoulders, his voice soft and warm and gentle. Something in them eased at his touch. They believed in him, Peter saw. Of course they were willing to believe in him, in anything, for even the thinnest promise of relief from the hard realities of a fast-changing world.

But Peter had known men like the Messenger before. At bottom, they were all the same. They were bullies who talked about fairness but all they really wanted was power for themselves and retribution against their enemies.

They continued on, Vance gripping Peter's arm again, his hand like a vise. Hollis was silent.

After the cabins came a square field of green grass, perhaps fifty yards across, ringed with pole lights. At the far side, at the end of the path, stood a large log building with a wing on each side, a deep front porch, and a bare patch at the eaves where a sign had been removed. As with the cabins, every window shone brightly.

"This was the lodge for the former Boy Scout camp," the Messenger said. "Now it's our main headquarters, with staff offices, rooms for counseling and medical care, and classrooms for the children. Beyond it are the group living facilities and more cabins." As if Peter had signed up for a tour and the Messenger was his guide. Maybe he thought Peter would become an investor.

"Here we have our armory and food storage," the Messenger said, nodding at a broad stone building. With its bulletproof exterior, steep metal roof, and tall narrow windows, it was built for minimal maintenance and would be easy to defend. Like a nondenominational church built by Stalin's favorite architect.

"Beyond are various shop and maintenance facilities," the Messenger said, pointing at a row of three hulking, utilitarian boxes clad with galvanized sheet metal, stretching away into the haze of falling snow. "Of course this is only a fraction of our land. We have dozens of greenhouses for year-round food production as well as livestock barns and grazing areas. A creek comes down the mountain, giving us abundant water. We are four hundred strong. No matter what happens in the outside world, we have everything we need to be completely self-sufficient."

"Tell me about the Dark Time," Peter said. "How will it happen?"

The Messenger's eyes twinkled. "That information is held close. Only a few can know the details. You are not one of them."

"That sounds like a man hedging his bets. The police know about you. They're coming."

The Messenger smiled and clapped his hand on Durant's shoulder. "Tom is my eyes and ears in law enforcement statewide. Thanks to him, nobody even knows we exist. And after tomorrow, the police will have more to do than they can handle. In a week's time, most will no longer report for duty. Make no mistake, friend, the Dark Time is coming. All the lights will go out for a very long time."

"You're full of shit," Peter said. "Just like every other nutjob predicting the end of the world. When it doesn't happen on schedule, your followers will leave. Your movement will fall apart."

"Respect the Messenger," Vance growled, then backhanded Peter across the face again, this blow harder than the last. He saw a bright flash and fell to his knees on the cold, wet grass.

The Messenger looked down at him with pity. "You are blind to the truth, friend. Economic mobility is at an all-time low. Inequality is higher than it's ever been, worse than the time of the robber barons. Drug companies are addicting us to their products. Artificial intelligence is coming for our jobs. The government has been captured by moneyed interests. There is no will to change when officials are busy lining their pockets. In the years to come, nothing will get better for ordinary Americans. They will only get worse. So I ask you, which is better, to be dead or to be enslaved?"

He shook his head gravely. "I think you and I would have the same answer to that question. In fact, you appear to be exactly the kind of person we need in our Movement. Strong, brave, loyal, relentless. Like Hollis here. Unfortunately, Hollis believes your loyalty lies elsewhere. He does not think we could ever trust you. Sadly, I must agree with his assessment."

Peter got one foot under him but Vance put a heavy hand on his shoulder, keeping him in place. The Messenger didn't seem to notice. "Don't you see, friend? The industrial world is on the brink of collapse. Storms and wildfires grow more severe every year. Heat waves and droughts last longer. Disease is rampant, one epidemic after another. Our civilization is impossibly fragile. The end is inevitable. All it will take is a nudge to bring it all crashing down. We are simply getting a jump on the apocalypse. When the lights go out, people will get hungry and cold. They will turn on each other. Humanity will devour itself, as it has been doing for centuries, ever since the industrial revolution. But those of us who are prepared, those with the strength and vision and will to survive, we will thrive by returning to the old ways."

"You have a pretty dim view of humanity," Peter said. "I've been to war. I've seen the worst that mankind can dish out. But

I've also seen the best of humanity, who we can be when we're part of something larger, when we're needed. I've also read my history. People aren't perfect, but they usually do the right thing eventually. Whatever you have planned, all you're doing is robbing us of the chance to make things better."

"I wish I could agree with you," the Messenger said sadly. "Unfortunately, you have the wrong reading of history, the wrong reading on humanity. Men are animals. We will only ever be animals. The Dark Time will prove me right. Sadly, you won't be here to see it."

"You talk about the end of civilization, but you're only four hundred people," Peter said. "What about the rest of the country?"

The Messenger smiled. "Our Movement is not alone. I am in contact with a hundred movements just like ours, across the continent and across the world, providing advice and assistance. Each has a plan and stands ready to execute. We are at the forefront. Once we begin, the others will follow our lead toward a simple, honest life on the land, the way it was meant to be."

"Ah, the good old days," Peter said. "Measles and dysentery, women dying in childbirth, a life expectancy of forty. You really are crazy as a shithouse rat."

Vance raised his hand to hit Peter again, but the Messenger shook his head. "Over the years, many have thought as you do. I will prove them wrong. Sadly, you won't be here to see it."

The Messenger gestured to his right, where a small cinder-block building stood aligned with the near corner of the armory. "You will spend the evening in our stockade."

But Peter was staring to the left where a wooden wall stood facing the meadow. Built of heavy planks nailed to a pair of thick posts, the whole thing was maybe ten feet wide and eight feet tall. The raw planks were stained dark in places. A half dozen ring bolts had been installed at the wall's top and bottom. Round rocks of various sizes lay in small piles at each side. Half the meadow's lighting seemed directed at the wall, as though it were a stage.

The Messenger saw him looking. "Ah," he said, as if seeing a birthday cake made just for him. "That is our punishment wall. At midnight, you will be chained to it. Your life will end as the Dark Time begins. You will be our blood sacrifice to the gods of our new world."

51

Vance grabbed Peter's arm and walked him toward the stockade.

Peter didn't fight it. With his hands cuffed in front, he felt better about his chances, but he'd have Hollis to deal with, too. Vance didn't appear to be armed, but Peter had seen the bulge of a pistol on Hollis's hip. Not to mention all the other people in the compound who bought into the Messenger's lunacy. Even if he managed to escape, they would only increase their security as they tried to find him. That would just make things harder for Lewis and Manny.

At the small block building, Hollis told Vance to stand guard. "I'll send someone to relieve you when the time comes." A barred window opening faced the punishment wall, as if to provide a preview of what was coming. The heavy steel door faced the armory. Beside it was another barred opening. Hollis unlocked the door with a key on a ring. Vance pushed it open and shoved a stumbling Peter inside.

The static flared at the size of the cell, plain cinder-block walls maybe eight feet square. There was no heat, no light except what shone through the two small windows. In a corner, a stinking black five-gallon bucket served as the toilet. A dark shadow resolved itself into Carlotta and Ellie huddled together on a cinder-block bench built into the wall.

"Hey, guys," Peter said, putting on a smile. "Nice place you've got here."

"Meatball!" Ellie jumped up, her face bright as a candle flame. She came to give him a hug, then stopped abruptly when she saw the handcuffs. "What the hell? You were supposed to *rescue* us."

"I traded myself for you. They're going to let you go in the morning."

"What about Ma—"

Peter put his finger to his lips, then pointed to the window opening, where the edge of Vance's broad shoulder was visible, and gave her a wink. "Nobody else is coming. They have no idea where we are."

Now Carlotta stood and hugged him. The human contact eased the static a little. In the dim glow of the dying day through the barred window, Peter could see that she had a black eye. "They're not letting us go," she said in his ear. "They already told us that."

"I know," he whispered back. "They're planning to execute me at midnight. At least the French Foreign Legion waited until dawn."

Ellie sat slumped on the cinder-block bench. "Dude, this rescue *sucks*. Did you get the speech from that freak show who calls himself the Messenger? That dude is bananapants."

Peter took a seat beside her, pulling Carlotta closer. "Manny and Lewis are coming for us. I'm not sure when, but it will be tonight. We need to be ready. Get some sleep while you can."

He tried to project confidence. But he was having trouble feeling it. Even if June could locate the compound, then find the stockade in the heart of it, almost everyone he'd seen was carrying a firearm. Manny and Lewis and June weren't going to bring this place down by themselves. That would take a Marine battalion. Breaking them out was the only option. But it had to be before midnight, when he was scheduled to die.

And if they somehow managed that?

They'd still have to figure out what the Messenger was planning.

Then figure out how to stop it before the shit hit the fan.

Thinking, hoping, he sat with Ellie and Carlotta on the bench in the dark, the three of them huddled close for warmth. The cell grew colder. The night deepened. Outside, the wet snow pattered down.

After a while, Vance unlocked the door to admit a young woman with a dirty face and plastic plates. White bread sandwiches with American cheese and mustard, congealed mac and cheese, carrot sticks. No utensils. The young woman was silent as a mouse and kept her eyes on the floor. She filled paper cups with water from a plastic jug, then took the jug with her when she left. Vance stood in the doorway for a moment, eyeballing Peter as if daring him to try something. He didn't.

Ellie looked skeptically at her plastic plate. "If this is dinner after the apocalypse, I don't know if I want to survive it."

Carlotta looked at Peter. He shook his head. He didn't trust the Messenger or his people. The food might be drugged. Carlotta took their plates and dumped everything in the toilet bucket so they wouldn't be tempted to eat it. Ellie scowled.

Peter went to the window. The big man stood before the door, arms crossed. "Hey, Vance."

The big man didn't turn. "Shut up."

"Come on, Vance. I'm a condemned man, talk to me. You really believe the Messenger's bullshit?"

Vance turned to face him with a cruel smile. "The man is a visionary. You have no idea how many people think the way we do. We shipped those black-tips all over the country. The Messenger has contacts all over the world. Once we get things started, the others will join in."

Peter felt his heart sink. "The Messenger said something about the lights going out. All that talk about the Dark Time. He means it literally, doesn't he? You're taking down the electrical grid. But it's all controlled by computer, so that must mean you have a hacker. Is he already inside the system?"

Vance's face went blank. "That's enough talking. Shut your mouth or I'll come in there and shut it for you."

Peter had hit a nerve. "Just tell me the fucking plan. I'm locked in a cell. You're going to kill me at midnight. What can I possibly do?"

Quick as a snake, Vance reached through the bars and tried to grab him by the neck. Peter danced back, feeling those thick fingers brush his skin, then caught Vance's wrist with his cuffed hands and pulled the big man hard against the rebar, torquing the elbow. For a moment he imagined breaking the arm. But that would get him nothing but a quick jolt of satisfaction and maybe an early death.

He let go. Vance pulled his arm back, rubbing the strained joint. "Midnight can't come soon enough," he growled.

52

The night deepened. Another guard came and Vance left.

Peter stood by the barred window, trying to keep the white static at bay. It didn't like the cell, or the fact that he was, for the moment, powerless to do anything useful. He stared out at the compound, hoping to see a friendly face.

Instead he saw a flurry of activity under the pole lights. A pair of four-door pickups pulled up beside the big stone armory. The trucks were rigged for rough travel with oversized tires, heavy-duty winches on their bumpers, and four rectangular five-gallon fuel cans mounted in each bed. Wherever they were going, they'd need more than one tank of gas to get home.

Men got out of the trucks. Peter recognized Hollis, Vance, Nickels, and Boxall. There were three more men he didn't recognize, and also a boy, Ellie's age or younger. They went into the building and returned carrying rifles, ammunition boxes, and other equipment. Getting ready, Peter thought.

Boxall and the boy made a second trip inside and emerged with a pair of black spidery-looking contraptions that Peter couldn't identify. As Boxall passed his contraption to Vance in the back of the truck, it was momentarily turned on its side and Peter saw the rotor arms and propellers. Two large drones. Probably the ones Reed had built.

The boy made a third trip into the armory and returned with a small case on a strap over one shoulder and a big smile on his face. Peter couldn't figure out why he was part of the group.

Two of the men got back into the trucks and drove forward toward the second building and under a high open roof that jutted out from one side. Beneath it were an old gas pump and what looked like the round end of a propane tank the size of a semitrailer. The wooden roof structure would keep the rain and snow off the equipment and the people using it. The other men walked up and began to pull the fuel cans from their racks and fill them from the pump.

"Peter?" Ellie came over to stand beside him. "What's the matter with all these people? What do they want?"

"I'd guess the Messenger wants power and doesn't care who gets hurt along the way. Maybe his inner circle, too. But I think the others are just frightened," Peter said. "Things are changing too fast. A lot of people are getting left behind. They don't feel like they have much control over their lives. And they're mostly right. The modern world is complicated and deeply flawed. But they're wrong to think that some earlier era was any kind of utopia. Even if they're successful, they still won't be in charge of their own lives, not the way they hope. They'll just be subject to the Messenger's whims, along with other forces like the weather or crop failure or disease."

She looked up at him. "So what's the answer?"

"I wish I knew, kiddo. All I know is that we've never had control over anything but ourselves and our reactions to the challenges life hands us. What we do have is the ability to make the best choices we can, and hopefully think further ahead than our next meal, our next paycheck, our next election. If enough of us work together, we can change the world."

"You sound like my social studies teacher, Ms. Olsen."

"A wise woman, I'm sure."

"I don't know about that. She's got, like, ten cats."

"Take your wisdom where you find it, kiddo."

Ellie returned to the bench to huddle with Carlotta for warmth. Peter stayed by the window, watching the men and boy finish filling the fuel cans, climb in the trucks, and drive away.

He was thinking about Garrison Bevel. From the brochure, Peter knew the man was an electrical engineer. He'd worked at PG&E, so he understood industrial power systems. And Vance had shut down when Peter had mentioned the power grid. That had to be the target.

The grid wasn't truly national, Peter knew, but three interlinked regional grids that covered the continental United States, along with parts of Canada and Mexico. Each regional grid contained many smaller subgrids, connected in a complex web of power lines and legal agreements. It was controlled by software that measured demand and shunted power from generating plants to wherever it was needed. The software also controlled multiple safety systems, including giant circuit breakers that would trip in case of overload so the huge electrical loads didn't melt power lines or blow up transformers.

But the software was notoriously full of bugs. The switches and circuit breakers were often forty or fifty years old. National security researchers had been talking about the grid's vulnerability for decades. There was speculation that the Chinese and the Russians had already hacked parts of the system.

Peter figured a brilliant coder like Geoffrey Reed was capable of doing the same. The engineering text on Reed's bookshelf, *Industrial Power Systems*, would have filled in any gaps in his knowledge about the grid. If Reed had finished his work before he died, all it would take would be a few keystrokes by any amateur to trigger the attack.

Except hacking the software wouldn't be enough. They'd have to damage the hardware, too. Power plants were hardened and secure facilities. But they wouldn't have to destroy the generating plants to create a national blackout. The electrical substations, where the power was stepped up for transmission over vast distances on high-voltage wires, were often guarded only by fences. With control of the software, if the Messenger's people managed to destroy substation hardware in a few strategic locations, they could create a cascade effect. Faulty circuit breakers and a few fallen tree branches had accomplished the same thing in the 2003 blackout in the Northeast. Fifty million people had been without power.

Of course, that blackout had only taken four days to repair. The Messenger seemed to think this damage would be permanent. How would he manage that?

It wouldn't be enough to just shut down the grid and wreck a few substations. To keep all those power companies from rebooting the system and bringing it back online, the Messenger's people would have to destroy a lot of hardware. The most vulnerable components were the high-voltage transformers at substations.

This wasn't exactly a secret, either. In the last few years, Peter knew, attacks on substations had more than tripled. Gangbangers and extremist groups shot up transformers with hunting rifles, killing power to towns for weeks, and using the chaos as cover for robberies and revenge killings.

Then Peter realized what the armor-piercing rounds were for. The black-tips would have no problem penetrating the metal transformer casings and shredding the copper coils beyond repair. Transformers were expensive, and power companies didn't keep many replacements on hand. Building a new one was a complex and expensive process. Most were custom-made overseas. There was no strategic national stockpile. It could take several years to replace a single specialized unit.

If the Messenger's movement had truly expanded its reach to other groups across the country? Together they could destroy hundreds of transformers, or thousands. Which meant restoring power could take decades or longer, and would require the combined resources of the entire industrialized world. And not everyone would be inclined to help the United States. China, for example, where most transformers were now made.

Dear God, Peter thought. Could these assholes actually pull this off?

He thought about what would happen if electricity stopped flowing nationwide. First, the heat would go out. The cold would kill many older people, and not just in the northern states. Food shortages would follow immediately after. The food supply network was nationwide, and with no electricity to pump fuel at stations and pipelines, delivery trucks were dead on the road. Few farmers stored their own seed and fertilizer over the winter months. Once food stockpiles were gone, America would starve to death in a hurry.

He really hoped June had figured out where the hell this compound was located.

Then he heard the sound of singing.

53

JUNE

Wildman Legal Services was in a modest townhouse condo in an older development that had seen better days. Beige vinyl siding, peeling paint on the trim, roof shingles turning green from the moss growing unchecked. The street-facing garages were the most prominent feature. The bright porch light was the only thing that differentiated Wildman's condo from the rest.

Lewis pulled the Lexus to the grassy verge in front of the building. "What's the play?"

June knew he would do anything for Peter. Manny, too. But she didn't know Faraday at all, except that, if he was working security for a tech billionaire, he almost certainly had a background in law enforcement.

June opened her door and got out. "Lewis and Manny, let's go. Faraday, you stay in the car. Keep the engine running." She pointed to the old gas-station maps that Peter had found in Reed's apartment. "Maybe take a look at those, see if you can figure out what those markings mean."

Faraday looked at her. She thought he would say something. Instead he just nodded and slipped out of the back seat to climb behind the wheel.

June marched up to the door, Manny and Lewis right behind her, grim and lethal. She pushed the doorbell but didn't hear it ring, so she pounded hard on the blue metal with the flat of her hand.

No answer. She pounded again, this time longer and harder. June was good at getting people to talk to her, it was an important skill for every journalist. But she was asking an attorney to open her client files to three strangers. Conversation wasn't going to be enough.

She was still pounding when the door jerked open to the limit of a security chain and a woman peered out at them from the shadows. She was middle-aged and plump in a faded blue twinset. Her voice was sharp with annoyance. "Don't you see the sign? No soliciting."

She stepped back to close the door. June stuck the toe of her hiking boot into the gap. "Are you Ann-Marie Wildman? Wildman Legal Services?"

"Yes," she said. "Who the hell are you?"

June kept her voice pleasant. "I'm sorry to interrupt your evening, but we need to ask you a few questions. It's about one of your clients."

Wildman's face pinched tight. "I'm an attorney. Client information is privileged. Are you the police? Do you have a warrant?"

"No, ma'am. But we desperately need your help. Two women have been kidnapped."

Wildman looked past June, scanning the street. "Are you filming? Is this some kind of prank? If so, I certainly don't appreciate your involving me."

"It's not a prank," June said. "The women's names are Carlotta Martinez and Eleanor Thorsen. Please, can we talk for a few minutes?"

"Without a warrant? I don't think so. Anyway, I don't see what those women have to do with me or my clients."

"This is taking too long," Manny said. He reached past June and wrapped both hands around the edge of the door by the chain. June pulled her toe from the gap, stepping back to give him room. Manny pulled the door almost closed, then, with a single explosive movement, slammed it open to the limit of the security chain.

June heard a crunch as the chain-plate screws pulled loose from the interior trim. Manny shouldered his way into the entry hall as the lawyer backpedaled up the hall, fear on her face.

"I'm not going to hurt you," Manny said. "But one of those kidnapped women is my wife. The other is a thirteen-year-old girl entrusted into my care. So either you tell us what we need to know or you'll have to watch as we go through your files one by one."

"If you do help us," June added, "we'll leave as quickly as possible."

Wildman already had her phone in her hand. She turned and ran toward the living room, punching the screen as she went.

Manny sprinted after her, caught her wrist, and plucked the phone from her hand. "She called 911." He tossed it to June and clamped his hand over Wildman's mouth.

June fumbled the throw, dropped the phone to the carpet, then picked it up and put it to her ear in time to hear a voice say, "911. What's your emergency?"

"Crap, I'm so sorry," June replied. "Everything's fine here. My five-year-old thought he was being funny."

The voice hesitated a moment, gauging her answer, then finally said, "No problem, ma'am. Have a safe day."

"Thanks, you, too." June put the phone in her pocket. At the end of the hall, the middle-aged lawyer struggled against Manny's grip, eyes wide. June sighed. This was not how she'd wanted things to go. "Ann-Marie, we don't want to hurt you. But we need information or people are going to die. Will you help us?"

Manny unclamped his hand from her mouth. The skin was red where his hand had been. She said, "I told you, it's privileged. If I help you, I can be sued. I could be disbarred."

Lewis had come inside and locked the door behind him. "Not gonna be a problem," he said. "Guy we're looking for ain't never gonna know we even talked to you, not unless you call the cops once we gone. You do that, it's public record. Maybe your other clients find out, too. Won't be good for your business."

Wildman shook Manny's grip from her wrist, then planted her hands on her hips and glared at them all, one by one. "So you're blackmailing me."

"It ain't like that," Lewis said. "Once we get what we need, we're gone. Then you do what you gotta do. I'm just laying out the possible consequences."

"The person you're looking for. If he really did what you say he did, kidnapped those people, who's to say he won't come after me next?"

Lewis looked at her. "He won't."

"How can you possibly promise that?"

Lewis gave her a tilted smile, the cold, hard version that didn't reach his eyes. "Because he'll be dead. That's a promise."

Wildman took an involuntary step back. Her lips thin and white, the tendons standing out in her neck. "You broke into my home. You're holding me by force, against my will. Now you tell me you're planning to kill someone? How are you any different from those kidnappers?"

It was a legitimate question, June thought.

Lewis's eyes softened. "We're plenty different," he said. "The three of us here, we trying to put out the fire. The people we looking for, they the ones lit the match. They already killed two people that we know of, probably more. They're heavily armed and planning some kind of attack. You want to be the person who coulda helped but didn't?"

"Crap." Wildman's mouth puckered like she'd just taken a bite of something rotten. "Fine. Come on." She turned to Manny and put a finger in his face. "But don't you touch me."

"Yes, ma'am," Manny said. "I'm sorry about that. And thank you for your help."

54

The living room was cluttered with too much furniture, a sign of someone who had moved from a much larger home. Ann-Marie Wildman led June up the stairs to an office in a small second bedroom. The walls were bare. Four file cabinets and a desk with a large monitor were the only furnishings. The single personal item was a framed photo on her desk of a middle-aged man grinning for the camera. Wildman pulled out the chair and sat. "What's the name?"

"Garrison Bevel," June said, looking over her shoulder. "Do you remember him?"

"The name's familiar. I have a lot of clients. I never actually meet most of them, we just email. With some, their affairs are more complicated, and I get a little more involved." Wildman hit a key and the monitor lit up. "Conventional spelling?"

"Yes. Would you have been involved in any real estate transactions? We're looking for a physical address, someplace rural, east of Tacoma. Maybe a former summer camp."

Wildman's hands froze above the keyboard. "Really? The old Scout camp? That's the kidnapper?"

"One of them." June found the brochure photo on her phone and showed it to Wildman. "Is this him?"

"I mean, he's older now, but yes. Those same eyes. I set up a few companies for him. But I haven't seen him in years."

"You met in person?"

"That's how he wanted it. He did everything in person. He said he didn't use computers. He even paid me in cash. With the purchase of the old Scout camp, he made me a corporate officer. I signed all the documents. His name's not on anything."

She clicked the mouse a few times, typed for a moment, then stopped and turned to face them. "I just want to say something. My clients are regular people who just want me to help them navigate the bureaucracy and, sometimes, keep their names off public records. People have the right to privacy. It's perfectly legal. If some of them choose to break the law, that has nothing to do with me."

"Of course not," June said. "But maybe some clients give you a bad feeling. Like this guy."

Wildman nodded. "Somehow he knew that my husband had passed away. He said all the right things, but he kept touching me, and he kept asking me questions. Was I all alone? Did I need a friend? The way he looked at me, it was like he could see right through me, all my sadness and pain. Like he was feeding off it."

She sighed. "My name is on all that paperwork. Am I going to be in trouble? If he does something bad?"

"You run a business. He was a client. If the police ever knock on your door, just answer their questions. You'll be fine."

"Like that's going to help me sleep tonight." Wildman hit a few more keys. "Here it is. I'll print a hard copy."

"Thank you. Can you give me everything else you have on him?"

"Sure." The printer hummed. June took the papers from the tray as they came out. The top document was for a real estate purchase on NF-54, which was a national forest road. Five hundred acres. The town was given as Palmer, Washington. June passed it to Lewis. "Is this in the right area?"

Lewis glanced at the pages, then did something on his phone. When he raised his head, his eyes were dark and his jaw was set. "It's right down the road from Nickels's place. Jarhead and I were practically on top of the motherfucker."

It was seven forty-five and well past dark by the time they got back in the Lexus. They were more than two hours behind Peter's captors.

Faraday pushed hard through the traffic, but it was slow going, even for Seattle. Manny sat in the shotgun seat with an oil-stained towel on his lap, field-stripping and cleaning his rifle, the smell of gun oil permeating the car. June was in the back with Lewis, who was looking at the hieroglyphics on the old maps Peter had found. Faraday hadn't been able to make any sense of the markings, but they all were convinced they meant something, if they could just figure it out.

June paged through the rest of the legal documents, hoping to find clues to the Messenger's plans buried in the printouts. Aside from the Tacoma storefront, the only other real estate the Messenger owned appeared to be an apartment in Rio de Janeiro. He'd set up two other companies with Ann-Marie signing as a corporate officer. One was a construction company, the other a farm. Likely done for tax reasons, to maximize their cash flow while they were building up their compound. They both had the same street address as the former Scout camp.

At least she figured out why the sale of a Boy Scout camp hadn't shown up on a simple internet search. The answer was in the closing statement, which listed the seller as a Belleview investment group. June looked them up on her databases and saw that they'd bought the property almost twenty-five years ago, when many rural newspapers hadn't yet gone digital. So June's research skills weren't completely broken.

She'd put her laptop aside and was studying the hieroglyphics on the paper maps when Faraday took the exit for the Auburn Mall. They had all agreed it would be good to collect the Tahoe, if they could find it.

Faraday turned into the parking lot. June pointed him toward the trees in the far corner, where Circuit Rider's text had told Peter to meet him. A minute later, she spotted the Tahoe standing alone under the beating rain. "There it is."

When Faraday pulled up beside it, June had trouble understanding what she was seeing on the ground. When she got out and walked over, she realized the wet heap on the blacktop was a pile of clothes. Peter's clothes. All of them.

Her stomach curdled with fear. She cursed, long and loud.

Those motherfuckers had stripped him naked.

They were going to kill him.

55

June had the Tahoe's extra key. Peter's luggage was still in the back, but there was nothing else. She and Lewis climbed in and led the way down surface streets toward the freeway and the old Boy Scout camp. Each of them had already downloaded a map of that section of the national forest, knowing cell signal could be spotty in the wilderness. On the way to the mall, Faraday had talked them through the layout of the compound. The main entrance and parking area, the cabins, the lodge and armory and greenhouses.

SR 167 was a parking lot. On 18, the rain was brutal and traffic was creeping along at ten miles per hour. They were losing time. Didn't these idiots know how to drive? June's stomach was sour with worry. She wanted to roll down the window and scream at everyone to get the fuck out of their way. She didn't. Raging at the indifferent world wouldn't help.

She checked Google Maps and saw a couple of accidents perfectly placed to bring everything to a halt. She found an overland route and directed Lewis off the freeway. Unfortunately, everyone else had the same idea, and the surface street maze was almost as bad.

In Covington, Lewis pulled into a mini-mall lot, ran into an auto parts store, and came back with two sets of tire chains, leaving one with the Lexus. "All this rain down here, gonna be plenty of snow up in the mountains."

They cut across 272nd Street toward Maple Valley. It was nine-thirty. To calm her mind, she opened the paper map of Washington state on her lap and tried to focus. It wasn't easy. At the moment, June didn't give a fat fuck about the Messenger's plan or the end of American civilization as she knew it. She cared about Peter, Ellie, and Carlotta. Once she got them free, then she'd give a shit about whatever those assholes were planning.

Still, whatever the Messenger was up to, June couldn't count on Peter having figured it out. When they got him back, she wanted to be able to tell him their next step. So she stared down at the clustered hieroglyphics and the lines connecting them, then at the long column of numbers running down one side. Finally, she picked a large circle of symbols outside of Kennewick, pulled out her notebook, and started copying down the pictograms.

One looked like a fat little rolling pin, kind of. Another was a jagged arrow curving up. Another was a jagged arrow that curved down. There was a tiny picket fence, and a tiny stick figure, and a dozen other little images that didn't look like anything, really. A box with an X in it. A box with a dot in it. Some boxes rendered in red, others in green or blue or black. Then circles with vertical lines, circles with horizontal lines, also in multiple colors. All linked to other groups of symbols by the ruler-straight lines.

Again, the whole thing reminded her of a corporate org chart for an extremely complex interconnected organization, or maybe a group of organizations. She stared at it hard, willing the answer to come, but it didn't. There was something to that idea, she could feel it. But she couldn't quite latch on to it.

So she opened her laptop and pulled up a map and zoomed in on that area, comparing the pictograms on paper to the online version. Because the scale was so large on the hard copies, she had to assume the locations were approximations. She scrolled and scanned, both in regular map view and in satellite view, looking for any object that might correspond to a symbol.

Nothing clicked. Fuck. She felt the Tahoe accelerate. She looked up and saw the traffic clearing ahead of them. They were heading into the mountains. On the windshield, the coastal rain had changed to sleet.

She turned to Lewis. "You got a look at these maps, right? Did anything make sense to you?"

He kept his eyes on the road. "Not a lick. And no pressure, but you got about twenty minutes before we ditch the truck."

"Understood." She picked another spot on the map and repeated the process, scrolling and scanning at the new location. Nothing. Lewis mostly kept his eyes on the road, but every few minutes he'd glance over.

"Our turn coming up," he said. "You figure out those numbers on the side yet?"

"Shit, I haven't even tried." She'd looked at them back at Stella's house, thinking maybe they were email addresses or account numbers or numerical passwords. Then Robert had called to say he'd cracked the burner phone, and she hadn't gotten back to it.

"They all the same number of digits?" Lewis asked.

She counted. "Yeah. Fourteen." Then the light bulb went on and she gave herself a dope slap. "Fuck a duck. They're GPS coordinates, but in digital format. How could I miss that?"

Latitude and longitude were usually depicted in degrees, minutes, and seconds. But they could also be depicted as a single number, which June knew from her reporting was a format often used in programming. The first seven digits were latitude, the second seven were longitude. Seven digits meant four decimal places, which would give an accuracy to about eleven meters.

She opened a new browser window and typed the first number into the search bar, leaving a space between the seventh and eighth digit. A map came up. She frowned. "China? Fucking Inner Mongolia?"

Lewis glanced over. "Right idea, wrong hemisphere. Second set of numbers, make it negative."

She went back to the search bar, added a minus symbol after the space, and hit return. A new map came up. The pin was in the middle of what appeared to be empty land, east of the mountains, just off Highway 17. She zoomed in and gained no new details. She zoomed out and that's when she saw it.

"Holy fuck. It's two miles from the Chief Joseph Dam."

She switched to satellite view and went back to the pin. It was the dead center of an enormous electrical substation. Zoomed in all the way, she could even see the power lines running from the dam to the substation, then out to the southwest, toward Seattle.

"The Messenger's going to hit the power grid," she said. But how? By blowing up the dam? It would be a catastrophe, but not exactly a civilization-ender. They'd have to destroy hundreds of power plants to make a dent.

Lewis slowed and took a right onto a low, narrow bridge and crossed the river. Below, the churning water was black in the headlight wash. After the bridge, the road turned to gravel. He accelerated again, the Tahoe bucking wildly over the ruts. Her fingers kept bouncing off the keys. "Pull over for a sec," she said. "Let me plug in the next number."

Braking, he turned his head and looked at her. There was no anger in that stare, but no kindness, either. Instead it was the stare of a seasoned apex predator, hard and flat and utterly without mercy. It didn't scare her. She'd seen the same look in Peter's eyes as he readied himself for a fight.

"You got one minute," he said. "Then we go get our people."

She typed the next number and hit return. She got the blue circle that meant some server somewhere was thinking. But the circle kept circling. She wasn't getting a result. She pulled her cell modem from her bag. The indicator light was off. They were too deep in the mountains.

"No signal," she said. "Fuck it." She knew enough. She opened her notepad to a fresh page and wrote a few lines, then added her master password and showed the whole thing to Lewis. "If something happens to me, use my computer and find those fucknuts."

"Roger that." Lewis glanced at his phone. "We 'bout three miles out."

He took his foot off the brake and the Tahoe rocketed uphill toward the camp.

After another mile of bad logging road, the forest rising steeply on one side and falling away on the other, they came to a derelict turnoff where scrub brush grew up between the tire tracks. Lewis hit the brakes and killed his lights. June had already put her laptop, her notebook, and the paper maps in her work bag. She got out and ran down to the Lexus and handed her bag to Manny through the window, quickly explaining what she'd found and how to keep looking, just in case. Then she returned to the Tahoe while Manny threw the Lexus in reverse and backed up the turnoff until the big white SUV was out of sight behind a curve.

Two minutes later, he and Faraday materialized out of the falling snow with their gear and hopped into the Tahoe. Nobody said a word. June's heart was pounding hard.

Headlights still off, Lewis put the vehicle in low gear and began to climb again, slower now, into the darkness.

56

A mile from the camp, they came to a wide point in the road where a stack of cut logs stood nine feet tall. Lewis reversed the Tahoe behind the pile, tucking the back end into the underbrush until the big SUV was fairly well hidden. The dashboard clock read 10:47. June's nerves were stretched tight as piano wires.

They gathered at the front bumper as Manny unpacked the duffels he'd brought, handing out body armor, weapons, ammunition, radios, and night-vision gear. The night was completely black and the wind had picked up, blowing the heavy wet snow sideways into their faces. The snow still wasn't really sticking, which meant their tracks wouldn't show. A lucky break, June thought.

Lewis left the Tahoe unlocked with the keys above the visor. After a quick look at the downloaded map to get their bearings, they pulled on their packs and Lewis led them single-file across the road and into the trees.

June's armor was heavy on her shoulders as she climbed, the land rising steeply beneath her boots. The forest was dense with towering pines and smaller firs and cedars beneath them. The air was perfumed with evergreens and the smell of decomposing mulch. June's night-vision goggles turned the world a surreal and grainy green. Without them, she would have turned her ankle on a rock or impaled an eyeball on a branch in the first dozen yards.

After forty minutes of rising terrain, the slope leveled out and the shades of green began to brighten as new light filtered through the overstory. They were coming to a clear-cut. Still inside the shelter of the forest, Lewis lifted a fist. They stopped, sank to a knee, and raised their goggles.

They looked out on a chaos of ankle-high stumps, evergreen seedlings, and high slashing tangles of bare blackberry canes, dense and tough and studded with thorns. Beyond that was a line of eight-foot chain-link that stretched to each side until it disappeared into the mist. Coiled razor wire gleamed at the top. The light came from a row of pole lights inside the fence, pointing outward.

Faraday pulled out his phone. They gathered closer. The downloaded satellite view glowed faintly, showing the overall layout. "We're here," he said. "This line of buildings stretching away from us, those are the workshops. At the far end is the armory. It's stone, and a fortress. Running parallel to the workshops on the right is a gravel road, then a row of greenhouses. On the left is the remains of the ground they cleared when they stood up the workshops, with raw forest after that. Ahead, past the armory, is an open green space they call the meadow, with the lodge on the left and cabins on the right."

June's hands were cold and wet on the rifle. Manny didn't have any gloves that fit her. The climb had warmed her, but now that she had stopped, the wind chilled her to the bone. "Where do you think they'll put Peter, Ellie, and Carlotta?"

Faraday put two fingers on the screen and zoomed in. "Just past the armory, off the right corner, there's a small cinder-block building. They said it was an old generator shed, but the window openings had bars on them. I didn't ask too many questions, but my guess is, that's their jailhouse."

It was in the heart of the compound. The muscles flexed in Manny's jaw, the only outward sign of his distress. "Okay," he said. "Let's hear some thoughts about how to do this."

"Any cameras?" asked Lewis. "Perimeter guards?"

"Not that I saw the last time I was here," Faraday said. "Might be different now."

"Either way," Lewis said. "We shoot out the closest light, cut an opening in the fence, and slide up the outside of that line of workshops, head for the jailhouse."

Unspoken was the fact that they were four people. Inside the compound were several hundred.

"And if the jailhouse is empty?" Faraday was playing devil's advocate, gaming it out.

"We try the lodge," Lewis said. "If they're not in the lodge, we try the armory."

"We're going to bump into somebody," June asked. "What do we do when they realize we don't belong?"

"Pull a trigger, but only if we got no choice," Lewis said. "That's how Peter would do it. So that's how it is."

"I'm good with that," Manny said. "Most people won't be out this time of night, anyway. Especially in this weather. Not unless they're seriously hard core."

They all looked at him. Nobody said the obvious thing, which was that a heavily armed mountain compound run by a lunatic with a messiah complex was the definition of hard core.

Faraday said, "And if they're not in the armory?"

"Then we're fucked," Lewis said. "Truth is, we're probably fucked as soon as we hit the lodge. So if we can, we grab the fucking Messenger. He'll tell us where they are. We keep a gun to his head until we find them. Then we beat feet for the Tahoe."

"Getting in will be easy," Faraday said. "Getting out will be a lot harder. Especially if we start shooting people. Everybody in there is armed, even the kids."

"Unless their attention is on something else," June said. "Faraday, you said there were buried gas tanks, a propane tank. Maybe we could start a fire, something like that."

Lewis gave her a tilted grin. "Ooh, I like that."

"Me, too," Manny said. "Faraday, you can find those tanks in the dark?"

The security man nodded. Manny looked at each of them in turn. "Anything else?" Nobody spoke. "Then I think we're good. Lewis, you and Faraday take the diversion, do some damage. June and I will find our people."

Manny checked his watch. "It's eleven thirty-five. Stay on your radios. Meet back here. If we're being chased, fallback one is the Tahoe. If that's compromised, fallback two is the Lexus."

June took out the light with a suppressed pistol. The snow dampened the sound. They waited for ten minutes, but nobody came to investigate. Manny pulled a pair of heavy-duty bolt cutters from his pack. "Let's go."

Bent low, they worked their way through the tangle of brush, blackberry thorns tearing at their clothes. At the fence, Manny bent and began to cut the chain-link from the ground up to his chest, then returned the bolt cutters to his pack and they slipped through. The breach was large. Any capable patrol would see it. But once they found the captives, they'd be leaving in a hurry.

Inside the fence, the clear-cut continued. They stowed their night-vision gear and walked toward the nearest building carved out of the trees. Eighty feet long, dull metal siding, metal roof with solar panels, no windows. On the right, a rough two-track ran parallel to the line of structures toward the brightly lit center of the camp. On the left, rocky ground with knee-high ferns.

They walked through the ferns to the far end of the building, where they saw a roll-up door and a weedy patch of hardpacked dirt between it and the next building. They didn't see a living soul. They continued through the ferns along the second building, which looked a lot like the first. At the far corner, Lewis peeked and waved them across another packed dirt patch to a third building, which was the same as the first two. They kept moving forward. Their boots tore at the soft, wet undergrowth.

At the far end of the third building, a low rumble rose through the hush of the snow. Lewis put up a fist and they all sank to the ground. He peeked and drew back. The rumble grew louder and resolved itself into engine noise, at least two vehicles. Then the thunk of heavy doors and men's voices rising and falling, although the words were too faint to make out.

The wind gusted cold along the edge of the building. June looked toward the trees and realized that the snow was beginning to stick on branches and undergrowth. Soon it would stick on the ground. So much for luck. The longer it took them to free the captives, the easier it would be to follow their trail.

She turned and peered past Manny and Lewis. Across the clearing, which was gravel, the fourth building was made of stone, with tall, skinny windows and a steep roof. The armory. Beyond it to the left, through a line of trees, June could see a large log building, all lit up. The lodge. They were close.

The men's voices came and went. June checked her watch. It was ten minutes to midnight. She heard car doors closing. As the engine noise grew closer, Lewis peeked again. Then the engine noise went silent. His voice came softly over her earpiece. "Two trucks, at least four men, maybe more. I think they're directly on the other side of this building."

Faraday said, "That's the gas pump and the propane shed. Maybe they're fueling up."

"Any action we take starts the clock," Manny said. "Unless there's a threat, we hold here."

"Roger that," Lewis said.

They waited. June's hands were frozen. She put them in her jacket pockets, clenching and unclenching to keep the blood circulating. She wondered if she'd have to kill somebody. She'd killed a man once before, out of self-defense. She'd thought about it for months afterward. She didn't want to do it again.

But then she pictured Peter, stripped naked in the rain in that mall parking lot, willingly trading himself for Ellie and Carlotta. She kept thinking about what the Messenger's people had done to him. What the Messenger might yet do to all of them, if she couldn't find them. And knew she was ready to kill any man or woman standing between her and Peter, Ellie, and Carlotta.

57

After what seemed like a very long time, the truck engines started again, then rumbled louder. Lewis peeked around the corner of the building. "They're leaving." The noise faded until it disappeared into the hush of the snow.

Manny said, "What do you think, Lewis?"

"Hold up," he said. "More voices."

Then June heard them, too. Just a few at first, then more and more. They were singing. She couldn't make out the words, but the tune was familiar. "What the hell?"

"It's a community thing," Faraday said. "That's what the Messenger said, anyway. Like their version of church. Sometimes after evening meal, they sing. But I don't know why they're doing it now."

June thought about her conversation with Troy Boxall. He'd told her they'd moved up the schedule. "It's happening," she said. "Whatever they're doing, it's happening now."

"We need to move," Lewis said.

"Agreed." Behind June, Faraday rose to his feet.

Manny did the same. "Okay. We go. Time to split up. Keep in touch."

After another peek around the corner, Lewis waved them forward, then slipped around the corner toward the gas pump. Manny continued across the clearing toward the stone armory. June followed, rifle up, heart beating fast. Behind her, she heard the crunch of a footstep in the gravel and glanced over her shoulder to see Faraday following Lewis. Now the clock was ticking.

As she got closer, she identified the song. "I Shall Be Released." She knew the Nina Simone version, but she wasn't sure who wrote it. As she crept along the side of the armory, the singers went silent for a moment, then began something new. She recognized it immediately. "This Land Is Your Land," by Woody Guthrie. She didn't get it. Fucking folk songs?

They reached the end of the armory. The line of trees helped hide them from the grassy meadow ahead and the lodge on the left. Manny crouched and peeked around the corner to the right. June leaned forward and looked over his shoulder. She saw a small cinder-block structure with a heavy steel door and a small window opening blocked by metal bars. No light came from inside. A single guard stood at the building's far side with his back to them, craning his neck to see something beyond. He wore a dark green rain slicker and carried an AK-47 over one shoulder. Snowmelt dripped off the roof onto his hood.

The singers launched into another verse. Manny turned to face June. "Wait here," he whispered. Before she could answer, he unholstered his pistol, crept silently up behind the guard, and cracked him across the skull with the pistol. The guard staggered. Manny grabbed his hood and pulled him back from the corner and whatever he was looking at there.

The guard tried to fight him. Manny hit him again and the guard dropped. Manny took a wrist and hauled him behind the armory, where he pulled a roll of duct tape from his pack. June looked at the guard's face. He was just a kid, no more than eighteen. Manny slapped a silver strip over the kid's mouth, then rolled him over and began to tape his wrists behind his back.

June crept up to the jailhouse window and peered inside. Several figures were huddled together in the dark. "Psst," June whispered, then put a finger to her lips. The figures separated and came to the window. Carlotta and Ellie, wearing their coats, eyes haggard but now hopeful. June reached through the bars and they clasped hands. "We're getting you out of here. Where's Peter?"

"They took him," Carlotta said softly. "Right after they started singing."

Manny came up, grinning widely at Carlotta as he took a heavy sledgehammer from his pack. "Wait," June whispered, then went to peer around the corner of the jailhouse, trying to see what the guard had been looking at.

She caught a side view of Peter standing before a freestanding plank wall. He wore an ill-fitting coat and pants, a stranger's boots without laces. His wrists were cuffed and raised over his head, held by another pair of cuffs to a large ringbolt set high in the wall. He did not look happy.

The singers were arrayed in front of him in a broad semicircle. Hundreds of them, men, women, and children. Each held a couple of rocks. Even the children.

June jumped back and put her hand on the big hammer, stopping Manny's swing. If he started pounding at the jailhouse door, the mob would come running. She pointed around the corner and he went and looked at the crowd. When he returned his brown face was pale.

June leaned close and whispered, "Got any ideas?"

Manny nodded and keyed his earpiece. "Lewis, if you're going to make some noise, now's the time."

"Thirty seconds. You gonna love it."

June said, "Give me those bolt cutters. When Lewis kicks things off, I'll get Peter. You get Carlotta and Ellie. If things get messy, we'll meet you back at the Tahoe."

Manny nodded, his face tight as he slipped off his pack and gave her the tool. Then he squeezed her shoulder. "You'd have made a helluva Marine."

"And I know why he calls you brother." She leaned in and kissed his cheek.

The singers came to the end of the song. After a moment, they heard someone begin to speak, projecting to the crowd. It was the Messenger, Garrison Bevel. June recognized his voice from that freaky-ass tape.

She peeked around the corner again and saw him standing in front of the crowd, wearing a raincoat and wide-brimmed hat. His back was to Peter. The snow was falling again. "Good evening, my friends. Today is a glorious day for our Movement. As I stand here before you, our friends are on their way to make history and change the world. Before the sun rises again, the Dark Time will be upon us. The future, our future, begins now."

On the recording, the Messenger's voice was compelling. In person, it was even more powerful. It rose and fell, warm and wise, like a loving father talking to his beloved children. Even knowing what she knew, June found herself falling into the cadence of it.

"This man before you has tried everything to stop us. He hates everything we stand for. He has already murdered two members of our Movement. He would murder us all if he could. Like the world we are leaving behind, this man is beyond redemption. And for that reason he must die."

June looked at the faces in the crowd. They could have been anyone. Her neighbors, her coworkers, someone she passed on the street. She wondered what had happened in their lives to bring them to this dire place.

The Messenger kept talking. "However, as hateful as this man might be, as much as he might deserve to die, his death will serve a much larger purpose. As our great project begins, his death will be an anointing, a blood christening of the new world we are making. And you, my friends, through your participation in this ancient ritual of sacrifice, will bring forth a fresh flowering of humanity like nothing the world has ever seen." He rubbed his hands together. "Now, friends. Are you prepared?"

A roar came from the crowd. They brandished their rocks, their faces clenched in anger. June didn't want to believe they might be evil. Surely something in their lives had broken them down, changed them. They didn't start out like this, she was certain of that. No baby came into the world already wanting to burn it down. It was the Messenger who had taken their pain and twisted it, distorting their hearts and souls. He had made them into this mob, ready and willing to kill for him. To trade their souls for any hope of easing their suffering.

But they had also chosen this path of their own free will. And choices have consequences. So June would do what she had to do to save Peter.

She keyed her earpiece. "Lewis, seriously, fucking go already."

"Roger that, Junebug. Better cover your ears."

At first, she didn't hear anything. A flickering orange light appeared behind the high roof of the armory, brightening the faces of the crowd. A minute later, she heard short disciplined bursts of rifle fire.

Then came a vast crackling *whump* and a huge red-orange fireball rose into the night sky.

June turned and looked at the crowd. They stood in shocked stillness, staring at the towering flames. June waited, wondering what they would do. After a moment, debris began to fall from the sky. Burning wood, scorched pieces of sheet metal.

Then the crowd broke, people running in every direction.

June sprinted toward Peter, pistol in one hand and bolt cutters in the other.

58

PETER

When the singing started, Durant came to the stockade door with three other men. They all had nightsticks. Peter was more than ready to fight them. Even with his hands cuffed, if he could get a stick, he'd have a chance.

Durant must have seen it in his face. "You come easy, the females stay safe. You make it hard for us, I'll give them to Vance."

He let Durant take him.

People had already begun to gather on the grass. They saw him and sang louder.

Durant's men hauled Peter to the plank wall, where the lawman took out a second pair of cuffs and clicked one end through a high ringbolt. "Raise his arms."

Now Peter knew how this would go. He struggled against the fists clenched in the fabric of his coat, but the others kept their grip. "Hold him, for God's sake," Durant said, then wound up with the nightstick and swung at Peter's head. He saw it coming and shifted and managed to take the blow on his raised shoulder. It felt like getting kicked by a mule. Durant raised the nightstick again. "You're making it hard. Is that what you want for those females? Vance is one rough bastard."

Fuck. Peter forced himself to allow the others to raise his arms. Durant closed the other cuff around the chain linking the shackles on his wrists, leaving Peter tethered like a goat.

A big Mercedes SUV pulled up the lane between the rows of cabins and the Messenger got out and walked through the crowd. He was standing in front of Peter when the singing stopped. He began to give a speech in the falling snow. Durant stood to the side and listened, head turning as he scanned faces, looking for signs of trouble.

There were plenty of guns in the crowd, Peter thought. If he could get free, he could at least do some damage before they killed him. And he wouldn't be a fucking sacrifice for the new glorious age of mankind. So he pulled hard at his cuffs, feeling his wrists burn and blood flow as the metal cut into them. He wasn't getting anywhere. The shackles were too tight and his hands were too big. He wondered how he might break his thumbs, and whether that would be enough to let him pull free. But then he'd have trouble firing a gun. He wondered where June and Manny and Lewis were. Whether they were all right.

In the crowd, people muttered and hefted their rocks. He felt his chest tighten. He closed his eyes and took a long breath in and pictured June on that beach. Tuning out the droning voice, he conjured up every detail he could remember. The summer sun, the lake lapping at the sand, her vivid green eyes filled with mischief. If he was going to die, he would die with a smile on his face.

Then, as the Messenger finished his rant, Peter heard the unmistakable sound of gunshots, maybe a hundred yards away. *Pop. PopPopPop. PopPopPop.* He opened his eyes. From behind him came the angry roar of a large explosion. A thick wave of pressure and heat washed over him, warming the planks at his back.

Then a chunk of burning wood fell to the ground between the Messenger and his flock. The crowd fell apart as people ran.

Most fled the fire, including the Messenger, with Durant beside him. A dozen or more men had rifles slung over their shoulders. They ran past Peter, headed for the explosion.

Then June was sprinting toward him, her face grim, a pair of bolt cutters in her hand.

He smiled. The cavalry was here.

She cut him down, then cut the chain between his cuffed wrists. He still wore the bracelets, but he could move freely. He wiped his blood-slick hands on his pants and scanned the frantically dispersing crowd. Nobody was paying any attention to them. "Did you get Carlotta and Ellie?"

A metallic thump carried from the stockade. "That's Manny now." She grabbed his coat and kissed him hard on the lips, then handed him her rifle and a spare magazine. She took her pistol from her pocket. "Where's that shithead Messenger?"

Peter pointed toward the row of cabins. "He went that way." As much as Peter wanted to collect those two assholes, now was not the time. "Hollis and Vance and six others drove off maybe twenty minutes ago. They had two big drones. They're pulling the trigger. We have to go after them."

"Well, we're sure as hell not sticking around here." June turned and jogged toward the stockade. Peter followed, scanning for threats ahead and behind, rifle raised, unlaced boots too tight on his feet.

He arrived to see Manny with a crowbar, levering out the badly dented metal door. Its knob and deadbolt lay battered and torn on the ground. Carlotta rushed out and wrapped her arms around Manny's waist. Ellie emerged behind her, saw Peter, and ran toward him.

He hugged her tight. "Got you," he said softly.

With June scanning their backtrail, Manny pulled them behind the relative shelter of the stone armory, rifle up and eyes out. Peter said, "Where's Lewis?"

Manny nodded toward the fire, which was now consuming the next building. "That's his work, him and Faraday. We'll pick them up on the way back to the truck." He explained the hole in the fence and where they'd left the Tahoe. "You good to travel?"

"Give me a sec," Peter said. The man who'd been guarding the door lay bound in the mud. Peter handed June her rifle, then rolled the guard over and pulled the tape off his mouth. "What size shoes do you wear?"

"Uh, size twelve?"

"Good man." Peter returned the tape to the guard's mouth, then bent and untied his boots. They were badly worn, but at least they were the right size. Even better, they had laces. "Sorry, buddy. I'm taking your socks, too."

With half-decent boots and dry socks, a man could conquer the world.

Manny led them along the wall of the armory, away from the center of the camp. Carlotta was right behind him with the guard's pistol, then Ellie, then June with her rifle. Peter was tail-end Charlie, armed with the guard's unsuppressed AK and two spare magazines he'd found in the guy's back pockets. In the momentary quiet, he heard Manny say, "Lewis, Faraday, time to go. What's your location?"

Ahead of them, the second building was fully engulfed in flames, throwing heat for dozens of yards. The trees to the north were steaming. Peter figured that big explosion had blown through the metal siding, igniting something flammable inside.

If he could, he'd burn this whole compound to the ground. If they were lucky, he thought, he might yet get the chance.

Then ahead, through the roar of the fire, he heard unsuppressed gunshots on full auto. The gunmen who'd run toward the explosion. And Lewis.

Three figures ran around the end of the armory at full speed, lit by the flames. The leader saw them, pointed back the way they'd come, and shouted, "They're in the first greenhouse. We're gonna circle around. How much ammo you got?"

Then he looked past Manny and saw the women and Peter. He raised his rifle. Manny shot him in the face, the suppressed rifle nearly soundless under the crackling roar of the blaze. Ellie flinched. The gunman dropped into the faint snow. The other two men realized what was happening, turned, and began to lift their rifles. Manny shot them both in the chest. They staggered back. Manny adjusted his aim and shot each man in the head. They went down.

Peter looked behind him and saw four dark figures round the corner from the stockade, eighty feet away. He calmly found the first silhouette in his iron sights and pulled the trigger twice, *BANG BANG*. The unsuppressed AK was too damn loud. He was acutely aware that he wore no body armor. The silhouette collapsed and the other figures retreated out of sight. Peter put two more rounds into the fallen person, then called over his shoulder, "Manny, we gotta go."

Manny leaned against the stone building, voice loud to be heard over the fire. "Lewis, Faraday. We're at the northwest corner of the armory. Hold your fire, we're coming to you. Repeat, don't fucking shoot."

Manny turned and looked at each of them in turn. "We're going to the nearest greenhouse. Move fast and stay close." He raised his rifle, took a quick peek around the corner, then left at a run. The others followed into the space between the buildings. Peter was last, both eyes on their backtrail.

The heat from the blaze was incredible. Absurdly, Peter wanted to stay and get warm but knew that was a bad idea. On the gravel pad, several bodies lay sprawled in boneless and bloody heaps, sad and undignified in death as all men were.

They left the shelter between the buildings. Backpedaling, Peter knew he was falling behind. He glanced to his right and saw several more bodies. He wanted more ammunition, but he didn't have time to search the dead. To his left was the semi-sized propane tank, scorched black and cracked open like an egg. Not far away, the shell of an old gas pump burned merrily, and four flaming wood posts marked the supports where the sheltering roof had once been.

He looked back the way they'd come and saw a man poke his head around the far corner of the armory. Peter stopped and aimed and fired twice. Chips flew from the stone and the head pulled back in a hurry. Backpedaling again, Peter kept firing until he ran out of ammo. He dropped the magazine, popped in a fresh one from his back pocket, fired another few rounds, then turned and ran.

The greenhouses were made of clear plastic sheeting over round hoops. The blast wave from the exploding propane tank had popped the plastic like a balloon, and it hung from the hoops in wet shreds like ghosts in the falling snow. Inside the frame were long metal planters, two feet tall, full of dirt and leafy plants that would not survive the cold night.

He leapt a planter and dropped to the ground, then braced his rifle, aimed back the way he'd come, and waited. He wanted those assholes to think hard before they came after him. Combat never left you. Right now, he was glad of that. Later he wouldn't be.

Two men sprinted around the corner of the armory, firing wildly. Peter aimed, pulled the trigger, dropped the first man, then the second. They fell in sorry heaps like the others. Stupid, stupid, stupid.

Peter counted to ten and nobody else appeared. He stood and ran crouching down the center aisle through a gauntlet of shredded plastic to the far end of the long greenhouse, where the others knelt in the dirt, watching him come.

Carlotta held Manny's hand and had her other arm around Ellie, who was flushed and breathing hard. June braced her AK's butt at her hip, looking like an Irish revolutionary posing for a photo. Lewis had his back to Peter, rifle scanning over the top of a planter on the left, covering the south and east. Another man covered the north and west. Peter didn't know him. He had brown skin and a black beard and eyes that glittered in the firelight. One pant leg was wet with blood and roughly bandaged below the knee.

Manny said, "That's Faraday. This is Peter."

Peter said, "Appreciate you being here. You okay?"

Faraday nodded. "I'll live."

At the exchange, Lewis turned and saw Peter. "Took you long enough." His eyebrows were singed, his jacket scorched, and his grin as wide as Peter had ever seen it. "You like my diversion? I made the boom as big as I could."

"Everybody good to go?" Manny scanned their faces, the veteran platoon sergeant getting his troops ready to move out. One by one, they all nodded. Then Lewis hoisted Faraday in a fireman's carry and Manny led them toward the fence and the forest beyond.

Each of them aware that this whole little adventure wasn't worth shit if they couldn't find Hollis and Vance and the others before they flipped the switch on the end of the world.

59

Manny had extra night-vision gear for the former captives, which let them move at speed through the dense, dark woods.

With Faraday still over Lewis's shoulders, they made it to the Tahoe without firing a shot. Nobody was waiting for them there. Probably because, while Lewis was hosing down the wooden propane tank enclosure with gasoline, setting it on fire, then putting a few bullet holes in the pressurized tank to light the candle for real, Faraday had gone to the parking lot to shoot out the tires of the vehicles there. The only one he missed was a silver Mercedes he'd spotted in the lane between the cabins, because he didn't want to start putting holes in buildings where children might be sleeping.

They piled into their ride, Lewis behind the wheel, and roared down the logging road, headlights off. Peter watched behind them but saw no pursuit. At a muddy turnoff, Manny and June helped Faraday limp up the side road. A minute later, the Lexus eased toward them. Carlotta and Ellie left the Tahoe and got into the back seat of the Lexus. The group had already decided that Manny would take Carlotta and Ellie to the cabin where Carlotta's mother had taken their girls, dropping the wounded Faraday at a hospital on the way. Once Faraday's phone connected to the network, he would reach out to a guy he knew at Homeland. Peter, Lewis, and June would go find Hollis and Vance.

As the Lexus pulled past, Faraday handed June's work bag, with her laptop and the old maps, out the window to her. "Stay safe, all of you."

Lewis drove them downhill to the blacktop and headed west toward the city. Once her hot spot lit up again, June turned on the dome light, then opened her laptop and unfolded the paper map of Washington state so Peter could see it from the front seat. "Okay, here's what I know." She pointed to the row of numbers written in the margins. "This first number is the digital GPS coordinate for the electrical substation outside the Chief Joseph Dam. That's here." She tapped her finger on a cluster of hieroglyphics, then swept her hand across the others. "My guess is, each of these is some kind of power plant. I haven't run the searches yet."

Now she ran her finger along Geoffrey Reed's ruler-straight lines stretching from the power plants toward Spokane and the coastal cities. "These must be the high-voltage lines that connect everything. This whole thing is a schematic of the grid in Washington state." She handed the map forward to Peter. "These, too. All of them."

With this crucial insight, Peter spread the map on his lap and looked again at the little symbols, the stick figures and picket fences, the various colored circles and squares marked with dots or lines. He was no engineer, but he'd wired plenty of houses with his dad, and he knew what an electrical diagram looked like. Grid systems were infinitely more complicated than basic home wiring, but the principles were the same. "These circles and squares must be switches and circuit breakers. Reed was marking which ones need to be open and which ones shut. Or something like that. Whatever they mean, this map is his plan of attack."

Lewis said, "If they can do it remotely, what the hell are they doing with those drones?"

"I have no idea." Then Peter explained his theory about the armor-piercing rounds. "A hack can eventually get unhacked. But if the grid is down and they shoot out enough transformers, the power will be out for years, maybe decades."

Lewis leaned in to peer at the map. "So outta these ten, which ones are they gonna hit?"

"With the Messenger's ego, he'll pick something big," Peter said.

"I'll plug in the rest of the coordinates," June said. "Read them to me?"

Peter read them out one by one. She typed each number into her mapping app and checked satellite view. "The substation for the John Day Dam. The substation for the Grand Coulee Dam. The Columbia substation. The Bonneville Dam substation."

"Grand Coulee," Peter said, finding it on the old paper map. "That's the biggest generator in the state, right?"

June checked Wikipedia. "Almost as big as all the rest combined. It supplies power to eight states plus parts of Canada."

"That's where they're going. A system failure there will have huge consequences down the line."

"What about Columbia," she asked. "That's a nuclear plant."

"For that reason, it'll be extremely well guarded. Anyway, they're after the substations, not the plants." Peter looked at the symbols again. "The little picket fences, the stick figures. That's substation security. See here, the Columbia substation has three fences and four little people. The Grand Coulee has a single fence and no people. No guards."

"Okay." June leaned forward between the front seats. "Are we good? We have a plan?"

Lewis kept his eyes on the road. "Let's go get those motherfuckers. Are we going west or east into the mountains?"

"Lend me your phone and give me the coordinates," Peter said. "I'll get us where we need to go."

June said, "They've got an hour's head start. Before we do anything, I think we should call your friend Kitzinger, tell her what we've found."

He dug Detective Kitzinger's number out of his memory. This time she picked up. She didn't sound happy to hear from him.

"It's one in the morning, Ash. Where the holy hell have you been? You dump all this information on me in a voicemail and then vanish?"

"Did you look into any of it?"

Her voice was indignant. "Of course I did. Not only is it my job, but Captain Durant hadn't shared any of it. In fact, he told me and O'Donnell if we talked to you or your journalist friend, or if we strayed from the existing avenues of investigation, he'd suspend us for insubordination. Nothing makes a cop more suspicious than telling her not to follow the evidence. Now where are you?"

Using as few words as possible, Peter told her about the abduction, handing himself over to Durant, and the raid at the compound. Then he told her about the maps and the GPS coordinates. She listened silently. He heard the scratch of her pen as she made notes.

"Durant was stalling, trying to wait out the clock," she said.

"That's my guess," Peter said. "Here's the upshot. We think they're going to take down one or more electrical substations. Geoffrey Reed built a couple of big drones, and that's how they're somehow going to set things off. We also think Reed hacked the various grid systems to set up some kind of cascading failure." He looked at June. "What am I forgetting?"

She said, "Does the Seattle PD have contacts at the big power companies? I'm guessing their software is compromised. Also, your forensics guys have Reed's laptop. If he's got any code on there, or passwords to any kind of code repository, somebody should take a hard look."

"I'll let our techs know," Kitzinger said. "As for the power companies, we have a liaison at Homeland. I'll call him next, tell him to wake up a bunch of his people and have them reach out to the power companies."

"Faraday is supposed to call his contact at Homeland, too," Peter said. "Hopefully a call from you will help speed things up."

"Good," she said. "I'll also brief our night commander so his people can start calling the local sheriffs, see if they can't get some deputies out to those substations. Can you send me those coordinates? And maybe pictures of those maps?"

June glanced at the list of numbers and started typing. "Working on it now."

"One last thing," Peter said. "Make sure you tell the sheriffs their deputies need to be careful. The bad guys have armor-piercing rounds."

"Got it," Kitzinger said. "You better get your ass to Seattle. Homeland will want to talk to you."

"You bet. Thanks for this, Kitzinger. Gotta go."

After Peter hung up, Lewis looked at him. "We ain't going back to Seattle."

"No," Peter said. "We go forward until it's finished, one way or another." He plugged in the coordinates for the Grand Coulee Dam, then looked at the routes on his phone. "If we stay on blacktop, we have to backtrack west all the way to Ravensdale and North Bend. Five hours if we really haul ass. But if we take

Forest Service gravel going east and cross at Stampede Pass, we can cut that time to three and a half, depending on conditions."

It was November in the mountains. Lewis said, "Do we even know if it's passable? The Forest Service doesn't plow."

"Forest Service website says the Stampede Pass Road is still open. Although this is dated a week ago." Peter downloaded the map because he knew they'd lose cell service quickly once they hit the gravel.

"Good enough for me," Lewis said. "Hold on." He hit the brakes and cranked the wheel. The Tahoe's tires screamed and the big vehicle slewed sideways on the wet pavement, ending up facing back the way they'd come. Even before they'd come to a stop, he stomped on the gas and they began to rocket toward the east.

They passed the turnoff to the compound, encountering no other vehicles. The pavement ended soon thereafter. Aside from their headlights, the darkness was complete. After a few minutes, they took the first left and began a gradual climb, black mountains looming close on both sides. There was maybe half an inch of fresh snow on the ground, but the gravel road had been recently graded and the Tahoe's traction was still good. Lewis was going forty, then forty-five.

At the next turn, the road became steeper, evergreens leaning close overhead. On their right, Sunday Creek flowed inexorably down to the sea. On their left was a clear-cut power easement, the tall metal towers and high-voltage wires invisible in the darkness except for the flashing red warning lights at their tops. The snow fell thick and fast, deepening as they climbed.

Lewis slowed to thirty. "You guys see what I'm seeing?"

Peter leaned forward. In the headlights, twin tire tracks had slowly materialized in the snow. Until now, there hadn't been enough snow to show tracks. A half hour from now, with all this accumulation, the tracks would be all but invisible. "Stop here."

Lewis hit the brakes and Peter got out and knelt in the road, looking at the tread patterns and snow scatter and the amount of accumulation over the impressions. "They're going uphill, too," he said. "Two trucks, and not that long ago."

Lewis was bent beside him, hands on his knees. "It's got to be them, right?"

Peter got to his feet, brushing wet slop from his pant legs. The wind howled through the trees. "Who else is dumb enough to be up here in the middle of the night? Although why they'd take this route I have no idea."

"Security precaution," Lewis said. "In case their plan got blown open, nobody would look for them on this road. But it means we ain't gaining on 'em."

"Not yet," Peter said. "I don't suppose we have any tire chains."

Lewis smiled. "In the back. Stopped just in case, after we learned where the compound was."

"Better break 'em out," Peter said. "It's only going to get worse from here."

They got the chains on and kept going. The road followed the power easement for a time, always uphill, crossing under the buzzing wires and back again, before turning away to the left and rising along the steep flank of a mountain. There were no guardrails. The evergreens seemed to glow in the headlights, their branches heavy and white. The snow grew deeper, then deeper still.

After another mile, the snow was faintly marked by bootprints where the men in the trucks had put on their own chains. A half-mile later, the road began to switchback up a precipitous slope. Rocks to one side, empty space to the other. June reached between the seats and gripped Peter's hand hard. By now the snow was at least two feet deep, and deeper in the drifts. Lewis shifted into low and dropped his speed to twenty, chains rattling, keeping his wheels in the tracks of the vehicles ahead, letting them break the path for him. Peter tried not to look out the window at the red power pylon lights below. It was a long way down.

The switchbacks grew tighter and steeper. Lewis slowed to fifteen, then ten. The tires began to slip on the uphill turns. The trees closed in, swaying in the wind. Then, after one final switchback, the land opened up and the road straightened out, rising and falling and rising again. To the right, more red lights floating in midair, power pylons stepping toward the east.

"I think we're at the pass," Peter said. "After this, it's five miles to the freeway and a hundred and seventy to the Grand Coulee Dam."

Lewis shifted out of low and began to pick up speed.

60

HOLLIS

Once they hit I-90, Vance set the cruise control at three miles over the limit. Behind them, in the second truck, Nickels followed suit. The last thing they needed now was to be pulled over by an overzealous state trooper.

Leaving the snow and clouds behind, they passed Cle Elum and the larger city of Ellensburg, both communities shining like bright islands in an ocean of night. The fertile Kittitas Valley seemed empty, but Hollis could see pinpricks of light marking houses and barns, wherever men and women had made their homes. Every bit of it a reminder of what would be lost when the Dark Time came.

Then the landscape grew desolate and empty. Aside from navigation lights atop wind turbines, a few tractor-trailers, and the highway itself, there was no visual evidence that man had ever existed. Just thousands of stars shining down with infinite indifference.

Hollis thought of what would happen when the power went out and the Industrial Machine died. And how many millions of people would die along with it.

He wondered again if he was doing the right thing. Not that he doubted the Messenger. The end was coming sooner or later,

Hollis could feel it in his bones. All you had to do was read the news. Mankind was eating itself alive. So-called progress led only toward their doom. But unlike the Messenger, Hollis's faith sometimes faltered. Who was he to make this choice? Who was he to wave his hand and turn out the lights?

Still, he had done as the Messenger had asked. With only a high school diploma, Hollis had figured out how to get things done. In the chat rooms of the dark web, he'd discovered Geoff Reed and his knowledge of the grid's weaknesses, and how to exploit them. He'd found Nickels and convinced him to build twelve hundred assault rifles and make twelve thousand armor-piercing rounds. He'd recruited Troy Boxall, the first member from the tech community, who'd made introductions to others like him. Reed had left Troy everything he needed to start the cascade of failure that Reed had designed.

Hollis knew he should be proud of what he'd accomplished. The Messenger had told him that repeatedly. Sometimes, when he looked around at what they'd built, the self-sufficient community on the mountain, he felt that lift of pride. Other times, mostly when he was apart from the Messenger, he thought of the Time of Undoing and wondered if it was the right path. If he had made the wrong choices. He no longer thought of himself as a person without worth. Now he knew he was intelligent, capable, resourceful. What else might he have accomplished in the world if he'd committed himself to it entirely, the way he had to the Movement?

Not that it mattered, he told himself. There was no room for second thoughts. The past was gone. The course was set. They were a few hours from changing the future.

They crossed the Columbia River at Vantage, then left the interstate at the tiny town of George, heading northeast toward Ephrata, where they would follow the Columbia up to the dam.

This was the Quincy Valley, irrigated by the river and filled with orchards, cherry and apple and pear. Hollis had recruited three farmers from the valley, convincing them to sell the land that had been in their families for three generations. It had happened before the Messenger's word had reached the tech community, whose subscriptions provided all the money they'd ever need. The Messenger's accounts still had millions they hadn't had time to spend.

Hollis checked his phone for the fourth time. He'd texted Durant to make sure the execution at the punishment wall had gone off as planned, but Durant still hadn't answered. He reminded himself that cell service was nonexistent up there. They had Wi-Fi that covered the central compound, but it came from a satellite connection that got spotty when the weather got rough. Durant's lack of response meant nothing.

They drove through tiny Lakeview and Soap Lake, then Coulee City, the town lights bright and cheerful in the depth of night. It wouldn't be long now. He looked at Vance behind the wheel. The big brute always seemed so certain, so convinced of the righteousness of their movement. For the thousandth time, Hollis wondered what was so broken in himself that his own faith faltered so often.

He glanced into the back seat, where Simon, their young drone operator, was curled up against his door, fast asleep. Beside him, Troy Boxall set aside his laptop and picked up his AK, fiddling with it. "This is going to be so fucking cool."

Hollis had never liked Boxall. He seemed to long for the destruction of the Dark Time. He'd once told Hollis he was looking forward to killing people. Unfortunately, for now, the Movement needed him.

Hollis said, "Remember, Troy, you have one very important job. Keep your mind on that."

"Are you kidding? The way Reed set this up, he's automated everything. He's already got worms inside all the systems. All I have to do is trigger his code. It will only take about five minutes for everything to propagate through the system. After that, it's all rock and roll, baby."

They came to Electric City, then the town of Grand Coulee, where the road split and Vance headed left on 174. The main substation was just ahead. They could see it now, brightly lit, wires feeding the huge metal high-voltage towers that marched west toward the coastal cities. Vance slowed for the turnoff, then swore and hit the gas and kept going.

"What the hell," Boxall said.

"Cops in the parking lot," Vance said. "At least six of them."

"Maybe they're running some kind of exercise," Boxall said.

"At three in the morning? No. Something's wrong."

Hollis checked his texts again, hoping for something from Durant. Nothing. Then his phone rang. It was Nickels, still behind them. "This ain't good, Hollis."

With the need to act, Hollis's certainty returned. "We knew this was a possibility, that the Industrial Machine would learn to defend its weaknesses. Stick to the plan. Past the curve, we kill our lights and Troy does his thing. Once that's done, six of us walk downslope and come up on them from behind. We're armored and loaded with black-tips. They'll punch through ballistic vests, vehicles, anything. Once they're down, we get the drones in the air and finish it."

"Roger that," Nickels said, and hung up.

Boxall whooped.

Beside him, twelve-year-old Simon blinked bleary eyes. "What's going on? Are we there?"

Boxall said, "We're gonna kill some fucking pigs."

Vance laughed. "And that's just for starters."

They found the turnaround and pulled over. Boxall pulled his computer onto his lap and hit a few keys. "Okay, I'm good to go." He giggled like a child taking pleasure in being naughty, then caught himself and cleared his throat. "Hollis? Should I do it?"

Hollis opened his mouth, not sure what would come out. His faith faltering again. All he'd ever wanted was some kind of home. People to care for, work that mattered. It's all any of them wanted. Was that so much to ask?

Vance watched him, then growled, "What the fuck are you waiting for?"

He was right, Hollis knew. Whatever doubts he might have, they no longer mattered. They had all done too much to turn back. They had nothing left to lose. There was no alternative. He unbuckled his seat belt. "Troy? Do it."

61

PETER

The dashboard clock read 3:17 when they rolled into the sleeping town of Grand Coulee and made the turn up the hill toward the main substation. After removing the tire chains and getting on the interstate, Lewis had pushed the Tahoe's speed to a hundred and twenty, hoping they could make up some time.

There was no snow on the ground here in the high desert, but the temperature was well below freezing. As they rounded the curve and left the last modest homes behind, a line of eight transmission towers rose before them like sentries against the night, their high tops crowned with the same red flashing lights. The dam itself wasn't visible because of the fall of the land. Lewis had already killed the headlights and pulled down his night-vision goggles so he could see the road.

"Slow it up," Peter said, looking at the map on his phone. "It's right on the other side of that hill." He pointed through the windshield. "Pull up that little gravel drive a ways, maybe find some bushes to hide us." If they had somehow passed the Messenger's men, he didn't want those assholes to roll up behind them parked on the side of the road. Hollis, Nickels, and Boxall knew the Tahoe. They would be sitting ducks for those armor-piercing rounds.

Lewis crept forward up the one-lane track, the ambient glow from the substation growing brighter. As he pulled into the waist-high scrub between two enormous metal lattice towers, the land fell away and the facility appeared in the distance, lit up like Santa's workshop on Christmas Day. Peter rolled down his window and raised the binoculars Manny had left him.

The substation leapt into view, a vast array of transformers, switches, circuit breakers, surge arresters, capacitors, and myriad other equipment, much of it from the previous century. The technology itself was even older, but still remarkable. As a kid, Peter and his dad had often driven past a much smaller substation on the outskirts of the town where he'd grown up. His dad always called it the lightning farm. Because, as his dad liked to say, mankind had learned to harness lightning and put it safely to work.

The facility itself was a quarter-mile wide and maybe four hundred feet deep, with a deeper section facing the road where an electric entrance gate and a maintenance building stood. The whole thing was surrounded by a chain-link fence, eight feet tall with barbed wire on top. Outside the gate was a parking area with six vehicles standing nose out across the far side of the lot, three or four feet apart. They were blocking the gate. Peter could see the low shape of the light bars across their roofs.

Kitzinger had made contact with the sheriff. The deputies had made it.

Half a dozen men milled around, weapons slung, looking at the vehicles and at small heaps scattered on the blacktop. Peter's binoculars weren't powerful enough to see details. Something wasn't right, but he couldn't quite figure out what it was.

A pair of fat-tired pickups appeared, turning brazenly down the access drive and into the parking lot. One man got out of each pickup and joined the others. Then Peter realized none of them were in uniform. And the small heaps on the parking-lot surface were dead men.

Shit. "The deputies are down. The bad guys are already here."

Lewis put the Tahoe in reverse but kept his foot on the brake. "If we come in hot, they'll hear our engines before they see us. They'll be ready. We've got no protection against those black-tips."

Peter nodded. "Surprise is our only option. We should go on foot from here." Cross-country to the parking lot, it was only a hundred yards.

"Works for me." Lewis opened his door. They'd already disabled the dome light. "Saddle up, motherfuckers."

Manny had left them most of his equipment. They geared up at the back of the Tahoe, keeping it light, just suppressed weapons, spare magazines, radios, flashlights, and night-vision goggles, in case they had to go hunting in the dark. The armor wouldn't help, so they left it behind. Each man's pack also had two rolls of duct tape and a first aid kit.

Peter was the first man ready. He raised the binoculars again, scanning the parking lot below. The Messenger's pickups were parked nose out for a quick getaway. The men had gathered at the cargo beds and were busy unloading something. He recognized the spidery skeletons of the drones. "We need to go now."

June grabbed his shoulder and turned him, then grabbed his ears and pulled him close.

He kissed her hard. The adrenaline burning in his veins. Alive, alive, I am alive. He looked at Lewis, who nodded his readiness. Then he turned and began to run, bent low in the knee-high grass and waist-high scrub, toward the bright substation and the killers assembled in the parking lot.

Lewis and June ran beside him.

The ground was uneven and he was careful where he put his feet, not wanting to trip and fall or, worse, break an ankle. But he kept most of his focus on the Messenger's men in the parking lot. One was the boy Peter had seen when they were loading the trucks at the compound. He was fussing around the drones now, bending to attach something to their undersides. Then two others each picked up a drone and held them above their heads. Red lights shone down from their fuselages, painting the men in a crimson glow.

The boy looked down at a dark rectangle in his hand and moved his fingers across it. As one, the black drones began to buzz loudly. Of course, Peter thought. The boy was the pilot.

The drones buzzed louder and slowly rose into the air. Something heavy hung between them, sinuous and gleaming, and Peter realized what it was. The motorcycle chains from the boxes in Reed's apartment, linked together into one long unit. The drones would lay it over a pair of high-voltage lines, where it would conduct a massive jolt of electricity between them.

That would be the catalyst, the event that would set off the whole cascade. A city-sized short circuit. But because of what Reed would have done inside the computerized systems, the fail-safe breakers wouldn't trip. The blast of electricity would shoot down the line, burning out switches and exploding transformers along the way. Which would in turn create new power surges that would propagate through the connected grids, doing more damage. The blackout would begin.

They were seventy yards out. "Take down the drones," Peter called softly. "Shoot the fucking drones!" The muzzle flash might give away their positions, but that couldn't be helped. Peter was betting his life that this was the right thing to do.

He knelt behind a shrub, aimed over the iron sight, and fired deliberate single shots. The others did the same. But the drones were moving targets and the AK-47 was not an accurate weapon at this distance. He heard the *whang* of stray rounds hitting the metal of the towers. If he had a decent shotgun, he'd have solved this by now. The red lights rose steadily higher, the drones growing smaller and harder to hit.

Rounds flew past his head, *zhip zhip*. He glanced down at the parking lot and saw four men with rifles raised in his direction, muzzles flaring. The drones were tiny now, the red lights shrunk to pinpricks. The four others had retreated behind the jacked-up pickups, where they stood with their necks craned, watching the flight. One was the boy with the controller.

Peter aimed for the device, knowing he might well miss it and hit the kid. He told himself the boy was a combatant, no different from a teenager in Fallujah staring down the sights of a rifle. And it was true. But if Peter killed him, he'd dream about the boy, anyway, like he did all the others.

More rounds flew past, *zhip zhip zhip*. Beside him, a branch fell from the shrub. He cleared his mind, aimed, let out a breath, and fired. The controller didn't move. The boy looked around, startled but unharmed. Peter had missed. He adjusted his aim to fire again, but the boy turned and ran through the row of sheriff's vehicles and disappeared behind a boxy SUV. Above him, the red pinpricks slipped sideways and began to descend. Maybe Peter had hit the controller, after all. He allowed himself to hope.

Then the night sky was lit up by bright white fireworks high in the air, a twin waterfall of sparks that kept renewing themselves like the world's largest arc welder. The drones were lit from below, their spidery black skeletons in stark relief, the linked motorcycle chains between them glowing orange from the high-voltage current in the wires it had bridged. The falling sparks were flecks of superheated metal from the wires and the chain. They bounced off vehicles and pavement and continued to burn.

Then a substation transformer blew with a spray of orange sparks and the thunder of an exploding mortar round. Another transformer went, then two more in rapid succession.

The sparks stopped abruptly. The substation lights blinked out. Peter glanced up to see the lights on the transmission towers go black one by one, the darkness marching west toward the cities of the coast. He looked behind him at the town sprawled across the low hills, just in time to see it vanish street by street until it disappeared entirely into the night.

There was no moon. He turned in a circle. Aside from the stars, the only visible illumination came from the headlights in the parking lot below.

Peter had failed.

The Messenger's people had won.

The Dark Time had come.

62

Partly concealed in the scrub, Peter bent his head and pulled in a deep breath. He'd failed to prevent this shitstorm. He couldn't undo the damage. But his mission wasn't over. It had changed. He would capture Hollis and Vance and whoever else he could get, and deliver them to the law in Seattle. After that, all bets were off.

He looked up to check on the gunmen in the parking lot. Lewis had already taken down one of them. The other three were advancing across the blacktop, backlit by the pickups' headlights, spraying armor-piercing rounds across the hillside. At fifty yards, Peter thought he recognized Troy Boxall, but not the other two. They all seemed to think their armor and weapons made them invincible, even though they couldn't see their adversaries in the scrub.

Watching them come, Peter keyed his radio. "Listen up. We're taking prisoners."

Lewis's voice was low and liquid in his ear. "Are you kidding? We should smoke these dirtbags and call it good."

"I'm with Peter," June said. "We need to know what they know. Also, taking prisoners is what makes us different from these assholes."

"I already know I ain't an asshole," Lewis growled. "Plus there's eight of them and only three of us, and we got no armor. I don't want to trade my life for these motherfuckers."

"We won't," Peter said. "Besides, I only want three of them, and they're not the ones shooting at us right now. So here's the plan."

First, Peter and Lewis focused on the advancing gunmen, who couldn't see them hiding in the scrub. The gunmen's torsos were armored, but not their heads or lower extremities. At forty yards, a couple of well-aimed rounds took out their legs and left them bleeding on the blacktop. They were still armed and firing, but lying prone, their armor didn't help much and they were easy targets.

Peter and Lewis made the kill shots, then turned and ran to the right, leaving June behind as they circled across the low curve of the hillside. Like the young drone pilot, the three men watching from behind the pickups had retreated through the line of sheriff's vehicles where the cover was better. They were all armed, but were evidently more cautious than the four dead guys.

Peter floated through the scrub, breathing easily, his legs strong and his boots sure on the uneven ground. Lewis was a shadow six feet behind him. Nobody was shooting at them. He heard June taking careful shots at the vehicles, punching holes in radiators and shattering windshields, keeping the remaining Messenger's men pinned in place behind the spaced line of sheriff's cruisers. Manny had given her his HK carbine when they split up. It was a much more accurate weapon than any AK-47.

Once Peter had gone far enough to be outside the beam of the headlights, the darkness became almost complete. He dropped his night-vision gear over his eyes and the world glowed a soft, familiar green.

A few minutes later, he stopped. They'd come ninety degrees from their previous position and were now even with the line of vehicles. Thirty yards out, he could see grainy green shadows crouched behind the two center SUVs, occasionally leaning out to one side or the other. They were peering through the row of cars to try to locate June's muzzle flash on the hillside, but had to keep ducking back to avoid her pinpoint return fire.

Peter assumed the remaining Messenger's men had night-vision gear, too. That's why he'd asked June to avoid punching out any headlights. When the others looked in her direction, that brightness would make their goggles flare for just a moment. Which made it harder for them to target her and easier for Peter and Lewis to approach unseen.

Peter keyed his radio and whispered, "June, hold fire in thirty seconds; repeat, hold fire in thirty seconds."

Side by side, they crept down the slope, rifles up and ready, silent as ghosts. Twenty-five yards. Twenty. Fifteen. June stopped firing. The shadows resolved into three men, bulky with body armor, the bulge of night-vision gear atop their heads. Peter couldn't see the boy. He took another step.

One of the shadows turned toward them. Peter assumed he meant to slip around the rear bumper of the SUV and fire at June. But along the way, he glanced in Peter's direction, saw something in the night, and raised his rifle. Peter knew by his enormous size it was Vance.

Peter shot him in the chest four times. He went down, punched in the armor with the force of a hammer blow.

The second man turned. Hollis. Lewis gave him two rounds to the chest plate, then pivoted and shot the third man twice in the back. They both fell. Lewis sidestepped to cover Peter as he ran up and kicked Vance and Hollis hard in the head, then tore away their rifles and threw them into the scrub. Lewis knelt to look at the third man, Nickels, who was already bleeding out. One of Lewis's rounds had missed his vest and torn through his neck. Die by the sword, Peter thought.

He pivoted to look for the boy, thinking it would be stupid to be shot by a child after all this, but felt something huge rise up in the darkness behind him. He turned, instinctively sidestepping, to see Vance swinging a big forearm toward Peter's head.

Vance connected. It was only a glancing blow, but it still buckled Peter's knees and knocked the night-vision goggles off his head. He backpedaled to bring his weapon to bear, planning to shoot the fucker somewhere permanent this time. But the huge man flashed out a hand and grabbed the rifle barrel, pulling it toward him and redirecting Peter's aim away.

Vance was incredibly strong. Peter had the sling around his neck and felt himself yanked forward with the gun. He didn't want to pull the trigger because he wouldn't hit Vance and he'd lost track of Lewis in the dark. In a tug-of-war for the rifle, Peter would surely lose. He set his feet, anyway, knowing if the huge man managed to pull Peter close, he was finished.

But this moment of resistance gave him an extra half-second to find the magazine release and let it fall. While it was still in the air, he ducked his head to free himself from the rifle sling and let go of the forestock. As Vance pulled the weapon away, Peter hooked the charging lever with the side of his hand, emptying the final round from the chamber.

Then Vance had the rifle but didn't seem to realize he had no ammunition. He spun the weapon and raised it to fire. As he pulled the trigger, Peter stepped closer and drop-kicked him in the groin.

The enormous man made a wordless bellow like a wounded bull facing the matador, but he didn't double over or even put a protective hand down to his crotch. Instead he threw the rifle away and moved sideways to put Peter between him and the night where Lewis would be trying to find a shooting angle.

Peter tried to circle left to give Lewis a shot, but Vance crabstepped right, matching him step for step. Peter couldn't see much in the dark, but he could see how the man moved, could see pale, heavy hands up and ready but his guard relatively open, as though no man had ever hit him hard enough to make him hurt. He was quick and strong and apparently unaffected by the blows he'd taken, but he was also weighed down by thirty pounds of body armor.

Then Vance rushed him, trying to run him down or trap him against the fence. Peter was ready. He feinted left, the way he'd circled before, then slipped right and drove a hard left fist under the huge man's raised chin and directly into his exposed Adam's apple.

Vance caught him in an outstretched arm to pull him close. But the damage had been done. With a single blow, Peter had crushed the other man's trachea, blocking his airway. Vance stumbled back, hand to his throat, trying to pull in a breath but only achieving a kind of awful wet wheeze.

Peter stepped in and kicked him in the knee. When Vance fell thrashing to the pavement, Peter sidestepped a grasping fist and kicked Vance in the throat. The huge man continued to thrash spasmodically, but the awful wet wheeze stopped and he began to suffocate in earnest.

Then Lewis was there with his rifle up, aimed at Vance's head. He pulled the trigger once and Vance stopped thrashing.

Peter looked at him. Lewis shrugged. "I didn't want to have to give that motherfucker an emergency tracheotomy or some damn thing."

"You just didn't want to have to lift him into the back of the truck," Peter said.

Lewis gave him a tilted grin. "That, too."

They heard a noise and turned together to see Hollis scrambling to his feet, looking around for a weapon.

Peter held out his hand and Lewis put the rifle in it. Peter aimed and shot Hollis twice more in the chest plate, hoping he'd broken a rib or two.

Hollis fell back to the pavement, keening in pain. Somehow Peter didn't feel sorry for him. He handed the rifle back to Lewis, then kicked Hollis onto his back and began to strip off his armor. "Lewis, you see the other one? The kid?"

Lewis bent and shined his flashlight under the SUV. "Boy, come up on out of there. Don't make me shoot your skinny white ass."

Peter pulled a roll of duct tape from his pack, rolled Hollis onto his stomach, and began to tape the older man's wrists, ankles, and mouth. It was harder in the dark. Lewis stepped out and waved at June, who went back for the Tahoe and roared down the access drive five minutes later, pulling around to the side so her headlights lit the area like a crime scene. Which, Peter supposed, it was.

He'd thought Hollis would try to talk, to justify himself, but he didn't. He'd probably read the expression on Peter's face and knew he was a hair's breadth away from a bullet to the head. Instead he just lay still and closed his eyes like a kicked dog. Peter was tempted to roll the man up in a tarp, just to let him experience how much fun it was, but reminded himself to be a better person than that.

He only wished Durant and the Messenger were there, too. To Peter, they were worse than the others. The Messenger for spinning his web of bullshit, and Durant for betraying his oath to serve and protect. He wanted them taken alive and healthy, so they could spend the rest of their lives behind bars. If some civic-minded convict didn't shank them first.

Then he realized he was still acting as if the lights would come back on like they always had, and society would continue as before. That there would still be police and judges and trials and prisons. Instead of looting and food riots and starvation. People dead in the streets and in their homes. So many dead that there wouldn't be enough humans left alive to bury them.

He saw Lewis's grim face and hooded eyes and knew he was thinking the same thing. If this was the new reality, they would need to get back to Wisconsin as quickly as possible. Peter's parents would need help. Lewis would want to be with Dinah and the boys.

They duct-taped Hollis and lifted him into the Tahoe's cargo bay. June pointed at the kid, sitting against the fence, eyes wide. He couldn't have been more than twelve. "What about him?"

Peter had taped his ankles, wrists, and mouth, too. There was no way to know whether he was a true believer or if his parents had pulled him into this mess. Either way, he'd rigged and flown the drones, so he was up to his neck in it.

"I got him." Lewis threw him over a shoulder, then carried him to the Tahoe and laid him down beside Hollis. "You best behave, boy, or you ain't gonna like what happens."

Peter walked the parking lot, looking at the sheriff's deputies crumpled on the blacktop in the forlorn postures of the dead. They deserved a decent funeral, and he hoped they would get it. The sheriff would come looking for them, or someone in their families. But he didn't want their loved ones to see them in this final indignity, abandoned where they lay like so many broken toys. So he did what he had done on many battlefields. He tried to restore as much of their dignity as he could. He rolled them onto their backs and straightened their clothes and their limbs. He closed their eyes and folded their hands across their chests. Noting as he did that the armor-piercing rounds had punched right through their vests. June and Lewis watched in silence.

When Peter was finished, Lewis walked toward the big pickups, pointing to the five-gallon fuel cans in their racks. "We gonna need those," he said. "We ain't got enough to get to Seattle. With the power out, we can't just pull over at a gas station and fill the tank."

"Find some rope," Peter said. "We can tie them on the roof."

When that was done, they climbed in the Tahoe and hit the road.

63

Somehow the blackout had seemed less strange during the gunfight. Peter had been on a lot of night missions as a Marine and seeing the darkened landscape through the green of the goggles had felt familiar.

But now, driving through town, it felt truly eerie. There were no streetlights or stoplights. No businesses lit up. No porch lights or yard lights. The only light came from the Tahoe. And when they passed, the darkness behind them was complete. Just the stars shining down through that cold infinity.

With Peter behind the wheel, June in the passenger seat, and Lewis in the back in case of a prisoner insurrection, they retraced their path, rolling through Electric City and Coulee City and Ephrata. Each town in its utter darkness feeling like something empty and dead. June kept checking her phone but there was no signal. They saw no other cars.

They crossed the flat plain of Quincy Valley, whose irrigated orchards fed millions. A hundred thousand fruit trees would die without pumps to raise the water from the ground. They stopped by the side of the road to fill the tank from the fuel cans on the roof, then kept going.

By the time they got to the interstate, it was almost five A.M.

Peter put the hammer down, not worried about speed traps, knowing the troopers would have plenty of other things to do tonight. The Tahoe ate up the miles. Even on I-90, they saw no other vehicles. He figured most night drivers had either made it home or run out of gas by now, and the early risers were sleeping in until the power came back on.

His adrenaline had long since leached away. They had all sucked down the energy bars, water, and cans of Coke that June had brought, but that was before the fight and now they were all yawning. He'd turned the heat down to help them stay awake.

They crossed the Columbia in utter blackness, rose into the badlands for a while, then dropped down into the next valley. Lewis put on his night-vision goggles to peer out the side window. "First real town up ahead," he said. "Might have to do a little B&E, but we need to get us some damn caffeine."

"I'm good with that," Peter said. When the Kittitas exit came up, he took it. At the bottom of the ramp, he turned right and his eyes found a glow. It was an independent gas station, windows and sign dark. The glow came from the parking lot, filled with cars and trucks circled around a bonfire. People stood on the gravel in ones and twos, hunched against the cold, looking up at the stars.

"This will be interesting," June said.

Peter pulled the Tahoe off the road and found a spot away from the pumps and the other vehicles. They got out with their rifles slung behind them and pistols in their waistbands, checked the prisoners, then walked toward the convenience store's door. A round-faced guy with pimples and a wispy mustache walked out to meet them, his breath white in the night. He was trying not to stare at their weapons, but not doing a very good job of it.

"Sorry, fellas," he said. "Power's out and the pumps don't work. Registers neither."

Peter's wallet was at the bottom of the retention pond at the Auburn Mall, but he knew Lewis had money. "How about cash?"

Three other men wandered over. They wore scuffed boots and dirty Carhartts. Two had pistols on their belts. One, older than the others, had a shotgun broken over his shoulder like a bird hunter. They didn't speak, just stared at Peter and Lewis, who stared right back.

The clerk said, "Cash works, but I can't make change."

Peter turned to Lewis, who peeled a hundred-dollar bill off a roll. Peter held it out to the clerk. "We just want coffee," he said. "And food." He looked at the other guys. "You want coffee? It's on us."

They shook their heads. "We're good," said the hunter. They were giving off a weird vibe, Peter didn't quite get it. He wanted coffee but he had no desire to kill anyone else that day if he could help it.

The clerk took the bill, glanced at it, then nodded. "Coffee's gonna be cold and old, but you're welcome to it." He opened the store's door and held it for them. "Come on in."

They left the other guys lingering outside and walked through the spotless little store, using the small tactical flashlights Manny had given them. The coffee was viscous and sour, but there was a full pot. Peter shared it out into three large cups and tucked them into a cardboard tray along with a handful of creamers and sugar packets. June was at the soft drink coolers. "Hey, they've got some of those Starbucks cans."

"Grab a few," Peter said. "And a couple gallons of water."

Lewis came over, loaded up with packs of assorted nuts and beef jerky. "Protein."

They dumped their haul on the counter. The clerk looked at the pile and began to punch numbers into his phone's calculator. "This all's gonna cost you a lot more than a hundred bucks."

Now the other men stood at the store entrance, partially blocking it. Peter turned from the register and let his hand fall near his pistol, aware of Lewis doing the same. "You guys are making me nervous. You mind backing away from the door?"

The hunter looked at him, sucking on his teeth. His face was thin and severe. "You guys military?"

"Marines." Peter tipped his head at Lewis. "Army."

"We were all Army, too," the hunter said. "So you know how it is. We're just making sure everything's copacetic and nobody gets hurt."

"Roger that," Peter said. "But I'd still feel better if you gave us a little space."

The men looked at one another, then shrugged and shuffled back a few steps.

Lewis pulled two more hundreds from his roll and held them out to the clerk. "This enough?"

Peter half-expected the guy to stuff the money into his pocket. His bosses would never know. Instead he pushed one bill back across the counter and slipped the other two into the register's security slot. "You got nine dollars and twelve cents left if you want something else."

"Keep it." Lewis counted four more hundreds onto the counter. "And share these out for anyone else who needs food or water. On us."

"That's real kind of you." The clerk pushed the grocery bags across the counter. "You folks have a real good day, okay?"

Outside, the hunter was staring at the Tahoe with the fuel cans tied to the roof. "No cell service. Radio ain't even playing that emergency message. You fellas know something we don't?"

"Power might be out awhile," Peter said. "If you've got family somewhere, you should go to them."

The hunter gestured at the other men. More people had begun

to collect around them. "We're all trying to get home," he said. "That's how we ended up here. Stopped for gas. But the pump don't work 'cause the vandals took the handles."

Peter recognized the lyric from "Subterranean Homesick Blues." He smiled. "You're a Dylan fan?"

The hunter grinned and his severe face suddenly looked twenty years younger. "Oh, hell yes. The missus and I seen Bobby play live twenty-three times. We drove to Ellensburg last year to see that movie, with Timothy whatshisname? That kid really nailed it, you know? Made me wish I'd been in Greenwich Village myself back in the day."

Peter turned to the clerk, who'd come outside to stand with them. "I don't suppose you've got a bucket, rope, and funnel, do you? And the tool to open the access hatch?"

The clerk looked at Peter with hunched shoulders and a glum look. "Mister, I'd give everybody all the gas they need, but it ain't mine to give. They'd be stealing it."

Peter held out his hand and Lewis put his roll into it without a word. He never left home with less than five grand. Peter handed the roll directly to the clerk. "My buddy's buying. Just keep track of how many gallons. You have a pen?" The clerk opened his coat and pulled out a ballpoint. Peter wrote his phone number on one of the hundreds. "Copy that somewhere you won't lose it. Give the gas to anyone who needs it, every gallon you've got. And if you need more money, just text me what I owe. I'm good for it, I promise."

"Gosh." The clerk blinked at the money in his hand. "I guess that'll work. That's real generous of you. I mean, we're all in this together, right?"

Peter nodded and clapped him on the shoulder. "How about that bucket, rope, and funnel?"

The clerk went back inside. The hunter looked at Peter. "You guys fill up first."

"We've got enough to get where we're going," Peter said. "We're in kind of a hurry, though. Something we need to do."

The hunter grinned again and the years fell away. "Well hell, us three can get this handled. And we won't let nobody get greedy, neither. By the way, I'm Wendell." He put out his hand and they all shook. "It's been real good to meet you all. Travel safe and take care, you hear?"

They walked across the gravel lot toward the Tahoe, standing alone under the bright canopy of stars. June put her arm around Peter's waist. "That was nice, wasn't it? Makes me think that, if we work together, no matter how bad this thing gets, we can make it through."

Peter thought of the incredible acts of generosity he had witnessed under the most horrific conditions. The other face of war, he supposed. An opportunity for selflessness. He pulled June closer, her hip bumping against his. "People never stop surprising you. They're usually better than you expect."

Lewis's tilted smile turned wistful. "Almost enough to make you believe in humanity, ain't it?"

They checked to make sure their prisoners were still breathing, then topped their tank from two of the fuel cans on the roof and set off again. The freeway was empty. They drank the cold gas station coffee and ate beef jerky and cashews.

Passing Ellensburg, everything was dark. Peter knew there was a hospital somewhere in town, that it would have power from backup generators until the diesel ran out. He looked for the light but he didn't see it. He wondered if the Messenger's contacts across the country had started taking down local transformers. Vance had mentioned people overseas, too. Peter wondered how far it had spread, how long it would last.

As they started the long climb up into the Cascades, leaving the high desert behind, the eastern sky began to brighten in the rearview. It was not quite six in the morning. They passed Cle Elum, then Easton, then the exit for the Stampede Pass, which they'd driven down from the Messenger's compound just five or six hours before. It seemed like a lifetime ago.

At Snoqualmie Pass, the ski resorts and condos were lightless and cold-looking. The snow on the mountains glowed an unearthly white. To the west, the clouds were gathering. Then the road tipped downhill toward the coast, following the South Fork of the Snoqualmie River down through the valley it had cut over a thousand millennia and more. If humanity was at a tipping point, Peter thought, and got knocked back to the Stone Age, at least the wildlife would return. Elk and moose. Bears, mountain lions, and wolves. Birds and fish and everything else mankind had hunted almost to extinction. Without eight billion *Homo sapiens*, the rest of the planet would be just fine.

June took his hand and squeezed it. In the back seat, Lewis stared out the window with his rifle on his lap. Thinking about Dinah and the boys, Peter was sure. After he delivered Hollis and the kid to the Seattle police, they'd start to plan the trip home to Wisconsin. It would get harder as the days passed and the blackout grew longer. Harder to get food, harder to get fuel. It didn't matter. They'd done much harder things before. Whatever happened, they'd make it work or die trying. There was a kind of purity to that.

They passed Tinkham Road, sweeping through the long downhill curves. It was fully light now, the clouds a pale gray shrouding the forested hills. Peter had made this drive a half dozen times over the years, and he'd always liked this stretch. North Bend was ahead, then Issaquah. He wondered if his Chevy was repaired yet. Even if it wasn't, he'd need the camping gear from the back. The old truck got lousy mileage. Maybe better to leave it in Ballard for good. The end of an era.

The thought made him inexplicably sad.

He knew it wasn't about losing the Chevy. It was about losing everything else. Going out to breakfast with friends. Dancing with June to a barroom jukebox. Seeing a movie in a crowded theater. The whole beautiful messed-up human world. Goddamn them, the Messenger and his people. How dare they end all this?

He wiped his eyes with the back of his hand. Mourning for his lost country. June leaned over and took his arm. The Tahoe threaded its way downhill toward the sea. There were no other cars. The freeway curved right, then left. Because of the trees and brush along the road, he saw no evidence of civilization.

As they came around one long curve, the landscape opened up and June's phone dinged in the center console.

Then it dinged again and again and again. Her face lit up as she grabbed it, staring at the screen. "I've got a signal," she shouted.

The phone kept making noise, notification after notification. She turned to Peter in wonder, a grin growing on her face. "Holy shit. Holy fucking shit!"

Then her phone rang. She hit a button and Kitzinger's voice came out of the tiny speaker. "Where the hell have you people been? The president's declared a national emergency. The Homeland guys are getting very worked up."

Ahead, there was a break in the clouds. Pale blue sky shone through. Maybe the storm had rained itself out for a few days. June was crying softly. Peter's vision was suddenly blurry and he had to hit the brakes and pull over. His voice box was tight; he couldn't get the words out. Finally he took a deep breath and cleared his throat. "We're coming up on North Bend. Where do you want to meet?"

64

The lights were on in downtown Seattle.

Lewis had no desire to talk with the authorities, so Peter dropped him off at the King Street transit station, then drove to the SPD's West Precinct with June at his side.

Because of the national emergency, nonessential workers were asked to stay off the roads. Traffic was almost nonexistent. But Belltown cafés and restaurants were open, and clumps of locals stood talking on the sidewalks, raincoats unzipped, lattes in hand.

Kitzinger was waiting outside the precinct's main entrance with two hard-eyed guys in crew cuts and cheap suits. The FBI had wanted to meet at their office, and Homeland at theirs, but Kitzinger had suggested SPD turf as a kind of neutral ground, and Peter had agreed. He liked local cops and he liked Kitzinger, too. She'd never stopped looking into KT's murder, and he knew she'd keep digging until she found everything there was to find.

Peter and June got out and shook Kitzinger's hand, then popped the rear hatch. "We brought you a couple of presents."

The hard-eyed men stared down at the prisoners swaddled in duct tape. Kitzinger said, "Who's the kid?"

"He flew the drones that blew the first circuit breakers." Peter reached in and thumped Hollis on the chest with his knuckles. "I'm pretty sure this asshole is the Messenger's right-hand man."

Kitzinger grinned. "I bet he's got stories to tell."

"What's the latest with the power outage?" June asked.

Kitzinger said, "Thanks to your friend Faraday's call to Homeland and your call to me yesterday, the utility companies managed to isolate most of the local grids to keep the blackout from spreading. Also, SPD techs found a hidden partition on Geoffrey Reed's hard drive. His code was there, along with his notes. He couldn't resist documenting his hack. That, along with the coordinates and pictures of those maps you sent, helped the geniuses reverse engineer the entire thing. Homeland commandeered a few spare transformers, so power should be back on in Eastern Washington in a few days. The National Guard is mobilizing with relief supplies and generators."

"What about the Messenger's connections across the country, across the world," Peter asked. "Did anyone take down the grid anywhere else?"

"Some groups managed to kill substations in a dozen states, but Homeland did a pretty good job of mobilizing local law enforcement," Kitzinger said. "That seemed to limit the damage. A few isolated incidents internationally, but not many."

"And the Messenger's compound?"

Kitzinger gave them a toothy grin. "SWAT teams went in two hours ago. There wasn't much resistance. Most people had already gone. But they didn't think to destroy any records, so we'll know who they are. If they really stoned people to death, they'll be held responsible."

"How about the Messenger? Did they get him?"

Kitzinger shook her head. "He wasn't at the compound. Homeland found his name on a private plane manifest with a destination of Mexico City. Captain Durant paid for the charter, we assume he was also on the flight. A Mercedes SUV registered to Durant was found in airport parking. The FBI has already contacted the Mexican authorities. The plane is still in the air. We'll have them in custody in a few hours."

Peter looked down at Hollis. "How does it feel to know your pal the Messenger ran away when things went bad? And took Durant instead of you?" Peter shook his head. "I guess you weren't important to him." Under the duct tape, Hollis somehow looked like a child who'd just learned the truth about Santa Claus.

Kitzinger opened the precinct door and held it for them. "We should go in. The feds are about to wet their pants in there."

Peter tossed the keys to the older of the hard-eyed guys, who plucked them out of the air. Both men climbed in the Tahoe and drove away without a word. Peter never saw the car, the men, or the prisoners again.

Peter and June spent four days being debriefed by Homeland and FBI agents, with Kitzinger as SPD liaison contributing the smarter questions. They spent their nights eating dinner with Ellie, Manny, Carlotta, and their girls, then retiring to a very nice hotel suite, where they made love in every room on every piece of furniture including the bathtub.

At mid-afternoon on the first day, there was a flurry of activity and everybody left the conference room. Kitzinger finally returned with a storm cloud on her face. "Somehow the fucking feds missed the Messenger. If he and Durant got on another plane or rented a car, it's in a name we don't know about."

June looked at Peter, her eyebrows slightly raised, asking a question. In the many pages of the Messenger's paperwork she'd gotten from the attorney Ann-Marie Wildman, she'd seen information about an apartment purchase in Rio de Janeiro.

Peter gave a very small shake of his head. June had given the feds all the paperwork. They'd screwed up Mexico City. If they couldn't come up with the Rio condo information themselves, he didn't trust their ability to find the Messenger there, either. Besides, when push came to shove, Peter still had unfinished business with the guy. Not to mention Durant.

On the afternoon of the fourth day, the lights were back on in Eastern Washington. The final death toll was twenty-seven. But only four people had died for reasons that could be directly linked to the power outage. Which seemed to Peter like some kind of miracle.

That same day, they got word that King County had fast-tracked Ellie's guardianship by Manny and Carlotta Martinez. The State Department still hadn't managed to locate her father, and he hadn't responded to repeated attempts to contact him.

Ellie and Carlotta were talking to therapists. Manny's dangerous roofers were on security detail, just in case. And the mechanic had finished repairs to Peter's truck, except for the bullet holes in the front quarter panel, which Peter thought he might leave as a reminder.

Congress had supposedly set aside partisan differences to work on a bill to fund upgrades to the electric grid. The FBI was focusing on homegrown terrorist groups and extremist cults. The Seattle mayor offered Peter and June the key to the city. They declined.

Unsurprisingly, the tech conference went on as planned. The only change, according to news reports, was a few hollow speeches about how technology existed to safeguard humanity's future.

Durant and the Messenger were nowhere to be found.

65

Four weeks later, Peter, Lewis, and Manny sat in a rented Range Rover with heavily tinted windows outside a Brazilian favela called Rocinha. Through high-powered binoculars, Peter watched a white-haired man a block away. He had a bullhorn and was speaking to a small crowd, drinking in their rapt attention like an intoxicating liquor.

He spoke in English, using simple language and pausing between sentences so a female interpreter could keep up. Behind him, a tall man with a dark mustache and a straw cowboy hat stood with an AR-15 slung over one shoulder and a pistol on his hip, head turning to scan his surroundings like the cop he had been for decades.

The tropical sun beat down, and the Rover's air-conditioning was turned up high against the stifling summer heat. They'd been watching the two men for nine days.

Rocinha was one of many such favelas, improvised shantytowns climbing the hillsides outside of Rio de Janeiro, inhabited by people with few other choices. Lewis had found a local police detective who'd given them the rundown. A drug gang ruled Rocinha with an iron hand, extorting money from businesses and individuals alike. The only water came from a few public taps. Open sewers ran down the sides of the narrow dirt streets. Electricity was pirated from power poles at the edge of the community. Poverty was endemic and schools were few and underfunded. For a child born in a favela, there was little future.

This was the place Garrison Bevel, the Messenger, had chosen to start his new movement.

In stark contrast with Rocinha, the Messenger had moved into the penthouse of a luxury apartment building on Avenida Vieira Souto, across the street from beautiful Ipanema Beach. Durant was his constant companion, always armed with an automatic rifle and a pistol. Whenever they left the flat, they were accompanied by a local four-man security detail in an additional vehicle.

On three separate evenings, however, the Messenger received a pair of attractive female visitors at his apartment. The women were different each time, but all young and similarly dressed in short-shorts and bikini tops that left little to the imagination. From the beach, Manny had taken photographs of them dancing on the balcony with the Messenger while Durant frowned through the sliding glass door.

The fourth time two young women arrived in a taxi, Lewis got out of the Rover and met them at the gate for a conversation. Somehow, Lewis spoke passable Brazilian Portuguese. After a bit of back-and-forth, a significant amount of money changed hands. Then the women buzzed the gate and Lewis waved Peter and Manny out of the Rover.

The building's security guards were not pleased to see three armed men accompany the young women into the elegant marble lobby. The women explained that these men were their friends, very nice men, here to make sure they arrived safely at their destination. More money changed hands. The guards went back to their posts. The two young women and their three nice friends got on the elevator.

When it arrived at the top floor, the young women led them to the apartment door. The men stood to the side and pulled suppressed pistols from beneath their shirts. The women rang the bell and waved cheerfully at the peephole, as if they did this kind of thing every day. For all Peter knew, they did.

After a long moment, Durant opened the door with a frown. He wore pale trousers and a striped linen shirt with the bulge of a pistol beneath it and his cowboy straw on his head. The women ran for the stairs as Peter pointed the gun at his chest. "Hands up and mouth shut."

Durant reached for his holstered pistol. Peter shot him in the hand. Durant stepped back into the entryway and shook his injured hand like he'd been stung by a bee. A galaxy of fine red dots appeared on the white walls and ceiling.

Peter followed him in. Durant turned and dove for the assault rifle on the entry hall table. Peter shot him in the back of the thigh, then leapt forward with a fierce grin and pistol-whipped him on the back of the head. Durant dropped like a sack of shit.

Peter tossed the rifle to Lewis and stepped over the disgraced Seattle cop with Manny right behind him.

They found the Messenger climbing from a chaise lounge on the sunny balcony, wearing only a tiny red Speedo stretched by a bobbing erection that had to be the result of some kind of prescription medication. Super-classy, Peter thought. He was sure there would be a bottle of knockoff Viagra somewhere in the apartment. "Hi, Gary. Remember me?"

If Bevel was startled at the intruders, he didn't let it show. Instead he just smiled and said, "Hello, friend. How can I help you?"

His eyes were still magnetic, his face still warm and expressive. Peter wanted to throw him off the balcony and shoot him as he fell.

Instead he caught the man's wrist in a control grip and frog-marched him into the living room, where Manny kicked him in the balls, then dropped him on the Persian rug, rolled him over, stuck a syringe into his butt cheek, and pressed the plunger.

Peter returned to Durant, bleeding on the white floor tiles while Lewis stood over him. Durant's tanned face had gone pale. There was a lot of blood. He wouldn't last long. Peter's leg shot had nicked something important. He didn't care. "Looks like you traded your integrity for a couple of hookers and a nice apartment. How's that working for you now, Captain?"

Durant stared up at him, dark-eyed and stern. "The Movement will go on without us."

"No, it won't." Peter leveled his pistol at Durant's head. "Kitzinger says hello, by the way." Then he pulled the trigger.

Lewis had already closed the apartment door so the neighbors wouldn't hear the ruckus and call the police. He found a set of apartment keys in Durant's pocket, then went down to the Rover to bring up the wheelchair.

Gary was awake but compliant, thankfully speechless, and blinking like a man just emerging from the deepest cave in the world. The drug was a hypnotic cocktail often used to subdue schizophrenic patients in a mental ward. Peter was going to say something to him but decided not to waste his breath. The man was either delusional or a con man of the first order. Or possibly both.

Peter searched the apartment for electronics, financial documents, and whatever else might be of use, throwing it all into an alligator valise from the closet. Manny found a kimono in the bathroom and wrapped Gary up like he was headed to the beach. When Lewis returned, they loaded the man in the wheelchair, slapped sunglasses on his face and a straw hat on his head, and took him down the elevator.

The girls were long gone. In the lobby, the security men turned away, pretending they didn't see a thing.

Outside in the heat, a passing cop stopped and opened the Rover's door so they could lift the glassy-eyed old man into the car. He even offered to load the wheelchair in the back. "Obrigado," Lewis said, smiling. "Muito gentil."

The sky was blue, but a line of clouds gathered on the horizon. Peter drove directly to Santos Dumont airport and pulled into the FBO facility, giving the guard at the gate a false name. The guard saluted and pointed them toward the VIP apron, where a plain white jet, newer than the others waiting there, stood apart from the rest.

As the Rover came to a stop, the cabin door opened and Faraday, wearing a cast on his injured lower leg, leaned out to deploy the integrated steps. Peter handed up his duffel and the alligator valise. Manny slung Gary over one shoulder and carried him up the steps into the aircraft. Lewis set the rest of their gear on the tarmac, then got back in the Range Rover and drove it toward the parking area, where the rental company would pick it up later.

The line of clouds was closer now. On the sun-blasted pavement, the tropical heat was thick with humidity. Peter handed up the remaining equipment to Faraday, who said, "Mr. Wilkinson's lawyer is on the phone with the FBI director right now. A team will meet us at Leesburg FBO when we land."

They still didn't know how Gary Bevel had slipped the noose in Mexico City. They didn't have a complete list of his US and overseas contacts, either. "Just tell me this asshole won't end up at some Club Fed," Peter said. "We don't want him to spread his bullshit to a whole new audience."

Faraday shook his head. "Nobody wants that. The feds are going to suck every last shred of intel out of him, learn about all the other freaky groups he knows, then lock him in a very deep hole and throw away the key."

Peter didn't particularly trust the feds not to screw this up. If Bevel was to be believed, he had allies everywhere. And if some grandstanding subcommittee chair called for congressional hearings and people started to cover their asses rather than do the right thing, the situation could go south in a hurry. Regardless, the feds were the only ones in a position to actually act on what they learned. And Peter still believed in the rule of law, even if it didn't always work as well as he'd like.

And when it didn't?

Peter would continue to live by the code of conduct he'd set for himself many years ago. No matter how screwed up things got, that code was his North Star. Take care of the people you love. Protect the people who can't protect themselves. Do the right thing, even when it hurts. Because liars and cheats are always temporary. Integrity is the only thing that lasts.

Faraday ducked back into the cabin and the engines began to wind up.

Now Peter could see the slanting gray shadow of rain falling from the approaching line of clouds. As the squall blew toward them, the land darkened below. The clouds grew closer, the flash of lightning followed quickly by the rumble of thunder. Soon he could see the heavy droplets advancing down the runway, splashing off the wet pavement as the water accumulated faster than it could drain away.

He turned back toward the parking area and watched as Lewis jogged across the tarmac, loose and lean in the tropical heat.

THE DARK TIME

He arrived ahead of the squall, his timing excellent as always. Halfway up the airplane steps, he turned to Peter, who remained on the ground in the rising wind, watching the storm come. "Let's go, brother. We want to beat this storm, we gotta get moving."

"On my way." Peter took one last look at the darkness sweeping toward them, then headed for the jet.

ACKNOWLEDGMENTS

Heartfelt thanks to writer pals Gregg Hurwitz and Robert Crais for talking me off the ledge during a challenging year, along with friends Kent Krueger, C. J. Box, Michael Koryta, and Lou Berney for offering additional much-needed encouragement, as well as with David McCloskey for our conversations about the general insanity of the writing life.

As always, special thanks are due to Don Bentley and Bill Schweigart—our friendship means the world to me, and really helped get me over the hump on this book in particular.

Big thanks to the Milwaukee writing crew, including the delightful Erica Ruth Neubauer, Andy Rash, Tim Hennessy, Liam Callanan, and Chris Lee, for drinks and book talk.

Additional thanks to Adam Plantinga (again) for his help with the police bits—you should read his books, they're excellent. Any inaccuracies, misrepresentations, or distortions necessary for the story are entirely my fault.

The truth is, I could fill a page with writers to thank. Crime writers are, by and large, kind and generous people, and I'm extremely grateful to be a part of this community of storytellers.

And the booksellers! I am so grateful for the many independent booksellers who put my work into the hands of readers. Local bookstores are the lifeblood of the book world, and their knowledge and passion have been instrumental in my success and the success of almost every other writer you love to read. Plus buying local keeps those dollars—and jobs—in your community, so please, please patronize your local independent bookstore!

Extra super special thanks, of course, as always, are due to Barbara Peters at The Poisoned Pen in Scottsdale and Daniel Goldin at Boswell Books in Milwaukee, who have been champions from the very beginning. I am forever in your debt.

Ongoing bazillion gazillion thanks to Erin Olson for our continuing conversations. I remain grateful beyond words.

At Putnam, thanks to editors Tom Colgan and Carly James, as well as to the superlative publicity, marketing, and sales teams—including, but by no means limited to, Katie Grinch, Alexis Welby, Ashley McClay, and Benjamin Lee. Thanks also to the visual artists who make my books both beautiful and readable—especially this cover!

Thanks to my mom, the indefatigable Lucia Petrie, for being an ongoing inspiration as well as the most effective unpaid member of the sales staff.

Thanks to my brother, Bob; my sister, Maryl; and the rest of my friends and neighbors for helping keep me sane in an insane world.

Thanks to my son, Duncan, for our grand outdoor adventures and for our many long conversations about the creative life and how to live it. You remain an inspiration to me.

And no acknowledgment would be complete without a massive shout-out to my Sweet Patootie, the magnificent Margret Petrie. You are truly an artist of everyday life and it has been great fun to spend the last twenty-six years married to you. I'm so very much looking forward to twenty-six more!

The deepest thank-you goes out to the many veterans who have trusted me with their stories of war, and life after war, over these last fifteen years. You inspire me every day. I hope you see yourselves in Peter Ash, because you are definitely part of his DNA. If you think there's something I've gotten wrong about your experience, or if you want to talk about anything else, please don't hesitate to DM me on my socials or shoot me an email—if you reply to one of my newsletters (you can subscribe at nickpetrie.com) it will reach my personal inbox.

And if you're a vet suffering from PTSD—and statistically, many of you are—please know that your suffering is real and you are not alone. If you're hurting, or haven't yet gotten help, please consider calling the Veterans Crisis Line at (800) 273-8255—or simply dial 988, then press 1. Thanks again to reader Tim Morgan for giving me this suggestion, and please accept my apologies for the fact that this paragraph wasn't in the first six books.

One more thing. For me, the best part of being a writer is my conversations with readers—whether in person at bookstores, libraries, festivals, and conferences, and virtually via social media, remote events, and email. You remind me that I'm not just talking to myself, and I'm very grateful. Thanks for being a fan of Peter Ash.

ABOUT THE AUTHOR

NICK PETRIE received his MFA in fiction from the University of Washington, won a Hopwood Award for short fiction, and his story 'At the Laundromat' won the 2006 Short Story Contest in the *Seattle Review*. His debut novel featuring ex-soldier Peter Ash, *The Drifter*, won numerous awards including the International Thriller Writers Award for Best First Novel in 2017.